"*Queen of Shadows* pulled me in . . . Dianne Sylvan's rich, dark, sexy reimagined Austin is filled with people I want to visit again and again. Dianne Sylvan's got voice, doesn't miss a beat, and rocks it all the way to the last note. Sit down. Shut up. And enjoy the show. It's intense, dark, sexy, with just the right touch of humor. Looking for a new addiction? Go no farther."

—Devon Monk, author of *Magic on the Storm*

"*Queen of Shadows* grabbed me on the first page and didn't let go. Miranda, the heroine, is vulnerable and gutsy, with magical abilities even she doesn't suspect. Vampire David Solomon is as powerful and heroic as he is deliciously seductive. Dianne Sylvan has created an original take on vampires that I thoroughly enjoyed, and I'll be looking for her next book with great anticipation. She's a skilled and talented storyteller who definitely knows how to deliver one hell of a book!"

—Angela Knight, *New York Times* bestselling author of
*Master of Fire*

0682

# QUEEN OF SHADOWS

DIANNE SYLVAN

ACE BOOKS, NEW YORK

**THE BERKLEY PUBLISHING GROUP**
**Published by the Penguin Group**
**Penguin Group (USA) Inc.**
**375 Hudson Street, New York, New York 10014, USA**
Penguin Group (Canada), 90 Eglinton Avenue East, Suite 700, Toronto, Ontario M4P 2Y3, Canada
(a division of Pearson Penguin Canada Inc.)
Penguin Books Ltd., 80 Strand, London WC2R 0RL, England
Penguin Group Ireland, 25 St. Stephen's Green, Dublin 2, Ireland (a division of Penguin Books Ltd.)
Penguin Group (Australia), 250 Camberwell Road, Camberwell, Victoria 3124, Australia
(a division of Pearson Australia Group Pty. Ltd.)
Penguin Books India Pvt. Ltd., 11 Community Centre, Panchsheel Park, New Delhi—110 017, India
Penguin Group (NZ), 67 Apollo Drive, Rosedale, North Shore 0632, New Zealand
(a division of Pearson New Zealand Ltd.)
Penguin Books (South Africa) (Pty.) Ltd., 24 Sturdee Avenue, Rosebank, Johannesburg 2196,
South Africa

Penguin Books Ltd., Registered Offices: 80 Strand, London WC2R 0RL, England

QUEEN OF SHADOWS

An Ace Book / published by arrangement with the author

PRINTING HISTORY
Ace mass-market edition / September 2010

Copyright © 2010 by Dianne Sylvan.
Cover art by Gene Mollica.
Cover design by Annette Fiore DeFex.
Interior text design by Tiffany Estreicher.

ISBN: 978-0-441-01925-0

ACE
Ace Books are published by The Berkley Publishing Group,
a division of Penguin Group (USA) Inc.,
375 Hudson Street, New York, New York 10014.
ACE and the "A" design are trademarks of Penguin Group (USA) Inc.

PRINTED IN THE UNITED STATES OF AMERICA

10   9   8   7   6   5   4   3   2   1

*For Laurie and Laura, who told me so*

# PART ONE

# Pomegranate Seeds

# One

The guy next to her in the checkout line looked kind of like a vampire.

Miranda didn't look at people. She kept her eyes averted, even while negotiating the chaos of the Austin city streets. She slipped into the empty spaces between bodies and went unnoticed, a messy ponytail bobbing in and out of focus, a pale, heart-shaped face drawn with years of insomnia. If anyone remarked on her presence, it was probably to say something about her hair; unconfined, her dark red curls spilled haphazardly down over her shoulders, a jeweled tone that caught fire on the rare occasion sunlight touched it. If they thought anything about her at all, it was probably that her hair was fake. They certainly wouldn't remember her eyes, for no one ever saw them.

She was very careful about that.

A woman walking down Sixth Street carrying a guitar case was hardly news in Austin, which had at some point proclaimed itself the "Live Music Capital of the World." Musicians here were like actors in Los Angeles, plentiful and mostly working in restaurants.

A woman standing in line at the mini mart with a guitar case was a little more interesting, mostly because she should have been bumping into people, but Miranda knew every inch of space around her, could feel the individual people on all sides, and she knew not to get too close. *Don't look up, don't touch. They'll regret it. You'll regret it.*

She shifted her weight from one foot to the other, shifting the red plastic basket in her hands, looking down, as always, at her purchases. Allergy medicine, hummus, pita, a small block of Cheddar carefully selected from the pile, oranges, six bottles of Shiner. She could have been anyone in Austin.

There were only a handful of people in the store, which was why she was there after midnight. The crowd at the club had been dense and restless from the heat, and she wanted nothing more than to sprint home with her guitar bouncing on her back and gain the safe silence of her tiny apartment off Lamar, scald the night off her body in the shower, wash down a couple of Benadryl with a Shiner, and fall into a short but welcome coma.

But her fridge was empty. She had been eating less and less, drinking more and more. Her hands shook with hunger on the neck of her twelve-string and nearly missed every other chord.

Not that it mattered. She could bang two sticks together, and still they would come.

She twisted one hand free of the basket handles and impatiently shoved a loose curl back behind her ear. She wasn't going to think about that. Not now. If it started, it wouldn't stop, and she'd never make it home. There was only one more person in front of her in line, and then it was two blocks from here to the bus stop, ten minutes to the apartment complex. She could make it.

Edging closer to the register, she snatched a pair of Snickers bars from the display and dropped them in the basket.

"I prefer Milky Way, myself," came a low voice alarmingly close to her left shoulder.

Miranda held back a scream and spun around, for once lifting her head and *looking*.

A young man had somehow come up right behind her and was standing only a couple of feet away, watching her with detached curiosity. He was oddly pale in the bright fluorescent lights and wore a long black coat that covered him from neck to ankles.

In Texas, in August.

She stared at him, heart pounding in her chest at the shock of being sneaked up on. No one ever came into or out of her presence without her feeling it. She could feel a pigeon blink at fifty paces. She relied on the knowledge even as she hated it.

He seemed unaffected by her reaction and simply stood watching her; that was when she realized how insanely blue his eyes were. They were dark, almost the color of blueberries, an impossible shade she'd never seen before. They had to be contacts—nobody had eyes that color. If she hadn't been so rattled, she might have smiled to herself; she was thinking the same thing about his eyes most people did about her hair.

"Are you all right?" he asked. There was something musical and compelling in his voice, almost soothing, and it contained an apology for frightening her.

She wanted to sob, *No, I'm pretty fucking far from all right*, but all that would come out of her mouth was a strangled half whimper. She took a step back involuntarily, and the strap of her guitar case started to slide off her shoulder. She groped after it, but it was either grab the instrument or hold the basket—no contest, really. She started to let go of the handles—

—and a pale, long-fingered hand shot out and took the basket from her smoothly, holding it out in front of her at a careful distance while she got herself back together. It was a strong hand, neatly manicured, and she couldn't help but compare it to her own, constantly trembling with nails bitten to the quick. Her right hand had decent nails so she could play, but she'd nibbled off the left for years.

Shaking, she took the basket back and mumbled her

thanks, returning her eyes to the ground where they belonged.

The cashier was giving her a pointed look, and she realized she was next. She stumbled forward and hoisted the basket onto the conveyor belt, turning to slide through the lane without whacking the guitar on the sides, simultaneously digging her wallet out of the blue embroidered purse she'd bought at a street fair back when . . . back when.

This was not how things were supposed to go. No one was supposed to notice her. The bored-looking blonde ringing up her food wouldn't even remember she'd been there. The only people who ever paid any attention to her were the ones who paid the fifteen-dollar cover charge and stood before and below her line of sight every Wednesday and Friday night at Mel's. They saw her, and they listened. Random strangers didn't do that.

She glanced back behind her, almost sure he would be gone, but he was still waiting patiently, no longer watching her. She dared take a second to size him up, just in case he came after her on the street. Taller than her, which didn't mean much to a five-four woman. Slender. Pale. Black hair that was shiny in the lights like a raven's feathers. No visible tattoos or piercings. Coat buttoned all the way up to the neck, almost clerical. She could see black leather boots.

He was holding one item: a pint of Ben & Jerry's Cherry Garcia. Something about that struck her as exceptionally weird.

She handed the cashier her debit card and waited, knowing when to take it back without looking up. Two plastic bags, and she all but bolted from the store.

She was sweating bullets as she climbed on the bus, and not from the brief run to catch it before it sped away. *Don't freak out, girl. Focus. You're almost home.* She brought her mind forcibly back to the present, away from the store, and concentrated. Music. In her head she rehearsed her latest cover song, and her fingers squeezed her thigh lightly, miming the chords. She wasn't satisfied with the bridge. *The minor fall, the major lift . . . the baffled king composing Hallelujah . . .* Her own thoughts and Leonard Cohen's blended together as the bus bounced all over the road.

*Hallelujah* . . . five more minutes . . . *hallelujah* . . . three more blocks . . . *hallelujah* . . .

She gathered up her bags and her guitar and disembarked, ignoring honking horns and shouted insults as she ran across the street against the light to her building, keys already in her hand.

Home was a first-floor one-bedroom in the corner by the pool. Home was small but comfortable, furnishings pulled together piece by piece in a kinder time, an eclectic sort of mix that went for comfort over unity of style. Home had a fantastic sound system that was worth more than all the furniture combined. Home had no plants or pets, nothing to demand her affection or attention.

She let her guitar slide onto the floor, along with her purse, and shoved the grocery bags into the fridge without unpacking them. The only thing she removed was a beer.

Miranda flung herself onto the couch, the desire to wash the stale cigarette smell and sweat off her body taking second place to the desire to get wasted as quickly as possible. Her apartment, barricaded and blocked from the world through years of unvoiced prayer and desperation, was the one place she could think in silence, the one place nothing could touch her.

For how much longer?

Her eyes, so used to sticking to the ground, lifted up the wall, following a crack in the paint that had been here as long as she had. It was comforting, that crack, always there, able to tease her gaze upward, to remind her there was a world above her waist.

Not that there was much of one below her waist. Even

her once-trusty vibrator, a powerful Hitachi she called Shaky, lay gathering dust beneath the bed, as day by day life contracted and the thought of ever caring about orgasms seemed laughably far away.

Cold. She was cold again. She reached sideways for the quilt that was always on the couch and pulled it around her. People who didn't eat got cold. She should eat.

Her last boyfriend had been Mike. Five years ago. They'd met at the insurance company where she clerked while she made her halfhearted attempt at college. The university had swallowed her, her freshman class larger than her hometown, and she had gotten lost, a foreshadowing perhaps of her life now. Mike had helped her move into this very apartment, and they'd had sex on the living room floor before she bought the couch. Six months later he'd proposed. She'd said no. It wasn't until that moment she realized she didn't love him, and really never had. Boyfriends were like the Freshman Fifteen; you were supposed to obtain them in college. She'd gained the fifteen, too, but those pounds were long gone. She looked a bit gaunt now, even more so than her mystery guy at the grocery store—

She shuddered. Blue eyes and a raven's feathers.

He hadn't been gaunt, though. Really quite nicely built, just—

She drank the rest of the beer without tasting it and immediately opened another. By the time she fell asleep on the couch, still fully clothed with her shoes on, she'd had four, and her mind was blissfully numb.


She was famous, and she was insane.

Her voice soared out over the audience, holding them spellbound and enraptured, delivering their hopes and fears tangled in chords and rhythm. They called her an angel, her voice a gift.

She was famous, and she was a liar.

They had no idea where her talent came from—critics

and journalists and experts of the industry postulated that she'd had a musical family, that she'd started in a gospel choir, that she had taught herself to sing. They were all stupid and blind.

Her extraordinary talent, as they called it, depended on them . . . and it was killing her.

Miranda had been playing guitar for only six years, but she had taken to it as if she'd been born with one in her hands, and it came as naturally as breathing. She taught herself out of books and a drive to do something, anything useful with her life. A friend of a friend had been dicked over by his roommates, left holding a three-bedroom apartment and a lease, so he'd sold off all their possessions. She'd bought a pair of speakers, and he'd thrown in the guitar for free just so he didn't have to look at it anymore.

In less than a month she hadn't wanted to look at it either. It was a piece of shit suited for a rank amateur. She gave it up on Craigslist and took an entire paycheck down to Strait Music for something real. When she told the salesman how long she'd been playing, he blinked at her as if she were speaking Farsi. She'd picked up a five-thousand-dollar Martin and shown him she was very, very serious.

Then, while he was ringing up her (considerably less expensive) purchase, out of curiosity she'd sat down at a piano.

"Are you sure you've never played before?" the salesman kept asking.

Oh, she hadn't been an instant virtuoso, but she'd made her way through the sheet music on display slowly, with only a few mistakes. The arcane notations on the page made sense to her in a way nothing else ever had. The second time through she played it perfectly.

Now she had a fairly sophisticated digital keyboard; her apartment was too small for a piano. She sat down one night with YouTube and drank in performance videos, staring at hands on keys, and after that it was easy.

All of that might have frightened her, but soon she had far more pressing concerns.

One night, back when she was still with Mike and had a social life, she was sitting outside Austin Java practicing playing and singing at the same time. She was sad—she spent a lot of time sad, so she couldn't remember now what particular sorrow had haunted her that night—and she sang quietly, not wanting to disturb the other patrons. The place was crowded with students poring over their textbooks.

At one point she paused and looked up. Every single person there was crying.

A little scared but fascinated, she'd repeated the situation on another night, in another place, with a different song, to the same effect. Whatever emotion she wanted to call up, all she had to do was put it in the music, and everyone around her felt it. She could take a happy song and use it to make people weep, or have everyone dancing a jig through the most emo crap she could think of.

It didn't take long to figure out there was more to it than that. If she concentrated, stretched out toward the people around her, she could feel hints of what they were feeling. She could take that, and amplify it, or change it. Once she knew what they were feeling, it was a lot easier to influence them.

At first it was fantastic. She played on the street for tips, and her cup overflowed with dollar bills. Then a guy who owned a bar downtown, Mel, offered her a paid gig on Wednesdays. The crowds had been minuscule at first, but after everyone walked out high as kites on the happiness she pumped into them, they came back, and they brought friends. Soon she was seeing her name in the *Austin Chronicle*, and Mel recommended she get an agent.

And if she had her doubts, if she wondered how ethical it might be to manipulate people's emotions so willfully with this funny little talent of hers, she quickly forgot those doubts in the glare of the stage lights and the adoration of the crowd.

Slowly, as the months went by, she noticed her control was slipping. More and more emotion seemed to flow through her head whether she wanted it to or not. She kept picking up on people's feelings at random, and sometimes they were so horrible it left her weeping—despair, fear, hatred, violence, rage, all tore through her when she least expected them. She started to know things about people she didn't want to know, and she couldn't stop it.

It was worst when she looked people in the eye. People held all their secrets in their eyes. They could smile and laugh like they hadn't a care in the world, but one look into their eyes and she knew . . . she knew. She could feel their guilt, their longing, their loss—emotions were clearer than speech if you knew how to listen. The weight of their heart's memories bore down on her own.

She knew the preacher on the corner had fucked his nephew. She knew the homeless man on the bus was a Vietnam vet who'd saved ten men and had his leg blown off for his trouble. She knew the crazy cat lady three doors down still talked to her dead husband's photo as if he were there. She knew the gangbanger passing her on the street had nightmares about his childhood dog.

All those secrets were in her head. Emotions, and memories bound up in emotions, filled up all the space inside her. If she touched someone, she learned more than whether they had sweaty palms. She learned of the deepest darkness inside them, and it made her want to scream and hide.

The only time she could control it was when she played. Then she could moderate the flow of emotions and work with them. Otherwise it was just her and the creeping madness that was eating her alive.

The one perk, she supposed, was that going batshit insane paid well. She had her two nights a week at Mel's, and a Monday night at a local café, and among them the shows netted her enough to live on, especially since she was hardly eating and had no social life. She'd been able to quit the endless round of clerical jobs filing in windowless rooms—no more pantyhose, no more burnt coffee smell and paper cuts. There had been a time when the prospect of leaving the nine-to-five world would have thrilled her.

The problem with feeling everyone else's emotions was that there was no longer any room for her own. As the ability had gotten stronger, she had become less and less of a presence in her own mind, unable to separate herself completely from other people without drinking herself unconscious. She felt like a thin candy shell over nothing at all, run through with cracks and ready to splinter at any second.

On nights like tonight, when the moon was heavy and full and all of Austin seemed ready to collapse under the weight of the hundred-degree summer air, as she stood in the wings waiting for her cue, she knew that time was coming closer and closer.

She folded her arms across her body tightly. Cold. Always cold. Her stage clothes, black and tight and made of shiny patent and Lycra, were starting to feel loose—if she didn't start eating she was going to look like a bag of antlers. She had always been proud of her body; she wasn't a supermodel by any means, but had a curvaceous figure that filled out a V-neck perfectly and hips that swung when she walked. Men had never been a problem, back when they mattered. Even when she'd been a little chubby in college she'd been lively and popular, known for her razor wit and gorgeous breasts. Now she was starting to look like she'd wandered off the set of *Schindler's List*.

Mel introduced her, and though she couldn't see the crowd she could feel them. Packed to capacity, the bar held about eighty people, and that was the biggest crowd she could hold at once. Any more than that and the emotions were simply too much, and she fell screaming to the ground with her fists jammed uselessly in her ears.

She was a talented musician but not much of a performer. She didn't banter with the audience, didn't show off or try to look sexy. She didn't really need to. When she walked out onstage, people stared at her—she could feel their eyes on her skin like a sheen of sweat—but as soon as she started the first song, she caught them all, and any doubts they had dissolved into dust motes.

She hated how easy it was. She hated that she'd let this happen.

She just wanted to go home.

But there was nothing else, not anymore. She couldn't go back to a normal job, not like this. There was nowhere she could go if she couldn't pay the rent, except back to her father's house or maybe to her sister's in Dallas, and madness seemed a small price to pay to avoid either of those places. Any hope of a real life with friends and aspirations beyond making it through another gig had long ago faded from her worldview. There was only this crowd, this song, this room full of oppressive heat and oppressive emotions.

She had to be careful or she was going to depress the audience so much they wouldn't come back. She deliberately shifted the mood for the next song, picking a cover of an old Sheryl Crow screecher that her voice could smooth out and lift up; soon, the crowd was swaying, and in a moment they'd be dancing, smiling. Happy.

It was small comfort to know that for at least this one night their troubles would be forgotten and they'd go home to their families and lives in a great mood, ready to take on the world. She didn't want to hurt anyone. She never had.

Hard to concentrate tonight. She kept the tone light and airy, feeding energy into the crowd to stoke it without making it burn too hotly; she'd made that mistake once and the happiness had spilled over into restlessness and then into anger. Bar fights weren't good for business, Mel said with a frown after the police had left. She should remember that.

About halfway through the set she managed to get enough control back that she could pick out individual energies in the crowd, and she didn't know whether to be pleased or chagrined—she recognized at least one.

Fuck, fuck, fuck. Kat was here. Miranda had forgotten all about her.

She shifted her focus, pulling back from Kat to avoid tampering with her emotions, and swept it around the room, reading everyone else, getting a bead on how the night was going. So far, so good. They were upbeat because she made them that way . . .

. . . except for one.

She tried to hone in on the individual presence, but couldn't; every time she got close it felt like her attention slipped on an icy patch and slid off him—or her—onto someone else. Frowning, she kept playing, trying to ignore it, but her mind kept coming back to that spot, a scab she couldn't stop picking. All she could say for sure was that whoever it was, they were . . . dark. Not depressed, not angry, but dark, with a frightening potential for violence. And whoever they were, they were staring right at her.

She didn't look. She was afraid to look. She dragged her attention away and finished the set.

By the time she came off the stage to another standing ovation, the presence was gone, and she felt like she could let out a breath she hadn't been holding. She left the stage with her guitar in her hands and clomped down the stairs in her platform boots, headed for the tiny space behind the stage that served as a dressing room.

Kat was there, waiting for her.

"Hey," she said, smiling. "That was awesome."

"Hey." It was an effort to speak, but she did her best. Kat hadn't seen her in weeks and was the closest thing to a friend Miranda still had after gradually cutting herself off from her once-broad social circle. They kept up mostly via e-mail—e-mail was safe. It was a lot harder to feel emotions over e-mail . . . but not impossible.

Kat leaned back casually against the table where Miranda did her makeup, looking every inch the Austinite in her faded jeans, sandals, and Indian print halter top. She fit the image of a musician far better than Miranda herself did; she had tattoos on her arms, a stud in her nose, and purple streaks in her blond dreadlocks. Kat did yoga and ate things like burdock and wheatgrass. She was also one of the most well-adjusted people Miranda had ever met. How they'd stayed friends was a mystery to her.

"You look like crap, though," Kat was saying as Miranda laid her guitar in its case and snapped it shut, then turned her attention to her clothes. She yanked the curtain across the "dressing room" entrance and bent to unzip her boots.

"Do I?" Miranda asked absently. A rubber band of pressure was starting to squeeze around her head. She'd overdone it tonight.

"When was the last time you ate? We should go grab a bite or something. Pancakes?"

Miranda's hands trembled. A restaurant full of people . . . God, there was no way. "I can't," she said. "I have to be somewhere."

"Come on, Mira, I haven't seen you in forever. What's going on with you? You never come out anymore, except here. You look like a cancer patient. You're shaky." Kat folded her arms. "Is it drugs?"

That was Kat, always to the point. Miranda missed her blunt humor and her sharp eye. Beneath her hippie exterior Kat was tough as nails, spending her days working with kids on the East Side, tutoring and mentoring and trying to keep them out of gangs.

"No, Kat, it's not drugs," she replied, peeling the Lycra off her body and replacing it with jeans. God, if only it were drugs! "I'm fine. Really."

"We all miss you, you know."

"I know. I miss you, too."

Miranda clamped down on the tears that threatened at the words. She never let herself think about where else she could be right now, the life she could be having. She was twenty-seven and felt like she was ninety. She should be lining up her career and looking for Mr. Right. Kat was her age—they'd met in a psych class—and had everything Miranda wished she could, except for Mr. Right, but only because Kat favored Mr. Right This Minute.

For just a second Miranda thought about telling her. Everything. Kat had resources, and she was hard to shock. She might be able to help.

"Come on, Mira . . . talk to me. I can help."

Miranda started, shrinking back from her friend's sympathetic hand. Had Kat come up with the thought herself, or had Miranda pushed it into her? The thought of doing to Kat what she did to the audience made her feel sick.

She pulled a T-shirt over her head and yanked her hair back into a ponytail. "I'm okay, Kat. I am. I'll e-mail you—we'll have lunch next week or something. I just . . . I have to go now."

With that she grabbed her guitar and her bag and all but ran out the back door, not looking at her friend's troubled face but knowing what she was thinking. Kat's desire to help was sincere, above and beyond any musical influence, but what could she really do? Even if Kat believed her, who else would? Who in the world would understand what was happening without thinking she was crazy?

*You are crazy. They're not wrong.*

They'd commit her. They'd lock her away just like her mama, and poke and prod her and drug her until she was a drooling mass of atrophied muscle and brain.

No. Never. She'd die first.

*Probably.*

Kat's concern stayed with her, rubbing around the edges of her mind, as she hurried along the four blocks from the club to the bus stop. It was almost one A.M., and for a Friday night downtown Austin was unusually quiet; she didn't realize why until she heard a crash of thunder that shook her out of herself long enough to look up at the billowing dark clouds that had blotted out the moon.

"Fantastic," she muttered, and picked up the pace. Her keys and a few loose coins jingled in her purse and her guitar case bumped her butt as she trotted along the sidewalk. A couple of people moved out of her way, avoiding a collision with the instrument by inches.

The first few fat drops of rain left dark circles on the still-hot pavement, and she felt them on her hair. The pressure in the atmosphere echoed the pressure building in her mind. She had to hurry, had to get home before every heart in Austin bled into hers and she got lost in their pain and petty grievances.

If only positive emotions were as strong as negative ones. They were, in their way, but they were so quiet that the bad stuff drowned them out. Sometimes she felt love, sometimes she felt joy, but they were quickly bogged down in the surrounding fear and anger of everyone around them. The few scraps of beauty she dug out of the dung heap had once been enough to keep her going—the potential in people for good was what she drew out when she played—but as time went on those small, sweet voices were lost, and the weeping of the world was all she knew.

It was starting.

Another day in paradise. Wasn't that a song? She started humming, trying desperately to concentrate on something, anything else: *Hallelujah* . . . Leonard Cohen understood her tonight. Her own thoughts had already started to submerge under the emotions of the rest of the city. *Someone was beating a child tonight . . . someone wanted steak for dinner and got meat loaf . . . someone was faking it . . . someone had "Angel of the Morning" stuck in his head . . . someone hated her mother . . . someone was going to pay . . . someone liked to be tied up . . . someone forgot to set the DVR to tape* Ghost Whisperer *. . . someone—*

*—someone was following her.*

Darkness. She could feel darkness. The same as in the club? Probably. A sane woman would have run, but she was so tired . . . so tired. Her legs suddenly felt like lead. It was as if she could see herself from a distance, and see what was going to happen, and there was nothing she could do but get out of the way of her fate.

*Hallelujah . . . hallelujah . . .*

There were four of them. One followed her from the club, the others emerged from an alley. Their minds were like oily black snakes, slithering toward her with the dull glow of lust and repressed rage. One of them liked her hair; another one was thinking about her breasts. A third figured she had money in her purse.

The hand that clamped on her shoulder was thick and meaty, and it yanked her backward off her feet. She cried out, but the noise was muffled as a second hand clapped over her mouth, and she was hauled back against a sweaty T-shirt with a pounding heartbeat beneath. None of them spoke until they had dragged her off the street, into the alley.

She watched the darkness of the alleyway close around her and heard the sound of her guitar case scraping along the ground. One of the men already had her purse and was rifling through it while the one dragging her threw her to the ground.

She wasn't afraid. Fear was for the unknown. She knew exactly what was going to happen.

*Hallelujah . . . hallelujah . . .*

It disconcerted them that she didn't fight, but they beat her anyway, a sharp kick to her stomach causing her body to involuntarily curl around itself to protect her abdomen. Another kick to her kidneys, and she cried out from the pain. One of the men dropped to his knees and hit her in the face, hissing at her to keep quiet or she was dead. She saw the flash of a knife, felt the blade held to her throat. *Don't scream, don't move. Do as we say and you get to live.*

She knew better.

They pushed her onto her back, and she stared up at the storm clouds she could barely see between the buildings. It was raining hard, but neither she nor her attackers noticed the downpour.

The night was hot and humid, but she felt cold when her clothes were ripped aside—cold, always cold.

*This is the way the world ends . . . not with a bang but a whimper.*

Zippers. Laughter. Hands shoving her legs apart.

Tears filled her eyes and spilled over, but she was still, just staring blankly with dead eyes up past the shoulder of the first man who forced himself into her body. The pain was a thousand miles away, as were their voices. All she could feel was cold, and all she heard was music, endless lines of melody filling her head until the world went dark at last.

First was the smell. Garbage, engine exhaust. The sickening musty smell of sex and an undertone of blood.

Then came sensations, one by one: pain first in her hands, then in her rib cage, then sharp and hot between her legs. Her face felt huge, her tongue swollen in her mouth.

Sounds. Men speaking. The voices were familiar and sent a knife of fear through her belly.

Someone nudged her back with a foot, but she didn't move, didn't betray her consciousness. She knew that if they saw she was awake, they would kill her. Why they hadn't already, she didn't know.

She heard a grunt and felt something hot and wet hit the side of her face. Oh. That was why. Another zipper, this one going upward, and a chuckle. He was done.

It wasn't over. She was still alive and they weren't leaving. *Oh God. Oh God.*

The numbness that had overtaken her before no longer shielded her from the horror of what was happening—fear crawled over her body and she fought the panicked need to run away. She wouldn't make it two steps, assuming she could even get to her feet. The pain told her quite well that she might be able to crawl, but that was it.

Movement, and someone seized her by her hair and pulled her upward, exposing her throat. She couldn't stop the scream from erupting.

"Well, look at that," the man with the knife against her jugular said, his breath fetid against her face. "Pretty little thing's awake."

He stroked the blade along her jawline. "You know, baby, you've got just about the sweetest little pussy I've ever fucked. Doesn't she, boys?"

Grunts of agreement all around. She wanted desperately to struggle, to bring her knee up into his crotch, to do anything; but it was too late. She was too hurt, too weak. The time to fight was long past. She'd let it pass. She had given up her life instead of trying to survive, and this was the end of it.

*The end. Please, let this be the end. Let them just kill me . . . at least then it'll be quiet . . . please . . .*

He was laughing, and withdrew the knife. She could feel his hips against hers, and to her disgust, he had an erection again. "Maybe we're not finished yet," he said. "I think I've got one left in me."

"Gordon, let's do her and get out of here," another of the men said anxiously. "Somebody's gonna come by."

"Keep watch," Gordon snapped. His free hand groped her breasts beneath her torn shirt, then dropped down to undo his pants.

He wasn't coordinated enough for the operation, though, and had to loosen his hold around her neck to force her back to the ground. For just a second, he lowered the knife.

Some instinct she had never felt before surged up through her battered body. Rage, red-hot and fanged, boiled her from the inside and seized the opportunity that chance had granted it. A sound she'd never known she could make tore from her throat—half scream, half snarl.

She threw herself backward into the man and knocked him off balance, then twisted her body toward him, clawing at his face. She felt something mushy beneath her thumb and shoved her nail into it, eliciting a scream from Gordon as he fought her off. She fell sideways, reaching out to grab the knife foolishly by the blade; it sliced into her palm, but she won it free, rolling up onto her knees in time to see Gordon scream again, his hands covering his eye, blood gushing from beneath his fingers.

She had his eyeball under her nails.

The other men, panicked, started toward her, but the sight of her covered in blood, half naked, brandishing the knife at them while their leader scrabbled at his punctured eye, gave them pause.

"Kill the fucking bitch!" Gordon shrieked. *"Kill her!"*

Other weapons came out. More knives, but no guns. Small-time thugs used to lording their power over vulnerable women. They'd found a perfect victim in her—small, frail, alone, and weak. She hadn't even fought. They had assaulted women as a team for years, leaving bodies here and there in Dumpsters and trash cans. No one had ever reported them to the police—because they chose women no one would ever miss, who could be used up, killed, and thrown away. Like her.

She could feel what they were feeling—Fear. Anger. Hatred. But mostly fear. They didn't know what to do, but there was no way she could fight them all, even if she weren't injured and cornered. They were going to kill her.

But she wasn't going to make it easy for them. Not again.

When they came toward her, all attacking at once, she stepped back, and her entire being screamed, *"NO!"*

The sheer force of her emotions flew outward, hitting them all like sledgehammers, and as one they were knocked backward by it, knives skittering across the concrete. She lashed out again and again, beating them with her agony the way they had with their fists, violating them with her violation. They were screaming, writhing. She didn't stop.

She stood over them in the now-pouring rain, blood oozing down her thighs, her hands fisted at her sides, and ground her emotions into them like putting out a cigarette in someone's arm. She made them feel the fear and pain of every woman they'd raped and killed, imagining their last thoughts. The women had mothers, daughters, boyfriends waiting at home who would never see them again. They had hopes and fears and possibilities that Miranda had never had. These pathetic little men had taken all of that away. Their hatred for women had made them bold.

One of them was begging for his life. She stared down at him, and he flinched from her eyes, eyes no one had seen in months. He had a wife, kids. Please. He offered her anything she wanted if she'd just let him go.

She stared, feeling nothing. "No."

She didn't know how she knew, but she knew what to do. The mind was tethered to the body, and she imagined reaching in and snapping the cord as if she were snapping his neck.

He stopped begging.

Now the others started. Even Gordon, who lay in a pool of his own blood not far from the pool of hers, where he had thrust his thick, blunt penis into her body over and over again, then watched and jerked off while the others did the same, begged for mercy.

Had the other women begged? Yes, most of them had. They hadn't fought, but they had appealed to hearts that were little more than lumps of rotten wood. Women always went for the emotions. Men went for fists. That was how the world worked.

*Snap. Snap.* Glassy eyes fixed on the walls. Struggling limbs put to rest. Those rotten hearts that felt nothing but contempt for those they destroyed shuddered into stillness.

She turned on Gordon.

She didn't hear his words, was unmoved by his begging, even when he crawled to her feet and sobbed. How many others were there? How many for Gordon? At least a dozen over the years; she could feel it. A dozen women's voices cried out to her as if they stood beside her. The choir of the dead, her own voice joining them, once an angel's song but now a scream.

*Snap.*

Slowly, she turned back around, her eyes falling on the one thing that made any sense: her guitar. They had left it unmolested on the ground, near the strewn contents of her purse. Cell phone, discarded; wallet, emptied; girl, fucked.

It occurred to some part of her to wonder what time it was, how long she'd been in this alley waiting to die. It was still wet, but the rain had passed. She was soaked, and the cold was gradually penetrating her mind, her body shaking so violently she couldn't stay on her feet.

She fell hard to her knees, feeling the pain distractedly. It faded into the din of other injuries. Her whole body was on fire, even her skin.

Her eyes lowered, as always, this time to her hands. They were bloody and filthy, her bitten nails crusted with the remains of Gordon's eye and dirt from her feeble struggles on the ground. Such small hands. Mike had always said she had lovely hands. He'd loved holding them, her palm disappearing into his broad one. Once, her hands could have done anything. She'd majored in psychology for a while, anthropology, even considered med school. She wanted to make a difference. She might one day have been a counselor assigned to a young woman like her.

She was sobbing quietly, but she heard the footsteps and froze.

Someone was coming toward the alley. Someone familiar.

She recognized it immediately: the darkness from earlier tonight, a time that felt like a thousand years ago. She knew it was the same person and wondered how she had mistaken it for the men who now lay dead around her. They were nothing alike.

Fear gripped her again, but she couldn't stand. She couldn't move. If he had come for her life, he could have it. It didn't matter anymore.

A shadow fell over her.

Suddenly something took hold of her mind, and the cacophony of emotions and voices that had moved through her the entire night cut off, the silence inside her so complete that it hurt. She would have screamed, but her throat was full of shards of ice. She didn't know what to do with silence. She no longer understood it.

The silence was followed by something else she hadn't felt in months: warmth.

She tried to shrink back from the hand that cupped her chin, but she had no strength left. She remembered— slender fingers, black cuffs, taking a basket from her. Those same fingers gently turned her head this way and that, looking her over, while she felt that warm energy gliding through her, cataloging her wounds, assessing her crumbling mental state. The touch was the most intimate she'd had in years, aside from what the men had done to her, but it was so different, she couldn't be afraid.

Finally, a third pulse of energy touched her, and it felt like her entire body had been massaged and oiled. Pain faded, and she collapsed, limp, into a fold of black held out for her.

She could barely see, but a faint red light caught her eyes, and she stared into it, wishing she could draw the glow into her . . . she lifted one hand and touched the light, feeling something cool and hard, like stone.

She heard him speak, but not to her. "Star-three." After a pause, he went on. "Faith, I need your team at these coordinates immediately."

Faintly she heard a woman's voice reply, *"As you will it, Sire."*

Then, his voice was directed into her ear: "Rest, little one. You're safe now."

Sleep rose up over her in sweet dark waves, and she gave in to it gratefully. The last thing she saw was a pair of midnight blue eyes.

# Two

The sentence was death, and he knew it, but he still ran.

At three in the morning on a stormy weekend it was eerily quiet, even in East Austin. The slap of his feet pounding the sidewalk was answered by a distant rumble of thunder and the faint flash of faraway lightning. It had rained all day Saturday, and off and on most of the night, turning a hot August day into a sauna that drove even the most stalwart Sixth Street partiers indoors.

The East Side was the poor side of town, the minority side, and there was nobody around at this hour but whores, dealers, and apostate vampires fleeing from justice.

Wallace raced along Stassney, eastbound, past houses in various states of disrepair. He hated this neighborhood and the people in it. Working families lived here, mostly Mexican immigrants and the sons of immigrants, fat wives who come morning would herd their children and hungover husbands out the door to mass *en español*. He passed a corner store with a white-painted trailer outside that boasted *pollo al carbon*, and indeed the greasy smell of roasted chicken filled his nostrils as he dove off the road and down past the storefront.

The last time he'd fed was on a cute little college girl in town for the second summer session at ACC. He remembered the way she'd slid to the ground, her fierce struggles ceasing, as the last few drops of her blood traveled down his throat. He'd left her corpse faceup in the middle of the street, knowing who would find it and how angry they would be. It was sort of the equivalent of shooting the governor the finger.

Finally he couldn't run anymore. Pain stabbed through both his sides and his legs started to give out on him. He blundered into a chain-link fence and grabbed it, holding himself up while he wheezed.

None of this would have happened if Auren were still Prime. When Auren had ruled the night over the southern United States, there were no rules—he could kill when he pleased, who he pleased, how he pleased. Auren had been the best kind of Prime: vicious, passionate about the hunt, with a blatant disdain for human life. That was perfect, in Wallace's mind. Everyone had thought Auren was invincible.

Not quite. Fifteen years ago, a blade had swung, and after that everything went wrong. Now killing humans was a capital offense.

Wallace had no use for such bullshit, and he wasn't alone. There were others who resented the new order, and the time was fast approaching when the old would be new again. He'd planned to be at the head of the pack, reclaiming his place in the world, but somehow he'd been found and followed.

He listened intently for a moment, expecting footsteps but knowing there would be none. The Prime's inner circle of warriors, the Elite, were silent hunters with no desire save dispensing the Prime's particular version of justice.

Half-drunk with fear, he looked around. It was as good a place as any to die. They'd be here any minute, and his blood would spatter all over the concrete.

"Good evening, Wallace," came a sickeningly familiar voice.

He raised his head, dragged himself to his feet, and smiled.

He was surrounded. Half the Court had turned out to execute him. It was kind of flattering, but then, if you pissed off the Prime you tended to be flattered by the grandeur of your own death.

A woman stepped forward: petite, Asian, with that frail-looking build that was almost convincing until her hands closed around your throat. She fixed her almond-shaped eyes on him, dispassionate.

"Evening, Faith," he replied hoarsely. "Fancy meeting you here."

"Are you finished running?" she asked. She, like all the rest of the Elite, traveled armed, but the gleaming steel blade at her hip stayed sheathed for the moment. If she wanted him to die quickly, she could have had him shot with a crossbow. If she had wanted him dead already, she could have walked forward and parted his head from his shoulders with her sword. It was the standard form of execution.

She did neither of those things. She stood and waited.

By the time Wallace realized what she was waiting for, the crowd was already parting, and any thought of bribery or clemency vanished. He was well and truly fucked.

"Sire," Wallace said tiredly. "Glad you could make it."

A man in black emerged from the darkness as if it had birthed him, and the Elite stepped back to a respectful distance.

The ninth Prime of the Southern United States was perhaps the most terrifying creature in the world to have standing over you at the moment of your death. He regarded Wallace through those impossible blue eyes, his expression cold and calculating. He was as always dressed impeccably, in black from head to foot, except for the heavy silver and ruby amulet that hung from his neck. In the darkness the stone glowed menacingly: the Signet, the Prime's badge of office. Few who saw that stone lived to testify that yes, it really did emit light. The myths about the Signets, and their bearers, went back thousands of years.

The most frightening thing of all was the dense aura of power that churned around the Prime like the storm clouds overhead. A vampire that strong could conceal it completely when he wanted to, and Wallace knew the display was for his benefit . . . and it had the desired effect. Wallace's heart pounded into overdrive, and he clutched the wires of the fence, desperately looking for an escape, any escape.

"James Theodore Wallace," the Prime said, his voice low, just loud enough to carry, though the psychic energy that underscored the words could probably be felt in the Panhandle. "You are under an order of execution for the murder of Patricia Kranek."

"Come on, Sire," Wallace began, trying to think of anything that could prolong the inevitable. "It was an accident. You know how it is—you get used to killing them, and then all of a sudden you're not allowed, and it's hard to know when to stop. Humans are so fragile."

"The law was established fifteen years ago, Wallace," came the reply. "You know it as well as every vampire in this territory. Hunt where you will, feed on whom you will—but a life taken, whether theirs or ours, demands a life in return."

"A fucking human! A cow! They're nothing to us!"

"Enough." That single word sent bone-chilling fear into Wallace's spine, and he pressed himself harder into the fence as if he could melt through it to the other side.

The Prime glanced over at his second in command and nodded once. A wicked smile spread over Faith's features, and she drew her sword and made a gesture to the others.

Beheading, then . . . but not until the others were done with him . . . assuming there was anything left to behead.

The crowd swarmed past their leader, their collective roar cutting off Wallace's weak protests. As they descended on him, he caught a glimpse of the Prime, who stood with his eyes closed, unsmiling, as if in pain.

The Texas Hill Country was the last place anyone would ever think to look for vampires, and that was precisely why it was ideal.

The Haven stood nestled in an oak-blanketed valley like a bird in the hands of a saint, its dark wood and brick edifice rising three stories from the surrounding gardens, stables, and other outbuildings that were all kept perfectly tended by a fleet of humans during the day. They came and went without entering the house, not caring who they worked for as long as they were handsomely paid. In the two centuries since the Haven was first built, perhaps a dozen humans had set foot inside; in his entire tenure, there had been none.

Until very recently.

The car slid around the circular drive, coming to a halt before the main entrance. One of the Elite jumped out of the front seat and came back to open the door for him.

As he emerged, the second car, carrying Faith and her patrol unit, pulled in behind. A moment later she fell into step beside him up to the heavy oak doors, which sailed open at his approach. His two personal bodyguards took the traditional seven steps back as they entered the building.

"Report," he said to Faith as they crossed through the Great Hall to the two grand staircases and headed for the second floor and his private wing of the Haven.

"The city is a tomb," she replied. "Word has gotten out about Wallace, and the entire Shadow District has shut down for fear that there will be more executions. I had the body moved to a field where it'll get full sun exposure in the morning."

"Good."

"I dropped the week's patrol reports onto your server as

well as the data sheets on the new Elite recruits. You'll also find an updated version of the map showing the locations of the attacks around the territory in the last ninety nights."

"Including the most recent?"

"Yes, Sire."

"Good." He thought of the images the patrol unit had beamed back of Patricia Kranek's body, her eyes open and staring up at the night as if she were simply stargazing. Seeing Wallace's head tumble onto the ground had not been nearly satisfying enough, especially knowing that there were more where he came from, and that without more evidence to lead to the source of the attacks there would probably be more deaths.

The unrest in the city could not be allowed to escalate into full-out war. That was unacceptable.

"Sire . . . about your . . . guest?"

He didn't speak until they had entered the East Wing. The woman stationed at the wing entrance bowed, and he nodded back to her; each member of the Elite guard that they passed did the same, and so did the lone servant making the rounds of the empty rooms with her feather duster. She had the wide-eyed look of a recent hire and was faintly awed at the sight of him; he knew she would tell her friends in the staff quarters that she had seen him, in the flesh, as it were.

The doors at the end of the hall opened into his suite. It, too, had its own guards. They bowed, and the one on the right, Samuel, held the door open for him and Faith to enter.

Once inside, he paused to remove his coat and hang it by the door. It was his second favorite. His favorite had been soaked with so much blood and filth that the only thing to do was throw it in the fireplace.

No matter. Clothes were easily replaced. A woman, on the other hand . . .

He took his usual chair and beckoned for Faith to take the other. "Now," he said, "go on."

She had managed to hold on to her professionalism, but now that they were alone, she shook her head and dropped her brisk demeanor. "With all due respect, Sire, you're completely off your nut."

"Tell me something I don't know." He leaned back, hands folded.

"How could you bring her here? She needs a hospital, a real doctor. She might have had internal bleeding or broken bones."

"Two ribs," he replied. "No bleeding. Did she wake at all while you bathed her?"

"No."

He nodded. That was his own doing; he'd kept the woman essentially in a coma until she was clean and safe, unwilling to risk her waking up naked under the hands of a stranger. He had instructed Faith to take care of her, and she had done so reluctantly, but without complaint.

The only thing he had helped with was the woman's hair; Faith had wanted to cut it off, as it was matted and caked with blood and God knew what else, but something in him had rebelled at the thought and he had worked for over an hour with a comb and half a bottle of conditioner, gingerly separating the long curls and scrubbing them clean. A few strands had been ripped out during the attack, but he salvaged the rest. He suspected that Faith's lowered opinion of his sanity had formed then.

"Come," he said, rising.

Faith followed him across the main room of the suite, to the adjoining door, which led into the small bedroom where their guest was currently sleeping. The room was normally empty. His predecessor, Auren, had kept a mistress there, as he had never taken a Queen.

It was an ideal place to house an injured woman. He could keep an eye on her and know that she was safe. The Haven was home to more than a hundred vampires at any given time, and though they were all in his employ and therefore carefully screened and monitored, he wasn't about to bet her life on their character.

He eased the door open, finding exactly what he expected: darkness. She had slept for an entire day and all of that night even after he lifted the compulsion that kept her so far under that she wouldn't even dream. She was sleeping naturally now.

He stood over the bed. She looked so small with her hair fanned out over the pillows. Her face was bruised, her lower lip cut, but he imagined that when she wasn't emaciated and battered, or terrified and despairing as when he'd first seen her, she was beautiful.

"I still think this is a bad idea." Faith sighed—she was used to her advice appearing to go in one ear and out the other, though he always listened.

They'd known each other a long time, he and Faith. She had come here with him from California when he had taken the Signet. Only she, of all the Elite, was familiar enough with him to voice her opinions freely, and did so practically every day. He was thankful for that—it was easy for someone in his position to believe himself invulnerable, above reproach, and that was what got them killed.

That was in fact what had gotten his predecessor killed fifteen years ago.

"Why are you shielding her?" she asked, frowning.

"This is why." He dropped the energy barrier he'd been holding around the woman's mind, and he knew Faith could sense the consequences—the woman moaned aloud, clapping her hands to her ears, trying to block out the emotions of everyone in the Haven . . . a hundred creatures whose histories were the fodder for nightmares anyway.

He restored the shield.

"Shit," Faith said. "An empath?"

He nodded. "A mothering-strong empath, and a minor telepath, for starters. She picks up thoughts and memories attached to feelings. It's tied in to her musical talent—she manipulated the crowd's emotions as easily as you or I would wield a sword. As soon as the music stops, she loses control."

"And she used it to kill those . . . men."

"Yes."

"I still think—"

He kept the edge out of his voice, but only just. "Faith, what do you think will happen to her if human doctors get their hands on her? Assuming she survives, she's going to need training far more than medical care. She certainly doesn't need more men jabbing at her and police officers dragging the details out of her. You know very well what happens to women like her."

Faith looked away. She did know. "Cheap shot, Sire."

"But on the mark."

"You always are." His second in command crossed her arms, staring down at the world of trouble in the bed before them. "How did you find her?"

"By chance," he replied, smiling a little at the memory. "We were in line at the grocery together."

"Meet-cute," Faith said, smiling back at him in spite of the situation.

"Not so cute. She was terrified of me, but that's normal. I saw right away that she was gifted and deteriorating quickly. She didn't know that while she was receiving, she was also projecting. I saw flashes of her memories, including the bar where she plays, and went back there last night . . . morbid curiosity, I suppose. I intended to follow her afterward. . . ."

"But I called you," Faith said, realization dawning on her face, along with guilt. "We needed you at the crime scene. God—if I hadn't done that—"

"This is hardly your fault."

"I know, but . . ." Faith shook her head. "So you looked for her after we finished at the scene, and found . . . them."

"Yes."

Another smile, this one grim. "How lucky for her, I suppose, that the most powerful vampire in the Western Hemisphere happens to have an ice cream addiction. A pint of Ben and Jerry's saved her life."

He sat down in the armchair beside the bed. "She saved herself first, Faith. She would probably have died if I hadn't found her, yes, but she was the one who stopped those bastards. I stanched the bleeding and brought her here to heal. She may not thank me for it." Over on the chest of drawers, he saw that Faith's team had delivered the human's guitar as well as the gathered belongings from her purse. By some miracle, the instrument was intact.

"Thank you, Faith," he said. "You can clock off now if there are no more loose ends."

She didn't look happy about leaving, but she bowed. "As you will it, Sire. Did you hunt tonight while you were out, or should I send in a bottle?"

He thought of the woman he had fed on before joining the hunt for Wallace. He had unconsciously selected a redhead from the teeming mass of youth and music downtown. She, however, had had blue eyes. He knew from a second's glimpse that the woman in the bed had clear green eyes the color of sunlight on leaves.

It had been more than three centuries since he had seen sunlight, but it was the sort of thing his kind never forgot.

Faith departed, closing the door quietly behind her, leaving him alone with a broken young woman who, he recalled, liked Snickers bars.

That was about all he knew of her. She was extraordinarily gifted, completely untrained, and had a singing voice like dark honey touched with cinnamon. She had green eyes that never left the ground. She drank Shiner Bock. He hadn't even had a chance to learn her name—it was something Grey, he remembered from the sign at the bar, but he had assumed, perhaps foolishly, that he would speak to her afterward and find out the rest.

There was nothing to do but wait. He didn't want her to wake alone in a strange house with no idea what was happening or who had claimed her from the streets of Austin.

He sat back and pulled the phone from his pocket to read Faith's reports . . .

Well, perhaps after a game of Tetris.


Everything was different when she woke.

She was warm, and comfortable. There were smells, but not blood and garbage; she smelled a wood fire, fabric softener . . . almonds, faintly, in some form of body wash or shampoo.

The air on her skin was clean and so was she. Soft fabric covered her, just the right weight, and it was warm . . . so warm.

Warm and silent.

Had she been more alert, the silence in her mind might have panicked her. Her thoughts seemed thin and stringy alone in her head, and didn't fill the space. It felt like being onstage solo in a concert hall meant to seat thousands.

She tried to move, but pain coursed through her body, a dull throbbing from a dozen epicenters. Her muscles were so weak they wouldn't respond to her commands, though with effort she could move her head and open her eyes. She half expected to wake to the storm-smudged sky back in that alley, bleeding to death in the dirt, but her vision gradually focused on what was above her—a ceiling.

She blinked, trying to make sense of it. Dreaming . . . oh, God, she'd been dreaming. The whole thing was a dream. Even her dingy apartment had all been the invention of her imagination; the bedroom there had a ceiling fan, and this one didn't. She was somewhere else, somewhere safe and far away from the nightmare . . . where?

Her mind barely had time to register the immense

relief of it all before reality began to settle back around her, heavy as a shroud.

Her body hurt. The left side of her torso sent pain through her every time she inhaled. Her face was swollen, the hand that had been cut with Gordon's knife pulsing with her heartbeat. When she shifted her hips slightly, an arc of white-hot agony tore upward between her legs.

She whimpered softly. Relief gave way to the yawning pit of desolation.

There was a sound to her right, and she turned her head—too fast, it turned out, as another wrenching pain seized her neck and shoulders. The room swam in her vision for a moment before righting itself.

She stared, everything else momentarily forgotten.

He was sitting beside her bed in a plush-looking armchair, his slender body as unconsciously regal as a cat's, reclining as if the chair—no, the *world*—had been created for his own particular use. As before he wore all black, perfectly hand-tailored to show off an almost inhuman grace. Raven hair fell into eyes that almost seemed to glow in the merry flicker of the fireplace at the far end of the room. He could have been a runway model—or, better yet, one of the gorgeous gay yogis she'd met during her brief stab at spiritual development a few months before everything went to hell. Everything about him was so perfect he might really have been something cooked up by her imagination. At the grocery store she had thought of him, vaguely, as handsome, but she was so focused on running away that the extent of his beauty had obviously failed to register.

The only anomalies were in the accessories: around one wrist, a flat featureless band of silver metal that reminded her of those slap bracelets that were popular back in the early nineties. Around his neck, a heavy silver chain ending in a fairly Gothic-looking amulet set with what was either the biggest ruby she'd ever seen or the gaudiest fake ruby she'd ever seen. The stone itself caught the firelight and glowed, too, so strongly she thought for a minute it had a tiny bulb inside.

He was staring down into the screen of an iPhone. Somehow that was every bit as weird to her as the ice cream had been a thousand years ago.

She stared, and stared—it was the longest time she'd been able to simply *look* at someone in months.

For a while he let her stare. She knew that he felt her eyes on him. Something about him kept teasing the back of her mind with knowledge she didn't want.

Finally he lifted his gaze to hers.

It felt like the bottom had dropped out of her heart as she fell into his eyes, seeing . . . and feeling . . . so much more than she should have, but still far less than she got from people off the street. This . . . man . . . had barriers around his thoughts, and walls of steel around his heart, and had drawn the circle of power around her that now kept her mind silent with his own hands.

"I know you," she whispered. Her voice sounded like it had been dragged over broken glass. "Where am I?"

His voice was the same as she remembered: low and musical, with a foreign cadence but no obvious accent. "We call it the Haven," he replied, speaking gently, keeping the peace of the room intact.

"It was you in the store, and in . . . in the alley. Who are you?"

He sat back, sliding the phone into his pocket and folding his hands, considering her question. "There are several ways I can answer that. How much of the truth do you want right now?"

She started to snap that she wanted it all, but another look in his face made her think better of it. This man had found her surrounded by the corpses of men she had killed, and not only had he not called the police, he'd brought her somewhere safe and was now shielding her mind. There was far more going on here than a chance meeting in an alley.

She shut her eyes hard. "Just give me what you think I can handle."

"Very well. My name is David Solomon. This, the Haven, is my home. You were brought here because you were injured, and because by striking those humans down with your power you inadvertently crossed a border into our world."

"Your world?"

"On one side of that border, the police and government agencies enforce their law. On this side, the law is mine. As far as I'm concerned you were the hand of justice last night. The scale is balanced."

"And you're what, supernatural police?"

He smiled, and though it was a very attractive smile, it sent a chill through her bones.

"I thought I could help you," he said after a moment. "I saw what you were and the road you were headed down."

She closed her eyes for a minute, fighting tears, her fingers clenching in the pristine white sheets that cocooned her. She sought inside her mind for the cold comfort of voices and emotions, of anything . . . but there was a blank wall, one she couldn't take down.

"It's quiet," she whispered. "It's so quiet. What did you do to me?"

He shrugged fluidly. "I shielded you. It's an energetic barrier that separates you from the emotions of others. If you had been properly trained to your gifts, you could do the same."

She didn't reply, but shut her eyes again, listening. Her hands gripped the sheets so hard her knuckles were white.

"What's your name?" he asked.

She didn't look at him. "Miranda Grey."

"A pleasure to meet you, Miranda Grey. Are you hungry?"

She shook her head. She'd throw up anything she tried

to eat right now. A moment later she asked, "What are you going to do with me? Are you going to fuck me, too?"

His eyebrows shot up in polite incredulity, and he said, "Certainly not."

Now she shrugged. "I don't think I'm much good for anything else."

His nails dug into the arms of the chair as he said sharply, "Don't say that."

"Why not? You don't even know me. Why do you care?"

He didn't answer, and she looked away, toward the shuttered window. All the light in the room came from the fireplace—in August, in Texas, as out of place as the long coat he'd been wearing. Who the hell were these people?

To mask her sudden fear, she stammered, "What's that thing around your neck?"

His fingers lifted to the stone almost unconsciously, and it seemed like the light flared subtly at the touch. "The Signet," he replied.

She waited for an explanation, but none was forthcoming, so she said lamely, "It looks heavy."

A smile crossed his face that was at once both wry and deeply, deeply weary. "It is."

A breath later his expression had returned to neutral; he smiled again, and rose. "There are guards outside this door. No one will approach you without permission. I have arranged for food to be brought to you by the servants. If you need anything, feel free to ask them, and it will be provided. I must ask you not to go poking around alone beyond these halls—I can't guarantee your safety outside the East Wing. When you are feeling better, you'll have a tour."

"Wait . . . am I some kind of hostage? What if I don't want to stay here?"

He turned back to her, one hand on the door, and met her eyes. "Where would you go?"

Again, she looked away, staring into the fire. "Nowhere."

"Rest, then, Miss Grey."

"But where are you going?" She was suddenly afraid, though whether of him leaving or staying, she couldn't say.

"It's sunrise," he replied. "I'm going to bed."

With that, he left, and she stared blankly at the fire with silence echoing in her mind until slumber tugged her back into its web and spun oblivion around her.

*Screaming. Groping hands. Laughter.*

Miranda struggled against the sweaty, covetous hands that gripped her, her wounds tearing and bleeding again, desperation overriding pain. She could taste blood in her mouth and feel it oozing down her legs . . . she was so weak . . . but she wouldn't be taken alive. Not this time. She screamed again and redoubled her efforts, but it was no use, they had her . . . they were dragging her to the lake to throw her body in . . . she felt the sickening lurch of flying through the air, and the freezing water was like a thousand knives in her lungs.

She tried to scream a third time but couldn't take a breath. The world was fading to black. In the background she could hear shouting, crowd noise, screams. Classical music. The chaos of a hundred songs played in the recesses of her brain.

Then she heard the sound of metal sliding against something, like a sword being drawn. A swish, and a thump, and her vision filled with a pulsating red light. The din around her cut off abruptly.

She woke to a pool of moonlight over her bed and the taste of blood lingering on her tongue.

The fire had died down to embers, but the room was still perfectly comfortable. It took her a second to remember it was high summer and she really should be burning up.

Strange—she hadn't realized the room had a window. Turning her head for a better look she saw there were some kind of metal shutters over the outside, just now slanted open so she could see the moon. To the left of the window, on the wall near the sill, there was a black button that she assumed operated the shutters. Had someone been in to open them while she was asleep?

More questions along those lines began to occur to her. She was clean—who had bathed her? Someone had bandaged her and dressed her, which meant someone had touched her naked, unconscious body. The way her palm was wrapped suggested someone knew what they were doing. Should she be angry about that, or grateful that they had taken care of her? Had it been David Solomon? The thought made her shiver. He'd claimed he didn't intend to assault her, but why should she believe him? What kind of crazy fuck took in a strange woman he'd just seen kill four people?

*God. Oh God.*

Miranda sat up slowly and painfully and put her head in her hands. That night came to her in flashes of fear and nausea, just like in her dream, but now it was punctuated with images of men at her feet, begging for their lives.

The scale was balanced, David had said.

Did she believe that?

No.

She couldn't think about it right now. There was too much, and it was too hard, and she was too fragile—it wouldn't take a lot to send her wailing over the edge, shield or no shield.

Instead, she focused on her body, and on moving it. She slid carefully over to the edge of the bed and dropped first one foot, then the other, over the side. Her feet didn't touch the floor; it was a tall bed, queen-sized, and she had never been a large woman. She was afraid that her legs wouldn't support her, but testing with one foot she found she could stand, more or less, as long as she held on to the bedpost.

First, she tottered over to peer out the window,

wondering where on earth she was. She expected to see buildings and busy streets, but the view presented to her was one of rolling hills, endless trees, and, closer to her, an expanse of gardens contained within a tall iron fence. Outside the fence, she could make out the silvery shapes of deer grazing along the treeline. There were several smaller structures as well, all built in the same style as where she was. She figured out, by craning her neck to the left and right, that she was on the second floor of an honest-to-God mansion, somewhere in the Hill Country.

Her knees felt weak at the realization that wherever this place was, it was definitely no-one-can-hear-you-scream territory. There wouldn't be any buses running out this far. If she wanted to leave without a ride, she'd have to hike in the Texas heat.

Without shoes. She looked down at herself, noticing her attire for the first time. They'd dressed her in a white T-shirt and black cotton pants that were too long for her legs. Her hair was hanging loose and her feet were bare, their chipped raspberry toenail polish poking out from the pants. Had they thrown away her clothes? She hoped so, although she'd liked her beat-up old tennis shoes, and she'd been wearing her favorite blue panties with the stars all over them . . .

Flashes. *Hands. Pain. "You've got the sweetest little pussy I've ever fucked . . ."*

She swayed backward and had to half turn and grab the bedpost to keep from passing out. She wanted to go back to sleep . . . she wanted a drink . . . she wanted to die. Anything to make it stop, to leach the memories from her and leave her alone.

Shaking her head hard against her thoughts, she turned her attention back to her surroundings and set about a slow exploration of the room.

It was about the size of her apartment bedroom and had the indefinable feel of a place that was kept clean but never used. The furnishings were expensive but not overblown, fairly traditional in style but not ornate. Bed, chair, matching sofa, fireplace, chest of drawers. Her guitar and purse had been left atop the latter.

Out of habit more than interest she opened the case and checked to see that her guitar had survived. It had, without so much as a broken string. Small favors.

She rifled through her purse and dug out her cell phone, which turned on obligingly even though the screen was cracked. No missed calls, no messages. She snorted softly. Who exactly would miss her? If she had died in that alley, it would have taken days for anyone to notice her absence. Mel at the club would probably be first, after she missed her next performance. The cops would probably identify her body from her driver's license and old student ID, then call her father, whom she hadn't spoken to in years. Eventually her sister, Marianne, would hear. Would anyone call Kat? Would Kat blame herself for not staying with her despite her protests that night?

*It doesn't matter . . . you're alive. Sort of.*

Nothing appeared to be missing—they'd even found her lip gloss. It was pearlescent mauve. Had there really been a time she'd cared about having shiny lips?

She wasn't sure exactly who *they* were, except that David had said *we* when speaking of the Haven, so it stood to reason other people lived here, too. He was obviously someone important, but it made no sense to her, and deep down she had a feeling she was better off not knowing.

One door: a small closet, empty. Another door: a small but well-appointed bath. She frowned. There was no mirror above the sink. Someone had, however, stocked the little room with new toiletries and towels, even including a package of elastic bands for her hair. She dug one out and reached up with stiff, aching arms to arrange the curly mass into a hasty braid.

She returned to the chest and looked in the drawers: there were two more sets of clothes identical to what she had on, plus some socks and brand-new underwear the same brand and size as her old ones, but all in white.

Miranda pondered taking a shower, but first she had to finish her inventory: there were two more doors.

The one that David had disappeared through she figured went out into the hallway, so she started with the other . . . but to her confusion, she opened the door to find herself looking into a marble-tiled hall lined with other doors.

The door immediately to the left was flanked with a man and a woman in black uniforms, each wearing a sword in a sheath down to their knees, and each with one of those silver bands on their left wrist.

The woman saw her and smiled, then actually bowed. "Good evening, Miss. My name is Helen and this is Samuel. Shall I call for your dinner?"

"Um . . . no . . ." she sputtered. "Just looking around, sorry."

"If you need anything, just ask one of us," the guard said. "We've been instructed to look out for you."

"By . . . by whom?"

The two exchanged a look. "By the Prime, of course," she replied.

"Oh. Okay. Thanks."

Miranda closed the door. She had absolutely no idea what the woman—Helen—was talking about. What the hell was a Prime? Who *were* these people?

And if this door went into the hall, where did the other one go?

She hesitated with her hand on the knob, then eased it open a few inches, almost dreading what she was going to find.

More weirdness. Beyond the door was simply another bedroom, this one enormous; the bed alone dwarfed hers, and was surrounded by heavy curtains. The far end of the room was a sitting area with a couch and two chairs facing a fireplace twice the size of the one in her room. Bookshelves lined the walls, laden with volumes and assorted objects from a variety of countries and time periods.

She felt rather like someone digging up relics from the *Titanic*, but ventured into the room anyway, careful not to touch anything. The books were not dusty, so either they were routinely read or there was one hell of a maid running around. The usual suspects were in attendance: Shakespeare, Milton, Thoreau, Keats; philosophy, history, even physics and engineering; but there were also at least two dozen software manuals spanning the entire life of computer technology, kept in meticulous chronological order, the most recent being a tome devoted to something called PHP.

Several weapons hung on the walls, all blades, including one that looked something like a samurai sword and a couple of long knives crossed over each other.

Ninja computer programmer?

She completed a circuit around the room, finishing at a large desk with a precise arrangement of electronics. Phone dock, MacBook, a set of Bose speakers designed for use with an iPod. Wireless mouse. Two external hard drives. There were also a few standard office supplies, including a slim silver pen that lay in a groove cut into the desk's surface. The pen was engraved, and she risked picking it up to read the inscription: PRIME DAVID L. SOLOMON, PHD.

Ninja computer programmer doctor?

"What the hell are you doing in here?"

Miranda's heart stopped and she spun around, or at least tried to, though her body wouldn't fully obey and she nearly ended up falling over. The voice had come from the doorway to her room, and she turned around to see the speaker standing with arms crossed, glaring at her.

It was a woman of Asian descent with long black hair in dozens of tiny braids, her brown eyes staring daggers at Miranda. She, too, wore the black uniform of the guards in the hall, but with the addition of a series of small silver pins on the collar, and several extra weapons—also blades.

Miranda started to stutter out another apology, but the woman cut her off. "I could be out in the city hunting for insurgents, but instead I am sent to check on the Prime's new pet."

Miranda felt the apology die on her tongue with a flash of irritation. "I haven't lifted my leg on the furniture yet."

Was it her imagination, or did the woman almost smile?

"You shouldn't be in here."

"I know," Miranda said, flushing. "I was looking around my room and found the door. It wasn't locked. I didn't realize whose it was."

She set the pen down where she'd found it and crossed the room, following the guard back into her own chamber, embarrassed to have been caught snooping. As she passed she noticed that up close, the woman was actually a hair shorter than she was, but a hundred times more imposing, weapons or no weapons.

Miranda made it back to her room before her legs got too weak to stand on, and she collapsed into the love seat with a quiet moan. She'd managed to forget the pain in her muscles and ribs for a while, but now it flared up again, and she leaned back to take pressure off her chest, shaky and exhausted.

When she looked up, the woman was staring at her as if seeing her for the first time. There was something like recognition on her face, and she reached into her pocket, retrieving a prescription bottle.

"These are for you," she said. "Vicodin."

Miranda regarded the bottle, which had her name in

bold print across the label, issued by a doctor she didn't recognize and picked up from a CVS on the west side of Austin.

"I also instructed Samuel to bring you food," she went on. "I know you're probably not feeling hungry, but you have to eat if you're going to heal."

Miranda didn't bother to protest. She knew that this was not the sort of woman to argue with.

"Also, I'm to give you this." The guard produced one of the wristbands that she and the others wore, and handed it to Miranda. "It's a voice-activated communication device. If you find yourself needing help, say the code number of the person you want to speak to, and it will connect you if you have sufficient security clearance."

"How do I know the codes?"

"Samuel is code nineteen. Helen, code twenty-three."

"What about you?"

She raised an eyebrow. "Star-three."

"Why a star?"

"The Prime is Star-one, and I am his second in command."

"Then why aren't you Star-two?"

"Traditionally the Prime is first in the chain, followed by his Queen, then their second. Our Prime has no Queen, so Star-two is vacant."

"What exactly is a Prime?"

She got the look of someone trying to find words to explain calculus to a hamster. "The Shadow World is divided loosely into twenty-seven territories," she began. "Each territory is controlled by a Prime, and ideally by a paired Prime and Queen, who set the law which is enforced by their warriors—us. Everyone living within that territory is required to follow the Prime's law on pain of death."

"Okay, back up. Shadow World?"

The woman looked taken aback. "What?"

"I don't get it. I've never heard of any of this, and your Prime guy was talking about your world like it's this whole separate universe. Are you all nuts? You really think there's some special kind of law just for you? Who is he? Who are you? And what the fuck is going on in this place?"

She fell back into the cushions, drained by the burst of questions, and stared at the guardswoman, who blinked at her in surprise.

Miranda waited for her to say something, her head starting to pound—normally the guard's thoughts and feelings would tell her whatever she wanted to know. This business of having to ask questions felt strange after months of knowing too much about everyone she met. She could even look the woman in the eye, if she wanted to, without being confronted with her entire life story, which for a woman wearing a sword was probably a good thing.

"And one last thing," Miranda said before she could help it, "if you guys are bodyguards, why don't you have guns? What good is a sword going to do you in the twenty-first century?"

Now the woman definitely smiled. "Bullets are useless against our enemies," she told Miranda, "but decapitation works for pretty much everyone."

"So, what, you're the Highlander?"

She took a deep breath and sat down on the opposite end of the sofa. "I think perhaps this explanation will take a while."

Miranda shut her eyes a moment. "I figured." She gestured weakly at the woman, who was sitting with absolutely perfect posture, ready at a moment's notice to leap into action . . . whatever sort of action went on here in Bizarro World. "Why don't we start with your name."

"All right. My name is Faith."

"Nice to meet you, Faith. Miranda. Now, tell me who you people are."

She tried not to let the statement come off as a command, but Faith's eyebrow quirked anyway. "It's complicated. You may not believe me."

"Then keep it simple, for now. Ten words or less."

"I can give it to you in three."

"Go ahead."

Faith smiled, and the entire universe, already perilously close to spinning wildly off its axis, ground to a halt as she replied, "We are vampires."

# Three

Her name was Maria, and she spoke no English, but the halter top and leather miniskirt said all anyone at the club really wanted to know.

He led her from the dance floor up the stairs to the balcony, where the guards were holding the space, keeping the rest of the crowd away. She followed gamely, her mind full of sex and tequila.

She was young and sweet and surprisingly innocent, here with her older friends for a wild night on the town before starting another week cleaning hotel rooms. He imagined her in her maid's uniform dancing in the hallways, a vacuum her partner, peeking in people's suitcases. The thought made him smile.

He also had another image of her: so drunk her eyes rolled in her head, being held down and fucked by the group of frat boys he'd seen moving in on her. Maybe she would remember, maybe it would just be a haze of booze and Rohypnol, but in the morning she would wake up hung over with the vague feeling that someone had been cruel to her, and it would never occur to a poor immigrant girl to get the police involved over being treated like a gutter whore.

He'd seen it a thousand times. They came to Texas for something better, and perhaps they found it—but the milk of human unkindness was as bitter in Austin as it was in Mexico.

Maria was nineteen, and her Spanish was lightning fast. She spoke of her friends still out on the dance floor, and of the guy who'd stuck his tongue in her ear an hour ago, and of the merits of Patrón over Cuervo. She was nervous. A handsome man in black had slid in behind her on the dance floor, his hands wrapping around her hips and drawing her back against him, and her will went completely slack. Her friends had elbowed each other, and he knew what they were thinking: *rich white man*.

The human mind was astonishingly easy to manipulate. They were almost always open to gentle suggestion, and few knew how to shield. It was that manipulation, ironically, that enabled his kind to feed without hurting anyone . . . when they bothered to do so.

He drew Maria to the corner and pressed against her, feeling her small hands and long fingernails clench his upper arms. She had no intention of saying *no*, but still, he turned so that if she wanted she could still get away, even as he took firmer hold of her mind and tilted her chin back.

The smell of her skin—perfume, yes, but beneath that soap and sweat and the intoxicating scent of the feminine and mortality—brought his hunger out full force. His teeth scratched lightly over her neck, and he lowered his head and struck.

Her body tightened, but his hold over her was too strong to allow her to panic. She moaned and ground her hips into his. He ran power through her, heightening her arousal until she moaned again; desire and pleasure strengthened the blood, and flavored it with an undertone of sex and chocolate, thick and hot. She also had the faint taste of frankincense—a good Catholic girl.

He drank until he felt the itch in his jaw fade, and until her heartbeat fell into rhythm with his. Beyond that point, taking more could injure her. This was all he needed, and would affect her about as much as donating at the blood and tissue center.

He lifted his mouth from her skin and licked the two tiny holes. They would be gone by midmorning.

Maria sagged back against the wall, and he held her up for a moment, carefully planting suggestions in her mind: She'd met a man, they'd danced and had a few drinks, and then she'd gone home. She could fill in the details with her own imagination. She was to get in the cab that would be waiting outside and return to her apartment, eat something, and then sleep.

He watched her walk back down the stairs in her stiletto heels, wondering for the thousandth time why women in this century hadn't jettisoned such patriarchal masochism. Once he saw her walk out of the club, where his guards would steer her into the Yellow Cab and pay the driver, he took the stairs and left himself.

The night was hot and humid from the recent rain, but for his kind it was just warm enough. The only real reason he wore his coat this time of year was to conceal his weapons from the teeming mortal crowd of Sixth Street.

He lifted his wrist and said into the com, "Star-three."

A chiming noise told him he'd connected. *"Yes, Sire?"*

"Report."

*"As you requested, I came to check on your guest. I'm there now."*

He blinked. "Still?"

*"Yes. We're . . . having a conversation about . . . things."*

Oh. *That* conversation. "How's she taking it?"

*"Unclear at this point. I'll keep you apprised."*

"Star-one, out."

He smiled faintly at the thought of how Miranda had reacted to finding out exactly what she'd blundered into.

He was about to call the car to take him back to the Haven, when a second chime, higher-pitched, issued from the com.

"Yes?" he asked.

*"Sire . . . Elite Twenty-seven here reporting from Patrol Three. We have a situation and request your intervention."*

Her voice was tense, with an edge of shock. His heart sank. There was only one reason the patrol would request his presence on an otherwise peaceful night: another attack. "Alpha Seven?"

*"Yes, Sire."*

"Location?"

*"The 360 entrance to the Barton Creek Greenbelt."*

"I'm on my way."

During daylight hours the Greenbelt was scattered with joggers and humans walking dogs. The ribbon of trees and brush itself wound around the water, beneath the highway and along the edge of town, and though it was a good place for a run or a nature walk, it was also, unfortunately, a good place to dump a body.

The car pulled up into the parking lot, and by the time he got out the two on-duty patrol leaders were already at his side, giving him the rundown on the attack.

"Is it the same MO as the rest?" he asked.

"No, Sire. It seems the insurgents have upped the ante . . . and they wanted to deliver a very pointed message."

"I suppose it's foolish to ask who the message was for," he mused, following them down the entry path that led to the Greenbelt itself. "How was it discovered?"

"Anonymous tip to APD. They recognized the signs and called it in to us."

He smelled the body before he saw it. As they turned a corner, the stench of old blood and decaying flesh hit him in a nauseating wave. Contrary to popular myth, vampires didn't get hungry just from smelling blood—it was the life energy contained within it that they lived on. Seeing blood splashed around a body wasn't any more appetizing to them than a pile of rotting fruit would be to a human.

The rest of the patrols were clustered around the scene, and as one they rose and bowed to him when he appeared. He nodded, and they returned to their work, gathering parts.

There were a lot of parts.

He stood with his arms crossed and pondered what was in front of him, anger forming a hard knot in his chest.

The Elite had unfolded a plastic tarp on the ground and were lining up the victim's dismembered remains. Each part was wrapped meticulously in white paper and sealed with masking tape. One of the Elite sliced carefully through the tape and unwrapped each piece to get a better look.

The knot of anger caught fire as he realized what he was seeing.

The human had been methodically butchered. There were no clothes, no personal effects, just parts hacked off at the joints with what looked like a cleaver. The white ends of bone were visible where the legs had been cut at the knee. Flesh had been sheared from the pelvis and wrapped separately from the bones. The rib cage had been sliced into segments, ready for barbecue.

Despite the obvious care taken to wrap the body parts, scavengers had already gotten to several, and so had insects. Flies buzzed everywhere, and at least three of the parcels had been dragged from the central location beneath a tree and ripped open. Blood had soaked through the corners of the packages.

One of the Elite turned away from the package he was opening, looking ashen and sick. At the Prime's questioning look, he gestured at the package and said, "Organs. Including the tongue."

"How long has this been out here?" he demanded.

Elite 27 joined him. "We're thinking since this morning, but it looks like it may have been refrigerated before the dump. I called for an APD forensics team to come in and claim the body—they can give us more details. But it was definitely a vampire—there are fang marks at the jugular. I'm guessing that was the cause of death and the poor bastard was hacked up postmortem."

"You're sure it was male?"

"Yes, Sire. The genitals were in their own package. There's also this . . ."

The Prime went with him over to the tree. Elite 27 pointed at the base of the trunk, where the skull had been left unwrapped.

He knelt next to it, wondering whose life had been stolen and whether he had died in pain—the traces of the human's death had already faded, which meant he had been dead several days. It was a blond, Caucasian, about 30 years of age, healthy looking—except of course for being disembodied underneath a tree.

"Look at his ear," the Elite suggested.

The human's left ear had been punctured and hung with a metal tag, just like those used by cattle ranchers, but instead of a number, it was etched with a symbol.

Each Prime had an official Seal. The tag in the human's ear bore the Seal of Auren, the Prime before him.

Apparently the old boy still had friends.

He straightened, clamping down hard on the rage boiling up his spine and the instinctive urge to spill blood. "Now we know who we're dealing with," he said. "I want a trace run on anyone connected with Auren's Court who survived the war. Allies, Elite, servants, everyone. Anyone you find, bring in for questioning. Anyone who resists, rip their heads off."

"Yes, Sire. I'm on it." The warrior seemed a bit surprised at his vehemence, but turned away to call the Haven and have one of the administrative support staff get started on the search.

He walked back up the path, feeling every year of his age and more, anger gradually giving way to frustration and then to weariness. In the last three months there had been seven murders by vampires who were making no effort to hide their crimes. Up until now in his tenure there had been occasional attacks, but nothing on this scale. It had taken a decade and a half for Auren's followers to organize themselves.

Harlan, the driver, bowed. "Sire. Back to the Haven?"

"Yes."

Harlan opened the door, his eyes on the white van pulling into the parking lot with the city coroner's logo emblazoned on the side. "These people must be barking mad to declare war on a Signet," he noted.

The Prime smiled grimly. "The bastards have no idea who they're dealing with."

"Obviously not, Sire. Or perhaps they believe all the legends about you are just that, legends."

He settled into the seat. "They'll learn better. Auren did."

As Harlan pulled away from the scene, easing the car into traffic, the Prime sat brooding, his fingers curled around the Signet he had plucked from Auren's headless corpse fifteen years ago.

No matter how many allies he had, no matter how much power and money and influence, there were always those waiting in the shadows for their turn at glory. Assassination attempts usually started before the old Prime's ashes were even scattered. The old regime and the new battled for control, sometimes for years. His Elite had taken ruthless hold of the territory inside two months.

Auren had been charismatic and strong and held a complete disdain for human life. Those who followed Auren were the dregs of the Shadow World: murderers, rapists, and thugs. If they had a new leader, they would be tough to put down. They would be after his blood, and soon, if they weren't dealt with, would make a play for the Signet.

He smiled into the darkness.

*Let them try.*


Miranda listened to Faith speak, peppering her with questions but mostly just . . . staring at her.

Her brain was stubbornly refusing to process anything the guard was saying. Thoughts looped through: *These people are insane. I have to get out of here. This isn't possible. These people are insane. Wait, what about garlic?*

Faith was matter-of-fact. Garlic: myth. Coffins: myth. Crucifixes: myth.

About thirty minutes into the discussion Miranda had to ask for a glass of water and a Vicodin. The damage to her body was draining what little resolve she had to run away. Assuming she made it to the door and assuming she could find her way out of this place, fatigue and pain would send her to the ground before she made it fifty feet.

So she let the painkiller dull her senses and let Faith talk, as if any of it were believable.

Vampires. She was in a house full of vampires. They had their own society, their own government, and their president slept in the next room.

Miranda held a cushion in her lap, the closest thing to a shield she could find between her and the crazy person on the other end of the couch.

"Metal shutters," Miranda muttered, looking over at the window. "They block out the sun."

"The windows are also coated with UV-blocking film. The shutters are a safeguard and for comfort—we have trouble sleeping unless the room is pitch black."

She put her hands over her face. "This is just . . ."

"I know. It's a lot to take in."

"Hold on . . . if you drink blood, why was the Prime guy buying ice cream?"

Faith smiled. "We can digest human food in small amounts once we've built up a tolerance. It helps us pass for human. Naturally we have an easier time with liquids. Some of us have things we still love—a sweet tooth is most common."

"But it doesn't do you any good nutritionally, right?"

A male voice spoke up from the doorway. "Not unless Ben and Jerry start making Mocha Plasma Chip."

Miranda looked up to see the Prime had arrived, silently opening the door between the bedrooms. He seemed to fill the entire room with his presence, as before, but tonight he looked a little worn around the edges, like he'd seen something horrible.

His blue eyes lit on her, and he smiled. "How are you feeling this evening, Miss Grey?"

"I don't think that's a fair question, Sire," Faith replied for her.

"I'm fucked up on Vicodin," Miranda told him, keeping the hysteria out of her voice by inches. "Otherwise there'd be a girl-shaped hole in that door."

He leaned sideways against the door frame, still smiling. "I understand."

"All right, screw this. Show me your teeth."

His eyebrows shot up. "I'm sorry?"

"If you're really a vampire, you must have fangs, right? Show me."

He nodded and came over to the sofa. Faith jumped up, bowed, and moved aside so there was room for him to sit. Miranda started to say something about it, thinking it unfair that she had to get up just because he was in the room, but then she remembered who she was talking to.

The Prime opened his mouth, reached up, and ran a fingertip over one of his canines. Miranda watched with her heart ripping its way into her throat as the tooth stretched lazily down half an inch, extending like a cat's claw, dangerously sharp. A few seconds later it withdrew, and she saw that even retracted it was visibly more pointed than it should have been.

Miranda glanced over at Faith, who was grinning a bit wickedly. The guard did the same as the Prime had, showing her teeth.

"Holy shit. Holy shit."

"Don't be afraid," David said softly. "You're safe here, perhaps safer than you've ever been in your life."

"But . . . but you eat people."

He chuckled at the phrasing. "In a manner of speaking. But we have laws against killing our prey."

"Prey . . . oh God." She shrank back as far into the corner of the couch as she could, causing her ribs to stab sharply, and gasped at the pain. Tears gathered in her eyes. "I don't think I can take this."

"Would you like us to leave you alone?" he asked.

"Please," she whispered. Sobs were building in her chest. Distantly she heard the Prime tell Faith he needed to speak to her privately. Miranda curled around the cushion, burying her face in it, and listened as the door opened and shut.

When she glanced up, David was still there, but standing, halfway between the couch and the door.

"If you need anything, I'll be nearby," he said. "Just knock on the door, or call with your com."

She nodded, unable to speak. He didn't look like he wanted to leave, but he did so, closing the door behind him.

Miranda lowered her head back to the cushion and waited for the tears to come, but they didn't. Instead she felt deadened on the inside, too overwhelmed for any one emotion to take precedence. Listening to Faith had kept the demons at bay for a while, just as it had distracted her from her injuries, but no longer—too much had happened, stretching all the way back to that day at the café when she'd made strangers cry. Her life had become a furtive hell that had fireballed into ash, and there was nothing left. She had nothing to go back to, and no reason to care.

They should have killed her. Maybe she could persuade the vampires to drain her dry. If she left the wing and ran around the house, would she find someone willing to kill her?

A few minutes later a metallic clanking sound startled her, and she looked up in time to see the shutters closing over the window. Mystery solved: They must be on a timer with the button as an override.

She sat and stared at the unlit hearth, cold gradually seeping back into her bones though the room's temperature hadn't changed.

She must have dozed off, because when she opened her eyes again her legs were asleep and her ribs and her palm hurt unbearably. The pill had worn off. She groped at the side table for the bottle and succeeded in knocking it onto the floor with her bandaged hand. As she tried to reach for it, her back seized up, and she slid face first off the couch onto the rug.

It hurt so much to move, she started crying. Finally the dam seemed to break and she wept into her arm, sobs racking her body like a child's, the hoarse sounds torn from her throat echoing in the empty room.

A thousand miles away she heard footsteps, and a shadow moved over her, a glowing presence kneeling at her side.

Warmth surrounded her in the form of a fuzzy blanket, and a light touch of energy tapped on the back of her mind, seeking entrance. She didn't know how to refuse and was too weak to try. The "hand" touched her, and soothing heat flooded her body until her muscles went totally limp.

She felt herself lifted, felt herself carried. Bed, sheets, comforter; he tucked her into feather pillows and fine linen, and she had time to notice that the bed smelled different before sleep claimed her.

The nightmares came thick and fast all that day. She struggled against dozens of assailants, saw dark water rising up toward her face. She tasted blood. They laughed at her as they bucked their hips at hers, bit her breasts, used her hair like reins.

Fanged monsters joined in, tearing holes in her throat. Her whole body itched as blood slicked down over her skin, and when she tried to run away she slipped and fell into the black water. Hands grabbed her legs and pulled her down, down into the darkness . . .

But once again, there was a flash of red light, and everything stopped.

She ought to have been used to nothing making sense by now, but when she opened her eyes this time, the world had changed again.

Another bed, not her own and not the one in her apartment. This one was far larger, surrounded by curtains that were open partway at the foot to reveal a magnificent fireplace alive with heat and golden light. The sheets over her had to have a thousand thread count.

On the far side of the room she could hear a rapid clicking noise. Typing?

She felt relaxed and recognized the blurry after-effects of the Vicodin. She'd had another pill at some point. When?

Miranda lifted the blankets from her legs and scooted down toward the foot of the bed, where she could see the rest of the room. Instantly she recognized her surroundings—even before she saw the figure sitting at the desk.

He spoke without turning around. "Esther brought you something to eat."

She saw a tray on the coffee table, and her stomach lurched painfully with hunger. She could have asked for help, but she gritted her teeth and forced herself off the bed and to her feet, biting back a cry. She felt bruised all on the inside even through the drugs.

It took several minutes to reach the couch, but she did, and fell onto it the way she had the one in her room earlier. Huffing and puffing from the exertion, she rearranged herself and managed to get the lid off the tray.

Tantalizing smells wafted up to her nose. There was soup, bread, and a bowl of sliced strawberries.

"It's vegetarian," the Prime said, his eyes still on the laptop screen.

"How did you know—"

A smile in his voice. "You don't smell like an omnivore."

For the life of her she couldn't decide if that was interesting or deeply creepy, so she focused on the food. She'd barely eaten in two days, and it was all she could do not to inhale it.

"Does someone around here cook?"

"It was delivered. There's a kitchen on the first floor but I don't think it's ever been used."

"What time is it?" she asked around a mouthful of bread.

"Four thirty in the afternoon."

"Aren't you supposed to be asleep?"

"I had some work to finish."

She tried to get a look at the screen, but all she saw was a window full of arcane strings of characters. He appeared to be editing it, and he stopped periodically to consult a notepad covered in precise handwriting.

She thought of the pen she'd seen earlier and resisted the urge to ask what kind of degree he had, and where from. Best not to admit she'd been poking around in his bedroom. A safer route was, "How does a vampire end up a computer geek?"

He stopped working and swiveled the chair to face her. "When I first became involved with the Signets, most Primes were still relying on outdated radio technology for intra-Elite communication. Our security system was obsolete, and there was no network among the Signets to share information. We tend to be . . . slow in evolving. I decided that in order to survive as a society we had to adapt."

"Why not hire someone to do all the technical stuff, then? Clearly money's not a problem around here."

"I don't trust anyone else. It only takes one slipped password to bring a network down. I'm the only person with full access."

"Where did you get these thingies?" she asked, holding up her arm, where she'd snapped the wristband on earlier.

"I developed the first version five years ago. This is the third. The original design was more like a wristwatch with a keypad. I reverse-engineered the touch screen technology of the iPhone and combined it with voice recognition software. The fabrication is subcontracted to a private firm via the Department of Defense, which was happy to make the coms in exchange for limited access to my designs."

"Um . . . did you go to school for this sort of thing?"

He inclined his head toward the wall, where she saw for the first time a framed diploma: a doctorate in engineering . . . from the Massachusetts Institute of Technology.

"MIT? Are you serious?"

Her amazement amused him. "Of course. My dissertation was on voice recognition technology and its applications in security and defense. That was twenty years ago, though—the research is Paleolithic now."

Twenty years ago, she'd been seven years old. He didn't look any older than she was. "When were you born?"

His smile faded. "1643. I was born and raised in northern England."

After everything she'd been through and heard in the last forty-eight hours, finding out he was over 350 years old barely even fazed her. She just nodded, and commented, "You don't sound British. Or Jewish. Isn't *Solomon* Hebrew?"

He nodded. "When you live for more than one human lifetime, it pays to reinvent yourself from time to time. When I left England behind, I also left behind my birth name."

"What was it?"

This time the smile was faint and held a bit of an admonishment, and she realized she had no business asking, and that he'd intimated he wouldn't tell her anyway. "Sorry," she muttered, trying to think of something less personal to ask. "Where did you go after that?"

"Valencia, for a while. Then Lyons, Rome, and Edinburgh. In 1920 I moved to the States and lived in California until 1989. I finished my postgraduate studies and then moved here."

Her stomach was getting full, and combined with the narcotics it was making her drowsy. She replaced the cover on the tray and sat back, appreciating how comfortable the couch was—not as comfortable as his bed, but still, it was soft enough not to hurt, and felt like reclining on a cloud. She rested her hands on her belly and asked a bit sleepily, "What did you do in California?"

"I was the Prime's second in command."

"Why didn't you stay there and be Prime, then?"

She heard him rise, and a moment later a lightweight blanket was placed over her, possibly the same one he'd wrapped her in before. His voice was as soothing as the couch was comfortable, although what he said was hardly comforting. "The Prime of California is a friend of mine," he told her, moving her about like a rag doll, bending her knees and putting a pillow beneath them to ease the strain on her back and pelvis.

"So?"

"The only way a Prime can lose his Signet is if he dies."

Her eyes shot open. "Does that mean you killed the old Prime here?"

He nodded. There was no triumph in his face, really, just resignation. "You and I are not so different. We both dealt death in the name of justice."

She made a sound that was almost a laugh. "Justice had nothing to do with it. I just wanted to live."

"Liar," he chided gently.

"They're going to lock me up," she murmured as she

began to drift off again. "They'll put me in the crazy house . . . I'm not just crazy now, I'm a killer."

Her eyes were already shut, but she heard him say, "Like I said . . . we're two of a kind."

# Four

*Rain, rain, go away . . . no, don't . . .*

Summer storms returned to Austin the next day, and Miranda slept to rolling thunder and the patter of rain on the metal shutters.

She spent most of the next few days asleep, in fact, sometimes crying her way out of nightmares and sometimes drifting in wistful memories of a time when the world made sense. She dreamed of college, of lying in bed with Mike on a Sunday morning sharing sections of the *Austin American-Statesman*. She dreamed of the early days with her guitar and the rush of applause.

Life reduced to its simplest factors: She slept, she woke, she ate, she showered, she slept again. Sometimes she saw Faith, and she spoke to the two guards who watched her door and brought her food, but for the most part she was alone, and glad of it. Safe beneath a pile of linens, she could forget where she was and what had happened . . . for a while, from time to time.

She didn't see David. She didn't know what sort of business occupied the strongest vampire in Texas, but it kept him away from dusk till dawn. Faith hinted that something was going on in the city, but didn't specify, and Miranda didn't ask.

At one point Faith asked for a list of things she wanted

from her apartment, and later produced additional clothes and Miranda's laptop. Miranda took a moment to e-mail Kat and Mel and let them know she was out of town indefinitely. She didn't log back on to see if there was any reply.

On the fourth day, or evening, she woke about half an hour before sunset from sleep that was almost restful and climbed out of bed to find that parts of her weren't as sore as they had been.

The rain seemed to have abated for now. She would have gone to the window to look out, but the shutters prevented it; these people were serious about their darkness. She supposed that if her skin would ignite within thirty seconds of exposure to sunlight, she'd be a bit paranoid, too.

*Any minute now I'm going to wake up in the mental hospital. Any minute now.*

She made her way to the bathroom and showered, taking things slowly. If she moved too fast, she hurt herself, or at least got dizzy. Staying focused on each tiny step of washing and drying kept her from having to think. It hurt to think.

Everything was so big and empty in her head that she kept catching herself sitting still, listening for voices that weren't there. The emptiness echoed within her until she had to start humming to drown it out.

Wet hair falling around her shoulders, she took out her guitar and sat back down on the bed. She didn't want to play, but what else was there for her to do? Her own thoughts weren't powerful enough to fill the space, which brought to mind not the peace of meditation, but the stricken silence after a nuclear bomb, just before the sirens began.

She tried. She lifted her fingers to the strings and tried to summon a song, any song, but nothing came.

For a long time she sat hugging the instrument to her body, head bowed, gripping the guitar's neck. She didn't cry; she had cried enough already. She felt dry and gritty on the inside, like sandpaper, rubbed raw.

She didn't hear any noise, but she felt him approach. Somehow through the shields and the silence, she was aware of him moving toward her as he moved through the room.

A hand touched her chin, and lifted; she looked up into the Prime's eyes.

"Come," he said.

"Where?"

"With me," he replied. "You need to get out of this room for a while."

She was inclined to disagree, but knew better, and set aside her guitar, standing up carefully. She grabbed her faded old blue cardigan from the chair and wrapped it around her, sliding on the beat-up pair of sneakers she'd had brought from home. "Okay."

He held open the door for her and allowed her to set the pace down the hall. The two guards bowed as they passed—that happened again when they left the corridor, and again when they took a left turn. Miranda noticed their deference distractedly. She was too busy taking in the grandeur that surrounded her.

It was more like a museum than a house. Statuary, paintings, and antiques lined the hallway, and the floor was polished marble. She felt like she'd stepped into a parallel universe of rich people with too much time on their hands. The farther they got from the bedroom at the end of the hall, the more ornate things were, presumably to impress guests. The Prime's room, and her own, were sedate in comparison. She wouldn't call the place tacky by any stretch, but it seemed to have been designed from the ground up for one purpose: the display of affluence.

David told her a little about the building's history as he led her along. Primes, he said, inherited the fortunes and property of their predecessors, so most of what was here dated back before his tenure. There had been eight

Primes in this Haven before him, each leaving his mark before losing his life. The primary structure's four wings housed the Prime, the Elite, and the servants, as well as any visiting dignitaries. The other buildings were for storage and warrior training.

"This whole wing is yours," she said incredulously. "What do you do with all these rooms?"

He indicated various doors as they walked by. "Conference room. Library. My workroom. Music room. That staircase is locked and leads down to the server room."

"Music? You play?"

He smiled. "No, but the seventh Prime's Queen did. I'll have the piano tuned for you."

"So why don't you have a Queen?"

His smile faded. "Some of us don't. It isn't up to me."

"Shouldn't it be?"

He tilted his head to the right, and she took the right-hand hallway. "Becoming Prime isn't merely a matter of strength and age. The Signets choose their bearers, and those bearers' mates. None of us really understand how. The system has been in place for over two thousand years, and its origins have been lost . . . but the Signet never lies. It knows, somehow, who we are meant to rule with, even if we have never met."

"Wait a second . . . you're telling me a *necklace* tells you who your soul mate is? And you just . . . believe it?"

The smile returned, and he said, "As did centuries of my forebears. You can see, perhaps, why I had such a difficult time persuading the others to adopt new technology. We're dependent on a system that relies on magic as old as history. The kind of person who is willing to abide by that isn't the kind who wants an iPod."

"Then where do you fit in?"

They turned another corner, and the hallway opened out into a huge open room; before her was a balcony rail, with a grand staircase winding down from each end into a ballroom. Everything was spotless, the wood gleaming. Miranda felt as if she'd blundered onto the Embassy Ball set from *My Fair Lady*. She suddenly wished she had on something more impressive than an old cardigan and a ratty pair of blue Chucks.

They took the right-hand staircase, but instead of leading her to the main doors, he angled right again, to a smaller door that led outside.

The rain had passed, at least for now, leaving everything clean and fresh. The night was warm, and she was immediately dazzled by the starlit sky that peered out between the silver-edged clouds; the garden path they walked along was lined with electric torches, but they were dimmed to allow the overhead view to shine. She stared up, and up, into the spaces between the stars, feeling the world whirl away from her, suddenly tiny in the vastness of this world she had come to, and everything that might lay beyond.

"Easy there," she heard him say, taking her arm.

She shook her head to clear it. "God." She wasn't used to looking up. It made her neck ache. She'd had her eyes on the ground so long she had forgotten there were stars. It helped that here, in the country, the sky seemed to go on forever without city lights or pollution to obscure its diamond-freckled face.

They made a slow circuit of the gardens, stopping often to let her rest. She noticed that the plants were mostly night-blooming, and that the trees were planted strategically to give the beds adequate shade from the relentless Texas sun. The path flowed organically along the rise and fall of the land, skirting the edge of the dense woods that surrounded the Haven. Once or twice she heard hooves thudding away from the path as deer spotted them and ran for their lives.

"Do you ever eat animals?" she asked, breaking the silence.

"We can. The life energy in an animal's blood isn't as nourishing as a human's, but depending on the animal, it can be adequate. Many of us live that way, believing it somehow ethically superior."

"You don't believe that?"

"No. If I feed on a human, I can give him or her energy in return—we give off a particular aura when we drink that keeps our prey from trying to escape, and it is . . . intensely pleasurable. It doesn't work on animals. There's nothing I can give a deer in exchange for what I take. Plus, the amount I need per night would kill a smaller creature, but barely even weakens a human."

"Does that mean everyone around here is going to want to hurt me?"

"They may, but they know better." David let her sit down on a stone bench to catch her breath—talking and walking were a little much at the moment. "I won't deny that there are those who don't like you being here, Miranda. Many of my people think humans are only useful for food, and the idea of you living among us offends them. But as long as you stay in the East Wing, and don't go anywhere alone, you'll be safe."

"I don't know how long I can live like that."

"Trust me . . . I don't want you here any longer than you have to be."

He must have seen the hurt on her face before she even realized she felt it, because he added swiftly, "For your safety, and sanity. This is no place for mortals."

She smiled wanly at the word *sanity*. It was probably years too late to save that.

"Nonsense." He contradicted her thought, offering a hand to help her back up. "You're perfectly sane."

She snorted. "Sorry, but hearing that from you isn't exactly comforting."

Miranda stared at his hand for a second, then reached up and took it. She expected his skin to be cold, but it wasn't. It was definitely cooler than a human's but not corpselike the way the legends said. She remembered Faith mentioning that vampires could control their body temperatures and that they hated to be cold. Miranda supposed it reminded them too much of being dead.

Were they dead? The Prime breathed; she had heard

his heart beating, and the fingers that closed around hers were full of life.

"We die," he told her, drawing her gracefully back to the path, "but to transform, not to decay. Dying is like hitting reset. It allows our genetic code to be rewritten. There's some research into exactly how the process works—I'll show it to you if you like. But we're as alive as you are, just . . . different."

She drew her hand away and wrapped her arms around her stomach, holding her cardigan tight against a sudden chill that swept over her. "Does it hurt?" she asked.

"More than anything you can imagine."

She held back another humorless laugh at that one. "Is it worth it?"

He smiled, and the starlight glinted off his teeth. "Definitely."

Miranda said little until they returned to the Prime's wing, where he had to leave her in the care of her guards. Then she gave him a quiet "Good night" and returned to her room, still hugging herself in the huge tattered sleeves of her blue sweater.

He was satisfied for now; her color was better, and she was growing stronger little by little, enough that the walk had tired but not exhausted her.

Still, it had been only a week since her world had been razed to the ground. She could hardly be expected to jump up and embrace life, grateful for a second chance.

He knew all too well how bitter life's second chances could taste.

Faith met him at the end of the hall, bowing. "Sire."

He took a deep breath and let it out slowly. "Is he here?"

"Yes. We've got him isolated in interrogation room B. Shall we?"

This time, the walk he took was for a much different purpose. With each step he felt himself shedding the human woman's comparatively easy companionship and returning to what he knew best.

He had not been exaggerating. This was no place for mortals.

They headed outside, this time taking a different path than he had with Miranda, toward one of the smaller outbuildings. Tonight he was supposed to be evaluating the new recruits, spying on their training session, but instead Faith had brought word that he was needed for something a little more urgent.

As he walked, he reached up and fingered the Signet, a habit he'd noticed almost all Primes had when they were deep in thought. He felt oddly preoccupied, and not remotely in the mood for the task ahead, though once upon a time the idea would have cheered him. Once, he would have looked forward to questioning a suspect all evening. When he had been second in command in California, he had earned the reputation that had followed him here, and since taking the Signet he'd kept it easily, but still, there were times . . .

He didn't allow himself to finish the thought. There was no room for doubt here.

"This way." Faith swung open the outer door of the cinder-block building and stepped back to allow him first entry. "We caught him in the act, blood still on his hands. The girl was still breathing, but she died en route to Brackenridge."

"Good," he said, ignoring her raised eyebrow. With the victim dead, the suspect was under a death sentence; he didn't have to worry about causing permanent damage.

Another Elite guard stood outside the metal interrogation room door. He bowed and slid the bolt back.

The Prime stood in the doorway a moment, allowing his presence to fill the room, knowing that the suspect would feel it. He reached out with his power and swept the chamber, his senses calculating: male, under a hundred years of age, and scared shitless.

Just like he liked them.

He walked into the room and towered over the suspect, who flinched as the Prime's shadow fell over him and tried to edge even closer to the wall. The chains around his wrists and ankles wouldn't let him go far.

David gestured for Faith to stay back. He looked down at the suspect.

"Name?"

The vampire stammered something unintelligible in Spanish.

"I'm sorry, could you repeat that?"

This time, in English, "I'm not telling you nothing. You're gonna kill me anyway."

The Prime raised his hand, and the suspect was immediately jerked upward and thrown backward against the wall. The shackles snapped off, allowing him to move, but he was pinned by the Prime's power, whimpering as he tried to struggle.

"You're absolutely right," David told him, stepping closer. The suspect cringed visibly. "You broke the cardinal law of this territory, and you're going to die. There are therefore only two questions remaining. One, do you want to die by my Second's hand, or by mine? And two . . ."

He reached into the man, seeking out the capillaries of his fingers and toes, and applied pressure, squeezing almost gently. The man's eyes went wide and he tried again to fight, but couldn't; as the tiny vessels began to pop, he made terrified animal noises and the drenching sweat of fear broke out over his face. It wasn't painful, really, though it would be as the burst capillaries became bruises—but the vampire could feel it happening, and knew he couldn't stop it.

"How long do you want it to take?" David concluded, doing it again. This time he saw a blood vessel burst in the man's left eye.

Barely expending any effort, he lifted his hand again, and the suspect screamed hoarsely as the fingers of his right hand began to crack, one phalanx at a time.

Faith said from the doorway, "Obviously not a trained warrior."

"No," he replied, watching the man writhe. Little finger; metacarpal. They broke so easily, like snapping twigs. David remembered how it felt to do the same thing with his bare hands; this was much less messy. "If he had any sort of Elite history, he'd have been taught to withstand pain. Was this attack as meticulous as the one at the Greenbelt?"

"Not this time. It was a straight-up slashing with the Seal of Auren carved into the girl's arm with a blade."

"Hmm." David moved closer to the man again, abruptly releasing him from the vise. "I would imagine that if he's familiar with the Seal, he may have one on him somewhere."

The man was panting, his eyes rolling wild in his head. "Don't—don't—"

"Shut up." With a wave of his hand, the Prime forced the man's mouth closed. "Speak when I ask you to or don't speak at all."

He reached up and unbuttoned the suspect's shirt, yanking it aside unceremoniously, frowning in distaste at the filthy state of what was underneath. "Your boss isn't paying you well enough," he noted. "You smell like the ass end of a dead rodent."

Sure enough, just over the prisoner's left pectoral muscle was a week-old tattoo: the Seal of Auren in black and red.

"So," David said, "let me go over this one more time just so we're on the same page. You're working for a dead man, or at least for his friends. You've committed at least one murder, which you were caught at, so your life is forfeit. Now you can either tell me who you're working for, and die quickly by decapitation, or you can keep pretending you don't know anything, and die slowly by decapitation. Slowly, and screaming."

To punctuate his words, he reached into the man and broke one of his ribs cleanly in two.

Predictably, the man shrieked, then hung shaking against the wall, suspended from invisible bonds, head bowed.

David gave him a moment.

Finally the man panted, "I'm Rico."

David smiled and replied in Spanish for the prisoner's benefit. "That wasn't so hard, now, was it? A pleasure to meet you, Rico. David Solomon, ninth Prime of the Southern United States."

On the next breath Rico snarled, "Fuck you."

The Prime sighed, "Language, Rico," and broke another rib.

"Fuck you!" This time with a scream. "My master would never have done this to his own kind! You're a fucking traitor and you're going down!"

"Do you really believe that?" he asked. "How do you think Auren took the Signet in the first place, Rico? By sending fruit baskets? He slashed and burned his way through the entire Court and raped and tortured the Queen herself before murdering her. Their Elite, their servants . . . everyone, dead within a week of the Pair's death. Auren was no God, no hero. He was just like the rest of us: a killer, heartless and merciless. Now tell me who you're working for, and I may contradict myself and show you mercy."

Now Rico began to laugh, the desperate mad laugh of someone with nothing further to lose, who was in enough pain not to care. Then he reared back and spat at the Prime.

David rolled his eyes and stepped easily out of the way, though the motion would have been a blur to anyone else in the room.

"This is my second-favorite coat," he told Rico calmly. "That's really why I don't want to bleed you—that, and I'd hate to make the servants clean it up. Too bad, really. Messy deaths are much more satisfying. I suppose I'll have to settle for this."

With that, the Prime made a slow, twisting gesture, and

Rico's bones started breaking with dull popping sounds. He dropped the man to the floor and let him writhe, the screams building, turning into the panicked, agonized wails of a dying animal.

Rico was still alive when his skull caved in, but by then he could no longer scream.

When every bone was crushed, the vampire's body lying in a crumpled heap, David motioned for Faith to come forward, and she sliced off Rico's head with one clean swing.

David looked over at Faith, who nodded. Her eyes were hard and fierce. The guard outside looked like he was about to vomit. That was the difference between a soldier and the second in command.

"Have him dropped near where the attack occurred," the Prime said to the guard as he straightened his coat. "I want his friends to see the consequences of their actions."

"Yes, Sire," the guard managed, letting him pass.

Once out in the free air again, David paused, drinking in the night. Out here the smells were of impending rain and night-blooming jasmine, not stale cigarettes and abject terror.

It had all been so easy, once. Back before coming here, he had meted out punishment and torture alike at his Prime's command without a second thought. He had served under two Primes in California, and the first, Arrabicci, had been as ruthless as Auren. Like many Primes he had cared only about vampires and had no qualms about his people killing humans. David had spent his years in Arrabicci's Elite hunting down vampire hunters, as well as rival gangs after the Signet.

Then had come Deven, Arrabicci's Second, who reluctantly took charge after an assassin's arrow sent all of California's Shadow World into bloody civil war for months. Deven had not instituted a no-kill law, but he had severely tightened restrictions on human feeding, and his fearsome reputation as a warrior helped him rule over the western states with absolute control. The gangs feared Deven like they feared God, and so there was little need to torture or execute anyone.

"Are you all right?" he heard Faith ask, and half turned to see her looking concerned.

"Peachy," he snapped before he could stop himself. Faith, however, was used to his moods, and didn't rise to the tone. She simply waited.

"Something about crushing a man's skull with my brain always aggravates me," he muttered, starting to walk again. Faith took up her usual place at his right hand. "And what have we learned? Nothing."

"Not entirely nothing," she replied. "We know that there's some kind of organization behind all of this. We know they're at least fanatic enough to get a dead Prime's Seal tattooed on their bodies. Fanatics aren't usually the smartest of criminals; they're bound to slip up."

"Yes, and how many humans will die before we stop them?" Had he been a more emotional creature he might have kicked something; irritation was prickling through his mind like the thorns of a particularly nasty cactus.

"Is this anger because of the insurgents, or is it guilt at killing that fool back there?"

He stopped and shot her an irritable look. "Stop being so goddamned insightful."

She shrugged. "That's what you pay me for. In the absence of a Queen, it's my job to question as much as support. I learned everything I know watching you in California."

In that, she hit the nail squarely on the head: the absence of a Queen. Primes were powerful, yes, and had many arcane abilities the average vampire did not. He was faster, stronger, and had sharper senses, among other things. He had been born telekinetic, a rare gift even among vampires that was extremely useful when it came to, say, interrogation; his telepathy was decent as long as he had some sort of connection to the subject.

A Queen, however, would have different skills; they

were tuned into the heart, and read people as easily as words. A Queen could have opened Rico's mind and lifted the truth out of him without hurting him at all, and then Rico could have been executed painlessly, instead of slobbering and spasming with his screams still echoing in David's ears.

He didn't have a problem with killing, in theory. He'd been a killer for 340 years. Doing away with his own kind, however, had gotten harder and harder since he'd come here. It was starting to feel like infanticide, no matter how richly deserved.

"You know," Faith said, bringing him back to the moment, "Deven once told me years ago that Primes aren't meant to be alone. Your power becomes debilitating if it's not shared."

"That's easy for him to say," David retorted with a shake of his head. "He only ruled alone for six months before Jonathan came along."

"Lucky him."

David started to respond, but he felt eyes on him, and lifted his gaze up from the gardens to the main building of the Haven itself.

There, in the second-floor window adjacent to his suite, Miranda stood staring out at the night, or rather, down at him; the firelight from her room caught the loose strands of her jewel-red hair, and in her white T-shirt with her pale skin she looked almost spectral, perhaps even angelic.

When she saw him, she smiled a little, then looked away as if embarrassed. Even at this distance he could see the faint touch of pink to her cheeks.

He might have read more into it, except that as long as he was shielding her he could pick up her outermost thoughts, and he knew she hadn't meant to stare. Movement below her window had captured her attention as she looked out at the forest.

A second later she glanced down again, probably feeling his eyes on her this time, and he inclined his head toward her in greeting. She gave a small wave and disappeared.

Faith was holding back a grin. "So, how is our guest?"

"I plan to start teaching her to shield tomorrow," he said, though he hadn't been planning any such thing until now.

"Is she strong enough already?"

"No way to tell until she tries."

She kept her tone professional, though he could tell she was trying not to laugh as she said, "You're in need of a Queen yourself . . . perhaps you've developed a taste for madwoman redhead?"

"Don't be disgusting," he replied mildly.

"I'm only joking," Faith said, becoming serious. "Besides, after what she's been through, I doubt she'll be interested in that sort of thing any time soon, even with somebody like you skulking around."

He smiled at the compliment, such as it was. "The best thing we can do for her is get her well enough to go back to her life."

A drop fell on his arm; the rain was coming back. He could sense it would settle in for the rest of the night after this brief respite from the downpour.

As he started to return to the Haven, he looked up at Miranda's window again; it was empty.

Yes, she needed to leave as soon as possible . . . for his sake as well as her own.


*Everyone dies alone, right?*

She dragged herself sideways, unable to feel her legs, pain lancing through her upper body from a dozen puncture wounds. One of the crossbow bolts broke off as she tried to move and drove deeper into her gut, and she moaned, then coughed, tasting blood.

Blood dripped from her face onto the pavement, and from her hands as she tried desperately to stay conscious. Her hands slipped and she fell, chin hitting the ground.

Behind her she could hear the others dying. Mickey, Jones, Parvati . . . she'd seen Mickey go down first and tried to bark out a warning to the others, but it was too late—they were surrounded and arrows rained down from the roof into the street.

Jones had screamed. She'd never heard him scream before. She'd known him a long time, slept with him off and on back when they'd both been green recruits still in awe of their own jobs, invincible with youth.

The Dumpster was only ten feet away. If she could get behind it, they might not see her, and she might be able to call home. She knew she was dying, but she had to warn the Haven. Ten feet . . . nine feet . . .

It was so cold . . . so much blood . . .

Eight feet . . .

They were coming. Footsteps. She heard Parvati's wailing death shriek as one last arrow was shot into her chest at point-blank range. The click of the crossbow, the scream, the heavy sound of a body hitting the ground . . . seven feet . . .

"Where's the other one? There were supposed to be four!"

Ambush. Her entire patrol unit wiped out in five minutes. How could they have been so stupid? The call had sounded legitimate. The network was infallible. Everyone knew that. There was only one way a fake distress call could have been placed over the coms, and she had to warn the Haven.

Five feet. They were looking for her, but in the wrong direction. She might have time.

She heaved herself over the last few feet, collapsing behind the Dumpster and pulling her now-useless right arm up near her head. Her voice was hoarse and she could hear death rattling its way up through her throat . . . not much longer . . .

"Star-three," she coughed into the com. "Elite Fourteen . . . Code One emergency channel . . ."

"Over here! I see something!"

*"This is Faith."*

"This is Elite Fourteen on behalf of Patrol Two West Austin . . . our unit has been ambushed. We received . . . a false call to these coordinates for backup . . . fired upon from above . . . all Elite down . . . the network has been compromised. I repeat . . . the com network has been . . . compromised . . ."

She heard Faith swear, then say, distantly, *"Hold on, Elite Fourteen. I'm sending rescue."*

"No need," she whispered as she heard footsteps behind her. "Just tell the Prime . . ."

Faith kept talking, telling her to hold on, that help was coming, but she barely heard. Someone seized her by the arm and dragged her backward, away from the shelter of the Dumpster, the Second's voice fading to a tinny murmur, suddenly silenced.

# Five

Miranda went into raptures over the library. It was larger than her bedroom, the walls lined with shelves from floor to ceiling, and even had ladders. It reminded her strongly of the library at the university, where she'd spent hours leafing through books, inhaling the musty smell of aged paper, puzzling over indecipherable tomes like *Les Miserables* in the original French.

It had been a long time since she'd simply sat down and read a book. Reading relaxed her too much, and relaxing, without a barrier of alcohol between her and the world, spelled trouble.

Her fingers traced the spines of classics, contemporary novels, and nonfiction in at least eight different languages. She'd thought the Prime's bedroom had a lot of books, but here were at least ten times that many. Given what he'd told her about the Haven, she wondered how many of these he had brought with him, and how many had been here as long as the building had stood.

Miranda pulled a yellowed copy of Shakespeare's comedies from the shelf and sought one of the window seats, grateful just to lose herself for a while in something that had a happy ending.

She handled the paper carefully, afraid it might crumble,

and read aloud to herself, her quiet voice echoing in the silent room, punctuated with the sound of turning pages.

"'I pray thee now tell me, for which of my bad parts didst thou first fall in love with me?

"'For them all together, which maintained so politic a state of evil that they will not admit any good part to intermingle with them. But for which of my good parts did you first suffer love for me?'"

A voice came from the door, and though she wasn't expecting it, for some reason she didn't start.

"'Suffer love!—a good epithet. I do suffer love indeed, for I love thee against my will.'"

Miranda looked up and smiled, continuing, "'In spite of your heart, I think. Alas, poor heart! If you spite it for my sake, I will spite it for yours, for I will never love that which my friend hates.'"

David smiled back. "'Thou and I are too wise to woo peaceably.'"

She closed the book and set it on the cushion, running her hand down the front cover. "This was always my favorite of his plays," she said. "Melodramatic, full of misunderstandings, but with a hearts-and-flowers finale. I used to pretend I was Beatrice and act out her lines in front of the mirror."

The smile widened a hair. "Not Hero?"

Miranda chuckled and shook her head. "No way. Hero was shallow and not very bright. She and Claudio would have had a bland life with bland children and a bland dog. Beatrice and Benedick, now *that* was a couple I could get behind. They would have had adventures together."

She noticed that he was dressed more casually than she had seen him before, and didn't have the coat. He wore actual jeans, faded in that designer way, and a long-sleeved dark blue shirt that set off the color of his eyes. The Signet lay glowing between his collarbones, wildly out of place with the rest of his attire.

"How are you feeling tonight?" he asked.

She thought about it. She was stiff, and sore, and hadn't slept well, but she didn't feel the edge of creeping panic she'd had every night so far. She could deal with being tired and in pain. That's what drugs were for. "Okay."

"Good. I'd like to begin your training tonight."

"Training?"

"Yes. You have to learn to control your gifts."

"And you're going to teach me."

"I am."

The idea of mucking with her "gifts," which was hardly the word for them, made her deeply uneasy, but he was right. She had to do something. She couldn't be the servant of her power forever. It would kill her inside a year unless something changed.

Learning to use it wasn't nearly as scary as the thought of ending up in the County Hospital D ward . . . wasting away with the choir of the damned as her only company. She had been in that place once, seen the vacant stares of the incurable cases, and even then, long before the voices began to penetrate her mind, she could feel the desolation that had soaked those dingy white walls.

"Miranda?"

She shivered and looked up at him again. "Sorry. Okay, let's do it."

He frowned, concerned, but didn't ask the obvious question. "This way, please."

She followed him back to the suite, into his bedroom, where he sat in one of the two armchairs that flanked the sofa and gestured for her to take the one opposite. She pulled her legs up and crossed them, wincing at the pain it caused her back.

"The first thing I'm going to teach you is how to ground," he said, folding his hands with his elbows on the chair's arms. "It's a technique as old as psychic energy itself. Once you're grounded you'll be able to work from a stable, secure foundation—think of electricity, and how if it isn't properly grounded it runs wild and can cause destruction. Your talent is the same way."

"But what am I supposed to do in an emergency, if I don't have time to do the grounding thing?"

"Ideally you'll become so familiar with it that you can do it instantly, no matter what the situation. It takes practice, but in time you'll be able to maintain a state of rational detachment where you can act instead of react."

"I take it you're grounded right now."

He nodded, looking faintly amused. "I'm always grounded. Keeping my energy flowing in an even circuit is the key to my emotional equilibrium."

"Emotional equilibrium. Meaning you never get angry and you're always perfectly calm."

"Yes."

She raised an eyebrow. "Are you sure you're not just boring?"

The Prime blinked at her, then laughed.

She'd never actually heard him laugh before, and somehow the sound made her feel better in a way she couldn't quite define.

"All right," David said, sobering. "Let's begin. Close your eyes, and bring your attention to your breath . . ."


An hour later, Miranda was completely exhausted, her head pounding so hard she could barely think, and she had the urge to punch her teacher in his perfectly sculpted jaw.

"Stop," she panted, putting her hands to her temples. "I can't."

He looked at her dispassionately. Though he'd been doing the same exercises as she was, demonstrating even more difficult techniques, he was as unruffled as before. She, on the other hand, must look like a funhouse mirror of him, her face red and sweaty and her hair hanging lank in her face. She was slumped in her chair while he sat as straight and regal as ever.

She was as angry at herself as she was with him. What he was showing her wasn't complicated, and she should have been able to get it. She could play two musical instruments, damn it! All she had to do here was ground herself, then draw energy up through her body and try to move it into a barrier around her mind. He showed her how to time it with her breath, inhaling to draw up energy and exhaling to move it, not forcing, but allowing it to flow so she could get used to how it felt.

Easy enough, in theory. It was a lot like what she did onstage. The trouble was that here she didn't have her guitar to hide behind. Instead it was just grueling repetition, the same exact exercise over and over and over until it felt like her skull was going to split down the middle.

"Again," he said.

She wanted to scream, but she tried to do as he said. And failed. The rudimentary shield she tried to raise flopped down around her like a dead fish.

"Again."

"Stop saying that! You sound like a fucking Teletubby! Let me rest for a minute."

The worst part was that he knew how tired she was, but she had no idea what was going on behind his mask of indifference. Didn't he care that she was in pain?

"We can't move on from here until you get this right," he told her matter-of-factly.

"Fine, but does it have to be tonight? I'm tired. My head hurts. My back is killing me." She fought back the angry tears that sprang to her eyes. "I don't deserve this. Not after everything."

"Life doesn't care what you deserve," he replied with all the warmth of an iceberg. "You didn't deserve to be raped, but it happened. The people who die out there on the street every night often don't deserve their fates. Veal calves don't deserve theirs. Do you want to spend the rest of your life as a victim, or do you want to be strong?"

"I don't know," she groaned. "Right now all I want is for my head to stop hurting. Just let me rest."

"Not until you get this right. Now stop whining and do it again."

Anger, poisonous and hot, boiled up along her spine. The feeling was familiar, and delicious, and it flooded her body with renewed energy, but she couldn't think—all she could do was feel, and she summoned all her meager strength and struck out at the coldhearted bastard who was making her do this. She flung power at him almost like a lightning bolt, and she could *hear* herself snarling.

As soon as the bolt left her body she realized what she was doing and tried to pull it back. Pain seared her mental "hands" and she cried out—too late. She tried to warn him . . .

. . . but it turned out she didn't have to. When the energy reached him, it hit his shields, and she could almost see the way they flexed and shifted around him to absorb the hit and ground it out without an iota of her rage touching him. She watched, fascinated, as the shield's energy compensated for the hit and rippled backward like an indestructible soap bubble, then returned to normal, without the Prime seeming to consciously react. It all happened in seconds.

They stared at each other. Her heart was hammering in her chest and she couldn't seem to catch her breath.

"Ground," he instructed calmly.

She was crying, but she ignored the tears and did as he said. Grounding was easy compared to the rest. When she was done, she wiped her eyes, the last of the anger gone, and put her head back in her hands. "You did that on purpose, didn't you?"

"It's important that you understand what's at stake."

"I'm sorry. I could have killed you."

There was a smile in his voice. "No, you couldn't have. A psychic attack may kill a human and completely incapacitate an ordinary vampire, but never me. The shields you saw are a part of what we, as vampires, are. Mine are stronger than most because I had to learn at a very young age to control my abilities."

"Young? How young?"

"I started manifesting talent when I was a child. It was . . . not accepted in that time and place. For most of my mortal life I never revealed to anyone what I could do."

"What can you do? I mean, besides . . . that."

His eyes moved from her face to the coffee table, and she stared, openmouthed, as the entire table quivered, rose off the floor by several inches, then lit back down. He didn't so much as bat an eye at the expense of energy.

"Holy shit. I take it not all vampires can do that."

He shrugged fluidly. "Some Primes can. We have powers that aren't found among lesser vampires. Still, mine are considered rare."

She stared at the table, almost waiting for it to move again. "So what happened, when you were human?"

He met her gaze, and for just a second, the mask seemed to slip, and she saw pain beneath it—years and years of pain that no amount of power or prestige had eased. Then his expression cleared and she almost believed she'd imagined it, until he said quietly, "A stranger came to town."

She tried for the lame joke. "A gunslinger?"

He returned her weak smile with one that was equally thin. "A Witchfinder."

Before she could ask, the bedroom door flew open, and Faith appeared, her face pale and grave.

"Sire, you're needed immediately," she said with a peculiar catch in her voice. "There's a . . . situation."

He held Faith's eyes for a second, then rose smoothly from his chair. "Go to bed," he directed Miranda as he pulled on his coat. "Tomorrow night you'll try again."

They departed without another word, leaving Miranda alone in the Prime's bedroom wondering what was going on. David had, of course, maintained that precious "emotional equilibrium," but she had this feeling that underneath it he was upset, and that whatever had just happened was only going to make things worse.

She found she was madly curious about the workings of the Court, like an anthropologist studying the Pygmies for *National Geographic*. She might as well have been hiding in the bushes with a video camera.

A voice erupted from the band around her wrist, and she yelped.

*"All personnel are advised that the com network will be down for maintenance until further notice."*

There was a click, and she felt . . . something change. The signal to the com must have been cut off; she hadn't realized she could actually feel it until now.

She started to get up and go to bed, as the Prime had commanded, but when she tried to stand, her legs wouldn't support her. It was strange how her body was so worn out after an hour of working nothing but her mind. The room spun around her, and she made it a couple of feet sideways until her calves struck the edge of the couch.

That would do. She let herself fall onto it, groping for the blanket she knew was still there, and though she didn't have the strength to stay awake, sliding into sleep she could feel a current of deeply troubled emotions that crept into the darkness of her dreams.

*". . . our unit has been ambushed. We received . . . a false call to these coordinates for backup . . . fired upon from above . . . all Elite down . . . the network has been compromised. I repeat . . . the com network has been . . . compromised . . ."*

Faith had worked for David Solomon long enough to know when he was pissed.

She replayed the message from Elite 14 to the tense

silence of the conference room, where all the other patrol leaders were gathered minus those who were out on duty now and the team she'd sent to recover the bodies. She watched as the Prime's face went from calm to steely, and the blue of his eyes went icy at the edges. A silvering of the eye color was a sure sign that a vampire was about to spill blood.

The aura of power around him swelled and darkened until it looked like a thunderstorm waiting to explode. The others took an involuntary step back.

She didn't. Running from fear only made it chase you.

The Prime took a deep breath, withdrawing his aura to its normal level. She'd always admired his control, but she also knew it wasn't infallible . . . and neither, apparently, was what he had built.

"Report," he said.

She nodded briskly. "The rescue team arrived to find four bodies, all shot full of wooden-shafted crossbow bolts. It appears they were fired on from the building across the street. There was no immediate evidence of who killed them, but we're running a check on the arrows to see if we can nail down the manufacturer and go from there."

"All right." David looked to each patrol leader in turn. "I'll be making an upgrade later tonight but not until I've found out where the leak is and we've dealt with him appropriately. I want all of you on high alert the minute you set foot in the city now. Obviously the situation is escalating. You'll be advised of further developments as they come. Dismissed."

A chorus of "Yes, Sires," and everyone but Faith left.

She leaned forward and put her hands on the table. "There was nothing we could do. By the time Malia called in, it was too late. The nearest team we had was ten minutes away."

He looked like he wanted to break things, but there

wasn't anything in the conference room that would do unless he wanted to fling furniture, and she knew he wasn't given to that kind of dramatic display. The going rumor was that he was incapable of emotion, and though she knew better, she could see where the story had come from.

"Come," he said, rising.

She followed him down the stairs to the server room, the nerve center of the network he had created from the ground up. That network was his baby, and the idea that someone had broken into it probably made him angrier than the loss of four Elite. Every Signet in the world knew that the Southern network was the pinnacle of communications technology. If word got out that it had been hacked . . .

"Have a seat."

She slid into a chair beside him while he took out his laptop and logged on to the main server. She wished she'd remembered how cold it was down here—he kept a sweater slung over his chair, and she really ought to squirrel one away in the cabinet.

Every single transmission sent over the coms, over e-mail, and over their phone lines was routed through this room, recorded and documented down to the word. Everyone who worked for the Haven knew there was no such thing as private communication except for between Faith and the Prime himself.

She smiled to herself. *You can't stop the signal.*

"How in the hell could someone hack us?" she asked, disbelieving. "As many layers of authentication as we have, and with the voice recognition built into the system, what kind of crazy genius could out-crazy-genius you?"

"That's the problem," he muttered, his eyes on the screen. "The more complicated a system is, the more likely it is that a complete moron can bring it down. The simplest route is usually the one that's overlooked.

Here . . . the logs for Malia's patrol. Everything routine . . ." He sighed as he read, and she moved closer to see what had been going on.

Everything was so normal it hurt. The patrol unit talked and joked with each other as they made their usual sweep of Austin's west side. It was the most affluent section of town, so there was rarely anything to do. That was why she'd assigned the youngest, least experienced Elite to the unit. That was probably why the attackers had chosen them, too.

Malia was a bright, cheerful woman, and while she wasn't the best warrior, what she lacked in fighting skill she made up for in leadership ability. Everyone liked her. She would have risen through the ranks eventually once she matured a little.

That would never happen now. She and Mickey and Jones and Parvati were all gone, all erased from the night in a few short minutes of vengeance and blood.

"We have to stop them," Faith said, surprising herself with the emotion in her words.

David looked up at her. "We will." There was a burning intensity in his eyes, and she believed him. His word was law.

"Here . . . right here is where the distress call came in, at 22:34. There was no verbal message, just coordinates sent via the emergency protocol. Well, that's not going to happen again. From now on all emergency calls will require voice recognition—I don't care if it slows the response time."

He was mostly talking to himself, which had always amused her to hear, and as he spoke his fingers were flying over the keyboard. At least four windows were up on the screen, and another two or three on the second monitor to the left, and he was working in all of them at once, tabbing between them with lightning rapidity. One was the network log, another the code for the emergency system, another some sort of logarithm he was actually working out in his head while he did everything else.

And people thought telekinesis was the scariest thing he could do.

Another window appeared. "I'm tracking the distress call," he said for Faith's benefit. "Location, frequency, duration . . . everything is normal. The encoding . . . son of a bitch."

He sat back hard.

"What?"

"Do you see that?" he pointed at the screen.

"That squiggly line with all the gibberish? You're going to have to translate it into Normal People-ese."

"This is the carrier signal of the false distress call. It's in-network. Passwords, voice recognition, everything passed security when they logged on, because the network wasn't hacked from outside."

"It came from one of us," Faith said, shocked. "One of the Elite sent the call."

"I designed this to be nearly impossible to break into from the outside, but apparently there's a flaw in our personnel screening methods. Somehow a mole slipped by the background checks, the applications, the evaluations . . . or, they changed allegiance after joining."

"How do we find them?"

"If this were a normal system, we couldn't. He or she is a skilled enough programmer that when I try to trace the signal to its location of origin, it reroutes itself and gets caught in a loop. But this system has a few fail-safes that our spy didn't count on."

"Such as?"

"This," David replied, unlocking one of the cabinets to his left and removing a small metal box. It, too, was locked, but with a fingerprint recognition system, which he opened, revealing what looked like an ordinary USB drive.

He plugged the drive into his laptop and closed out

most of the windows on the screen. A new program started running.

Faith tried to interpret what she was seeing, eyes narrowed. "What the hell is that?"

He smiled grimly. "Have you ever looked at the underside of your com?"

"No . . . it's blank, just like the front, right?"

"There's a sensor built into it that tracks the wearer's personal energy signature. It's a combination of psychic aura, body temperature, and a tiny sample of DNA from the skin cells that rub onto the band. This database holds the records of everyone who's ever worked for me and cross-references them with the data from the coms themselves. That's why the coms are issued to only one person and destroyed upon death. They send in new DNA info every time that person logs on for duty—not a full scan but enough markers to match it to the issued wearer."

He made a few clicks and the computer ran a search comparing the night's DNA readings with the database of everyone who had ever worn a com. "The person who made the distress call could get around the voice recognition system and the password database, but this fail-safe is completely unknown to everyone outside this room. In a moment we'll have the identity of whoever was wearing the com the distress call came from."

Faith gaped at him. "How in the hell did you do this?"

He looked at her as if she'd asked the dumbest question in history. "I'm brilliant."

She knew she wasn't going to get any more of an answer. She mentally added biochemistry and genetics to the list of things he had learned at MIT.

A beep, and the search completed, much faster than Faith would have expected. A name popped up.

"No," Faith said. "It must be wrong."

"It's a perfect match." David's eyes were growing pale again. "Have a team ready in five minutes. I'll meet you there."

* * *

Miranda woke to a feeling of cold anger coupled with dread in the pit of her stomach.

She looked around, trying to figure out what was going on that felt so wrong, but realized it wasn't coming from her—the dread was, but it was in reaction to the wrath, which emanated from someone else, someone she hadn't expected to ever see angry.

She got up, pleased that her body felt a lot less weak after her nap, and made her way over to the door, cautiously turning the knob to peek out.

Everything seemed normal.

"Do you need something, Miss Grey?" Helen asked. She and Samuel were at their usual posts, keeping watch.

"No . . . I don't think so, thanks."

As she started to shut the door again, Miranda froze.

A group of four Elite walked around tne corner into the hallway, deadly purpose in their steps. Faith was leading them, and the Second's face was set with a gravity that made Miranda's stomach lurch. Something was very, very wrong.

To her left, Helen tensed.

A few seconds later, the Prime entered the hallway, and again Miranda's insides flipped around in fear. This Prime was not the same man who had walked with her in the garden. He wasn't even the same man who had sat opposite her and drilled her in energy work only an hour ago.

This was the most powerful vampire in the southern United States.

Seeing him surrounded by others made it even more obvious, but she would never have mistaken him for any other in a crowd with his aura showing in her mind as a burnished silver, shot through with black and bloody red. His eyes were strange—they looked paler, grayer, as if they'd gone from deep azure to silver. When he was halfway down the hall, she realized that was exactly what had happened.

This was a creature with blood on his mind.

"Elite Twenty-three," Faith said, coming to stand in front of the door, "stand down."

Miranda wanted to retreat into the bedroom and hide until it was over, but she couldn't move.

Helen, on the other hand, could.

The guard threw herself backward, into the doorway, knocking door and Miranda both back into the room. Miranda was so stunned she couldn't react until Helen had her arm around Miranda's throat and hauled her upright, using her as a human shield.

"Stay back!" Helen cried.

The rest of the Elite, including Samuel, who had been about to jump at Helen, paused, turning back to their leader.

In a different situation Miranda might have thought the look on David's face was funny.

"Let her go," he said very, very calmly. There was a light in his eyes, a killing light, and the stone of his Signet was glowing noticeably brighter. "Don't make this worse for yourself than it already is."

"Why not?" Helen hissed. Her voice sounded odd, and Miranda realized her fangs were out. Icy fear gripped Miranda's entire body.

*Not again. Not again. Oh God please . . .*

"You're going to torture and kill me, right? I might as well take out this pretty little meat puppet while I'm at it."

A guttural male voice echoed in Miranda's head. *". . . pretty little thing's awake . . ."*

She could hear a zipper sliding down, feel sweaty hands on her breasts. The warm, firelit bedroom and the chaotic scene melted away, and she was back in the alley again, her bare back grinding into the cold concrete.

*Not again.*

She couldn't breathe. Helen was choking her.

It didn't matter.

Miranda reached into herself for the rage that had given

her the power to kill the men in the alley, their faces and voices playing over and over again in her mind, amplified by her own screams, until the voices drowned out everything, and all that she could hold on to was *feeling*.

She struck.

David had had shields standing between him and the wrath of a violated woman; Helen had no such thing. The power that the Prime had deflected so easily roared into the guard before she could even attempt to protect herself.

Helen made a choking, gurgling sound, and her arm fell slack. She threw up both hands to scrabble at her forehead as if she were trying to claw something out and whimpered in childlike terror with her eyes huge and rolling. Helen fisted her hands in her hair, clamping her eyes shut, the whimpers building toward screams until David stepped forward, seized her, and broke her neck with an audible crack.

Miranda toppled forward, coughing, gulping air in great lungfuls, her vision swimming. She landed on her hands and knees and let her forehead touch the cool floor, still trying to catch her breath as behind her she heard the Elite coming into the room and surrounding Helen's body.

"Let's move," Faith said. "She'll be conscious again in an hour. Get her up and to the interrogation room."

Miranda looked up. How could she not be dead?

"She's a vampire," David said from the doorway. "We're hard to kill."

The Elite who grabbed Helen's arms and dragged her out of the room cast Miranda strange, half-fearful looks on their way.

"I'll get her restrained and ready for you," Faith told the Prime.

"I'll be there in a moment."

Miranda lay shaking on the floor, only barely aware that David knelt beside her.

"You didn't have to do that," he said. "I could have stopped her."

She shook her head miserably. "All over again . . . I

could feel it, it was like . . . like that night, and . . . I couldn't help it. I wanted to kill her. I *tried* to kill her."

She'd thought she was done weeping, but now she wondered if she ever would be. She broke into hoarse sobs, her hands fisting on the floor.

His hand touched her shoulder lightly, asking permission, but she didn't care what he did. She didn't struggle as, once again, he lifted her up off the floor and carried her back to the couch; but this time, instead of simply laying her there, he sat down, still holding her, and let her cry.

She would never have expected to be grateful for that, but she clenched her fingers in his shirt and wept into his shoulder completely unself-consciously.

His chest moved beneath her hand as he sighed.

"This is my fault," he said. "It was too soon to start our work tonight—you needed more time for the memories to move away from the surface. Exhausting you like this let them take over."

She took a deep breath and, by some miracle, got herself together enough to try to ground. It wasn't a terribly successful attempt, energy-wise, but she did feel calmer and asked, "What did she do?"

"She's a traitor, Miranda. Because of her, four of my Elite were murdered tonight. She's also been working with those who have killed humans all over the city and want to drive us to war."

"What are you going to do with her?"

Another sigh, this one full of regret. "She'll be questioned as to her involvement with the insurgents. It may be that she was coerced into helping them, or maybe not. Either way, her actions have earned a death sentence."

"Are you . . . Faith said . . . what exactly does 'questioned' mean?"

He met her eyes. "Don't ask what you don't want answered."

She sat back, suddenly realizing she was in his lap, and

moved away from him, sickness gathering in her stomach where the fear had been before.

He wasn't human. None of these people were. They drank blood, they were immortal, and . . . he was going to torture Helen. She *knew* Helen. So did he. To become a guard in this wing she must have been with the Elite a long time, and he was just going to walk in there and . . . and then kill her.

The way Miranda had tried to kill her. The way Miranda had killed those men.

"I think I'm going to throw up," she groaned.

He didn't say anything as she stumbled away from the couch, but when she reached the door he said, "To your left," keeping her from vomiting in his closet.

She fell to her knees painfully in front of the toilet, retching, but nothing came. She closed the lid and leaned her head on the seat, afraid to get up just yet.

If there had ever been a time when life made sense, that time was far fled. She had blundered into the rabbit hole, and there was no going back.

"If I asked, would you kill me?" she whispered to the empty bathroom. "How would I taste? Like a sad little girl? Or am I damaged goods now?"

There was no answer. She forced herself to her feet and over to the sink, where she washed her face with ice-cold water, wishing she could see herself and hoping she never would again.

When she returned to the bedroom, he was gone. The door to her room was standing open, and she could smell food. Her stomach growled even though it had been in a tumult only minutes before.

Numb, too tired to care anymore, she went to her room to eat.

"God*damn* it."

The Prime stormed out of the interrogation room into

the waning night, leaving the corpse of a once-trusted ally in a pool of her own blood.

"I don't know what happened, Sire," the Elite who had been watching the cell said, pleading in his voice. "No one went in or out of that room before you arrived."

David whirled around on him and caught him by the throat, lifting up slightly. "If you're lying to me," he hissed, "I will cut out your lungs and feed them to you."

"I swear . . . I swear, Sire. Question me however you need to."

He dropped the guard, who looked like he was about to piss himself, and stalked away from the building. He was halfway across the garden by the time Faith caught up with him.

"We searched her while she was unconscious. I don't know where the stake could have come from, much less how she managed to get it through her own heart."

He stopped, taking a breath, appalled by his own lack of control. "Have the car brought around. I'm going into town to hunt."

"It's getting late—"

"Just do it."

Faith nodded once and stepped away to call Harlan while David stood brooding beside the driveway.

Helen had deliberately ripped off the sleeve of her uniform to display the Seal of Auren on her shoulder before she'd somehow staked herself, alone, in a locked room with a guard. How long had she been working for the enemy? Almost every attack had occurred somewhere that a patrol unit had conveniently been absent from. She had to have been sending the duty schedule to her masters. But why had they chosen to up the stakes and start killing the Elite now?

Whatever their game, it was working. They were finding and exploiting holes in his security, and by doing so learned where he was weak. He would be impossible to kill outright, but if they kept poking and prodding, they'd find a place to slip in, as he had done with Auren. If they weren't eliminated, it was only a matter of time. He'd seen the strategy before.

He paused midstride and narrowed his eyes. *Seen it before.*

"Star-three," he said into his com.

Faith popped up at his elbow. "Yes, Sire?"

He turned to her. "While I'm in town, I want you to go into the archives and pull all the files on the Blackthorn syndicate."

Her eyebrows lifted. "You don't think . . ."

"This is starting to sound too familiar," he replied. "The feints, the slowly rising body count, starting with humans . . . the Blackthorn took responsibility for Arrabicci's assassination, and I'm well aware that they hate me."

"But Prime Deven had them all executed," Faith insisted. "The entire cult was wiped out. There aren't any Blackthorn left."

"Perhaps not. But either a few survived the wars, or someone has been taking a page from their playbook. Regardless, I want to see the files."

"Yes, Sire. Are you sure you don't want me to accompany you into the city, things being as they are?"

He shook his head. "Even assuming they can kill me, they're not going to try yet. They'll work at chipping away my authority so that when they do take me out—theoretically—there won't be a huge resistance."

She didn't like it, but he didn't care. He had already fed once tonight, but the energy he'd expended trying to teach Miranda had left him hungry again. He couldn't think clearly with his veins itching and burning in his throat, and a yawning emptiness in his stomach.

He settled into the car, directing Harlan to one of his usual hunting grounds.

Just before they pulled away from the curb, he signaled

for Harlan to wait and rolled the window down, beckoning to Faith.

"Check on Miss Grey when you finish with the files."

And if there was a knowing little smile on his Second's face as he rolled up the window, he chose to ignore it, for now.

The myth was that vampires could not catch or carry disease. It was close to truth, but not true.

Their lives depended on speed, ironic considering their lives and physical ages never moved. They could regenerate skin, tissue, even bone within a matter of hours, sometimes minutes, depending on the wound and the strength of the individual. It was that rapid healing that kept them from dying unless their bodies were completely destroyed by fire or sun. Severing the head meant there was no time to heal and no way to focus power enough to recover before death took its toll.

Wood was another matter; something in the cellular structure of wood slowed down the healing process almost to the rate of a human. The heart was the most popular strike because it caused almost instant death, but any major artery pierced by wood could be fatal if the stake wasn't removed and the bleeding wasn't stopped fast enough.

By the same token, communicable diseases were killed by their white cells as quickly as they could heal a bullet wound, but if the disease was advanced in the human it came from, it could linger as long as several hours.

Diseased blood tasted bad. That was another way they avoided it. Every human's blood held layer upon layer of taste and scent, conveying a full profile of the human's health, living environment, and habits. Many of those same flavors could be scented as well so the predator could avoid tainted prey.

He could tell at ten meters if someone had a cold, allergies, or an unusual diet; vegetarians tasted cleaner, but sometimes a greasy burger was exactly what was called for. He could smell drugs, cigarettes, alcohol. He could taste ancestry as easily as he could taste cancer. They all had their preferences, but there was no reason to be indiscriminate.

Drugs and alcohol worked the way diseases did. He'd fed on a lot of hippies in the sixties just for the high. Everything humans did with their bodies and their energy affected how nourishing they were to his kind.

Sex, too, had its own range of tastes. Vampires drank desire, pleasure, and pain in the blood, often with equal abandon.

He didn't ask her name. She didn't ask his.

The club crowds were thinning by the time he got to the city, but there were always places to find suitable prey. The mortal population of Austin had no idea how many of its Sixth Street bars and dance clubs were owned by vampires who set up the perfect hunting grounds for their real clientele. The bouncers let in only the healthy and clean. They provided cheap drinks and kept out the scum. Ignoring the fact that entering such an establishment was likely to end in holes in one's neck, they were safe places for humans to enjoy themselves . . . with a hidden cover charge.

She was in her midtwenties, shorter than him, with small hands and intelligent green eyes. She had been about to leave after a hard night of partying. Her boyfriend had dumped her that very day and she'd come to get wasted with her friends, hoping to hook up with someone to make her forget.

He was well acquainted with the club. He owned it. He had his own booth and his own private room in the back that he had used at least once a week as long as he had lived in Austin.

It was three hours before dawn when he escorted

her into the room, and two hours before dawn when he escorted her out.

She had such soft skin, pale and sweet like vanilla ice cream. Her nails dug into his shoulders as he parted her thighs with an expert hand, teasing her. While he stroked her body, his power caressed her mind, and she cried out, her muscles tightening around his fingers.

She was already sweating by the time he peeled the tight T-shirt from her torso, exposing the flat plane of her belly and the swell of her breasts to his mouth. Too flat, almost . . . he would have preferred she were softer, with more curve at the hip, perhaps fuller lips . . . but she tasted like summer, like a woman who had never seen death or deliberately caused anyone pain, and he drank in that innocence, then drank her blood.

His teeth found purchase in her throat, and to distract her from the pain, he opened her legs again and entered her, the combined pleasure of it almost too much to bear for them both. She wrapped her legs around his waist and lifted her hips to meet his, and thank God, she didn't bother with the theatrical moaning most human women did. It would take a far greater fool than he not to recognize a faked orgasm.

The real thing, though, was almost as good as blood. Life energy was their true nourishment, and the most usable form for his kind was the blood, but there were other forms that, though lacking in staying power, were far more enjoyable.

He lifted his lips from her throat and licked delicately at the wound to speed its healing, his senses reeling with satisfaction. Everything else simply melted away.

He was so grateful that he brought her twice before finishing himself, then again before releasing her. Women, he had always felt, had gotten a raw deal sexually speaking. It was so easy for men, but women took work, and they put up with a lot from the dicked gender. The least he could do was make it worth their while.

She was breathing hard, the last tiny tremors still

running through her body, her eyes shut tightly. Neither felt the need to speak . . . but as he lay on top of her, supporting himself with his arms, he looked down and realized for the first time that she had red hair.

# Six

"I want to go for a walk, please."

The new door guard, a dreadlocked man named Terrence, still seemed a bit bewildered at his sudden promotion, not to mention nonplussed as to how to handle his charge. He never knew whether to smile at her or bow or what. She found it oddly endearing.

Samuel grinned at her. He'd never been rude, but after Helen's arrest, his attitude toward Miranda had gotten much warmer. She wasn't entirely sure why, but as with so many other things here, she just didn't ask.

"Terrence here can accompany you," Samuel said.

Miranda sighed, but she knew there was no way around it. They were under orders not to let her venture out alone. All the stubbornness in the world on her part wouldn't persuade them to disobey their Prime. "Okay. I'll be ready in five minutes."

She went back into the bedroom and put on her shoes and cardigan, then pulled her hair back into two quick, slightly puffy braids. When she opened the door again, Terrence bowed, then let her lead the way out of the Prime's wing.

Things had changed in the week since Helen's death. Miranda had woken from her nightmares with something new fluttering weakly around in her heart. She didn't know what to call it, but it got her out of bed and drove her to practice grounding even though David had decided not to push her for a while. He'd told her to practice whenever she felt up to it, and to let him know when she was ready to learn more. That sudden kindness after the way he'd come at it the first time made her wonder about him, though she wasn't sure what exactly to wonder.

After that he'd disappeared. She barely saw him for days. Whatever was happening had apparently gotten much, much worse, and the Court simply didn't have time for her anymore. There was a tension in the Haven she could practically taste even through David's shield.

It hadn't taken her long to start exploring. A guard followed her everywhere, but they kept their distance as long as she didn't try to get herself in trouble or wander off somewhere forbidden. None of the Elite had a clue what to make of her, this battered little woman with her frightening power. Those who had seen what she did to Helen had passed on the story, and now she had a reputation.

Miranda couldn't decide if having a reputation here was something good or bad, but as the days went on, she decided she liked it. She felt safer knowing that she made them nervous.

At first, their deferring to her the way they did to the Prime bothered her, but after a few days it became second nature to her. So did inclining her head at them in acknowledgment of the bow . . . which was exactly what David did.

"Why are they treating me like this?" Miranda asked Faith one night as they took a stroll through the gardens. Faith had come to see her several times, checking on her welfare and then, to Miranda's surprise, engaging her in conversation, trying to learn more about what made the Prime's new pet tick.

Faith knew exactly what she meant and glanced over at the guard who had been shadowing them on their walk. "Promise not to freak out over what I tell you?"

"I promise."

They took the long path that looped around the garden perimeter and over toward the stables, an area Miranda had not yet ventured toward. It was another hot night, but not blisteringly so, and signs pointed toward an early fall this year. The end of the summer was apparently quite a celebration among their kind—longer nights and a decline in the crime rate made life easier for the Shadow World.

Faith walked alongside her, her eyes on the splendid riot of color that surrounded them—all shades of green, all depths of shadow, the ethereal whites of the night-blooming flowers that released their heady scents into the warm wind as they passed.

"There's a rumor," Faith went on. "After word got out of your abilities, people began to talk. You shouldn't make anything out of it, Miss Grey—"

"Miranda, please. Miss Grey sounds like I'm a substitute math teacher."

A smile. "All right, Miranda, you mustn't give these rumors any more credit than exactly what they are, the idle gossip of a houseful of vampires where you are now living in the mistress suite off the Prime's bedroom."

"The mistress what now?"

"Your room. The last Prime to live here had no Queen, but he kept a series of mistresses in that room throughout his tenure. The last one was reported to have been showing signs she might become more than a mistress."

"I'm sleeping in the Slut Suite of Whore Manor?"

"You can see, then, why rumors might fly. Add to that your abilities, and . . . the most popular theory now is that you're being groomed to take the Queen's Signet."

Miranda flopped down on a bench, astonished. "But I'm human!"

"Rumor has it it's only a matter of time."

Tonight, Miranda followed those thoughts almost against her will as she followed the path that she and Faith had taken along the outermost edge of the gardens.

*Ridiculous.* It was the sort of wild speculation that

surrounded the British royalty or the latest talentless Hollywood celebutantes. Surely the people here had more important things to worry about than what she was doing here. Gossip was usually a mindless distraction from a far too serious world. Clearly the same forces were at work here.

If it was so mindless, then, why was she angry about it?

Miranda shook her head and took the path back toward the Haven, determined to practice her shielding tonight. They were going to keep talking as long as she was still here. She could deal with the stares and the bowing, but she'd always hated being whispered about.

Had David heard the rumors? What did he think of them? Probably nothing. He had to be used to the chatter; that was part of how Primes built their empires, using their reputations to bolster their power. She'd seen that much already. Faith had told her a few of the stories that surrounded him—he could vanish into thin air, move faster than darkness, and probably breathe fire and turn people into gerbils. Given what Miranda had seen him do so far, it was probably easy to foster such legends beyond the Haven's walls.

She took the stairs back to the second floor, pretending not to notice the Elite behind her, and gave the guards a nod of thanks before shutting and locking her door.

Miranda took a minute to work a bit more antifrizz goop into her hair; the humidity had been high for Austin this year, and she could only imagine how wild she looked . . . not that she could be sure. She was looking forward to having a mirror again.

A mirror, and a life would be nice, too. Strange that she was starting to think that maybe, just maybe, she might find the latter someday.

The time before the Haven had already become a blur of pain and fear—this place was so far removed from the day-walking world that she didn't even feel like herself anymore. That horrific night in the alley had broken her heart into a thousand pieces, but it had broken her

life neatly into "before" and "after." It had been so long
since she'd had her mind, so long since she'd felt any tiny
flicker of hope for the future . . . all she had to do was get
strong enough to shield for herself, and she could return
to Austin, and . . .

What, exactly? Go back to performing? Would that be
safe? Could she even play without relying on the emotions of others for fuel? If not, what would she do, get a
job like a normal person?

She stood for a moment with her brain reeling. *Normal.* She had no idea what that even meant anymore. Yes,
there was hope . . . and that hope brought with it a new
kind of fear that she simply wasn't equipped to face right
now.

As if fate knew she needed the distraction, she noticed
that there was a light coming from under David's door.

That was unusual this early in the evening. He was
almost never there until nearly dawn. Curious, she ventured over to the door and opened it a crack to peek in.

She expected to find him at his desk working some
sort of technological wizardry, but when he wasn't, at
first she thought he'd just went off and left the light on.
Then she caught sight of his dark head at the end of the
couch—he was lying down.

Miranda opened the door a little wider and crept over
the threshold just to make sure he was okay; it wasn't like
him to be here this time of night, let alone to relax in any
form at any time. Something had to be wrong.

Inching closer, she got a better look. He was, indeed,
stretched out on the couch, in casual clothes like he'd
worn the night he'd shown her how to ground; the coffee
table was spread with papers in tidy piles, and there was
an open file folder over his stomach, one hand holding
it down. She smiled when she saw the empty ice cream
carton on the corner of the table: Ben & Jerry's Chunky
Monkey.

He was asleep. She'd never actually seen him sleep

before. It made him look younger, less grave, almost . . . cute.

She wondered if he'd ever been happy, if he'd ever smiled . . . if he'd ever been young. She remembered her grandmother saying once that she was a sad child, born old. She had a feeling that David had been born that way, too.

She started to retreat to her room, but he shifted slightly, startling her so that she froze like a rabbit under the gaze of a snake. The faint touch of peace on his face hardened, his brow furrowing, and he shook his head slightly, one hand flexing on the couch cushion. His lips moved, almost a tremor, words barely audible.

"Lizzie . . ."

Miranda held her breath and listened, her heart in her throat as she leaned closer, straining to hear.

"Lizzie, take Thomas . . . hurry . . ."

In that moment pain flashed through Miranda's head, and she stepped backward involuntarily, clapping her hands over her ears the way she once had to try to block out the voices. This time, though, it wasn't a voice invading her thoughts, it was an image: a little boy with brown hair down to his collar, running with his arms outstretched, giggling. He wore some kind of Pilgrim-looking costume that was stained around the hems, and he was barefoot, his skin nut-brown from the sun.

The boy ran along some kind of dirt path and was swept up into the arms of a woman waiting for him; she wore a muted dress with a high collar and her hair was pulled back in a stark knot, but her smile was warm, and beneath the dull-colored clothes she was young and beautiful, with sparkling brown eyes.

The scene began to fade, and Miranda smelled something, or rather, remembered the smell of something: smoke, and the acrid stench of . . . something burning. She heard a cacophony of shouting and wailing, and terror gripped her; she turned and ran, taking the path back from where she'd come, but there was nowhere to go, nothing but fire . . .

"Miranda?"

She flailed out at the men who tried to seize her arms—they were going to kill Thomas, she had to hide him before—

Someone shook her gently, and she gasped, her vision clearing as suddenly as it had appeared.

She was backed up against the bedroom wall, and David was standing in front of her, his hands lightly resting on her shoulders. He was pale, even for him, and looked more worried than she'd ever seen him. His eyes were an even deeper blue than usual, smoky.

"Sorry," she stammered. "The light was on and I didn't . . . didn't mean to wake you."

He shook his head and guided her back to the couch. "What happened?"

She had no idea where to begin. As long as she'd been cursed with voices, they'd been just that, or feelings; she'd never *seen* things before, especially not random events that could have been history, or just brain garbage.

"Wait," she murmured. "Were you dreaming just now?"

He looked away. "Why?"

"I saw a little boy, and a woman. Then there was fire."

David looked at her sharply. *"What?"*

"They were kind of . . . colonial, I guess. I don't know history that well. But they both looked so happy. Then it's like I was her, and I was afraid they . . . somebody was going to hurt the little boy."

The expression of suspicion on his face faded into recognition, and then something like sorrow, and he looked away from her again. "Yes. Somebody was."

"What did I see?"

He sat back, eyes on the ground, and crossed his arms almost nervously. "You saw my wife."

"And the boy . . ."

"Our son."

"Do you . . . do you dream of them often?"

"No," he answered, still not looking at her. "Not often."

A thousand questions whirled in her head, but she knew she was prying and was fairly sure it wasn't a subject he would feel comfortable talking about. Whatever drove a person to become a vampire, it couldn't be pretty. She couldn't imagine what would persuade her to give up her humanity that way . . . the thought made her feel queasy. She couldn't even look at the needle when she got a shot.

"Oh, come now," he said, picking up on the thought with genuine amusement in his voice. "It's no more disgusting than the things you humans eat."

"Not me," she returned with a grin. "Vegetarian, remember?"

Now he was definitely smiling. "Cheese is the coagulated lactation of a ruminant mammal. It's not even made from human milk, which would make far more sense. Eggs are essentially the menstrual period of a chicken. Honey is mostly bee spit. Shall I go on?"

She grabbed a throw pillow and threw it at him. "Oh, gross!"

The tension of the moment was effectively broken, thank God. She knew better than to revisit the subject. There were some things . . . no, a lot of things . . . she didn't need to know.

"How are you tonight?" he asked. "It's been a few days."

"Not awful." She drew her legs up under her chin; it no longer hurt to do so, and a few of her more visible bruises were fading. Her ribs and back still ached if she stayed in one position too long, and one of her wrists throbbed if she tried to play guitar for more than half an hour—not that she had, really. She'd picked at the instrument here and there when she was bored, but nothing else. "I think I might be ready to start lessons again."

An eyebrow quirked. "Are you certain?"

"I think so. I've got grounding down pretty well, and I've been working on moving energy around."

"Very well, then. Tomorrow night."

She eyed the array of files on the coffee table. "Do you need help with whatever this is?"

"No." He leaned forward and started compiling the papers into a single stack. "I was just looking over old patrol reports and field notes from my time in California. It wasn't getting me anywhere."

"So you still don't know who's behind all of this."

He raised a curious eyebrow. "How much do you know exactly?"

She shrugged, and replied, "I know what you've said, and Faith has hinted. And I get these . . . feelings . . . sometimes, not exactly voices but impressions that tell me things. I think it's bleed-through from the shield you have around me."

David looked confused, frowning. "That shouldn't be possible. Shields like mine don't leak."

Miranda felt him reaching through the shield, and it surprised her, but didn't scare her; she held still to let him do whatever it was he was doing. To her mind's eye it was as if he ran a hand along the outside of the shield he was holding up around her, and then along the barrier between her and himself, checking for flaws. She envied the way he made it look so easy, but then, if she'd been doing it for 350 years she might have been that good, too.

He shook his head, speaking almost to himself. "No leaks . . . and the barrier between us is thinner than it would be between me and an outside person, but still, there shouldn't be any crossover."

"Do you get stuff from me?" she asked.

"Occasionally, but that's to be expected since I'm the one holding the shield. Sometimes you think loudly," he added with a smile. "You're easily as strong a projector as you are a receiver, which is how you can both sense emotions and manipulate them. We'll work on honing your projective skills as soon as you can keep yourself separate from the rest of the world."

He finished his inspection and withdrew to the other side of the barrier. "I should have asked first," he said with chagrin. "You don't need anyone poking around in your aura right now."

Miranda shrugged again. "It doesn't bother me. Anyone else it might, but I guess I'm used to you."

She knew it was strange. Two days ago she had been out walking in the garden and tripped over a stone, and Terrence had appeared beside her to grab her arm and steady her; she'd wrenched away from his grasp and nearly decked him, settling for a mild panic attack. His hand had been too big, his grip too firm. She'd apologized for the freakout, and he'd apologized for the liberty. She didn't want anyone touching her. She'd always been a rabid defender of her personal space, but now the minute anyone—especially anyone male—got within ten feet, her heart started to pound.

David was different. The only thing she could figure was that having his mind bordering so closely to hers day and night made her instincts accept him as nonthreatening. Perhaps it was because every time he'd physically touched her, she had gotten the psychic sense of him asking for her consent, never assuming. Perhaps it was because nothing about him reminded her of . . . those others. Of everyone in the Haven, she was the least afraid of him.

She was well aware how ironic that was, considering he was by far the scariest bastard she'd ever met.

"Well, I'm glad you're used to me," he said, and then seemed to regret saying so; she hadn't been looking for any sort of subtext in the statement but . . . had there been? Was it her imagination, or did he actually look a little *embarrassed*?

The two weeks she'd been at the Haven she had been trying to make up her mind about David Solomon. At times she wished desperately to hate him for trying to save her, and in almost the same minute she wanted his approval; other times he terrified her. Still others, she found herself wondering if, in another time and place, if he were human, maybe . . . but part of her mind had still been trying to settle on an opinion, until now. The ever-so-faint sheepish undertone in his voice swung the jury. *Yes . . . I like you . . . fangs and all. If someone asked me who you were, I would say, "My friend."*

"Do you want to tell me about what's going on?" she asked then. "Maybe I can help."

He rose, and for a second she thought he was going to kick her out of the room, but instead he walked over to the corner by the desk and opened a cabinet. The lamplight picked out the edges of a row of bottles and another of glasses. He filled one, then turned to her with a questioning look.

"Got any margaritas?"

"No," he replied, "but I can call for some if you like."

She shook her head quickly. That's exactly the sort of thing someone who was used to having servants would do. "No, that's okay. What about Coke?"

"With or without rum?"

"With. Lots."

There was a small fridge beneath the bar, and he retrieved a soda. As the door was closing she caught a glimpse of a thick plastic bag with a white label. Her stomach twisted.

He saw her staring. "Emergency supply," he explained as he poured her drink. "It's only good for about four days after it's donated before the life energy leaches out, but it's still stronger than animal blood. We have a contract with the blood and tissue center for a limited amount per month. It's saved more than a few lives here."

"Do they know what you're using it for?" She tried to sound nonchalant, but the thought still intruded: God, he *drank* that. It was in there because he drank it. He probably liked the taste, the smell.

"Of course," he said, returning to the couch and handing her her drink. She kept herself from shooting it out of sheer force of will, and took a sip, letting the alcohol burn her tongue and the bubbles fizz merrily along with it. "My people are known to the United States government on several levels. It's a relatively recent phenomenon, but keeping good diplomatic relations helps us all coexist. My predecessor wasn't so open-minded, so when I took the Signet I had to do a lot of damage control."

She took another swallow of her drink, this one bigger. She still couldn't shake the mental image . . . David, bending over someone's neck . . . using those teeth to pierce a human's flesh, and sucking from it, his lower lip stained red. His eyes had gone silver when he was angry; did they do the same when he fed?

Then there was the human. The bite would hurt, but he had said vampires used their psychic power to keep their prey calm, and that it was . . . what had he said? *Intensely pleasurable.* Was that why so many people thought they were romantic?

He was watching her again, and she felt herself flush. She knew he could hear some of her thoughts.

"It's all right," he told her, staring into his drink, then lifting his eyes to her. "I don't blame you for feeling revulsion. Any sane person would. But we do what we must to survive. At heart, we want the same things as your kind do."

"Really? What do you want?"

He lowered his glass, clearly surprised by the question, but thought about it a moment before he said, "I want peace in my territory. I want whoever is behind this brought to justice so no one else dies."

He told her, then, what was going on, or at least an abridged version of it: the attacks in the city, growing more frequent and more violent; Helen's betrayal and the holes in security it had exposed, which he was now confident were filled; and, in less detail, the street war in California and the vampire cult known as the Blackthorn.

"They began as a single family, around the time I was leaving Britain. Imagine Puritan vampires, if you can—religious zealots who favor austerity of lifestyle, feeding on those they consider sinners. They were all but extinct for over a century, then reappeared in California and assassinated the Prime there, expecting to put their leader in the Signet. Needless to say, the stone didn't wake for him. The territory fell into chaos. I helped the deceased Prime's Second end the war, and the Signet chose him. One of his first orders was to exterminate the Blackthorn. Any member of the syndicate we found, we killed. If any survived, they ran from California and didn't return."

"And you think they're here," she concluded.

"I don't know. Certainly the methodology is the same. They gradually undermined Arrabicci's authority, killing off his Elite until we were spread so thin that the Queen was left unguarded just long enough to take a crossbow bolt to the heart." He again got that haunted look on his face, then added, "I saw it, but I couldn't stop it. Everything happened so fast."

"Did they shoot the Prime after that?"

David shook his head. "They didn't have to. A Pair—that is, a Prime and his Queen—is bound by blood and soul. What kills one kills both. The Queen went down, and in less than a minute Arrabicci just . . . fell, dead, without a scratch on him. The bond between them enables them to share their power, but in doing so they also share their fates."

"That sounds awful," Miranda observed, sucking the liquor off an ice cube. She'd become a lightweight these past few weeks, and he'd had a liberal hand with the rum. She was feeling a bit blurred around the edges.

He smiled. "It does, doesn't it? From what I hear, it's wonderful."

"Your friend, the one in California, does he have a Queen?"

"A Consort."

"What's the difference?"

The smile turned wry. "The difference is, if you called Jonathan a Queen, he'd break your neck."

"They make gay Primes?"

"Only one, as far as we know. As I've said before, vampires are slow to evolve."

"I'll bet the Blackthorn loved that."

"That's part of why they singled out Arrabicci in the first place. Deven was his most trusted ally, and probably the single most accomplished warrior vampire kind has ever seen. The Blackthorn demanded that he execute Deven or be killed himself. I think his exact words were, 'Go fuck yourselves, and I'll see you in hell.'"

Miranda nodded, understanding. "And you're friends, so they hate you, too."

"For that and a dozen other reasons, not the least of which is that I helped wipe out their entire clan. If there are any left, they'll be out for vengeance as much as for their crusade."

She leaned sideways into the couch cushions, yawning hugely. It was a good thing she hadn't had any painkillers so far that evening. It took so little to wear her out. She remembered a brief time back in college when she could outdrink a fraternity pledge, but like everything else in her life, it had become a shadow, an indistinct ghost from Before.

"Do you miss your wife?" she asked sleepily.

It was several seconds before he answered. "It was a long time ago."

"Did you love her?"

"Yes. Very much."

"How did she die?"

He finished his drink, but didn't set the glass down. "She was convicted of witchcraft and burned alive in the village square."

Her eyes shot open. "Oh my God."

David nodded. "My son was sent to another town, on the other side of Britain, adopted by relatives. He died of cholera at age thirty-two."

"But . . . where were you?"

"I was in prison," he replied. "I was sentenced to die as Elizabeth had, but someone intervened. Afterward, I thought it best to leave Thomas to his life, believing me dead, instead of forcing him to face what I had become."

"I'm sorry."

She nearly dropped her glass, and he reached out and rescued it from her, moving too fast for her tipsy mind to register. One second the glass was in her hand, the next it was safely on the coffee table. He might even have done it with his mind.

"Perhaps you should have a nap," David told her, amused.

"I feel like I spend all my time asleep on your couch."

"You need your rest. You've been through a lot."

"Yeah." She pulled her knees back up to her chin, groping for the throw blanket and pulling it around herself haphazardly. "'Specially if you're going to work me over tomorrow like you did last time."

"I'll try to be gentle."

"That's what they all say."

She drifted off, smiling, aware that his eyes were still on her as her own fell shut.

It was a beautiful, clear morning in April when Lizzie died. The smoke had to have been seen for miles.

It was the last morning he ever saw, and he had only a glimpse of it through the bars of his cell. He was lucky; he didn't have to see her beautiful young face obscured by a column of smoke, or her rosy skin blackening. He didn't have to watch her scream . . . but he heard her. He heard all three of the convicted shrieking as the flames licked their bare, broken feet. He heard the crowd cheering, heard the drone of the reverend's voice.

One by one, the screams had become less and less human . . . then they had faded. David learned, years later, that in all likelihood the victims had died from

smoke inhalation, so they had been blessedly oblivious to the stench of their own flesh barbecuing. Perhaps
their feet had blistered, skin charring and cracking, but
the poisoned air would have starved them of oxygen,
and the agony may not have been as excruciating as he
imagined.

Or perhaps this time the smoke hadn't been enough—
the wind may have been wrong, the wood so dry that
flames raced up the pyre. Perhaps Elizabeth had died
cursing his name, or begging God for release. Had her
last thoughts been of him? Of their boy, already spirited
away in the night, out of the pernicious influence of his
demonic parents?

He remembered Lizzie as he had known her, laughing,
eyes sparkling, hair coming loose from its bun. She'd been
such a free spirit that she'd married later than her sisters.
The men of the village thought she was difficult. Fiery,
they'd said. She'd died, then, the way she had lived.

Richard Cooke, who had taken the last shift as jailer
before David was to follow Elizabeth's steps up to the
pyre, whispered to him through the bars that though the
other two condemned had sobbed and begged for their
lives, she had spat on the reverend in contempt and held
her head high as they lashed her to the stake. That was
his Lizzie.

Hanging had been a more common fate for witches
back then, but the Witchfinder who came to their village—
who was paid per conviction—had favored a more barbaric method that would remind the witnesses of the
inferno that awaited them in hell should they stray from
the path of righteousness.

Twenty-first-century Austin was both far more mon-
strous and infinitely kinder in comparison.

David stood in the warm night wind, staring down
at his city from the roof of one of its tallest buildings,
watching traffic move along the streets below. From here,
there was the illusion of order; things moved in straight
lines, according to signals. Horns blared, and the wind

carried to him snatches of music from the bars and clubs that lined Sixth Street, all of them filled to capacity on a Saturday night in late summer.

Kinder, yes . . . and yet the same ignorant hatred that had ended Lizzie's life had dogged his steps all the way to the twenty-first century. Either humankind had learned depressingly little in the last few centuries, or he was singularly cursed.

Somewhere out there was the gang he intended to find and eliminate. They were, he was sure, planning their next assault as he stood there.

For months the California Blackthorn had been phantoms. They appeared, killed, and dissolved before they could be identified. The Elite had been unable to track them until luck finally fell their way: One of the members dropped a matchbook at the crime scene. That matchbook led to a vampire bar, which led to David exercising his interrogation skills, which led to the rest of the syndicate. Blood had flowed on the streets of Sacramento until the night was silent again.

There had been nineteen human deaths and four vampires so far this time . . . five, if he counted Helen. The only good thing to come of it was that now the com network was so secure God himself would need a password to log on.

Again he thought of Lizzie's face. He thought of her often, but rarely in any depth. It had been over three centuries, and he had loved since then. Hundreds of people had tumbled in and out of his bed, and though he'd given his heart rarely, it had happened. He had known Lizzie for less than a decade total. Why had she returned to haunt his dreams now?

More important . . . how had Miranda seen her?

He'd shielded others before, and this had never happened. The only explanation he could think of was that Miranda was a good three times more powerful than anyone he had ever trained before. Psychically she was already as strong as half his Elite. It was also possible that she had some mostly untapped power as a medium, just as it was possible she could see and hear parts of him that no one else he had ever trained could . . . possible, and extremely unnerving.

His phone rang.

He reached for it absently, stepping back out of the wind. "Yes?"

"Let me guess," came a familiar, deep voice with a cheerful British accent. "You're standing on top of a building in a long black coat, brooding."

David smiled into the darkness. "Not at all, my Lord," he replied. "As it happens I'm at a topless bar with my face between a brunette's thighs."

"Liar," was the laughing reply. "Your voice isn't muffled."

"To what do I owe this honor?" David asked.

Jonathan Burke, Consort of the Prime of the Western United States, had spent most of his immortal life as a bodyguard for royals, and in his spare time he was rumored to bite trees in half with his teeth. A tall, broad blond whose nose had been broken a few times, he looked far more like a linebacker than like a vampire. He was a good ten inches taller than his Prime, his polar opposite in more ways than one; Deven was quiet and serious and had fooled many people into thinking he was fragile.

David imagined Jonathan sitting with his feet propped up on his desk at the Haven outside Sacramento, drinking a beer with his free hand.

"I e-mailed you the files you asked for," Jonathan said. "I don't know how much help they'll be. Your intel is probably vastly superior to ours."

"Thank you. I want to look over them regardless to see if there's anything I missed."

"You're looking for a matchbook," Jonathan surmised. "I hope you find one. I hate to think any of those cockroaches slipped through our fingers, but it's possible."

"That's not why you called," David pointed out.

"No, not really." The Consort seemed to be looking for

words, which was a bit unusual for him, but David waited until he said, "I saw something."

*Shit.* Consorts were almost all gifted with precognition, and Jonathan's gift was very strong. He'd foreseen Arrabicci's death, but he was on the other side of the world when it happened and didn't even know what he was seeing. He'd foreseen David taking the Signet—in fact, that vision had been what convinced David that the waiting was over and it was time to take Auren down.

"What did you see?"

"It was vague," was the reply, amended with, "but it felt urgent. I don't even know if it will make any sense to you. I wasn't going to call, but Dev said I had better, and you know he's always right."

"Go on."

"There was a woman," said the Consort. "I couldn't see her very clearly, but I could hear music."

David's hand clenched the phone so tightly he was amazed it didn't break. "And?"

"Black water. Cold. It felt like drowning—well, I think it did. I've never actually drowned, but still, if I could . . . anyway, I also saw a Signet Seal, not one I knew. I think it may have been Auren's, which makes sense given the situation. The stone drawn in the center was red like yours. It was painted on something, and it was burning."

The Prime nodded to nobody. "What else?"

"The woman . . . she was sad. She made me think of honey and rain."

"What happened to her?"

"She died, David. That much was certain. I saw her blood on your hands. My advice is, if you meet this woman, get her away from you as fast as you can."

David was dimly aware that he'd stopped breathing. "Is that all?" he managed.

"No. There's one other thing." Jonathan delivered the rest hurriedly, as if he were trying to exorcise the knowledge from his mind by saying the words aloud. "At the end, I saw you, turning the pages of an old book. Between two pages you found a drawing of a woman, so old it was falling apart. I didn't recognize her, but she felt . . . wrong. Then you turned the page again, and there was a note someone had written you, still folded."

"Did you see what book it was?"

"No. It may not even have been a real book—you know how these things are. Sometimes they're literal, sometimes they're metaphoric, sometimes they're rubbish. I wish I knew more."

"Thank you," David said, "I think."

"Don't thank me," Jonathan told him, and he could hear the weight of too much knowledge in the Consort's voice. "Never thank me for seeing things, Lord Prime. I don't want this, I never have."

"I know." David smiled into the phone despite the way his heart was lumbering around in his chest. "But just think of what you'd be missing if you didn't have it."

"There is always that." Jonathan's voice perked up a little. "Speaking of which, I must go. My presence has been humbly requested in the bedroom."

David rolled his eyes, chuckling. "Humbly requested, my ass. Give the Prime my best before you give him yours."

"As you will it, my Lord. Good hunting."

"Good hunting."

Jonathan's words replayed over and over through David's mind as he left the bank tower and directed Harlan to return him to the Haven. He grunted noncommittally when Harlan asked if he'd had a good hunt; he was too preoccupied for conversation. The whole trip back, as the city's bustling nightlife gave way to the scrolling central Texas hills, he thought about it, unable to banish the knowledge that arose from his very bones as much as it had from the Consort's gift.

He was going to get Miranda killed. The longer she stayed at the Haven, the more danger she was in. One way or another she had to learn to shield, and fast. He already had the lives of enough innocents burned into his soul; he wouldn't have hers, too.

The problem with visions was that they were born from a single instant in time. As soon as they were seen, the universe began to change around them. They showed what was most probable if the course of events went unaltered, but they weren't set in stone. Jonathan had told him, and because of that, he would make one choice or another, veering closer to or further away from the vision itself. Right now, the deck was stacked against Miranda's life. He had to do everything in his power to change those odds.

That meant getting her back to Austin. It also meant stopping the war before it escalated further.

Of course, Miranda being back in the city might be what got her killed; there was no way to know. So he would make sure she was safe in her mortal world until he was confident that she didn't need a guardian. That would be easy enough.

It might be better if she left his territory entirely. He could arrange that, and it wasn't as if she had a full life here to miss. The Blackthorn wouldn't lower themselves to chase after a mere human, assuming they even knew she existed.

That thought did something strange to him, though. The idea of Miranda leaving Austin set off a dull ache, and a kind of wild desperate clawing in his throat, as if he were holding back a cry of pain.

He shut his eyes and rapped his forehead lightly against the car window, feeling like a fool.

By the time he was back at the Haven and had taken the usual patrol reports and updates from Faith, it was nearly dawn, and he had a splitting headache. Every time he exerted a tendril of energy to ease it, it returned moments later; if he left it alone it would be gone in an hour, but in the meantime he had to put up with it, and that left him snapping at Faith and acting generally bitchy toward everyone else.

"Sire?" Faith said at the end of the patrol meeting. "Permission to speak freely?"

"Since when do you ask for permission?" he scoffed, forehead planted firmly in his hands.

She ignored the statement and said, "Sire, go the fuck to bed before I have to kill you."

For once, he did as she said without protest and tried not to look at anyone he passed lest he scare the servants.

He paused with his hand on the door to his suite, suddenly dreading the prospect of finding Miranda still asleep on the couch. He thought back to that ache he'd felt in the car and had half a mind just to bed down in one of the other rooms in the wing, but that smelled strongly of cowardice to him, and he was willing to have just about any vice except that one.

To his surprise, she wasn't in the bedroom. She must have woken and returned to her own bed. Relieved, he stripped off his coat and poured himself another drink. He needed a shower; it was hot in the city, and though vampires didn't sweat easily, he still felt coated by the humid air.

A sound reached him, and he stood with the bottle of bourbon still in his hand, listening.

It was coming from the adjacent room: music.

Hypnotized, he set down the bottle and followed the sound to the door, which stood ajar by an inch or so. Light was coming through it. He leaned to the left to see in without moving the door.

*"Strange how hard it rains now . . ."*

She sat on the edge of the bed, the light of the fireplace outlining her silhouette and catching her hair as it had at the window once before. Her guitar, a black acoustic he remembered from the night he'd brought her here, gleamed, and her fingers danced slowly over the strings while her bare foot tapped lightly on the side of the bed as her legs weren't long enough to reach the floor.

Her curls were falling into her eyes, but that didn't matter; she played with them closed, concentration on her heart-shaped face. The bruises had all faded, though there was still a cut healing on her forehead. What was truly remarkable was her expression: As she sang, the dark sweetness of her voice wrapping like a lover's hands around the lyrics, she was smiling, completely at peace in a way he hadn't thought she was capable of.

He wanted so badly to back away, but he couldn't. Without even trying she had caught him in her spell.

*Oh God. No, no, no.*

She wasn't working energy consciously, and a half-hearted check of the shield showed it as strong as before, but she didn't need power for this. Perched on the bed, dressed in a threadbare Austin Celtic Festival T-shirt, she was, he suddenly realized, the most beautiful thing he'd ever seen.

*"But I'm still alive underneath this shroud. . . ."*

It took more effort than he would ever have thought possible, but he pulled his eyes away and shut the door, fighting the urge to lock it.

Then he proceeded to the liquor cabinet and drank himself to sleep.

# Seven

**TO:** Miranda Grey (mgrey82@freemail.net)
**FROM:** Kat (katmandoo@freemail.net)
**SUBJECT:** MIA?

Hey girl,

I know you said you were out of town but when you get
back can we please have lunch? I really think we should talk.
I'm worried about you, Mira-Mira. You don't have to deal
with this stuff alone. Just let me know you're okay, okay? I
miss you lots, sugarbean.

Hugs,
Kat


**TO:** Kat (katmandoo@freemail.net)
**FROM:** Miranda Grey (mgrey82@freemail.net)
**SUBJECT:** Re: MIA?

I'm okay. I'm staying with a friend in the country. I promise I'll
call as soon as I get back into Austin. Please don't worry about
me (even though I know you're going to anyway). Miss you too.

~M

She clicked SEND and watched, amazed, as the message flew out of her outbox and into the digital ether a hundred times faster than it would have the last time she worked on her laptop.

"You're pretty handy to have around," Miranda commented.

Across the table, David looked up from the computer he was fixing and offered a smile.

She had mentioned, in passing, that her computer was a dinosaur; she'd bought it used off Craigslist, and though she'd loved it, it was slow and lumbering and almost full to the gills with music files. David had offered to have a look at it before they started their training session that night, and in approximately thirty minutes had it purring like a brand-new machine. While she tried it out, he cracked open the case of some server or another and spilled its guts all over the table, going after it with a set of tiny screwdrivers to replace some kind of . . . chip? She couldn't even begin to name the small, rectangular piece of hardware.

As usual he felt her eyes and said, without looking up, "It's a security device to help keep predators out of the network."

"Has anyone else broken in?"

"No, and they won't."

He was being a little short with her tonight, though she sensed it wasn't anything she had done . . . although he had been giving her some odd looks when he thought she didn't notice . . . speculative looks, almost wary, and what in any other person's face might have been interpreted as fear.

She hummed softly as she cleaned out her inbox until she glanced up to see him looking aggrieved. "Do you mind?" he asked.

"Sorry," she muttered. She almost started doing it again just to piss him off, but decided that probably wasn't a good idea.

What was left of her good mood evaporated when she saw the sender of the next e-mail.

**TO:** Miranda Grey (mgrey82@freemail.net)
**FROM:** Marianne Grey-Weston (marianne.weston@comtex
.dallas.com)
**SUBJECT:** Dad's birthday

Miranda,

If you're planning to attend Dad's 60th birthday party next month, please let me know so I can send an accurate count to the caterer.

I hope you're doing well.

Sincerely,
Marianne Grey-Weston

She stared at the monitor for a long moment, biting her lip, before she shut the computer and pushed it away from her.

"What's wrong?" David asked, finally looking up from his work.

"Oh . . . nothing. Just my sister." At his surprised expression she added, "Older sister. She still lives in Dallas where we moved after our mother died. We don't talk much."

"Why not?"

She ran her finger around the Apple logo in the center of the laptop, trying to talk around the heavy feeling that always formed in her stomach when she heard from Marianne.

"We've never been close." She knew he could hear the lie in her voice, but he didn't comment. A moment later she said, almost unwillingly, "There was this thing, when we were younger . . . our mother, she . . . went crazy, sort of."

"Crazy," he repeated, the coolness of the tone he'd used all night warming just a tad. "Crazy like you went crazy?"

"I don't know. Maybe. It happened when we were kids. Nobody would ever tell me what was really wrong with her. She was always so normal—she packed lunches, she went to school plays, all of that. Marianne was involved in everything. She was the good daughter."

Miranda let her eyes drift around the room as she talked, staring at the servers, the monitors, anything but him. "Then one day Mama just sort of . . . stopped. She stared off into space and didn't recognize any of us. They did every medical test they could think of and found nothing. Dad put her in the county hospital, and she died there when I was fourteen."

"I'm sorry," he said. "That must have been hard for you, so young."

"The worst part was Marianne and Dad. They both wanted to pretend nothing ever happened and act like she was dead even when she wasn't. They were embarrassed. I think she caused some sort of scene in public once. They were both more concerned with what people thought than with what happened to Mama. I went to visit her once, but I couldn't go back there. It was . . . it was hell. It was hell and she was locked up there forever."

Miranda swallowed her tears, forcing her voice to stay steady. "Marianne and I had a lot of fights about it. Dad refused to talk about it at all. He still won't. So I moved back here to Austin as soon as I graduated high school. I only see them once a year or so, and it's always miserable. When I see her, all she wants to know is if I'm getting married and how much money I make, even though for years it's been the same answer. She just has to lord over me the fact that she's a rich pediatrician with a lawyer husband."

"Then why do you talk to her at all?"

She smiled helplessly. "I have no idea. They're like . . . they're like Hero and Claudio. The Blandersons of Blandville."

"Then don't answer," David said reasonably, snapping the case back on the computer, then zipping the tools into their own case. "We don't get to choose how we're born, Miranda, and very rarely how we die; but we get to choose how we live. Life is too short to spend in dread and guilt."

She cocked her head to one side and gave him a look. "You do realize that you lack any sort of credibility in the 'life is too short' cliché department."

"Conceded," he replied, rising. "But I'm still right. Shall we?"

Miranda sighed. "Now that we're one for one on sharing our life stories, I guess we should get to the fun part of the evening."

She slipped her laptop back into its bag and slung it over her shoulder, following him out of his workroom and down the hallway. She expected him to take her back to the suite, but he headed in the opposite direction, stopping in front of a locked door that was almost hidden in a corridor.

Like most doors in the Haven, it had an electronic lock. She had watched the Elite hold their coms up to the locks to open them; apparently the locks were programmed to check security clearance before admitting someone. David did the same, and the red light on the lock changed to green.

Whatever she was expecting from the room, what she found wasn't it. Peering in she saw nothing but two armchairs, just like the ones near the fireplace in his room, but there was no hearth here; in fact aside from the chairs there was no furniture at all, and the floor was bare of rugs. There were no windows and only the one door, no decoration of any kind.

When she crossed the threshold, her knees almost buckled. It felt like walking through a wall of water; for a second she couldn't breathe as power engulfed her, pushing at her nonexistent boundaries like a living thing trying to learn her shape.

She started to fight against it, but something dragged her forward—David's hand.

On the other side of the threshold, the air felt normal, if a little too clear. Looking back at the doorway it almost seemed there was a veil of . . . not light, but diffusion, again like water.

"It's a shield," she realized. "I've never seen anything so powerful."

He nodded and gestured for her to take a chair. "This is a protected room devoted to psychic training. There are several in the Haven, but this one belongs only to me. Primes have used it for centuries, so the walls are imbued with energy that keeps out unwanted influences and keeps in whatever we do here. That way if you lose control, no one outside this room will be hurt, and no one can attack you while you're vulnerable."

"Why are we working in here this time instead of in the suite?"

"Last time was all groundwork. This time, I'm going to lower your shield, and you're going to rebuild it. If we tried that in the suite, you would have every mind in the Haven running through yours."

"A hundred vampires in my head," Miranda said, feeling cold. "Bad idea."

"Precisely."

They settled into their chairs. David looked to his left, and the lights dimmed slightly, mimicking the soft ambience of candlelight. There were no candles—no open flames, no lamps that could be knocked over, nothing to break or explode. She wondered if he had learned to work his telekinesis in a room like this.

She still hadn't decided whether it was weirder that he was a vampire or that he could move things with his mind.

Actually the weird thing was that she now had a relativity scale for weirdness, and that just being a vampire wasn't automatically at the upper limit of that scale.

"Let's begin," he said. "Ground."

She did so, first slowing her breath, then connecting her energy to the earth beneath her, following the movement of inhalation and exhalation with her awareness. The world slowed down, and the agitation she was starting to feel about facing another lesson grew still, not disappearing, but no longer grasping at the limelight.

"Very good," David told her, warm approval in his voice.

She smiled in spite of herself. "I've been practicing."

"All right. Now, keep your breathing steady, and try not to clench your energy. Act as though you're still totally shielded and remember, in this space you're safe."

She nodded and did her best to stay calm. She was familiar enough with energy now that she could essentially see what he was doing: He parted the barrier around her mind like a curtain and drew it back, leaving her completely unshielded for the first time since she'd come here.

Panic seized her. There were no voices, no marauding emotions from outside, but it felt so . . . exposed. She tried to keep her ground, but she was a rodent in the middle of an open field with hawks circling overhead; the vastness of the sky and the need to hide were overwhelming.

"Put it back," she moaned, clapping her hands over her ears. "I can't. I can't."

"Breathe, Miranda. In and out. Come back to your breath. There's nothing here that will harm you. I won't allow it. You know that."

"No, no . . . please . . . it's too much. Put it back!"

A note of hysteria entered her voice. For two weeks she'd had the comfort of his power standing between her and the madness, but now it was just her will, and she knew it wasn't strong enough. She'd never been strong enough. Just like her mother . . .

"You can do it. Listen to me, Miranda. You can."

"I can't . . . I can't . . ."

The protected room wasn't enough. Any second now the walls would fall and the voices would pour into her, and that would be the end of it—she'd go mad, she'd die, and never have that precious silence again—

Heart racing, gasping for breath as if she were drowning, she flailed in her chair, panic so thick and black around her that she could no longer hear anything, or see, and there was nothing left but screaming.

She came back to herself slowly, barely even aware that she was once again shielded and no longer cold.

For a moment she kept her eyes shut, listening. There was a drum beating against her ear, and everything else was so quiet . . . she clung to the tentative peace jealously for as long as it lasted before awareness crept back in.

She blinked and tried to make sense of her surroundings. She was still in the training room, but everything seemed very tall all of a sudden, and the chair was hard beneath her butt.

Floor. Not chair.

Miranda moved her hand over smooth fabric, squeezing slightly, feeling muscle beneath. There was an arm around her. She was leaning into someone's shoulder.

She drew back and looked into his stormy blue eyes. "I'm sorry," she said hoarsely.

One of his hands was in her hair, toying with a few strands. "You have to do this," he said to her softly. "You can't stay here forever."

"Are you sure?" she kidded wearily.

Something passed through his eyes, and he sighed. "I'm sure." The hand moved down to her arm, then lifted to brush a stray lock of hair from her eyes. "No one can save you except you, Miranda."

"You saved me once."

He smiled briefly. "No, I didn't. I only brought you in out of the rain."

"But what if . . . what if I learn how to do this, and I get better, and I go back to Austin, and . . ."

"There's no way to know the future except to step into

it. But I promise you, I won't let you go until I'm sure
you'll be safe."

She laid her head back on his shoulder and closed her
eyes. "Don't let go yet."


Miranda sat on her bed with her guitar, her fingers
absently plucking a few notes, her heart, as her mother
would have said long ago, as low as the rent on a burning
building.

She stared off into space without thinking for the better part of an hour before a knock at the door made her
look up.

"Come in," she said listlessly.

Almond-shaped eyes and shining black hair announced
Faith's arrival, as did the light glinting on her weapons.

The Second looked her up and down and said, "He
wasn't kidding. You do look like hell."

Miranda shrugged. "Just losing my will to live, thanks."

"I take it the lesson ended badly."

She rested her chin on her guitar. "You might say
that."

"Try again tomorrow," Faith said. "This kind of thing
takes practice—nobody gets it right overnight."

"I think I'm hopeless."

"You are if you say you are. If I were you, I'd say
something else."

Miranda wanted to throw her guitar on the floor in a
fit of pique, but the instrument didn't deserve that kind of
treatment. There was nothing in the room she was willing
to break, either—the servants would just end up cleaning
up after her, and she didn't like that. "Everybody around
here is just full of clever advice," Miranda muttered irri-
tably. "It's like a house full of Goth Yodas."

"I'm not here to give you advice. I was thinking
more along the lines of a distraction." A hint of mischief
appeared in Faith's eyes. "Want to see something fun?"

"Only if it involves getting blind drunk."

"Come on," Faith urged, taking the guitar from her and putting it in its case, then pulling her to her feet. "Grab your sweater and get moving or I'll be late."

Miranda knew a lost argument when she came up against one. She didn't waste her remaining energy protesting.

For such a small woman, Faith covered a lot of ground very quickly. Miranda had to practically run to keep up with her as they left the Prime's wing of the Haven, then left the building itself. Miranda was familiar with most of the garden paths by now, but Faith took her along a different one, leading toward one of the larger outbuildings.

"Now, you have to stay where I put you, and keep out of sight. Got that?"

"But where are we going?"

Faith opened a locked side door with her com and ushered Miranda inside.

"Over here."

At first it was too dark to see, but she could definitely hear; there were the sounds of a crowd, maybe dozens of people, above and before her, milling around and talking among themselves. Slivers of light penetrated the gloom, and Miranda puzzled out that she was under some sort of bleachers. She chose not to think of the possibility of spiders.

Faith tugged her arm and maneuvered her into a corner where a larger pool of light was falling. "Stand here, and you can look without being spotted. Can you see?"

Miranda looked out through the gap in the slots at the huge room bordered on all sides by bleachers like the ones she was hiding under. It strongly resembled a gym, down to the geometric figures painted on its floor—there was a central circle and several marked-off circles beyond it.

"Vampires play basketball?"

"No, no. Those are sparring rings. This is where the Elite holds group combat training. If you look over to your right, you'll see the latest batch of cadets."

She did. Seven people stood more or less in a line,

some looking very nervous. They were all dressed identically in a simpler version of Faith's uniform, dyed gray instead of black. None of them wore a com. There were four women and three men of a range of physical ages and ethnicities, but the one thing they all had in common was that they were in fantastic shape.

"Stay here until I come back for you," Faith instructed.

Then she was gone before Miranda could ask what the hell was going on.

At the far end of the room, a pair of double doors swung open, and Faith marched in, flanked by several more Elite. The room fell silent.

Miranda scanned the crowd. Were all of them here? How many Elite were there, anyway? If there were that many working for the Prime, how many damned vampires lived in Austin, and how in the world did they all stay fed?

"Welcome," Faith addressed the assembly. Her voice carried easily throughout the broad expanse of the room. "Honored Elite, you have been called here tonight to witness the final selection of three new brothers in arms. Each of you has stood here awaiting this moment, and each of you triumphed. Tonight we cheer the triumph of the new guard."

The crowd applauded.

The Second turned her attention to the seven recruits. "Twenty of you began this trial a month ago. Now you are seven. In an hour you will be three, and you will join the best of the best in the Shadow World. You will be inducted as full Elite warriors, pledging your lives and your loyalty to the Prime of this territory.

"To be a part of the Court is to be exalted among vampire kind. Allies of the Signet have always been the strongest, fiercest, and most cunning. To be Elite is to stand out even from the exalted—we are the Prime's hundred swords. Those of you who are victorious tonight will take your places in an Elite that is the envy of the world."

Miranda watched Faith, fascinated by how utterly she

held the others in her sway. Not one dared to look away from her, and they didn't look like they wanted to; if they were the best, Faith was better than the best, and seeing her among them, Miranda finally saw it. The weapons didn't make the Second—the Second made the weapons.

She envied Faith. She envied them all their shared purpose and strength.

When her speech concluded, the Elite applauded again, this time with cheering, and Miranda could feel the sincerity of their shouts. These weren't a mindless army of soldiers just obeying orders. They believed in something. They were willing to die to defend their leader and their home.

The crowd went quiet again as the trial began. First, the recruits were pitted against each other; there was some sort of rating system at work, like at the Olympics, but Miranda had no idea what went into it. As the recruits fought, Faith and several other Elite observed them, making notes.

Right away Miranda could see two standout warriors among them. The first was a middle-aged-looking black man, the second a rail-thin strawberry blonde who looked like she was about sixteen. They had radically different fighting styles, but both were a blur of motion with and without blades.

After about fifteen minutes Faith called a halt to the sparring, which Miranda realized had mostly been a warm-up; now Faith ordered one of the recruits into the main ring, and one of the Elite went up against him.

Miranda had never been athletic. She'd taken ballroom dancing in college on a lark with her boyfriend, but that was about it. She watched the fighting mesmerized, the graceful figures like a ballet—well, a ballet with swords. The clang of metal on metal was sharp and rhythmic, the vampires moving faster than in any movie martial arts she'd ever seen.

Her heart was in her throat, constricted with strange regret. Things would have been so different now if she had known how to do any of this that night in the alley. She imagined herself as the strawberry blonde in the ring, spinning around to kick a man in the stomach, knocking the blade out of his hand. She imagined what it would be like to be so strong that no man would ever try to hurt her again.

The crowd *ooh*ed and *ahh*ed as if they were watching a football game. Adrenaline was thick in the air.

The young-looking recruit sent her opponent to the ground bleeding. A cheer went up.

Faith nodded to her, and the girl stopped, bowed, and returned to the line where the others stood.

It went on like that until each of the recruits had fought one of the Elite. Then Faith spent a moment conferring with the black-clad warriors, some of whom looked a bit worse for wear, some of whom had won their matches—and announced two cuts from the list. Miranda didn't see where the two eliminated recruits went; they were there one minute and gone the next. Hopefully they were just escorted off the premises and not anything more sinister.

Miranda was pleased to see that both of her picks were still in the running. She wondered if any of the Elite had bets going; this was way too much like *Ass-Kicking American Idol* for them not to.

The best was yet to come. Next, the five remaining recruits had to face Faith.

All at once.

Each of them took up a position around the edge of the central sparring ring, with Faith in the center.

Now the crowd couldn't keep still. The minute the fight began, they were shouting, some chanting Faith's name, others whooping and hollering. A great many were on their feet.

At first the recruits didn't seem to know what to do. Nobody wanted to go first, Miranda supposed, and it hadn't occurred to them to take her on together. They were too worried about their own skins and their futures to consider cooperation.

The man Miranda had been betting on finally lost his patience and dove in.

That was a mistake.

Faith stepped sideways, letting the man's momentum carry him past her, and dropped to the ground, her leg flashing out. The man stumbled over it, his inhuman grace suddenly becoming a very human clumsiness, but he corrected himself and turned in time to avoid stepping over the line. He got himself back together and attacked again, this time with considerably more acumen.

Meanwhile Miranda saw one of the others looking pale and scared witless; his nerves were going to make him careless, too. He drew his knife and lunged at Faith while her back was to him.

Miranda almost gave herself away yelling a warning to the Second, but it wasn't needed. Faith knew exactly what the kid was doing, and she parried a swing from the older man and spun around, steel flashing toward the kid on the follow-through.

Blood. The recruit lurched to the left, dropping his knife as his hands flew to his side. Crimson soaked his gray uniform. He tried to pick his blade back up, but it slipped out of his bloody hands, and before he could try again Faith whirled and kicked him hard in the shoulder, sending him sprawling, half in and half out of the ring.

The crowd booed the recruit. Miranda wanted to boo, too. He'd done a cowardly thing trying to stab the Second in the back. Cowardly and incredibly stupid.

An Elite grabbed the recruit by the arm and dragged him bodily out of the ring, and that was the last Miranda saw of him.

Faith didn't miss a beat. The other man came at her as she turned to face him, but his fist met only empty air. Still, he hadn't lost any strength or speed, and he'd recovered nicely from his first fumble. After another minute

Faith spoke to him, and he froze where he stood, then bowed and stepped back to the edge of the ring.

Faith hadn't even broken a sweat.

They were down to four now, which meant only one was left to eliminate. Faith took on the blonde girl next, and as Miranda expected, she did well; Faith disarmed her twice, but never knocked her off her feet, and Miranda thought she saw approval in Faith's face.

The other two were a man and a woman, the former Hispanic and the latter black, and it was clear after Faith engaged the man that he wasn't nearly as skilled as the others. He was good, no doubt about it, but there was some elemental grace lacking in his movements that the rest had in spades. She didn't send him away when she was done with him, but Miranda knew that unless the last woman was dreadful, he'd be gone in a minute.

Luckily the last woman, who was a tall and insanely gorgeous dark-skinned goddess that every man in the room was staring at, didn't disappoint. To the shock of everyone assembled, the recruit actually managed to disarm Faith.

"Hand to hand," Faith retorted. The recruit nodded and dropped her own weapon.

Now the true talent showed itself; Faith was wicked with blades, but her straight-up martial arts skills were unbelievable. She seemed to have four arms, all of them spinning at once, never standing still long enough for the woman to land a punch. It was almost as if Faith could see the woman's moves before they were made, and simply not be there. Was it some sort of psychic gift of vampirism, seeing just enough of the future to know how to fight?

Finally, Faith raised her arm, and the din in the room faded again. She was neither panting nor slouching, unlike the recruits, who all looked like they were about to fall over.

"Honored Elite," Faith announced, "We have chosen

our three new brothers. Will each of you step forward, please."

She read each name, and a round of enthusiastic applause followed the recruit to the center of the sparring circle. The strawberry blonde, the older black man, and the Hispanic man all took their places behind Faith, who praised their skill and perseverance, then introduced them each by name to the rest of the Elite. The applause was thunderous.

Miranda frowned. Why had they picked that last guy? The woman was a superior warrior—even Miranda recognized that. The woman looked shocked, but she didn't embarrass herself; one of the Elite took her arm and led her back away from the others. Unlike the first few culls, she wasn't taken out of the room. Maybe there was some kind of consolation prize or understudy role for her.

Then the double doors sailed open again, and silence washed over every mind in the room, all conversations cut off midword, as the crowd, as one, turned to face the door.

Miranda's heart leapt.

David Solomon entered the gym, followed by his own personal guards at a respectful distance. He wore his long coat, the Signet out where God and everyone could see, the light that shone from it brighter than usual. Every inch of him radiated the regal bearing of one born to the crown.

He strode into the room, across the floor, to the sparring ring where Faith stood with the three new Elite-to-be. As he passed each section of the bleachers, everyone on it stood, until every vampire in the room was on his or her feet in the presence of the Prime.

When he stopped, his gaze swept over the crowd, and as one, they bowed to him. He gave them a nod in return, and they were free to sit back down.

Then he faced the three, his cold eyes fixed on each of them in turn. They were clearly terrified of him, but to their credit they didn't try to avoid the steel of his gaze.

He moved slowly toward them, walking from the strawberry blonde, past the older man, to the last man chosen.

Miranda's eyes didn't even have time to register the movement. Without a word, David turned, reached under his coat, and with a flash of steel, spun around and sliced off the man's head with a curved sword.

A gasp went up, and Miranda jumped back with a cry and almost lost her footing. Even over the noise she heard the sound of the head hitting the floor, followed by the body.

She dove back for the gap so she could see again, just in time for Faith to seize the man's sleeve and jerk it back, revealing a tattoo that caused another roomwide gasp.

David never spoke. He simply let the others see, allowing the tattoo to speak for itself, and stood by while two Elite dragged the corpse away by its feet, leaving a smear of blood behind. Miranda didn't see what happened to the head.

The Prime gestured, and the other recruit was nudged into the spot where the man had stood. Her face was pale, but she swallowed hard and took her place, standing up straight. When David's attention returned to her, she held his gaze and bowed. He smiled at her, approving, and inclined his head toward Faith.

The Second was completely unfazed by the execution. "Kneel," she commanded, and the three obeyed.

"Swear now, before these witnesses and before your Prime. Repeat, and take these words to heart: I do hereby pledge my blood and my life to the Signet."

They repeated, and she went on. "I swear everlasting fealty to the Prime of this territory and to all his allies. I will uphold his law and lay down my life for his if the moment comes. This oath binds me until my last breath, either in battle on the side of the Signet, or by swift execution in the event of my disloyalty."

All three gave the oath with full conviction.

Faith went to the Prime, who handed her a box from

his coat containing three flat strips of metal. One by one Faith fastened a com around each new Elite's wrist. The three of them were practically beaming by then.

Finally, David addressed them. "Welcome," he said, his voice ringing off the rafters with absolute authority. "You may now take your place among your brothers and sisters in arms as full Elite."

The applause was deafening. The three new Elite hugged each other and shook Faith's hand, then bounded up into the bleachers to an empty spot, where they looked around in a daze, grinning from ear to ear.

David allowed the cheering to continue for a moment before stepping to the center of the room. The Elite came back to rapt attention once more.

"My warriors," he said, "these times are dark and dangerous, and those of you new to my service have come to us in a moment of challenge. We face an enemy determined to destroy the hard-won peace of our world and return to an older, barbaric way of living for our kind. We have already lost friends to this threat, and I cannot promise we will not lose more; but I give you my word, as I stand here before you, that I will not rest until every last one of these cowards is put down. As you have sworn to fight for me, I will fight for you."

With that, he bowed to them. Another roar of applause went up, this one thunderous, and the entire Elite stood, cheering for their leader, who drank in their allegiance from the epicenter, smiling slightly, before saying, "Dismissed."

A herd of footsteps descended the bleachers over Miranda's head, the sound deafening when coupled with the chatter among the departing Elite. She couldn't see the Prime anymore thanks to everyone filing out of the room, but she caught glimpses of Faith speaking with the three new recruits, assigning them somewhere with another Elite as their superior.

Everyone was carefully walking around the pool of blood where the executed man's body had fallen.

There was a beeping noise, and Miranda shrank back into the shadows as the door behind the bleachers opened just wide enough to admit a single figure.

"I thought I felt you over here," David said, a smile in his voice. She could barely see him in the darkness.

"Are you upset that I'm here?"

"No. I suspected Faith would bring you. What did you think?"

Miranda looked back through the gap again as the last thirty or so made their way toward the exits. Faith and the new recruits had gone, and a pair of uniformed servants was mopping up the blood. They didn't look disgusted or even unhappy at their task. It was entirely possible it was a routine thing for them.

"That was amazing," she said. "I mean, you see them walking around the halls with swords and you know they're good, but . . . Faith especially. She's fantastic. And the others . . . they really love you. It's not just a job for them." She looked back over her shoulder at him. "What about that man, the one you killed?"

"Last night we took a suspect into custody who's working for the insurgents. She told me, after gentle persuasion, that they had another agent trying to work his way into the Elite to take Helen's place as their primary informant. I looked back over the training logs and decided on the most likely candidate. The suspect in custody confirmed my suspicions. I wanted to make it crystal clear how traitors will be dealt with."

"Is the suspect dead?"

"No. We're still holding her. I promised her an easy death if her information turned out to be accurate."

She crossed her arms and leaned against the side wall of the bleachers. "Does it ever bother you, killing people?"

He sounded the tiniest bit hurt that she had asked. "Of course it does, Miranda. I'm not made of stone."

She didn't say she doubted that, but she thought it extra loud.

He came to stand beside her, looking out the gap himself at the now-empty training room. "When Auren was Prime, humans all over the South died every night to satisfy the bloodlust of his Court. It was kept out of the media because they feared Auren's wrath, but eventually our world would have been exposed and the entire territory would have been swarmed with vampire hunters. These people want the no-kill laws lifted so they can take lives again—hundreds of innocent lives. If I have to break the bones of every last insurgent to prevent that, I will, and though I may hate doing it, I won't waste one second on regret."

His eyes were hard, glittering in the dim light like shards of obsidian, and he added harshly, "I don't expect you to understand what I face every night. I am responsible for every vampire under my influence and every human they feed on. That means making difficult choices. Judge all you like—you would do the same in my place."

"What do you want me to say?" she demanded. "You're right, I don't understand. I'm never going to understand. I'm just a human, remember?"

He glared at her wordlessly for a moment before saying quietly, "You'll never be just anything, Miranda Grey."

Behind him the door opened again and Faith said with studied nonchalance, "Everything all right in here, Sire? I was going to take Miranda back to the suite before I went to the patrol leaders' conference call."

Eyes still fixed on Miranda, David said to Faith, "That's fine. I'll meet you in the conference room."

With that, he turned away from Miranda and walked past the Second out into the night.

Faith watched him go, then gave Miranda an impressed look. "Nice work," she said. "Not many people can get under his skin like that."

Miranda tried, and failed, to come up with a clever rejoinder. All she could summon was a sigh. "Let's go. I'm hungry."

"You two are so cute," Faith remarked as they walked.

"That's not exactly the word I'd use."

Faith walked with her hands clasped behind her back, ostensibly looking up at the cloudy night sky. More rain was on the way. "You know," she said, "When I met the Prime, he was a lieutenant in Arrabicci's Elite, and a very different person. He was arrogant, even cruel at times. War was a game to him, and consequences were for humans."

Miranda frowned. "What changed?"

"I don't really know. He's never been one to share the details of his past—for the most part vampires don't talk about that kind of thing. We all have a tacit understanding that everyone has a painful history." She held open the Haven door for Miranda. "All I know for sure is that the Signet changed him. I don't think any of them realize what a burden that thing is until they have it around their necks. They take the power, the responsibility, and the fame, and there's no way out but death."

Faith gave her a sidelong look and concluded, "If you ask me, he needs a Queen."

Miranda groaned. "Not you, too! I thought you said all of that was just rumor."

"It is. But it's still a nice idea. It's almost a fairy tale, or some sort of archetypal myth. You're Persephone, wrenched away from spring and taken to live in the underworld, where you eat the pomegranate seeds and become the Queen."

Miranda rounded on her. "You've got to be joking. Has everyone around here conveniently forgotten what happened to me a couple of weeks ago? Do you really think now's a good time for matchmaking? And what, I'm supposed to give up being human for a *man*? When I don't think I'll ever want one to touch me again? There's so much that's insane about that I don't even know where to start, forgetting about the fact that nobody in their right mind would ever, ever want to live like you. God, Faith, please just *let it be*."

Faith looked neither taken aback by her outburst or the least bit sheepish. She shrugged. "I didn't say you should go jump his bones right this second, or in a month or a year. I'm just saying . . ." She nodded to the suite door guards and, again, held the door as for Miranda as she said, "Don't deny yourself the possibility of happiness one day because you're broken right now. At least consider the pomegranate seeds. Who knows? Besides . . . I hear Hades is spectacular in bed."

Faith was laughing as Miranda slammed the door on her.

# Eight

The insurgent had apparently never seen a Prime before.

He struggled in the grasp of the two Elite who held him on his knees on the wet concrete, his eyes huge and white, whimpering under the gaze of the black-clad man who stood watching him impassively and waiting for him to shut up.

David was running out of patience. The spy in the recruits had been dealt with and the informant executed, but so far none of the captives had provided any useful information leading to the rest of the syndicate. The attacks had died down, turning back on humans again, but their viciousness was increasing. The last victim had been flayed, her skin stretched like a cow's at the tanner and branded with the Seal of Auren. David could only hope that she had been dead when her flesh was peeled from her bones.

The next step was to take the interrogation to the streets of Austin, and so he had come to the Shadow District where the vampire-only bars and businesses were, to go through all of this again, this time out in public where the others could watch from their hidden corners and carry the news to their friends.

"Are you finished?" he asked.

The insurgent was gaping at him and his mouth was

working soundlessly, making him look rather like a fish on dry land.

"Let's make this quick," David went on. "I have better things to do than stand out here in this godforsaken weather and torture you. Now, tell me who you're working for and where I can find them."

No answer. He hadn't really expected one. He was starting to think that the reason none of the captives had told him anything was that they honestly didn't know. He was sure Helen had been higher on the totem pole, but the rest . . . all their tattoos had been fairly new. They couldn't have ranked too highly in the organization yet. They were expendable, and so they knew little of the real plan or the leadership. Chances were this fool had no idea whose service he was in.

He decided to take a different approach and motioned for the guards to loosen their hold on the vampire. The insurgent all but tumbled to the ground with a grunt, catching himself with his hands.

David crouched in front of him, leaning in to catch his eye. "Let's just talk, then. What's your name, lad?"

Confused by the sudden change of tone, the kid—and kid he was, he couldn't have been over ten years immortal—muttered, "Rollins."

"How long have you been a vampire, Rollins?"

The kid didn't meet his eyes, but said, "Three years."

"So I take it you've never seen me before."

"No, *Sire*." There was both fear and contempt in the last word.

"What did your new friends tell you about me?" David asked.

Rollins looked from left to right at the guards who were still blocking his escape and judged the odds were not in his favor. "They said you were the enemy. That you want to tell us all when to feed and what we can feed on. That pretty soon we'll all be living in camps out at the Haven standing in line for blood."

"I see. Do you know who's behind all of this, Rollins? Where those stories came from?"

"We're fighting for our freedom. The Shadow World is rising up against tyranny. You think I'm going to tell you anything? This is worth more than my life."

David nodded. "Righteousness is satisfying, isn't it? Sometimes having a cause to believe in is what makes this all worthwhile. But then you have to wonder: When it comes right down to it, are you really willing to lay down your life for a creed, especially one given to people you've never seen?"

Rollins looked up at him, baffled.

"Let me give you what you want, then, Rollins. Release him."

The guards clearly thought their Prime had lost his mind but did as they were told, stepping back from the kid to let him stand.

David straightened. "Here's your chance," the Prime told Rollins, holding out his hands. "Be a hero. Kill me, if you can. Everyone else, stand back."

The boy's eyes narrowed, understandably. "This is a trick."

"No trick." David pulled back his coat and drew his sword, handing it hilt first to the nearest Elite. She held it like it was Excalibur. "Hand-to-hand combat to the death. Show me how strongly you believe. Kill me and take the Signet back to your masters. I'm sure the rewards will be great."

Rollins stood staring at him, thunderstruck, trying to gather his wits and his courage; he had to know how ridiculous the idea was, but at the same time, if he really did buy into what these "freedom fighters" were selling, he couldn't pass up the chance. There had to be some kind of standing order to slay the Prime on sight.

The minute stretched out interminably as Rollins panted, his eyes wide, his hands fisting at his sides. David simply waited, letting his power-aura expand to show the boy exactly what he was facing: the full complement of darkness and death that bent only to the Prime's will. The Elite watched on full alert. They were ready to pounce on the boy the second he twitched if it looked like he might actually harm their leader, although it would hardly be necessary. Even if he did try to attack, it would take a much greater vampire than Rollins to defeat a Prime in anything like a fair fight.

Finally, Rollins lowered his eyes. Fear choked him and he shook his head dumbly.

David smiled, this time without any trace of compassion. Rollins went even paler at the nastiness of the expression. "Kneel to your Prime, boy," he snapped.

Instantly Rollins dropped to his knees.

"Now tell me what you know."

Rollins took a shaking breath and stammered, "They . . . they don't tell us much. Just what the next mission is. There's a woman in charge of my group. I don't know her name but I heard one of the others call her Black . . . Black something. We meet in a warehouse on East Nineteenth. It used to be some kind of downtown hippie commune or something. There's paint everywhere and it stinks like pot. Please don't kill me . . . please. I told you what I know. Please."

"Thank you, Rollins. That will do." David turned to the Elite, who gave him back his sword; the guard gave him a questioning look, and he nodded silently back, then turned and walked away, sliding the curved blade back into its sheath inside his coat.

Behind him, he heard a faint scuffle and a whimper, then the swing of steel and the thump of something heavy hitting the street.

"Star-three," he said into his com.

*"Sire?"*

"Faith, I need a search run on any female Blackthorn of rank within the syndicate, whether they're presumed dead or not. Cross-reference with the list of Auren's known supporters and see if there are any commonalities.

Also have a unit run recon on the old Austin Art Collective warehouse on Nineteenth. The insurgents may be using it as a meeting point for their lower-level enforcers. Have a scan run for heat signatures while you're at it to see if anyone's living there."

*"As you will it, Sire. I'll send the scan results in fifteen minutes."*

"Thank you. Star-one, out."

He walked up the street to one of the less seedy bars in the Shadow District, and as he passed he heard movement in the alleyways, footsteps retreating as he neared.

Yes, let them run. Let them creep back under their rocks. He was going to have a drink.

The bartender at Anodyne knew him, of course, but unlike a great many others he didn't so much as bat an eyelash at the Prime's arrival. There were a few places where David never deigned to set foot, but this one was frequented not only by him, but by most of the off-duty Elite.

The businesspeople who understood the bigger picture knew that running a vampire bar in a Signet-controlled city was a wise idea; if they were on the Prime's good side they never had to worry about violence or intimidation from gangs battling for the district. Their patrons could drink in peace. That was one reason why Haven cities tended to have much greater concentrations of vampires, and the Signets focused most of their resources on those; he had to worry about vampire crime a lot more in Austin than, say, Little Rock. The only other city in his territory he was often compelled to visit more than once a year in person was New Orleans. Vampires plus voodoo tended to be a treacherous combination.

Inside, the bar catered to three of their kind's favorite things: darkness, privacy, and beverages. Most of the room was cordoned off into booths, only a few of which were populated on a night like tonight.

The bar itself was empty except for a single man who saw the Prime approach and immediately decided to take his drink to a booth.

David took one of the stools while the bartender came over. "Evening, Sire," he said, his accent a familiar comforting combination of Hispanic and Texan. "What can I get you?"

"Good evening, Miguel. I'll have a Black Mary."

"Top shelf?"

"Stoli, please."

Miguel measured vodka into a shaker, then retrieved an opaque bottle from the fridge marked O NEGATIVE and filled the glass the rest of the way. He glanced over at David and asked, "You want Tabasco or Cholula?"

"Cholula."

He slid the drink over to David, who took an experimental sip and said, "Perfect."

He smiled to himself, thinking how Miranda would react if she saw—or better yet, smelled—what was in his glass. He could picture the face she would make.

His smile faded. That very reaction was the proof of how impossible it all was. He could think about her all he wanted . . . and he had been unable to stop for the past few days . . . but in the end, she was human. Even if by some miracle she was ever interested in sex again, and even if that interest were to turn to him, the fact was, it was doomed before beginning. She would grow old and die. He wouldn't. He was a predator. She wasn't.

He could tell himself that all he wanted, but it apparently made no difference to his body. He had caught himself staring at her, his eyes following the sweet line of her neck and shoulder, remembering the sight of her fingers on the guitar and wondering what it would feel like to have those fingers ghost over his skin. Every time she spoke, the curve of her soft lower lip occupied his thoughts for hours.

He had to fight with himself every night not to seek out her company, and he tried to be content with the time before and after their training sessions when they sometimes just talked for a while. He hadn't known anyone since Lizzie who could make him laugh so easily.

Miranda was far smarter than she gave herself credit for; there were times when she offered an insight into something weighing on his mind that made everything crystal clear. She made him laugh, she made him think, and she made him want desperately to tear the clothes from her body and taste the sweet flesh of her thighs . . . and her mouth . . . and the copper-cinnamon of her blood.

It was slowly driving him mad.

"Rough night, Sire?"

Thankful for the distraction, he looked up at Miguel. "You could say that."

"I hear there's a war coming. Bad for business."

"That depends on who wins," David replied wryly. "I don't suppose you've heard anything about these bastards."

Miguel shrugged. "Their kind don't come in here. They don't mess with me, I don't mess with them. They know your people are my best customers."

"I figured as much."

He had to get back soon. Miranda was expecting him for another session. After almost another week she still wasn't progressing nearly well enough for his peace of mind, although she had finally stopped having a panic attack every time she tried to shield. He wondered if perhaps, subconsciously, he was trying to sabotage her efforts by setting the bar too high, trying to keep her with him longer; but surely his subconscious wasn't that stupid? The longer she stayed at the Haven, the more danger she was in. Before long the enemy would know all about her, and she would prove another vulnerability. Networks could be upgraded, but Miranda's life was a risk he wasn't willing to take.

"Another?"

"No, thank you, Miguel."

The bartender raised an eyebrow and said casually, taking his empty glass, "Why do I get the feeling like you've got something on your mind more important than war?"

"What's more important than war?"

Miguel laughed. "Everything you're fighting for, Sire. But most of all: women."

"Women."

"Damn right. You got woman trouble?"

"Women are always trouble."

"I'll give you that. But if you've got a woman, what are you doing here?"

"I don't have a woman," David told the bartender, tossing a folded twenty on the bar and standing up, "but I'm afraid she has me."

"Shit! Lost it."

Miranda fell back against the cushions, gasping for breath, sweat pouring into her eyes. She reached for the bottle of water beside her chair and resisted the urge to pour it over her head instead of drinking it.

"That was better," David said. "Now tell me why it didn't work."

"The back. I put too much into the front and it got unbalanced. Again. Fuck."

She cursed a lot more when they were in the training room. She didn't especially care if she offended David's delicate sensibilities. He had yet to complain.

Despite her failure that first night—and her continued failure—David hadn't let up on her. In fact he seemed more determined than ever that she master her powers, and though his methods weren't nearly as relentless as they had been at first, he still drove her every night, sometimes for an hour and sometimes two, until she was so exhausted she wanted to cry, and often did.

But she was getting better. She could get her energy into the shield, though keeping it up was proving the bigger challenge. Shielding demanded 360-degree awareness, and she had no idea how she was supposed to manage that and do anything else at the same time. David had promised her that once she got the trick of it, it would become second nature. She tried hard to believe him.

After another forty minutes of brain-frying effort, he called a halt, and she sagged in her chair with her water bottle in her lap and her hair falling out of its ponytail.

"Drink," he reminded her. "Remember the headache you got last time."

She shuddered inwardly. A psychic overexertion migraine plus dehydration had added up to a truly miserable morning that two Vicodin had barely eased. Thankfully the rest of her body was mostly healed except for the cut on her hand, which still bothered her after she'd been playing guitar for too long. She hoped it would heal by the time she left here; if she decided to go back to performing, she'd have to be able to handle more than a couple of songs.

That was still a pretty big *if* at this point, but she had decided not to rule anything out just yet. The future was too big and terrifying to contemplate, so she focused on here and now, and the twin tasks of learning to shield and trying not to smack her teacher.

She finished off her water and capped it, staring at her hands. They didn't seem quite as useless as they had Before.

To her surprise, David asked her, "What are you thinking about?"

She raised her eyes. "Do you think I'll ever have a real life?"

"Define *real*."

"You know . . . a job, a family, a house, stuff like that."

He laced his fingers together. "Is that what you want?"

"I don't know. I used to think the idea of normal was awful, but maybe that was just because I never thought I could have it. If I can really do this, and I go back to the world and can live like other people . . . I don't know."

"Well . . . I don't want to disappoint or frighten you, but it's been my experience that powerful people are rarely left alone." There was something odd in his eyes as he said, "You're a bright flame, Miranda. Flames attract others to their warmth and light. You can hide it all you want, but even a blind man could see you."

"I always wished I could just disappear." She picked at a loose thread in the arm of her chair for a minute before asking, "Have you ever wished you could be human again? Live a normal life?"

"No," he replied. "I accepted what I am a long time ago. This life is where I belong. But there have been times when I've wished for . . . things that could never be. It does nothing but hurt to dream of the impossible."

"How do you know what's impossible? Can't things always change?"

"Some can. Some can't. For all that humans are limited in life span, you have more choices than we do . . . and you don't have to live with those choices, or your mistakes, nearly as long. You can take a risk and fall on your face, but if I hurt someone, or lose someone, I have to live with it forever."

She could hear that loss in his voice, and it made her chest hurt; on those rare occasions when he showed genuine emotion, it always affected her. It was a consequence of being so close to his energy, she was sure. "Are you thinking about Lizzie?"

He met her eyes. "No."

She broke contact first, feeling a bit disarmed and not sure why. "I think you're probably right. I don't really see myself in the suburbs with a husband and two point three kids. I think I'm probably too damaged for that."

"I don't think *damaged* is the word," David said.

"Then what is?"

He was smiling at her; she could tell even without looking. *"Extraordinary."*

Damn it, her face grew hot, and she smiled at him, her heart squeezing a little at the affection in that single word. "Thanks."

They held each other's gazes until David abruptly

looked away, saying, "We should head back. I'm expecting an update from Faith and this room screws with the com reception."

As usual they walked back down the East Wing hall together, but Miranda paused after a few minutes and said, "Did you say there was a piano around here?"

He gestured at one of the doors and unlocked it for her.

Miranda took one look inside the music room and nearly fainted. All her exhaustion vanished into thin air.

It was even more wonderful than the library had been. A full-sized grand piano occupied its center, and chairs and benches were arranged around for small performances, but there were also shelves and shelves of sheet music, both bound and loose in folders. There were reams of staff paper ready to write compositions on. Everything was meticulously organized and kept scrupulously clean, even though she knew no one had used this room in years and only the servants had been inside.

The acoustics of the room were so perfect she couldn't wait to bring her guitar in here. Her fingers positively itched for that piano.

"I could spend every night here," she breathed, her neck craning up to see the carved ceiling. It reminded her of the salons where great composers previewed their newest works of genius for select arts patrons.

"Let me see your com," David said.

She held up her wrist, and he took it in one hand, the sudden contact of his fingers on her skin doing something weird to her stomach. With his free hand, he took something out of his coat.

"How many pockets do you have in that thing?" she asked.

"Why do you think I wear it?" He attached the small device to her com, then ran a short cable from it to his iPhone. "Give me twenty seconds."

She was used to him doing random geeky things by now and just stood still while he used the phone to perform some sort of technomancy on her com. His mind continually fascinated her; she never knew, when he was staring off into the fireplace, if he was thinking about patrol reports, an upcoming conference call with the Signet outposts in other cities, how to increase the efficiency of the solar panels that provided the Haven's electricity, the 400th digit of pi, or the new flavor of Häagen Dazs.

"There." He unplugged and stowed both phone and device. "Now you have access to all the doors in this wing instead of just ours and the library. That way you can come here whenever you like."

She practically beamed at him. "Thank you!" Before she could stop herself, she flung her arms around him in a hug.

After a second's hesitation, he returned the embrace, holding on to her as long as she let him, releasing her as soon as she moved. Again . . . she felt nervous when he touched her, though there was no intent toward anything more sinister; it was just a hug. Touch had been such a loaded subject for her for so long, and now it was far worse. She didn't know how to be touched without panicking, but somehow, David got in under her radar.

She decided, then, to do something she hadn't ever expected to do. "Do you have a few minutes?" she asked. "I could play something for you."

David had been about to make some sort of excuse, but at those last words, his protestations died on his lips. "I . . . I would be honored."

She sat down at the piano, exposing the keys and running her fingers over them reverently, pressing a few and finding that David had been as good as his word: The instrument was perfectly in tune.

"God," she murmured. "Is this what I think it is?"

"It's a piano."

"Not just a piano," she said, smiling. "This is a Bösendorfer Imperial Grand, model two-ninety. She has ninety-seven keys, not eighty-eight—here on the left, see the black keys? They're sub-bass notes that extend her range. Look at her . . . she's beautiful. And she's probably worth a quarter of a million dollars at least."

His eyebrows shot up. "I had no idea it . . . she . . . was that valuable."

"Whoever this Queen was, she knew her instruments. One of my favorite artists plays one of these. They have a darker and more complex voice than the other major makers. I read somewhere that these are built out of wood from the same forest as the Stradivari violins. I've always wanted to see one in person, but I didn't want to torture myself."

He was smiling at her enthusiasm, but unlike every boyfriend she'd ever had, he didn't seem to be tuning her out when she got to babbling about music. Mike, for example, had only been to see her play a couple of times, and he'd done the nod-and-smile but never paid much attention.

"Any requests?" she asked.

"Whatever you like." One of the chairs, at the front left of the room, seemed to have been placed specifically for the Prime; it was much more comfortable looking than the others. David took it and leaned back, elegant as always.

Miranda wondered what the seventh Queen had been like, and how often she had been in this very spot with her Prime and other members of the Court listening to her performances. Perhaps she had played for him alone sometimes, saving a romantic piece for her lover. Perhaps she could feel his eyes on her, enraptured by her beauty and talent, as she played.

Classical or Baroque seemed most appropriate for this room, but Miranda didn't care much about tradition; what the piano needed was attention and energy. It was a crime for such a fine instrument to have been left unloved for so long.

Miranda reached up and yanked the elastic from her

ponytail. For some reason she'd never been comfortable playing with her hair up.

She laid her hands on the keys and began to play, feeling something she hadn't in a long time. There was a trancelike element to music for her, even before she started using it to siphon and spin emotion from the audience. Back when playing was something she did because she loved it, not a last bastion of sound between her and insanity, she had let it take her deeper, to a place beyond the world where the movement of her hands and the sound from the instrument fused with some part of her heart that amplified even the shallowest pop into something worthy of a backup choir.

She leaned into the music, and it was almost as though the piano were alive and elated to be played again; it responded to the pressure of her fingers almost before she reached the notes. A moment later, she lifted her voice into the room's still air.

Faith heard the singing as she entered the hallway toward the Prime's suite, and though she was on an urgent errand, she found herself drawn to the threshold of a room that, as far as she knew, hadn't been opened in twenty years or more except by the servants who kept it clean.

Several other Elite were hovering at the door, hanging back so they wouldn't be seen; Samuel and Terrence were there as well as the East Wing guard, Saylor. They all looked up guiltily when they saw the Second, but she was too curious to reprimand any of them for leaving their posts, and besides, their job was to guard the Prime and his guest, and clearly they were all doing just that.

Faith leaned her head around the door frame to see what was going on.

First, she saw Miranda, the source of the unbelievable singing. She looked almost dwarfed by the instrument she played on, which had to be twice as long as she was tall.

Still, it seemed like the aura of the human had expanded to include the piano as if they were one creature merged in common purpose.

Miranda's voice was both sweeter and darker than she would have guessed by hearing her speak, and she was so wrapped up in the music that she played with her eyes shut tight, swaying forward and back as her fingers hit the keys harder or softer. As she finished the song she was playing she went into what Faith assumed was an improvisation on its theme, a complicated line of melody and harmony that seemed to move in slow spirals around the piano. Faith had never heard anything like it.

> *Years go by, will I still be waiting*
> *for somebody else to understand . . .*

Faith looked over to the chairs and saw the Prime, and she couldn't help it: she grinned.

She'd known him a long time and had never, ever seen the expression on his face before. It was beyond captivated, somewhere in the wild land between rapture and dissolution, underlined with a longing that was as painful for Faith to watch as it was satisfying to finally see him lose himself to.

She could have told him he was doomed the minute he brought Miranda to the Haven.

No, now that she thought about it, she knew he was doomed when she saw how he reacted to the idea of cutting off Miranda's hair. He had spent an hour working through it strand by strand with the focused attention he brought to debugging network code, and with the singular devotion of a monk praying the Rosary. He would never have done such a thing for anyone else.

Yet he was still fighting it. Faith wanted to shake him sometimes.

Luckily, one thing vampires had was time to wait.

Faith moved out of the doorway and leaned back against

the wall. She needed to talk to David, but a few minutes wouldn't be the end of the world. Let them have this moment while they could.

Faith knew with the certainty of two hundred years that the worst was yet to come.

# Nine

The following Wednesday night, Faith asked quizzically, "You want me to do what, again?"

David gestured at Miranda, who stood in the center of the training room. The furniture had been pushed to the perimeter, where he sat now in his usual chair. "I want you to poke her."

"That's not really my thing, Sire. If you want, I could ask Lindsay when she gets back from patrol—"

"Psychically poke her, idiot," the Prime said.

Miranda spoke up a little nervously. "I can hold my shield myself pretty well now—"

"—but she has to be able to do it under duress," David said.

"Which means, under attack," Miranda finished. "We need someone I'm not used to working with to push at my boundaries and see if I can push back."

Faith still looked dubious, but she wasn't the type to contradict an order. She went where the Prime had indicated, a space a few feet in front of Miranda.

"All right," David said. "Go ahead."

He shifted his vision into the sideways sight that allowed him to "see" energy; the sight was different for everyone with psychic powers, but to him it registered like waves of heat, sometimes in color, sometimes merely temperature and texture. Faith's energy was cool, watery; Miranda's had the shimmer of autumn fire.

Miranda grounded flawlessly, and he watched with a critical eye as she slowly raised the barrier he had shown her how to create. She had finally caught the trick of keeping it all the way around her and not just in front, and this week they had worked on her keeping it up for longer and longer periods. Soon she would shield herself automatically and not have to constantly remind herself to keep the energy flowing, but she needed experience with the pressure of other minds, and he wasn't about to let her work outside the training room until he was sure she could at least defend herself against Faith.

"Okay," she said. "I'm ready."

David directed Faith to start simply by aiming her telepathy at Miranda and seeing if the human could block it out. Miranda's primary gift was empathy, which dealt in emotions while telepathy dealt in words; the two were otherwise difficult to distinguish from one another, and often having one gift meant having both in some measure. Emotions were by far the harder to filter out, but the shield was meant to do both.

He watched, trying not to speak up, as Faith framed a thought and sent it strongly toward Miranda.

The first time, her shield buckled, the front sagging under the pressure but not quite vanishing; Miranda hauled it back up again, breathing hard, her nails digging into her palms. At David's signal, Faith tried again.

This time, it held, though the effort showed in the sweat running down Miranda's face. After several more attempts her T-shirt was soaked, clinging to her breasts.

David did his best not to stare. Now wasn't really the time to act like a horny teenager.

He asked Faith to pause and took a moment to point out where Miranda was leaking energy. "On your left," he said. "You need to divert from the front to the sides."

"But then how will I deflect the hit?"

"Balance," he replied. "Remember how my shield rippled the night you attacked me?"

"You attacked him?" Faith asked, incredulous.

Miranda shrugged. "It didn't work."

"Exactly," he said. "If the entire shield is equally strong, the back and sides can take pressure off the front. Then the entire sphere supports itself, absorbing the impact and grounding it out instead of shattering. That's why we visualize it as curved instead of angular; curves follow the design of nature, and nature knows how to bend without breaking. Now try again, but this time, Faith, use emotion instead of thought."

"I'm not exactly an empath. You're going to have to explain that one a little more."

"Think of something really sad," Miranda told her. "So sad it makes you want to curl up in a ball and weep. Then throw it at me like you're trying to force me to feel it, too."

Faith was at a loss, but after a moment she thought of something and gave it a try, to no avail.

"Am I supposed to think of something that makes me sad, or something that would make *her* sad?"

"Your emotion, your experience. She has to hold firm where she stops and you begin."

Faith frowned, and then something seemed to occur to her. She looked over at David, and he could tell exactly what she was thinking, and also what a horrible idea she thought it was.

He agreed, but though his heart practically screamed in protest, he gave his Second an almost imperceptible nod.

She swallowed and turned back to Miranda.

"Okay," she said. "Here goes."

David took a deep breath and held on to the arms of the chair. He saw Faith reaching into herself and digging up a memory from the distant past; it wasn't one he had ever heard her speak of in detail, but he still knew it existed, and he knew exactly what it was going to do.

Faith gathered the energy of that memory for a minute, steeling herself, before releasing it, letting the despair of that moment in her life hit Miranda full force.

The echoes reached David seconds later: cries for mercy, laughter, the sound of cloth tearing, the terror of knowing her life was in the hands of those who thought she was less than dirt. A young girl on the streets of Edo, hurrying home alone at night, was nothing more than fresh meat . . . and afterward, her body bruised inside and out, she endured her father's shame knowing he couldn't give her to any man who wanted a virgin bride. That shame had turned to rage, and she had nowhere to go but the streets. There were plenty of brothels specializing in girls dolled up as geishas.

All of this hit David in a heartbeat, and a heartbeat later, Miranda was sobbing.

As she fell to her knees, he was on his feet, but Faith grabbed his arm and held him back.

"No," Miranda wept over and over. "No, no, no . . ."

He nearly shoved Faith aside, but the Second refused to budge. Miranda doubled over beneath the force of shared pain, and Faith's eyes were full of tears, but still, Faith wouldn't let him go to her.

Miranda's hands on the floor curled slowly into fists.

"No," she murmured. "No."

David watched, heart in his throat, as she breathed in . . . and out . . . and *pushed*.

The collapsing shield around her began to expand. Every time she exhaled, she fed more and more energy into it, until Faith's memories and the grief they brought with them started to lose their hold over her. Her whole body shook with the strain, but the shield held.

It *held*.

Miranda lifted her head. There was fire in her eyes.

With one last breath, the onslaught of emotion exploded into nothingness, and it felt like the air in the room had been scoured bare, as if a storm had swept through and lightning had struck.

Faith broke the silence. She whooped and punched

the air, diving to Miranda's side and hugging her with the kind of outward affection he'd never seen her display toward anyone.

"I'm . . . going . . . to fucking . . . kill you," Miranda panted. "Both of you."

"You did it!" Faith exclaimed. "I knew you could!"

"I did it," Miranda said to herself, staring down at her hands on the tile. "I really did it."

"You're still doing it," Faith pointed out. "You're still shielded."

Miranda's laughter was bright and joyful, and it tore him inside even as it brought an upwelling of joy to his own heart. She looked up at him expectantly, her green eyes sparkling, sunlit.

Without speaking, he crossed the floor and knelt in front of her, opening his arms; she threw herself into them, still laughing. He held her as tightly as he dared and kissed the top of her head, inhaling the scent of her humanity, shampoo, and the unmistakable whisper of warmth and spice he knew was hers and hers alone.

"What did I tell you?" he said into her hair. "Extraordinary."

When he looked up at Faith, she was giving him that mischievous little grin he'd come to recognize, and he pulled one hand away from Miranda's waist to give his Second the finger.

"I think we should celebrate," Faith said. "Break out the good Scotch and let's get fucked up."

"I have a better idea," David replied.

It started with margaritas but devolved quickly into tequila shots.

"So how old were you?" Miranda asked, plucking a slice of lime from her mouth and tossing it in the bowl on the coffee table.

"Nineteen," Faith replied fuzzily around her margarita glass. "Already a decrepit old spinster."

"God, can you imagine getting married at nineteen?" Miranda asked. "When I was nineteen, I didn't even know how to do my own laundry." She added, for David's benefit, "You know, laundry? Washing your own clothes? There are people who do that."

He rolled his eyes. "I know how to do laundry. I watched my wife do it dozens of times."

Miranda snorted and poured herself another shot. The room was spinning quite happily around her, and she intended for it to keep doing so as long as possible. "How did you turn into a vampire?" she asked Faith. "I mean, how does it work?"

"Well, there's blood involved."

"No shit, Sherlock."

Faith waved her hands vaguely, and if there had been anything left in her glass, it probably would have sloshed over the edge. "It's not like in the movies. It's a process. The main thing is you have to die with vampire blood in your veins. Right, Sire?"

"Right." David didn't seem to be as far gone as she and Faith were. He was remarkably relaxed for him but managed to stay sober enough to mix drinks without getting the proportions horribly awry.

"You exchange blood," Faith went on. "Sometimes we do that for sexy reasons. It, ah . . . what am I trying to say?"

"Gets you off really hard," David concluded for her. "And it creates a psychic connection. But in a few days, if you just let it go, it fades and everything is back to normal. There are basically two ways to get it to stick. Either your sire drinks you to death the first time, then feeds you her own blood, and you die and wake changed in about a day; or you swap once, then you start drinking human blood to strengthen you, then die some other way to complete the transformation."

"The second way sounds like it sucks."

David made a face at the pun, unintentional though it was. "It takes longer and hurts a lot more. The best way is the first way. You sleep through most of it. That's usually how it's done—about three quarters of the time the human dies permanently in the second method."

"Yeah? How did you do it?"

Faith said, "First." David said, "Second."

"But you survived," Miranda noted unnecessarily.

David nodded. "Only because I wanted vengeance. I forced myself through the change by killing the men who sentenced Lizzie to death. They were my first blood— they tasted like moldy sacramental wine."

She could see him starting to brood; she refused to let him slide into melancholy tonight. "How did you two meet?" she asked, pointing from the Prime to Faith and back again.

Faith chuckled. "I kicked his ass in the Elite trials. I would have ended up Arrabicci's lieutenant if the old bastard hadn't been such a sexist pig."

"He was not a sexist pig," David insisted. "He was a racist pig. You're lucky he didn't fire you during World War II."

"He wouldn't have, with Deven vouching for me. If Dev had told him pigeons fucked monkeys, he'd have looked outside for little hairy birds."

"This Deven guy sounds like an interesting piece of work," Miranda observed, downing her shot of tequila and stuffing another lime wedge in her mouth.

"Definitely," affirmed the Prime. "You'll have to meet him someday. His Consort, too. They're the kind of people you want to have on your side."

Suddenly, Miranda's mind brought itself back to clarity long enough to realize that in all likelihood she never would meet Deven. She could shield now. She wasn't perfect, but in a matter of days she'd be able to leave the Haven and return to Austin.

Back to Austin . . . back to the world. Her time at the Haven was almost over.

"You okay?" Faith asked. "You look like you're choking."

Miranda blinked back the burning in her eyes and said, "No, I'm fine. I think I've had one too many, is all. Everything's fine."

Even as she said the words, and smiled heartily to back them up, something inside her was crying.

A few nights later, under a sky that was heavy and threatening with more rain, Miranda walked outside in the garden, alone.

Terrence had gotten used to the paths she took, so he maintained a greater distance and kept an eye on her from farther away than he had the first week he'd been on guard duty. She was grateful for the consideration. Being followed, even by someone who wanted her safe, made her uneasy, especially now that there was no external shield around her that would warn the Prime if she was in trouble.

He had taken it down the night before, just as an experiment, and she had left the training room completely under her own power for the first time. So far things were going well, though she hadn't dealt with more than two people at a time. She was anxious at the idea of going outside, but she still had her com, and if anything went wrong, Terrence would be at her side in seconds.

September was doing its best to cling to summer as long as it could. The days had been scorching—according to the weather report—and the nights were humid and thick. Everyone was looking forward to the approaching front and its resulting storms to give some relief from the heat. It was the first tumultuous moment of autumn, and Miranda, like anyone who had lived in Texas for years, knew it would be another month before things genuinely cooled off.

She had been at the Haven for a month now, though it felt like years. Her little room had come to bear the stamp of her personality and habits, and she was a familiar sight to the Elite as she took the halls to and from the garden, library, and music room.

She felt a pang of loss at the thought of leaving the Bösendorfer. She had only been playing it for a week, but it felt like a part of her . . . like so many things here. Somehow the Haven had crept into her brick by brick, and the Stephen King–esque strangeness of life here had become normal. Austin, with its thousands of humans and daytime schedule, seemed alien in comparison.

Faith had intimated more than once that she should stay. Even David had hinted, without really meaning to, that he didn't want her to leave, but he had also said flat out that she was at risk here, and that the best thing for her safety was to return to the anonymity of the city.

Miranda wasn't totally sure she believed that. Surely the safest place for her, if vampires wanted to kill her, was with the Prime? But he was adamant, so much so that she had to wonder if there was something he wasn't telling her.

As if summoned by her thoughts, David emerged from the Haven, pausing at the head of the path to look for her. She waved.

He crossed the garden to her, stepping adroitly between plants and around a fountain, and joined her with a smile of greeting.

"I'm going into town tonight, but I wanted to see how you were," he said.

"Not bad. How does it look?"

He scanned her quickly. She felt the light touch of his energy again, and when it was gone, she missed it terribly. She'd gotten so used to the embrace of his power, her security blanket, that living without it was much harder than she had expected.

"Good," he answered. "You need to bolster your right side a little, but overall the flow is pretty consistent."

Miranda took a moment to feel around where he'd indicated and breathe more energy into the shield; she never would have believed it, but he was right when he said it got easier. He'd been so proud of her. She was proud of herself.

"Any news?" she asked.

He made an indefinite move with his head. "Nothing concrete. We've had the warehouse under surveillance for days with no results. They move their meeting spots around, never the same place more than twice."

"What about the mystery Blackthorn woman?"

"She doesn't fit the descriptions of any of the clan's women, and there weren't many. The Blackthorn didn't let their female members ascend very high in the ranks. There are two unaccounted for after the California wars, but without more evidence we can't be sure which one she is, or if she is at all."

"But the attacks have stopped—do you think they're planning something?"

"They must be. I've stepped up patrols all over the territory, not just in Austin, but anywhere there's been a related murder."

She saw the frustrated look on his face, and said, "You hate that they've got the next move."

"Yes. Until something breaks, they're in control, and I find that rather distressing."

"What about the citywide sensor network you were talking about?"

He made an impatient noise. "It's going to take months. I'm still working bugs out of the prototype system, and after that it has to be manufactured, then installed, calibrated, tested . . . not to mention I have to convince Washington to loan me another satellite. Still, it's the only workable plan we've got. Once it's running I'll be able to track every vampire in the city down to a one-block radius with only a two-second delay."

"I guess you could always catch one and put a GPS collar on him before releasing him back into the wild."

He chuckled, but looked thoughtful. "It's an idea."

His com chimed, and a voice said, *"Sire, the car's ready for you."*

"Five minutes, Harlan," he replied.

David turned his gaze to Miranda, and she could tell there was something he needed to say but didn't want to. Even through her shield—and his—she felt a brief second of confusion mixed with apprehension, even a little embarrassment; but of course, it was all smoothed over and put away before she could say anything.

"I'll be back in time for our session later," was all he said. "Try to get some rest."

"Good hunting," she said.

To her surprise, before he left, he reached down for her hand and lifted it to his lips; again, she was sure he was going to say something, but all he did was release her hand and step back, saying, "Be safe."

Then he walked away. She stood staring after him, her hand held up to her heart, the skin tingling long after he was gone.

A low rumble of thunder brought her back to herself, and she started walking again, this time almost furiously. Out of nowhere her thoughts went to what Faith had said that night, about her becoming Queen one day, and helpless anger roiled in her stomach the way the oncoming storm did in the sky.

Damn Faith for dangling such an impossible idea in front of her. It did nothing but feed on the niggling little fear in the back of Miranda's mind that no matter what she did, she would never fit in among other people, and that here, the Haven, could be her home.

*Sure. I'll go out and start drinking blood right now. Then I'll come back with fangs and a melanin deficiency and rule the world. And also, David will fall so madly in love with me that the Signet will pick me as his Queen and we'll live happily ever after in bloodsucking bliss among the sparkly unicorns.*

She wished she had something to throw.

She shoved her hands into the pockets of her cardigan, ducking her head against the rising wind. Looking back over her shoulder at the Haven, she felt even angrier and shook her head violently, trying to put as much distance between herself and the building as possible.

She walked past the stables, where the paddock was empty—the horses were inside like sensible creatures. There were two glossy blacks in there, she knew, a stallion and a mare, and though she was afraid of horses, she had been pleased at how much David cared for them. They followed him around like giant puppies when he came down to ride or groom them, prancing sideways and tossing their manes when they saw him, nosing his coat for sugar cubes. Animals by and large were leery of vampires, but he had raised these from foals. The stallion was named Osiris, the mare Isis.

The Lord of the Dead and the Queen of Heaven.

She snorted. Damn David, too, for good measure.

Impulsively she veered off the cobbled path and onto a narrow track that wound its way into the woods. She'd been out here once with Faith, who had showed her where the creek ran alongside the Haven grounds; the Second moved with confidence in the darkness, grabbing her hand more than once when she was about to blunder into a tree. They'd seen deer slipping shy and silver through the brush, and a white barn owl soaring silently overhead. The sound of the water would be soothing to Miranda's jangled nerves, and if she got rained on, well, she wouldn't melt.

*"Miss Grey."* Terrence's voice issued from her wrist. *"Please don't leave the path alone. The woods aren't safe for you at night and it's about to storm."*

She sighed. "Follow closer if you want. I'm not going far, I promise."

They'd had a few minor clashes of will, and she always won. Most of the time she regretted pitting her desires against his orders, and she ended up apologizing, but tonight she didn't care. Nothing was going to happen to her here; this was the Haven, and she was . . .

She stopped. A strange sound had managed to make its way through her irritation to her conscious mind.

The sound was a lack of sound. There was no noise—no birds, no deer, nothing. It was quiet, in the woods, at night.

*Oh fuck. Miranda, you moron.*

Slowly, she took a step back, and another. Swallowing the atavistic fear that clawed its way up along her spine, she turned on her heel and walked back toward the garden, dismayed at how far off the path she'd strayed in her mental tantrum. It was so dark . . . what had she been thinking, coming out here without a flashlight? The clouds had obscured the moon, and she could barely see through the trees, but there was enough light that she knew it wasn't much farther.

*Don't run. Walk. Just keep walking. You'll catch up with Terrence in a minute and have a good laugh. Don't run.*

She was fighting thousands of years of fight-or-flight instinct that clamored in her ears for her to bolt. She could feel it watching her . . . something in the trees . . . something hungry . . .

. . . just the way someone had been following her that night . . .

Panic gripped her, and she ran.

Branches snapped and leaves rustled behind her, and she blundered into a thick knot of bushes and had to fight her way through, feeling thorns scrape her arms and pull threads from her sweater. She broke free and ran faster, but somehow she'd gotten turned around and what she'd thought was the garden was actually the break in the trees around the creek.

The ground disappeared beneath her feet, and she tripped, a sharp pain shooting through her ankle. With a cry, she tumbled onto the bank, reaching for something to stop her fall, roots ripping her clothes until with one last sickening lurch she slid off the bank and into the burbling water.

By some miracle, she didn't lose consciousness when her head struck the exposed limestone at the bottom, and by another miracle, the water wasn't that deep. She fought her way upright to find herself only submerged to her hips. Miranda tasted blood; she'd bitten her lip during the fall.

A twig snapped above her. "Terrence?" she called. "I'm down here!"

There was no reply, so she tried to get to her feet. Her ankle gave way and sent her back to the ground, pain coursing through her leg. Broken? She didn't think so, but it was badly sprained and wouldn't hold her weight.

She expected Terrence's head to appear over the bank, and when it didn't, she tried her com. "Elite Twenty-nine."

It chimed, telling her the com had connected to Terrence, but he didn't respond. She repeated the code, adding, "Terrence, this is Miranda. I'm in the creek and can't get out without help."

Something moved up in the trees, and fear prickled her scalp. Her heartbeat stepped up.

Her com chimed, and a soft, ghostly voice said, *"Terrence can't come to the phone right now . . . but I can see you, Miranda."*

She looked around frantically. "Stay the fuck away from me!" she yelled into the night.

*"Do you taste as luscious as you look, little girl?"*

It was coming closer. She backed up against the bank, feeling around for a weapon, her fingers closing around a chunk of rock lodged in the mud. As thunder rattled through the trees, she worked to pry the rock free, knowing it was an inadequate defense against what was coming—but it was something. Desperate, she said into her com, "Star-one!"

*"He's not going to find you, baby. I've already got you. I'm going to hold you down and fuck your pretty body, then drain you till you shrivel."*

Why, oh why had David taken down the shield? If it

were still up, he could find her anywhere. He'd already be on his way. Maybe, just maybe he was monitoring her frequency, and knew something was wrong.

*"He wants to taste you, too,"* the voice went on, cold and heartless. *"That's all you are to us . . . all you'll ever be."*

She couldn't fight a vampire. She couldn't run.

She let the old anger rise up through her as it had when she'd struck at Helen. She had been here before. Compared to what had already been done to her, death was nothing.

"Come on, then!" she challenged the darkness, yelling to be heard over the wind, brandishing her rock. "Come get me, you bastard!"

*"Poor little lost girl, thinks she's so strong. She has no idea what's really out there in the dark . . . close your eyes, pretty baby, it'll all be over soon."*

Just then a voice erupted over the network. *"Guess again."*

Lightning split the sky, and Miranda saw a second's glimpse of someone on the bank, saw them leap down at her—

Her mind had no idea how to interpret what happened next. The air in front of her seemed to shimmer, then coalesce, each mote of darkness igniting and fusing. A shadow formed among the shadows, and solidified.

The Prime appeared, standing between her and her attacker.

It couldn't change course in time to avoid him. David snarled, another flash of lightning catching on the silver of his eyes and the gleaming white of his teeth, and seized the attacker and flung it into the side of the creek, where it hit with the deafening crack of broken bones.

Miranda shrank back, falling into the creek again, her knees hitting the bottom hard enough to bleed.

The attacker was struggling up out of the water, but David was already on him; he dropped on the figure like a striking hawk, and she heard her attacker's agonized cry. A few minutes later, there was a loud splash as the Prime dropped the body in the water.

The rain let loose. Lightning flashed again, and she saw blood on David's mouth. They stared at each other in the darkness.

Miranda let the rock fall from her hand.

Turning away, David bent, lifted a handful of water and washed the blood from his face, then demanded of her, "What the hell are you doing out here?"

Her anger flared again. "I'm fine, thanks. Bleeding, but that's always awesome."

Faith's voice interrupted. *"Um . . . Sire?"*

"What?" he snapped.

*"Where are you? I turned around and you were gone."*

"At the Haven," he answered. "Get back here immediately. There's been another security breach and there are two Elite down."

*"Yes, Sire."*

Miranda was aware, then, of the fact that she was soaked, and that her entire body hurt like it had been beaten. She sagged against the bank, heedless of the mud. "Where's Terrence?" she asked.

"Dead," was the terse reply.

He stripped off his coat and wrapped it around her, not that it did much good; but at least it kept the rain off her face. "How did you find me?" she asked.

"Terrence's signal stopped, sending up an alarm. As soon as I heard it I began listening to the entire network. I intercepted the traitor's transmission—he knew too much about us, but not as much as he thought, or he would never have spoken to you over the coms." He scanned the bank, then looked at her. "Come here. I'll have to carry you out."

She wasn't happy with his tone, but there was no time to argue; she was beginning to tremble from the chill, and she was bleeding in several places that were going to need attention. She stepped into his outstretched arm, and he lifted her up and held her to his chest, his other arm reaching overhead to grab a root that hung over the creek.

Even in the situation they were in, she marveled at how casually strong he was. She wasn't a big or heavy woman, but he lifted her one-handed and climbed out of the creek without appearing to exert any effort at all. Once on land again, he set her down to test her ankle, but there was no way she was going to be able to pick through the woods without falling and making it worse.

Sighing, he picked her up again, this time with both arms, and carried her straight out of the trees to the garden, where the full brunt of the storm hit them once they were out of the shelter of the wood. Neither of them made any attempt to speak until they'd made it to the Haven.

Once inside, several guards appeared, along with a cadre of servants, to offer their assistance.

"Retrieve Terrence's body from the forest," David ordered. "Bring in the traitor's corpse as well, then gather whatever evidence you can from the scene before this weather erases everything. Be careful. Have Terrence prepared for the standard Elite funeral tomorrow night, with honors. Esther, is Miss Grey's dinner in her room? Good. Draw her a hot bath and stoke the fire, as well as my own. As soon as Faith gets here, send her directly to my suite."

Miranda was rocking back and forth on her unsteady feet, unsure whether she was going to pass out or just throw up. The noise and fuss happened around her, not to her; dimly she noticed herself being picked up again like a sack of old potatoes, borne down the long hallway and into the comfort and safety of her bedroom.

But how safe was it, now? They had come for her at the Haven, when she was supposed to be under guard. Was anywhere safe?

She knew the answer to that, and it was breaking her heart.

He sat her on her bed, removing his coat and tossing

it carelessly on the ground, where it clanked as the concealed sword inside struck the marble floor. She let him
examine her, his hands rough and clinical, deeming her
wounds superficial and her lucky to be alive.

Esther, the lead servant for the East Wing, came in and
made a beeline for the bathroom, where Miranda heard
her turning on taps and laying out towels.

The normally cheerful little woman emerged with
Miranda's comb. "I thought Miss Grey might want to get
those tangles out first," she said diffidently. "And maybe I
bring bandages for your knees?"

"Thank you, Esther," Miranda said before David could
speak for her. He was never unkind to the servants, but
the mood he was in would probably result in hurt feelings. "I think bandages are a good idea. It's nothing serious, but it never hurts to be sure."

Esther nodded and gave Miranda a motherly smile
and pat on the cheek. "We don't want our *reinita* getting
hurt," she said, and departed on her errand.

Miranda looked up at David. *"Reinita?"*

He wouldn't meet her eyes. "Little Queen."

"Is that . . . is that what everyone thinks?"

"I don't give a damn what everyone thinks."

"Then what do you think?"

He stood facing the fire, which had been obligingly
stoked so that it cast its merry warmth around the room.
He didn't seem to feel the cold that had to be down to
his bones by now; they were both soaked, and his fine
linen shirt was pasted to his torso, stuck to the muscle she
knew was there, outlining his body. She hadn't realized
just how well built he was.

Through the wet shirt, she could barely make out the
edges of what looked like . . .

"Is that a tattoo?"

He sighed again, and without answering, unbuttoned
his shirt and dropped it on top of his abandoned coat. He
turned back toward the fire, allowing her a full view of
his back and shoulders.

His entire back was inked in the stylized shape of a bird of prey: a black-and-red hawk. Its wings spanned his shoulders, its tail reaching all the way down past his waist.

"That's beautiful," she breathed. One of her hands couldn't help but reach out, wanting a chance just to touch the lines of ink, to see if they were smooth, or raised like Braille. If it was in Braille, could she read him then, with her fingers, and learn all the mysteries? Or would the story end too soon?

"Do you need help getting in the bath?" he asked.

She shook her head. "I can manage."

"Good. I'm going to go change."

He grabbed his shirt and coat off the floor and stalked off to his room, the curves of the tattoo shifting as he moved.

Miranda got to her feet carefully and hobbled into the bathroom, yanking off her sodden clothes on the way, grumbling to herself the whole time. Who the hell did he think he was, treating her like she'd done something wrong, when she'd nearly been killed?

She lowered herself painfully into the steaming tub, thanking whatever deity might be listening for Esther, who knew exactly what temperature she liked. Right away the hot water began to soothe both her injured ankle and her wounded pride. She washed the scrapes on her knees and elbows and then lay back for a while, closing her eyes and trying to stay grounded.

But the reality of her situation made grounding hard. Terrence was dead because someone wanted to get to her, which meant that the insurgents not only knew she existed but considered her a threat, or at least worth killing. She was in danger and unless she spent every moment with the Prime they were probably going to try again, and again. Worst of all, her attacker had been one of the Elite. Any of them could be Blackthorn, and that meant that the Blackthorn could find the Haven.

It was supposed to be hidden, all signals monitored

coming and going. There were no unauthorized radios, computers, or other forms of communication—the security system could detect them. New Elite recruits were brought in from Austin unconscious so they couldn't trace the route back, and learned the location only once they were initiated and, supposedly, trustworthy. So little was left to chance . . . but that little was going to cost her her life.

She looked up at the bathroom walls in the midst of scrubbing stubborn bits of dirt from her arms and legs. She'd taken a lot of long baths in here, and she loved the muted tile with its mosaic accents. She'd gotten used to not having a mirror—there were mirrors in the real world. She'd have to look at herself again . . . and she'd see the sun. The prospect should have pleased her.

She levered herself up out of the tub, yanking the stopper with her good foot, and dried off, toweling her hair and letting it dry down over her shoulders. She dug out her old yoga pants and a T-shirt from Book People that read KEEP AUSTIN WEIRD, and took a moment to smear some of the antibiotic ointment Esther had brought onto her knees and elbows and a nasty scrape on her forearm. Only one knee really needed a bandage and felt badly bruised beneath the laceration. She was probably going to be black and purple all over tomorrow.

She stared at the array of possessions on the chest of drawers, then with numb hands took her backpack from a drawer and began to pack.

She didn't have that much. A couple of journals where she'd jotted ideas for songs; her phone, her iPod, and her computer, which all went into the laptop bag; miscellaneous toiletries; clothes. Her guitar was already snug in its case. There were a few books that needed to go back to the library and a folder of sheet music she'd taken from the music room to study. She stacked them up carefully.

Her hands closed around the spine of Shakespeare's comedies, and she lifted the book and pressed it to her chest.

After a moment she set it down and dug a pen out of her purse, opening up one of her journals; she took a deep breath to steady herself and wrote a few lines, then ripped the page out of the journal and folded it.

As she was sticking the note inside the book, she heard the door to the suite open.

"Faith has volunteered to drive you back to town," David said. "I've arranged a hotel room for you while your new apartment is being prepared."

"What's wrong with my old apartment?" she asked without looking up.

"It's not safe for you to go back there. Don't worry— all your things will be packed and moved for you in the next few days."

She wanted to protest, but she didn't have the energy. What difference did it make where she lived, anyway?

"I'm scared," she whispered.

He came to her and put his arms around her, and she buried her face in his neck, trying to breathe in the solace that wrapped her in its protecting wings. "You're going to be fine," he said. "I know it."

"Will I ever see you again?"

He didn't answer at first, and when he did his voice was full of pain. "It would be best if you didn't."

"Screw what's best," she said. "Promise me I'll see you again."

She stared into his eyes, willing him to understand, and he said softly, "I promise."

Miranda nodded, satisfied, and reached down, unhooking the clasp of her com and placing it in his hand. "I guess I don't need this now."

"You have my phone and e-mail, if you need anything. And this is for you . . ." He fished something from his pocket: a Visa card.

"I don't need money," she tried to say, but he interrupted.

"Take it. I'm the reason your life is being uprooted

again. I couldn't keep you safe here. Let me do what I can for you, Miranda. Please."

She lowered her eyes, accepting. "You've already done so much for me," she said softly. "Thank you."

"It was my pleasure."

She laughed a little. "Liar."

He smiled faintly in return. One of his hands came up, fingertips brushing the line of her jaw, and for once she let herself really feel the ache that arose at the touch.

There was a knock, and Faith said, "Sire, we're ready to go."

"Have Samuel take Miss Grey's things down to the car," David told the Second. "She'll be there in a moment."

"I'll be waiting outside," Faith replied.

Miranda picked up her purse and her guitar; Samuel spirited away everything else, leaving her to gather the strength to walk out of the little bedroom and not come back.

David was still standing beside the chest, his hand resting on the book, when she said, "Good-bye, Lord Prime."

She barely heard his answer. "Good-bye."

Miranda shut the door behind her and followed Faith down the hall, giving the servants and Elite she passed a small wave and what she hoped was a brave smile. Any of them might be in collusion with the enemy, but only the Prime and Second knew where she was going; all the others would know was that she was gone.

The rain had slackened enough that she didn't make a mad dash for Faith's car. She had to grin—the Second drove a sporty red Honda hybrid with California plates. Samuel was stowing the last of her handful of bags in the trunk. Miranda thrust her guitar and purse into the backseat, then opened the passenger door; Faith was already in the driver's seat with the engine running.

Miranda turned back to look up at the Haven one last time, half-expecting to see David's silhouette in the bedroom window, but the room was dark.

She started to get into the car, but then the Haven

doors opened. The Prime emerged, pushing past the door guard's surprised expression, and hurried down the stone steps to the driveway.

Miranda gasped as David came to her, drawing her to him, his heartbeat thundering against her chest; his hands wrapped around her waist and the back of her neck, and before either of them could summon a denial, he covered her mouth with his.

She barely had time to return the kiss before he broke away, releasing her and stepping back, his hand lingering on the side of her face for just a second before he turned around and walked away.

Miranda didn't call after him. She sank into the seat of the car, tears running down her face. Samuel shut the door for her.

Faith offered her an encouraging smile and pulled away from the Haven, taking the long road back to Austin in the rain.

# The River Styx

# Ten

October was hell.

For a week Miranda remained cloistered in her room at the Driskill, sitting in the darkness with cable TV and room service. She didn't even go down to the world-renowned Driskill Café for dinner, despite the fact that everything was paid for. She stammered her order into the phone and waited with her eyes averted for room service to come and go.

The minute the waiter or the maid or anyone came into the room, she curled up in a chair in the corner and focused so hard on her shielding that inevitably she got a splitting headache as soon as they were gone. She split her last bottle of Vicodin into half pills and doled them out only when the pain was unbearable. She was terrified of losing her protections; there was no one to help her now.

There was no one to help her. No one asked after her welfare. No one came to visit her. She was alone.

She tried to keep herself company with her guitar, but once again, the music had left her. So she watched movies, she nursed her bruises, she slept, and she waited for news.

Finally, six days into her stay at the hotel, a messenger came to her room to let her know that her apartment was ready and a car would be there in the morning to take her to her new home. She sat up all that night, her bags already packed and by the door, and come dawn she bolted down to the lobby without stopping, avoiding the elevator just in case she got stuck on it and had to speak to someone.

As she rushed outside to the car, the sunlight blinded her and she dropped her purse. A middle-aged man passing by on the street stopped to help her. She muttered her thanks.

"You okay, darlin'?" he asked, putting a fatherly hand on her shoulder.

The touch made her cry out and leap back. *Hands in the dark . . . laughter . . .*

She dove into the car and trembled like a leaf the entire way to the apartment complex.

It was a high-class place in South Austin, right off the bus route up Lamar that would take her to all her old haunts; she stopped at the office long enough to pick up the keys and sign the lease, then let herself in, barely acknowledging the friendly driver who carried her bags for her.

Once inside she shut and locked the door, and there she stayed for most of the month.

At first she told herself she was busy unpacking. All her possessions from the old place had been boxed and transported for her, labeled in neat black letters as to what room its contents had originated from; they'd put her furniture in a logical arrangement, but she didn't like it and spent several hours moving things around until it felt right.

The apartment was gorgeous and way out of her normal price range. It had two bedrooms, a huge bath, and an open floor plan that flowed from kitchen to living room. The living room boasted half a dozen windows and a patio. Molding crowned the walls, and the doorways were arched. The carpet was plush, the walls a creamy color that went with everything, the appliances top-of-the-line stainless steel.

She hated it.

There was too much light. She could no longer sleep with light coming into the bedroom, so she had to hang what curtains she had over the two small windows in there, leaving the living room exposed except for the wood blinds, which she kept shut all the time. She could never get the temperature right—she was used to cool air and warm fires balancing each other. Her new apartment didn't have a fireplace.

She even missed her dark, cheap little one-bedroom from Before. She missed the crack in the wall.

She worked her way from one box to another, trying to remember where she had acquired many of the things she owned and what they were for. The kitchen especially confounded her. Had she ever really used a toaster? Why did she have so many wineglasses and so few plates?

Whoever had moved her stuff had thoughtfully stocked both fridge and pantry with the same kinds of food she'd eaten at the Haven. Everything was bright and shiny and new. It should have pleased her, but it only made her sad.

There was too much noise in the city. All day and night there were cars, sirens, people walking by outside talking and laughing. People slammed doors, and apparently her upstairs neighbors were into indoor bowling.

Every time there was a sudden sound she nearly jumped out of her skin. For three weeks she was constantly afraid . . . her nightmares returned with a vengeance, so while it rained torrents outside, she cried torrents in her bed.

One evening at the end of the third week of October, she decided to try walking down to the corner store for a Coke. She'd been living off Chinese delivery and pizza for more than a week, having stretched her groceries as far as she could to the point of eating crackers with butter for dinner, but she couldn't bear the thought of a supermarket yet. Best to start small. She could walk two blocks to the Shell station and get a soda and maybe some chips.

She poked her nose out her front door for the first time since she'd moved in. It had been pointless trying to change her sleeping habits, so it was just after sunset and the air was rapidly cooling down. Somewhere in the time she'd lost hiding under her bed, fall had begun.

Miranda bolstered her shields, then did it again after she closed the door behind her. Every time someone walked past her she strengthened them even more, but not so much as an iota of external energy reached her.

*You know what you're doing, remember? You can do this. Just keep walking. Don't panic. Breathe in, breathe out. You know how to do it.*

If anyone noticed her unkempt appearance, they paid it no mind. She hadn't brushed her hair since waking, and though she wasn't as pitifully thin as she'd been Before, there were huge dark circles under her eyes. She hadn't slept through the day since she'd come back to Austin.

She needn't have worried. Out here, in a metropolitan area of 1.6 million people living out their lives and wrapped up in their own mortal concerns, she was nobody again, invisible.

It was so strange being able to see her reflection. She'd stared at herself for long minutes in the hotel, and again in her new bathroom, trying to make sense out of her features. Was this really who she was? Were those her green eyes? She had a scar on her forehead just below her hairline from that night. She'd had no idea until she saw it in the mirror.

She made it to the store and bought a twelve-pack of Coke and an armload of junk food. She handed her Visa to the clerk and signed the receipt without speaking, though she was pretty sure he was trying to flirt with her. She didn't know how to react to that.

On the walk back she took a moment to notice the weather; there had been a break in the rain, and the air was clear and crisp, a few stars peeking out of the darkening blue of the sky. What day was it? Friday? No, Thursday.

Once home, she expected to have to fight off a panic attack, but she felt remarkably calm taking the chips and candy out of her bag and stowing the soda in the fridge.

"Well now," she said to herself. "That wasn't so bad." She popped the top on a Coke and took a bag of Doritos to the couch to watch reruns of *Buffy the Vampire Slayer.*

The next night she took out the trash. When she got back, she turned on her computer and checked her e-mail. Once again, Kat had written trying to find her; after thinking about it for a minute, Miranda wrote back.

TO: Kat (katmandoo@freemail.net)
FROM: Miranda Grey (mgrey82@freemail.net)
SUBJECT: Re: Re: Re: MIA?

Hey Kat,

I'm back in town. I moved to a new place. Want to come over for pizza tomorrow? Let me know.

~M

Five minutes later she had a reply. It was only two words long: *HELL YES!*

"Rehab," Kat said around a mouthful of cheese. "I had a feeling it had to be something like that."

Miranda picked a black olive off her slice and dropped it in the box lid; Kat immediately scooped it up and stuck it on her own. "Yeah."

"You were looking like a junkie when I last saw you. Thank God you've gained some weight back—you'll be hot shit again if you keep it up, although the Doritos and Pizza Hut Diet might not be the way to go."

Miranda took another bite and said, "I know. I've just

been kind of a shut-in since I got back. I'm going to the grocery store for some real food in a day or two. It's hard to adjust to the real world after . . . all of that."

"But you're feeling better, right?"

"Yes," she said hastily, trying to believe it herself. "Much better. I'm going to be okay, Kat, I really am. It just . . . things got bad. Really bad. So it's going to take some time."

Kat nodded, tucking a stray dread behind her ear with her non-pizza-laden hand. "I've seen it a lot with my kids in the program. Sometimes they have to totally hit bottom before they realize there's a way back up." She reached over and squeezed Miranda's arm, looking worried when Miranda flinched. "Just promise that if I can help, you'll ask. Okay?"

"Okay."

She wanted to tell Kat the truth. She wanted to tell someone.

Most of all she wanted to talk to Faith, and she wanted to see David. She wanted to go back to her cozy little bedroom and watch the seasons change from a second-story window overlooking the hills. Her windows here overlooked the parking lot.

"So you said in your last e-mail you were staying with friends," Kat mentioned. "Does that mean you met somebody at the clinic?" She waggled her eyebrows suggestively. "Someone special?"

Miranda threw a pillow at her, and Kat laughed. "Oh, come on," the blonde said. "Plenty of people hook up in rehab. What else is there to do if you don't smoke? Besides," Kat added, "you're blushing. That must mean I'm right."

Miranda shook her head. "No, it's not . . . I mean . . . there was somebody . . . well, maybe. But it wasn't like that. We were just friends, or . . . well, more than that, but . . . I don't know." She took a swig of her beer, trying to find words, but how on earth could she explain any of it without saying too much? "Let's just say I met someone, and he helped me get better. But nothing was ever going to happen."

"Why not?"

She smiled ruefully, ripping the corner of the label off her Corona bottle. "We're from two very different worlds."

Kat's smile turned mischievous, and for a moment she looked a lot like Faith. "If you're not going for it, then, I know somebody you should meet. He's a music teacher—dark hair, blue eyes, smoking-hot ass."

"No, thanks. I don't think I'm up for that kind of thing right now. It's too soon."

"Why? You went in to get off drugs, not porn."

Miranda shuddered inwardly at the thought of some man, smoking-hot ass or not, touching her, trying to get his hands in her pants. She thought about being naked with someone, spreading her legs, having someone invade her body, fingers pushing into her, the sound of a zipper . . . suddenly cold, she groped for a throw blanket that wasn't there.

"What's wrong?" Kat was asking. "Mira . . . that look on your face just now . . . is there something you're not telling me about all of this?"

*God, is there ever . . .*

She hated lying, even when there was no other way. "Before I went in, something . . . the night you came to see me play, I was walking home, and . . ."

Kat's mouth dropped open, and her eyes filled with tears as the pieces came together. "Oh, fuck, honey . . . fuck, I'm so sorry . . ."

She pushed herself off the floor and put her arms around Miranda, who didn't shrink away from the hug, but couldn't quite return it.

"It's okay," Miranda reassured her. She could feel the guilt radiating from Kat's whole body. "It wasn't your fault. Don't blame anybody but the people who did it, okay? I'm all right."

"But why didn't you call me? Why did you just

disappear like that? I could have done something—we could have gone to the police. You should still go to the police. It's not too late."

"Yes, it is. Please, Kat . . . let's just not talk about it anymore."

"But—"

"Please." Miranda silently willed her not to press; she even risked leaning on Kat a tiny bit with her energy, just to change the subject. The less Kat knew, the better; there was always a chance that even here Miranda wasn't safe, and she wasn't going to risk Kat, too.

She squeezed Kat around the middle, finally returning her hug, saying, "It's okay. It's . . . it's all over with now."

There were not enough redheads in Austin to make him forget her.

There were not enough redheads in Houston, either, or New Orleans, or Oklahoma City. There weren't enough in all of Georgia.

In early October he essentially went on tour, visiting the major cities of his territory, greeting new Elite, upgrading various systems, and making his presence known. Most other Primes didn't bother with that kind of hands-on involvement, but he had learned from the best as well as the worst. Pretending there was only one city in the South allowed gangs to build up strength in other places, and Auren had barely kept up with the onslaught even at his peak.

It was the same everywhere. Arrive, meet, confer; hunt, fuck, leave.

There was no relish in any of it.

On the other hand, being home was no better.

He had closed and locked the door of the mistress suite and not set foot inside it since; he'd done the same to the music room. He'd entered the latter long enough to turn out a light Miranda had left on, and her presence was still palpable, her scent lingering in the air strongly enough to drive him to the bottom of a bottle of Jack. The next night he'd gone into the city and torn into the first auburn-haired woman he could find, drinking her so deeply he nearly killed her.

He wanted to call. He didn't call.

*Forget her. Forget her and move on.*

Forgetting was one thing vampires simply couldn't do. They had extraordinary memories that made their life spans seem interminable; he supposed it was an apt punishment for cheating death.

After the man who attacked Miranda—Elite 70, who had been working for him for three years and had an impeccable service record—was disposed of, his blood-drained corpse dumped in the Shadow District to wait for the sun, the attacks in Austin came to an abrupt halt.

David didn't trust the tenuous peace. Perhaps being thwarted in their attempt on the human had made them wary, or perhaps they were planning something even bigger. Either way, he concentrated on the citywide sensor network he was creating and kept the doubled patrols active until further notice. He wasn't about to get sloppy like Arrabicci and Auren had.

There had been absolutely no evidence of perfidy in Elite 70's quarters. He shared his room with Elite 25, who was as shocked as the rest of them were. David had tracked 70's movements back six months over the com network and found nothing untoward. Elite 70 hadn't ever separated from his unit, had never wandered off alone to meet anyone. His com signal had never wavered.

There had been a thorough search and interrogations throughout the Haven, but David still had no idea if 70 had kept in contact with his masters, much less what he had revealed about operations at the Haven. Elite 70 was of low rank compared to Helen and didn't have access to much sensitive information, but he might have been there as a pair of extra hands for her. Unless they found another traitor in their midst to question, it was too late to find out why 70 had been at the Haven.

David hated being played. That was exactly what these people were doing: making him suspect his allies, baiting him, making him expose his underbelly to their tiny poisoned spears.

He stopped his work long enough to make his journey around the territory, but as soon as he was back in Austin, he threw himself into the sensor network again. More than once Faith had to remind him to feed and sleep.

As a plan, creating the network was doable. As a distraction, it was woefully inadequate.

Every place, every corner of the Haven reminded him of her. Even in town, lying between the thighs of another nameless human woman waiting for her to finish coming while her blood sang through his veins, he thought of Miranda—her lips, the one time he'd tasted them . . . her hair, wound around his fingers . . . her bright laugh, so rare, that brought life into what now felt like a tomb instead of a home.

One night he made the mistake of sitting on the couch and leaning back into a pillow, releasing a wave of her scent. He had buried his face in it for half an hour, then thrown it in the fireplace.

At this rate he should buy stock in Jack Daniels.

He was in his workroom a few nights later, painstakingly wiring a sensor into its weatherproof housing, when his phone rang. His first inclination was to ignore it, but he glanced over to see who it was and decided he had better not.

"Yes?"

The voice wasn't British, and it wasn't cheerful like Jonathan's; it had, in fact, the faint lilt of an Irish accent and was gentle, if grave. But he could feel the same power and energy echoing from it even hundreds of miles away. "David, have I told you lately that you're an idiot?"

He put down his screwdriver and sat back. "Nice to hear from you, too, Sire. How are things in the Golden State?"

"I have two lectures prepared for you: one on the perils of ignoring your destiny and the other on gluttony, specifically related to drinking your weight in Jim Beam every night."

"I'm not drinking."

He could practically hear Deven roll his eyes. "I'm intimately acquainted with your vices, David."

"It's Jack, not Jim."

"Fine. Which lecture do you want first? I have a conference call with Western Europe and North Africa in fifteen minutes, so I'd like to move this along."

David rubbed his forehead, where a headache was forming—he'd been having a lot of them lately. "Deven, your own Consort told me to send her away or she'd be killed. What else was I supposed to do?"

"Jonathan reacts to these things emotionally. I'm sure if he'd realized you were in love with her, he would have thought differently. Besides, you know as well as I do that the future is malleable. Did you try letting her touch the second Signet?"

"Why would I do that? She's human!"

"Return to earlier point in conversation regarding you as idiot."

"You think I should have brought her across," David said. "After everything she's been through, and knowing the life she would face, I can't believe you of all people would say that."

"What I'm saying," Deven told him firmly, "is that I know how you love, how we all love. It's not just going to go away. The longer you fight it, the more misery you bring down on both of you. Trust me, dear one. What if the vision comes true, and she does die? Every moment you didn't spend at her side will haunt you forever. We all know how long forever really is."

David leaned his head in his free hand. "How about the second lecture?"

He could hear Deven rolling his eyes over the phone. "If you're going to become a drunk, at least spring for the good whiskey. Jack Daniels? Honestly. Have I taught you nothing?"

"Anything else?"

"Yes, one more thing, or rather, an addendum to the first. Consider it the official diplomatic recommendation of your oldest ally.'

"Let's have it."

"Quit fucking around and go see her."

When David hung up, he heard someone clear her throat in the doorway and saw Faith waiting to speak to him, the very picture of professional courtesy.

He shook his head in exasperation. "Thank you, Faith. Now I have *both* of them to contend with. Better yet, they're giving me conflicting advice when I don't want any at all."

Faith shrugged. "I thought you might listen to him."

He glared at her. "Do you think this is easy for me? Don't you think I want more than anything to go see her?"

"Then why don't you?"

"It would make everything so much harder in the long run to drag this out instead of having a clean break. She has a chance to live her life now and be happy. I'm not going to show up and keep reminding her of what happened here."

"But what if . . . and this is just a thought, obviously . . . what if she feels the same way about you?"

He lowered his eyes and went back to the wires and tiny screws. "Then I pity her."

Faith made an exasperated noise and stood there for a minute, but he ignored her. Finally she said, "The night's reports are on your server. I'm off."

"Fine."

Alone again, David tried to keep working, but he broke the same wire three times before he gave up. He picked up his phone and scrolled through the contact list: twenty-six Primes, several Queens, one Consort, the White House, the governors of all eight of the territory's states, Downing Street, the Department of Defense . . . and the mobile number for a human female, Miranda Grey.

He stared at the entry for a long time. All he had to do was hit a button and he'd hear her voice.

Cursing under his breath, he shoved the phone into his pocket and pushed himself back from the table, snatching his coat from the back of the chair and heading to the suite to find the good whiskey.

"I'm in for the morning, Samuel," he told the door guard. "See to it I'm not disturbed."

"As you will it, Sire."

He shut the door and hung his coat on its usual hook, removing his blade to hang beside the door and running his hand along the sheath with a sigh. He'd had many weapons over the years, but this one—a gift from the Pair of California the year he had taken the Southern Signet—was his favorite. It was shorter than those used by the Elite, with a slight curve, exquisitely forged and polished like a diamond. The edge had never once gone dull, and it was perfectly balanced. Over the years it had parted dozens of treacherous heads from shoulders. He didn't know all that much about metallurgy, but he was aware that it was worth a small fortune.

He glanced over at the fireplace, where another sword, much older, hung, still gleaming even in its retirement. It was about the same size but heavier, made of a lesser grade of steel back in his lieutenant days in California. The last thing he had used it for was to kill Prime Auren.

He remembered that night well, a mere blink of an eye past for his kind. He had taken the Prime by surprise, but that was no guarantee of victory. Auren was a skilled warrior. The fight had gone on for almost an hour, but David had been watching him for months, learning his weaknesses in battle.

The crowd that gathered to see him take the Signet from the body had stared in openmouthed bewilderment. No one had expected Auren to die. His reign was supposed to last for centuries.

David walked over to pour himself a drink, digging

out the new bottle of Jack he'd had Esther bring up—to hell with what Deven thought.

As he drained the first glass and started working on a second, he crossed the room to a wood cabinet set back in the corner and unlocked it.

Remnants of his past were kept inside: Lizzie's wedding ring, stolen from her newly dug grave; a handful of letters; a silk scarf that still smelled softly of jasmine; a few valuable items from his travels that he couldn't quite give up but didn't want to look at every day; the first clumsy circuit board he'd ever built.

He reached up to the top shelf and removed a black metal lockbox; inside that was another box, about six inches square, hand carved from ebony with the Seal of the Southern Prime worked into it. Each Prime had his own Seal, but it was a variation of this one, a stamp of his identity as well as his territory.

Carefully, he opened the wooden box, revealing a large red stone set into silver and hung on a heavy chain. It was almost identical to the one he wore, though just a shade smaller; and where his stone glowed faintly from the touch of his power, this one was dark, the mystical force inside it asleep as it had been for many years.

David put the outer box back in the cabinet and locked the doors, taking the Signet with him to the sofa, where he sank down into the cushions, staring at the dormant bloodred stone.

No one alive knew for certain where the Signets had come from or who had made them. He had asked, in the beginning, but was met only with silence as his answer. Somehow over the centuries that knowledge had been lost, and as far as he could tell no one cared all that much what the truth was. Only David seemed to understand that any force powerful enough to create the Signets had to be stronger than a Prime, and that meant they weren't at the top of the food chain the way they believed themselves to be. Somewhere, at some time in history, there had been a greater power at work among vampire kind. It may even still exist.

He had seen a Signet choose its bearer at least twice before his own. He thought back to the last night of warfare in Sacramento, when they had taken over the base of operations where the Blackthorn were hiding out, recovering Arrabicci's stolen Signet and returning it to the Haven where it belonged. He had handed the Signet to Deven for safekeeping, and the stone inside it had blazed to life, the light flashing like an alarm until it was around his neck. He could still remember the stunned look on Deven's face when he realized he had been chosen, and he remembered the enormous surge of power that had swept through the whole building, wrapping itself around the new Prime.

Only a few months after that, a chance meeting in a bar had led the Prime to his Consort. As soon as the Signet recognized Jonathan it began to pulse again, and later they found the second one doing the same safe in its box at the Haven. The two vampires had known each other for all of ten minutes, but the second the Signet flashed, they both smiled like the moon coming out from the clouds. They could feel the connection between them instantly, and it was, as were all Signets, a perfect match.

David had spent his remaining years in California happy for his friend and yet insanely, poisonously jealous. Leaving had been a relief.

He touched the sleeping stone with one finger, and a drowsy flicker of light appeared in acknowledgment. It knew him, of course. The stones weren't exactly sentient, but they definitely had a will. He could feel his like a quiet murmur of energy in the back of his mind, never invasive, but always with him. Again, he wondered who could have created such a thing.

Only a vampire could wake the Signet, but it was possible, however unlikely, that contact with someone who could *potentially* bear it might do . . . something.

And if he had shown it to Miranda, then what? What if he took the leap of faith and changed her, and the Signet didn't respond? Was she supposed to live in the mistress suite for all time on condition that he never found his true Queen? He knew she would never be content with that, and he wouldn't ask her to become a vampire unless he knew for sure he was hers.

What were the chances of that? There were a million vampires at last census, and of those only one could possibly be his match, assuming she was even born yet. Assuming circumstance ever led them to each other, it could be a hundred years from now.

He slammed the box lid shut and put it on the coffee table. This was stupid. He was torturing himself, and for what? Let the others go on about destiny all they liked. Destiny was just a way of denying responsibility for one's own actions. People lived and died by their choices, regardless of what a blinking rock had to say about it.

There was no time to wallow in self-pity, not with so much at stake. People could be dying in the city while he sat here moping over things that would never be.

She wasn't coming back. She had her own life to live, and he had his.

Enough was enough. He had work to do.


There was no way around it. Her keyboard was simply not a Bösendorfer.

Compared to the grand old dame in the Haven, her digital instrument sounded small and tinny. She could have hooked it up to the world's biggest amplifier and it still would have sounded like a toy xylophone after she'd had a chance to play the Imperial Grand.

She had spent hours on the bench in front of the grand, feeding her sorrow and longing into the keys as well as using the music to soothe the frustrations of an immortal warrior/diplomat. The piano was as regal as the Prime, as rich as the Haven itself, and she had adored every inch of it. She tried fiddling with the settings on her Yamaha to approximate the sound, but the most she could do was make it sound like she was playing at the bottom of a well.

She patted the keyboard and told it, "Don't feel bad. She was like a vacation. You're the real thing, baby."

The real thing, like real life, was a pale imitation of what she had lost.

Days dragged by, and she dragged herself along with them. She went through the motions and tried valiantly to feel more than passing interest in her old life. She hung out with Kat; she finally went to the grocery store; she did laundry and checked her e-mail. She even got in touch with Mel about going back onstage.

She expected him to be angry at her disappearance, but she'd never signed a contract, and musicians weren't known for their reliability in this city. In fact, she'd created enough buzz while she was still performing that when she vanished, she became the talk of the town. Rumors flew, mostly involving drug addiction and nervous breakdown. Mel was more than happy to have her back, given how many people had asked him about her while she was gone.

Her first gig was Friday. She had until then to convince herself it was a good idea.

So far her shields had held up. She'd been working on refining her technique while she was at home, figuring out how to thin the barrier out and pick out a single person's surface emotions without intruding. Still, she hadn't been around a big crowd yet. She'd even gone food shopping after midnight when the store was practically empty, just as she had always done Before.

Miranda paged through her collection of sheet music, trying to decide on a set list. She had actually been working on a few original songs, but none of them were anywhere near ready.

She came across her faded old copy of Tori Amos's "Silent All These Years" and found a lump rising into her throat. It was the first song she'd played on the Bösendorfer, the first song she'd played for David.

She shoved the song back into its folder and tossed it on the floor. Not that one. Not now.

A knock on her front door made her start so hard she nearly fell over.

Wary, she approached the peephole from the side, her heart pounding. For just a split second she held out a hope that maybe . . .

When she saw who it was, she smiled broadly and threw open the door.

Faith, caught off guard by the hug Miranda bundled her into, grunted in surprise, then laughed. "It's good to see you, too."

"Come in!"

It was a little weird seeing Faith out of uniform. She had come into the city in a leather jacket over dark jeans and a wine-colored sweater, her myriad braids clipped back from her face. In her high-heeled boots she looked sophisticated and exotic, not deadly, but Miranda would bet she had at least one knife on her somewhere.

Faith looked around the apartment with interest. "Not bad," she commented, taking off her jacket.

Miranda ushered her to the couch and offered her a beer, which she accepted. "I'm getting used to it. I had to get curtains in here, though. I wish I knew where to get metal shutters."

Faith chuckled. She scrutinized Miranda for a moment before saying, "You're looking much better."

"I guess."

"How are you?"

She held Miranda's gaze for a second, and Miranda knew what she was really asking. "I'm okay. I never thought I'd say so, but I miss the Haven."

The Second smiled again. "It gets in your blood, this life. I've lived on my own, and I can't imagine doing it again."

They chatted for a while about Miranda's apartment and what she'd been up to for the last two months, then moved on to Haven gossip; Faith told her that there had only been three attacks by the insurgents since she'd left, but that everyone expected all hell to break loose any second.

"Is the sensor network up yet?" Miranda asked.

"No, but it's getting there. The initial tests went well. It's probably going to take another month to get it live, though."

She knew that every day that passed, every human who died would torment David, and he would do everything he could to get the network running even if it meant he gave up luxuries like sleep.

"Make sure he's getting some rest," she said.

There was a pause, Faith holding her beer up to the lamplight, then clearing her throat. "Can I ask you something?"

"Sure."

The Second licked her lips a little uncomfortably. "Do you love him?"

Miranda gripped the arm of the couch. "I don't know."

Faith raised a quizzical eyebrow. "What do you mean, you don't know? I saw that kiss, and I saw the way the two of you looked at each other. Everyone knew, except maybe you two."

Frustrated, Miranda found herself blinking back angry tears—damn it, she'd sworn she wasn't going to cry over this anymore—and stood up, walking over to the window. "What kind of person would I be if I loved someone who kills people?"

"You've killed people."

Miranda smiled bitterly. "Exactly."

"People love soldiers and police officers. The president has a wife, and he's given orders that got people killed, all without getting his hands dirty. I guess it's more civilized if it's out of sight, out of mind."

She sighed. "I have no idea. It doesn't make any difference now anyway."

"It makes all the difference in the world. You could come back."

"No, I can't. I'm stuck here in the human world for the rest of my life, even though I know there's more out there. What do I do with that, Faith?"

"The way things are now isn't how they have to stay."

She faced Faith. "What about you? If I asked you . . . would you turn me?"

Faith's eyes went wide. "Turn you into a vampire?"

"No, turn me into a frog. Could you do it?"

Faith finished her beer in one long swallow. "I might be able to, physically. But I wouldn't."

Miranda had known she would say that, but still, her heart sank. "Why not?"

She laughed. "Because my boss would kill me."

Miranda turned away again, muttering, "Forget I asked. It was dumb."

"Yes, it was, but not for the reason you think. Look, Miranda . . . nobody would like to see you come home as much as I would, but right now you're not thinking clearly. Remember what you said? That you wouldn't give up your humanity for a man? Because here's the thing—just one reason, even love, isn't enough. Neither is being lonely or depressed about your life. You have to know with every fiber of your being that it's what you want."

Miranda couldn't look at her; there were tears on her face again. "I don't know if I can do this."

Faith stood up and came to stand next to her at the window. "What is it they say about learning to crawl before you can walk?"

Wiping her eyes, she nodded. "I'm sorry. I'm just scared and confused, and I guess I'm looking for a way out of reality." She looked at Faith and tried a smile. "I'm glad you came."

"So am I. Is there anything you need? Anything I can help you with?" she amended, knowing full well, as Miranda did, that what she needed, she couldn't have.

Miranda took a deep breath. "Actually there is something. Do you think . . . could you teach me to fight?"

She was almost pleased. She'd managed to surprise Faith more than once in one night, a thing unheard of. The Second crossed her arms and considered the question.

"I don't think I'll have time," Faith replied reluctantly. "I'm on duty most of the week, and on call when I'm not on duty—but I can introduce you to someone who can. A specialist, you might say."

"Good. I'd like that."

"Why the sudden interest?"

"I have to learn to take care of myself," Miranda told her, hearing the hollowness in her own voice. "Nobody else is going to do it for me. I've barely left the house in two months. I can't live like this anymore. Maybe if I know I can defend myself I won't be so afraid all the time."

Faith was looking at her keenly, but nodded. "I think you're right. I'll give you her card."

"Thanks." Miranda returned to the couch and sat back down, forcing herself to ask the question she'd had in mind since Faith had knocked on her door. "So . . . how is he?"

"A miserable bastard," she answered, "which I'm sure you knew."

"This is pathetic, isn't it? I sound like a moon-eyed teenage girl. I'm not even really sure how I feel about him, and . . . God, it's even making me sick. Next thing you know I'm going to start writing poetry and wearing too much eyeliner."

A laugh. "It's not so bad. Of the two of you, you're definitely handling it better."

Miranda's eyes fell on the folder of music she'd thrown

to the floor earlier. "Just take care of him for me, would you? You're the only one we can trust."

Faith smiled oddly at the word *we*. "Don't worry," she said. "You have my word."

# Eleven

Miranda's to-do list for the week included finishing her set list, cleaning the bathroom, and murdering Faith.

She stood in front of the unmarked, unlit door in the side of a warehouse building that had tufts of weeds growing up along its foundation, checking and rechecking the card Faith had given her to be sure this was the right address.

Unfortunately it was. Faith had sent her to the scariest part of town on a bus after dark for this with the assurance that it would be worth the trip.

*As soon as I learn how to kick ass, hers is first on the list.*

Screwing up her wavering courage, Miranda knocked on the door and waited.

A minute later, just as she was about to give up and run back to the bus stop as fast as her feet would carry her, a voice demanded, "Password?"

Miranda took a deep breath. "Dingoes ate my baby."

She heard the sounds of several heavy locks shooting back, and the door swung inward to reveal Faith's "specialist."

Miranda blinked.

To all outward appearances she was looking at a teenage girl with a doll-like face coated liberally with eyeliner and mascara. The girl's maroon-painted lower lip was pierced three times with silver spikes, and so were her eyebrow and nose. She wore a surfeit of black leather, including enormous boots covered with buckles. She was even shorter than Miranda, and looked like a stiff wind would blow her over.

She looked Miranda up and down with a skeptical eye, clearly unimpressed, and shook her razor-cut black bob. Her voice was an icy soprano with a hard edge. "You better be glad I owe Faith money. Come on."

Miranda followed her into the building, down a long dark hall that opened into a huge, mostly unfurnished room. The walls were lined with an astonishing array of edged weapons, and at the far end was a complicated-looking panel of switches and dials. It was the kind of room that Miranda would have expected to see lined with mirrors, but of course there were none, just swords, daggers, scary star-shaped things, and wall sconces.

"Um . . . you're Sophie?" Miranda ventured.

"That's me."

"How old are you?"

Sophie rolled her wide brown eyes. "A hundred and forty-eight," she replied. "I got to live back when women couldn't vote, isn't that awesome?"

"How old is . . . I mean . . . how old are you, body-wise?"

Another eye roll. "I came over at fifteen. Now shut up and let me look at you."

Miranda's mouth, halfway through forming another question, snapped closed, and she stood awkwardly in the middle of the room while Sophie made a slow circle around her with her arms crossed.

It hadn't been obvious at first, but watching the vampire move, Miranda could see that her petite build was deceptive, just as Faith's was; Sophie had real muscle on her compact frame and moved with the same uncanny grace as the Elite, a combination of poetry and precision.

She brought to mind a lynx meandering through the forest, tail swaying lazily side to side.

"So I'm supposed to teach a human how to fight like a vampire," Sophie said. "Am I wasting my time?"

"I don't—"

"Stand up straight!" Sophie barked. "Only humans slouch."

"But I *am* human," Miranda pointed out acidly, bristling at the superior tone coming from someone who looked too young to drive . . . but standing up straighter nonetheless.

"Not while you're here. If you want to fight vampires, you have to be more than human."

"I don't really plan on fighting vampires. I just want to protect myself."

Sophie snorted rather indelicately. "What do you think you're protecting yourself from, girl? You get mixed up with the Signets, they paint a target on your head. Anyone who wants to hurt the Prime will go after his people first. Angry little mortals in dark alleys are the least of your problems now."

Miranda felt the familiar sweep of energy that meant Sophie was looking at her with more than just her physical eyes.

"Your shields are good," the vampire noted, "but not good enough. I'm guessing you were taught by, what, a telekinetic?"

"How did you know that?"

"Some people think a shield is a shield. It's not. Whoever trained you didn't think you were going to use your gift in combat. All the gifts have their own flavors and need their own fine-tuning. I can tell your teacher was fucking strong, probably a guy, really old; if I had to be specific I'd say it was Solomon. I can see from the structure he's got you using that he fights a lot, but the way the layers are set up make it easy to reach out to objects, not people. So he throws things."

"I'm an empath," Miranda said defensively. "How am I going to use that in combat?"

"How did you kill those bastards that raped you? It wasn't with your hands, was it? Empathy can be even deadlier than telekinesis if it's strong enough. You can snap a lifeline with it, sure, but you can also cause pain like no other on earth. People can be taught to withstand physical torture, but emotional torture is a whole different critter. Using it won't replace good fighting skills, but it can make you that much more badass."

"And you can teach me that?"

"Fuck yeah. You're in pretty sad shape, but give me six months and I'll have you taking out lower-shelf Elite at least. Give me a year and you'll be able to give Faith a run for her money. You're built like me and her, which is good. We rely on speed and agility, not brute strength. Humans think fighting is just hacking at a hunk of meat until it stops moving. Humans are slow and stupid. While you're here, forget you're human. It'll just get in your way."

Not knowing what else to say, Miranda nodded.

"All right. Let's see how much this is gonna suck."

"Could I ask you a question first?"

Sophie tilted her chin down and looked up at Miranda with barely concealed impatience. "What?"

"Is it a good idea for you to have all that metal in your face if you're in a fight?"

Sophie actually smiled, the sharp points of her canines flashing. "Nobody hits me, baby. Now let's get started."

The woman in the mirror looked calm, capable. Her hair was loose in wild curls and gleamed in the low backstage lights with the aid of the Bed Head product line. She met the green of her own eyes steadily, and if it weren't for the purple smudge beneath the left, she might have looked confident. She absently reached up to run her finger along the scar below her hairline.

The club was packed to capacity. She could hear the crowd as if it were a hundred-armed animal waiting for its dinner, and though she had her barriers up as always, she could feel their anticipation all the way backstage.

She cursed to herself and tried again to cover her black eye with makeup. She was lucky she hadn't injured one of her hands yesterday—certainly the rest of her body felt the stiff and painful aftermath of three hours of being pummeled by a tiny barracuda pixie. If she'd been smart, she would have scheduled their meeting after her performance, not before. Now she was dreading not just playing in front of people again after so long, but having to stand upright for over an hour without dropping her guitar.

Now her to-do list was narrowed to cleaning the bathroom and murdering Faith, but "murdering Faith" had several gold stars next to it in her head.

Assuming tonight went well, it was going to be a busy winter. Sophie wanted to see her twice a week, and had given her a workout regimen as well as several acerbic recommendations about her diet, such as, "If you come in here smelling like pizza next time, I'll kick you in the stomach."

Goddamned vampires.

"Five minutes, Grey," Mel called from outside the curtained nook.

Miranda decided there was nothing more she could do for her eye. She stood up and stretched, grounding quickly before her nerves got the better of her, and took her guitar from its case.

"Okay," she said into the mirror. "Let's do this."

Her reflection nodded as she nodded. She told herself there was determination and strength in her eyes.

She waited in the wings for Mel to announce her, gripping the neck of her guitar tightly. The last time she had stood on this stage had not ended well. She tried to put it out of her mind, but she remembered that one of the men who had attacked her had been in the audience that night.

So had David.

As she walked out on the stage to a roar of applause, she swept the room with her senses, just on the off chance that she might feel a familiar dark presence among the teeming mass of humanity, but there was none.

That was all right. He had promised they'd see each other again, and she knew he wasn't the kind who made promises lightly. He had his work to do, and she had hers.

Smiling out at the audience, she lifted her guitar and struck a chord.

Weeks later the applause and adoration were still ringing in her ears when she left the club after ten o'clock, bag over her shoulder and guitar bumping her butt, and headed for the bus stop.

She was also smiling—no, a more accurate term would be *beaming*. She was still so high off the crowd energy that she could barely keep her feet on the sidewalk.

Yes, yes. Now she remembered why she had started performing in the first place. Those first few long-ago weeks when she had learned what she could do but hadn't let it consume her yet had been some of the happiest of her life. She had left the stage each night feeling like a goddess, or better yet, an artist. She had taken the dross of human emotion and spun it into the gold of harmony.

Miranda laughed to herself. She was even starting to sound as pretentious as an artist.

It wasn't until she had found a seat and the bus lurched away from the curb that it occurred to her she should be afraid.

She should be staring at the floor and fighting off the voices in her head. She should be counting the blocks from club to home and repeating them like a mantra.

Here it was, late December; the weather had finally turned cold, and another hard freeze was forecast for Monday night. She had been back in the city since early

October, and back onstage since Thanksgiving. The first few shows had been hard . . . she had trouble balancing the emotional flow of the audience without losing her shields, and the effort had cost her two-day migraines with accompanying hangovers.

Still, she refused to give up, and after a week, her training started to come back to her. Now she found herself actually excited before a show, and working with real enthusiasm on her original material. She was thinking of debuting the first song at the next gig.

A few days ago a woman had come up to her after the set and asked about representing her. Her card was still in Miranda's wallet, the reality of the slip of stiff paper almost too good to be true; she'd Googled the woman and found out she was legit, and was strongly considering accepting her offer. Denise MacNeil had said that she could get Miranda into at least three more venues and, if she could get a demo made, probably land her a recording contract.

If things kept up, she might end up in the studio by spring. The thought made her beam even wider.

She looked around at the other people on the bus with her, letting her shields thin out just enough that she could assess whether any of them were a threat, but unless the old woman in the walker was hiding a gun, there was nothing to worry about.

Reclaiming her own mind, it turned out, was all she needed to start living her own life.

She looked people in the eye now—sometimes she didn't want to, but she forced herself, to make sure she didn't start to slip again. Most of the time people smiled. Some looked away. Those were the ones to keep an eye on. They were hiding something.

She was grateful to have the rest of the night free. She made it a point never to schedule sessions with Sophie the night after a show; she liked to have some downtime. Plus, whenever she tried to work out after she'd been performing, she was inevitably tired and distracted and

Sophie ended up beating the crap out of her. On other nights, she was finally able to hold her own . . . for a few minutes, anyway. She was far from a warrior, but she was making progress.

Miranda also wanted the night off because there was something she needed to do.

She let the bus carry her past her stop, down Lamar; past the mammoth Whole Foods flagship store, past Book People, past the University of Texas campus . . . all the way up past Thirty-Eighth Street, with a dozen stops in between.

Yanking the stop cord, she swung to her feet and bumped her way past the few people still on the bus. Then she stepped out into the frigid night air, pulling her coat tighter around her, and stood in front of the Travis County Psychiatric Hospital for a long minute, just thinking.

The intake desk was open twenty-four hours. She picked her way along the tall hurricane fence that surrounded the industrial gray buildings, not in any hurry to go inside, but eventually she faced the glass doors of the main lobby and had to make a decision.

When the doors shut behind her, she stopped and grounded to quell the first stirrings of anxiety in her stomach, and she forced twice as much energy as usual into her shields as soon as the whispers began in her head.

She could feel them rubbing against her mind—light fingers of ghostly presence, some crawling with madness, some just . . . empty. Hollow people, scarecrow people, full of nothing but screams . . . how the doctors and nurses could bear it, she couldn't fathom. Maybe they were numb. So many humans were.

For the hundredth time she considered giving up on this little mission and trying proper channels . . . but that would involve filling out endless paperwork, and worse yet, dealing with her father. She'd much rather break the law.

The whole place was government-issue circa 1970, the predominant color hospital green. Everything was dingy despite the pathetic attempts to liven up the place with encouraging posters and announcements on neon paper. There were hardly any patients here anymore; the county facility had given way to a more modern, more politically savvy building farther from downtown that looked more like a school than a concentration camp. This place was slated to close next summer.

A bored-looking young woman sat playing solitaire on the front desk computer, but Miranda walked right past her to the building map. It looked for a second like the receptionist might have noticed her, but Miranda paused, infusing the energy of her shield with what Sophie called a *deflector*, the subtle mental suggestion to look the other way, and the woman went back to her game with a yawn. It was one of the little shielding tricks Miranda had been working on and apparently was one of the primary ways vampires moved through the city unnoticed by humanity when combined with their incredible speed and grace.

Miranda's speed and grace were questionable, but one thing she did have was power.

She scrutinized the map until she found what she was looking for, tucked her guitar case behind a listless potted ficus tree, and walked right down the hallway, her boots clomping purposefully on the linoleum floor. She was still in her stage clothes because they made her feel tough and untouchable: she'd borrowed the look from Sophie and rather liked it, at least for a few hours a night. Black pants, black boots, black corset top with rivets and buckles, heavy silver jewelry, and a lot of makeup she'd retouched after sweating it off onstage . . . all she lacked were the piercings. She'd even invested in a long black coat to sweep around in.

Of course, after an entire show in that getup, she couldn't wait to pry the top off and put on her sweat pants, but in the meantime, it was nice knowing that she looked a little scary.

The hospital's layout was miraculously precise. Most of the government buildings she'd been in had seemed designed by monkeys. She found 48-D without too much trouble.

A security guard was making rounds of the hallways. He was more alert than the receptionist and wouldn't be so easily fooled by her tricks. She would have to be more direct.

She strode right toward him, and he looked totally flabbergasted that a random civilian was wandering the halls of the nuthouse at this hour. "Excuse me, ma'am, this area is off limits—"

She smiled her most winning smile, which wasn't terribly winning, and looked him in the eyes. She had learned how to open her shields only a tiny bit, enough to let selected people in, and how to thin them and change their texture so she could screen out some emotions and read others. It was all energy, all subject to her concentration and will. She reached out to the guard, a balding man of about forty-five whose most pressing desire, aside from getting rid of the troublesome redhead in front of him, was to have a cigarette.

Child's play.

Miranda took delicate hold of that desire with a wisp of her power and tugged at it lightly, saying in a low voice, "It's all right, sir. You're on break. You need to go outside and have a cigarette."

He frowned. He wasn't a terribly strong mind, but he didn't want to lose his job. She didn't want to cause him any trouble, really—she was the one doing wrong, not him. So, she revised her plan, and said, "Go finish your round. I'll be gone when you get back. You won't think of me again, and no one will ever know I was here."

Finish his round—that he could do. He walked off without looking back at her, his steps slow and purposeful as before, the edge of anxiety that arose when he had seen her eroding into the usual boredom of his shift.

Miranda nodded, satisfied. Now she had to hurry.

It was, of course, locked; the medical records department was open only from eight to five on weekdays, and this was a secured file room for old cases, a dumping ground for records from all over the county. It was likely nobody had been in there for a month or more. So much was going digital these days, and ancient files like these were the lumbering dinosaurs that kept getting shoved from one building to another. No one cared much about patients who had been dead for so long. When the building was emptied in a few months, it was likely all these histories would be destroyed, their statute of limitations on usefulness long since passed.

She smiled to herself. Personal medical histories were kept under lock and key here, but in a very literal sense— there was no key card, no electronic pad, no combination. Perhaps the Haven should loan some of its technology to the Department of State Health Services instead of just the Department of Defense.

Miranda dug in her purse for the object Sophie had lent her for this little mission: a lock pick.

Breaking and entering hadn't been on their training agenda, but Sophie had offered to show her how. Sophie's opinion was that a woman should be able to get herself out of any situation she encountered, from a bad date to a prison sentence.

Miranda had wanted to smack the smugness off of Sophie's perfect little face for about three weeks, but once her body stopped complaining about the work and began to respond to all those hours in the gym, she found that she was starting to like, or at least appreciate, her teacher . . . in a smack-the-smugness-off-her-face kind of way.

A few pokes and prods had the door open in a few seconds. She was a quick study.

As she had hoped, the case files were stored alphabetically and identified by the first three letters of the patient's last name, then the first three digits of his or her social security number, then the year of admittance. It didn't take long to find the one she needed.

She left everything as she had found it, tucked the

folder into her bag, and locked the door behind her, walking back out past the receptionist, who never once looked up, even when Miranda paused to retrieve her guitar.

Flushed with success and the thrill of a teenage hoodlum leaving his first graffiti tag, Miranda climbed onto the last bus up Lamar and hugged her bag tightly to her the whole ride home.

She checked her watch as she made it back to her apartment complex: midnight, and sure enough, Faith was waiting for her at the front door of her unit. The Second flashed her a conspiratorial grin, and then her eyes widened.

"Whoa," she said. "That's some outfit."

Miranda looked down at herself. "Stage clothes," she explained. "I was nervous about this and figured if I looked like a serial killer people wouldn't mess with me."

Faith laughed. "Actually you look like a vampire."

"Is that a compliment?"

"Absolutely."

"Thanks, then." Miranda fished out her keys, let them both in, and set her guitar in its usual spot, hanging her coat by the door. Faith did the same using the second hook. The apartment was blessedly warm.

"Give me a minute to change," Miranda said. "There's beer in the fridge."

A few minutes later, clad in something much more comfortable although not exactly impressive, Miranda plopped down next to Faith on the couch with folder in one hand and a bottle of water in the other.

"How did it go? Any problems?" Faith asked.

"No." Miranda shook her head. "It was almost too easy. That invisibility stuff Sophie's been teaching me is amazing. I felt like a secret agent. And a criminal, which I am. It's funny—I never even broke the speed limit until I met all of you. Now I've got breaking and entering in a government facility and theft of private records to add to my voluntary manslaughter rap."

"You should tell your sister about it next time she e-mails."

Miranda almost inhaled her water laughing. She slit the sticker holding the file shut and opened it gingerly, though the paper wasn't nearly old enough to fall apart.

The first thing she saw was her mother's face.

"Oh, God," she whispered, taking the photo out of the paper clip that held it and holding it up so Faith could see. "She looks just like I remember."

"She looks like you," Faith noted. "Right down to the big sad eyes."

Miranda stared at her mother, her fingers touching the picture's face as if there were real skin there. She had been beautiful, once. Her red hair was cropped short around her face to manage the curls, but it was the same odd color as Miranda's. Her eyes were the same oak-leaf green, and though she was smiling in the photograph, there was, as Faith had said, sorrow behind her eyes.

The next photo was her hospital intake photo, disturbingly like a mug shot. There was no smile in this one. All the light had gone out of her face, and the last bit of life had burned out of her eyes. She stared blankly toward the left of the camera, looking distracted and distant, her skin sagging, dark circles heavy under her eyes. She reminded Miranda of herself the first time she'd looked in a mirror after returning to Austin.

Miranda's eyes ached with tears as she paged through the first few pages of forms, all filled out on the first night her father had taken her mother to the hospital.

"Marilyn Suzanne Grey," Faith read over her arm. "Preliminary diagnosis . . . paranoid schizophrenic . . . delusions . . . unresponsive to medication . . ."

A lot of what she read was medical and psychiatric jargon, but a picture began to form: About six months before she was sent away, Marilyn Grey began to hear voices. She claimed she could read minds, and though her knowledge seemed uncannily accurate, her behavior became more and more bizarre. She said the voices were getting louder, drowning her own thoughts out.

One evening she accompanied her husband to an office Christmas party, and after one drink began screaming— she claimed that the corporate president had molested his son, and made a variety of other accusations against personnel. Her husband, Miranda's father, had been fired from his job, humiliated.

"She was like me," Miranda said softly. "She was gifted and couldn't shield, and nobody ever taught her how. This would have been me . . . it almost was. It took longer because I had music to help control it, but . . . this could have been me."

She imagined her mother locked away in a tiny room, staring off into space as the minds of all the crazy people in the hospital clamored into hers. As surely as Miranda's body had been raped, so had her mother's mind, constantly, until she just gave up and stopped eating. The hospital, so helpful, had put her on a feeding tube, but Marilyn had somehow gotten her hands on a bottle of sleeping pills and put an end to their efforts.

Her remains had been dutifully claimed by her husband. He had buried her here in Austin and then moved to Dallas with his two daughters.

"Does it say where she's buried?" Faith asked.

Miranda nodded, swallowing, and pointed to an address. "I'll go there tomorrow," she said, sniffling. "I'll go before my session with Sophie. I'll take flowers. No . . . I'll take rosemary."

"Why rosemary?"

"Mama used to read Shakespeare to me. Her favorite character was Ophelia, and there's this line in *Hamlet* where Ophelia says rosemary is for remembrance. Poor Mama . . . God, poor Mama. I wish . . . I wish she were still alive. I wish I could have helped her, or even just held her hand and told her I knew how it felt."

She closed the file but kept the smiling picture of her mother out. She was pretty sure she had a frame in the closet it would fit. It was the only family picture she had, or wanted.

"I think she would be proud of you," Faith said. "You could have ended up like her, but you didn't. Now you're living on your own and getting along just fine. Hell, in a couple of years you could be on tour and selling millions of CDs. Or you could be . . ."

Miranda interrupted sharply, "I could be a lot of things."

Faith made an I-know-better face but didn't contradict her. "So this means you passed Sophie's assignment. She should be pleased."

"God only knows what she'll have me do next. She said she's going to start me on weapons this week. Imagine— me, with a weapon! I told her I'm going to chop someone's kneecaps off."

"I doubt that. She says you're doing fine."

"You talk to her about me?"

Faith grinned impishly at her expression. "I just e-mailed her yesterday to check on your progress. She said, and I quote, 'She doesn't suck.' Coming from her that's high praise indeed."

Miranda went from outrage at the idea of the two vampires discussing her performance to the warm glow of pride—Faith wasn't kidding about Sophie's penchant for criticism, but it meant that when she gave a compliment, it was a real one, and a rare thing.

"You haven't . . . you haven't told David what I'm doing, have you? He'd just worry."

"No. We don't talk about you at all. In fact we don't talk much, period, these days. He's been hell-bent on finishing the network and getting it installed. He's a man possessed, and he looks like absolute hell, but you know how he is when he gets the bit between his teeth about something." Faith saw her look and added, "He's feeding, and sleeping. I make him. But that's about it. There've been two more attacks this past month, and he feels like it's a race against time."

"I should be there," Miranda muttered. "I could help. I could help track them down with the things Sophie's teaching me."

Faith's eyes narrowed. "Don't get any vigilante ideas in your head, missy. The Prime sent you away from the Haven to keep you from getting mixed up in this. He'd have my ass on a platter—and Lindsay's—if you got in trouble."

"Lindsay?"

The Second cleared her throat. "The Elite who is absolutely not keeping guard over your apartment at a discreet distance."

Miranda rolled her eyes. "Oh, like I didn't know about her. She follows me everywhere. You think I don't know when a vampire's tailing me now? I've had to stop myself from waving at her. I'd hate for her to feel like she's not doing her job."

Faith's smile returned. "She won't hear it from me."

"Whatever. But you know, you still haven't told me how you know Sophie. Did you meet in California?"

She started to reply, but suddenly her com beeped. Faith frowned and said, "This is Faith."

*"Second, your presence is required at a disturbance at Westgate and Porter."*

"Situation code?"

*"Alpha Seven."*

"Shit," Faith said. "Has the Prime been called in?"

*"Not yet."*

"I'll do it. I'll meet you there in twenty."

*"Elite Twelve out."*

Miranda's stomach flipped. Alpha Seven was the code for a body found: human, suspected murder by vampire. The insurgents had struck again.

Faith held Miranda's eyes as she said into her com, "Star-one."

Her heart did a pirouette in her chest at the low, familiar voice. *"I'm on my way, Faith."*

The Second rose quickly and grabbed her coat. "I have to go," she said apologetically.

"I know. I understand. Just tell me what happens, okay? E-mail me."

"I will. Stay safe, Miranda. And remember what I said—don't do anything stupid. These woods are dark and dangerous."

Miranda stood in the doorway watching Faith literally break into a run as she hit the sidewalk; in a matter of seconds her shape seemed to blur and vanish.

She shut and locked the door, and though the thought of another murder was at the forefront of her mind, part of her had to admit that it made her feel better to have heard David's voice again, even just five words to someone else.

The woman had died trying to save her child.

They would have killed him first and made her watch, and while she screamed and begged them to take her instead, and fought like a desperate animal to tear free of their grip, they sucked the little boy dry and drew the Seal of Auren with a knife into his tiny pale chest, then turned on her.

An icy cold front had hit that week, and the boy was wearing a San Antonio Spurs jacket over his gray turtleneck. A knit cap with the Spurs logo was still on his little tawny head.

At least, based on the small amount of blood that had run from the carving, the child had already been dead when it was drawn. As small as he was it wouldn't have taken long, and it was unlikely the child had been in much pain.

David stood over the bodies silently while the Elite searched the scene. He kept a tight rein and an iron shield over his emotions, but no one dared approach him.

Faith knelt beside the two—posed deliberately with

the woman's arms around her ten-year-old and his shirt and jacket torn open—and dug into the woman's purse for her ID. "Kimberly Mason," she said quietly. "And Charlie." She removed a small photo and held it up, showing Kimberly, Charlie, and another woman smiling for the camera at a lakeside picnic, probably that very summer. "This is Susan Davis, her partner."

The link among the victims had arisen after he'd put a team on researching their identities: most of them were gay or lesbian; one was transgendered; one woman worked at Planned Parenthood. The rest were Jewish. It was classic Blackthorn, purging the world of perceived sin via a blatant disregard of the Sixth Commandment.

He wondered if Susan Davis was still waiting for her wife and son to come home tonight. Was she worried yet? Time of death had only been three hours earlier. There had been movie stubs on the victims, and the latest Pixar film was playing at the Westgate Cinema—were they due home yet, or had they been on their way to grab dinner?

"The police are on their way," Faith added. "They'll handle next of kin."

He could just imagine that. This was Texas. The police would look for someone else besides Susan Davis to call, and it was possible that she would end up hearing from an estranged relative that her world had just come to an end.

Children tasted young and sweet and full of life. They were so innocent and still so full of possibility. Their minds and hearts were still unjaded by decades of grinding reality. But they were dangerous—addictive— and tended to bring down the law much faster than dead adults. The drive of the species was to protect its young.

The little boy had blue eyes just like his mother.

Suddenly the Prime felt very, very old, and very tired.

In thirty-six hours there would be a sensor network covering the entire Austin metropolitan area that read the heat signatures of every living thing that passed through it. It was keyed specifically to follow the lower body temps of vampires and could track their movements, creating a

near-real-time grid of the city accurate to a single block.
The last thousand sensors were being installed tonight,
and after a day and a half of calibration and final tests, the
whole thing would go live . . .

. . . too late to save Kimberly and Charlie Mason.

The Elite all froze when he moved. He stepped forward and went to one knee next to Faith, then reached
over and closed first the child's eyes, then the woman's.

David looked up at the others, and when he spoke
it was calmly, firmly, and with deadly purpose. "As of
tonight," he said, "we are at war."

# Twelve

Scott had been single for two days, and there was a condom burning a hole in his pocket. Restless, he haunted the bars all night, looking for somebody, anybody, to take home who didn't remind him of Kenny. No blond hair, no blue eyes, no skinny soccer players. The perfect thing would be a huge hairy top in biker leather, but those were thin on the ground in Austin.

He'd never been good at the bar scene. He and Kenny had met at the library, for fuck's sake, both reaching for the same Proust. It turned out they were in different sections of the same lit class at UT. The pretense of being "study buddies" had lasted about an hour before they were screwing like mad rabbits. Scott had only been out since he'd moved here for college. Kenny was a senior and had a Tantric master's gift for giving head.

Scott left the Torch Song half-drunk and irritable, the remains of his third—fourth?—martini leaving him a little green around the gills.

"Fuck this," he mumbled, digging in his jacket pocket for his cigarettes. He'd started again about an hour after he'd come home from class early and found Kenny in the shower with that bony jerk-off from the lacrosse team. At least now there wouldn't be anybody bitching about the taste of tobacco on his breath.

It was a cold, nasty night, promising sleet. He was starting to really hate Texas; it was unbearably hot in the summer and messy and wet in winter. Spring and fall each lasted about four gorgeous days. He'd spent the last warm afternoons of the year out at the lake with Kenny and his friends. They'd skinny-dipped and made out passionately, smelling of cocoa butter and sex.

He puffed the cigarette angrily and stalked down Fourth Street, ducking his head against the damp wind. What was anyone doing out on a night like this? Hell, what was he doing out? Even if he did get laid, it was so cold he'd probably get his dick stuck to someone's tongue.

His car was in a paid lot a few blocks away, and though in the back of his mind he knew he probably shouldn't be driving, he didn't much care—the streets were virtually empty.

He came around the corner of the Spaghetti Warehouse, and started, gasping. "Shit! I'm sorry, I didn't see you."

The young woman standing in front of him tilted her head to one side, her brown hair falling limply into her too-bright eyes. "No problem."

He stepped to one side to let her pass, feeling a little uneasy under her unwavering gaze, and she continued to stare at him as he started walking again. There was another reason to transfer schools: Austin was full of freaks. Worse yet, they were proud of it.

He heard a footstep behind him and turned, head snapping around hard enough to make him dizzy.

The girl was standing a foot away from him.

"Is there . . . do you need help?" he ventured. She was starting to really creep him out—she looked like she was on drugs, or like she hadn't slept in a year. She was incredibly pale, with hooded eyes that seemed hyper-aware, and her body barely seemed to move as she stared at him.

"Actually," she said, "I'm hungry. How about we have a bite?"

He forced a smile. "Wrong tree, honey. And worst pickup line ever, by the way. Excuse me."

Her hand shot out and seized the arm of his jacket, and he tried to wrench away, but her grip was like iron. To the left and right he heard more footsteps, and before he knew what was happening he was surrounded.

*Oh God, I'm gonna get bashed. I should've called a cab. Where's my phone? Should I scream? Oh God.*

They half dragged, half carried him off the street toward a shadowy area next to a building that was roped off for construction. He tried to fight—he was in good shape, he should have at least been able to throw off the girl—but they were insanely strong, and there were three of them. The darkness beyond the building yawned at him, and some instinct told him if they got him over there, he'd never come back out.

A hand clamped over his mouth just as he took a breath to shout for help.

The only coherent thought he could seem to summon was the Hail Mary. He hadn't said it in at least five years. Those Rosary beads were long gone.

*Please, Jesus, please, they can have my wallet, just please don't let me die . . .*

He struggled again as the shadows surrounded him, and whimpered desperately.

"Shut up, faggot," one of them hissed. "If you're good, we'll make it quick."

Another one laughed. "Right."

They pushed him to the ground, one grabbing his face and wrenching his chin back to expose his throat.

"I'm first this time," the girl said with a wicked smile. To his horror, as he watched, her teeth started to grow longer, curving down over her tongue.

Raw fear made him writhe as hard as he could, which only made them laugh. Their ghostly white faces grinned down at him like baby demons.

Then, suddenly, everything . . . stopped.

The three heads hovering over him snapped up,

nostrils flaring wide as if to catch a strange scent. The girl's fingernails dug into his arm until he could feel himself bleeding, but the pain came to him from a distance—his heart had all but stopped in his chest, and time had slowed to a crawl.

Something yanked one of the two men up off Scott and hauled him backward, flinging him into the bright orange pylons that tumbled over like bowling pins.

The other two leapt up, growling like animals, but in the next second there was the sound of metal singing through the air, and with a gushing spray of blood, the second man's head flew off.

Scott screamed and rolled backward away from the blood, and though it mostly missed him, he felt hot droplets strike his face. He scrambled away toward the opposite wall and curled up in a ball, bile climbing the back of his throat.

He heard the girl's strangled cry, and he looked up in time to see her beheaded as well.

There were five people in the alley with him now, all dressed identically in black uniforms of some kind. They all had swords.

Swords.

He'd heard that trauma could make people insane.

One of the figures separated itself from the rest, cleaning the bloodied blade of his sword on the shirt of one of the dead . . . people. He was dressed differently than the others, in a long black coat, and his eyes were a strange deep blue ringed with silver around the irises. He carried himself as if he were their leader, and indeed, as he scanned the wall above the bodies, his voice had the clear authority of a seasoned military officer.

"Paint it here," he said. "Leave them beneath it. Elite Nine, see to the boy."

Scott found himself being helped to his feet by a brawny, dark-skinned man whose grip was surprisingly gentle. The man set him on his feet like he weighed nothing at all and looked him over, and though his eyes were as alien and cold as those of the girl, he made absolutely no move to threaten Scott. "He's not hurt, Sire," the man called back over his shoulder. "This time we beat them."

The dark man, the one with the coat, turned his head slightly in acknowledgment. "Good. Give him cab fare and send him home."

"Wait a minute," Scott stammered. His tongue was thick and unresponsive in his mouth. "What the fuck is going on? Who are you people? I mean, thank you for saving me, don't get me wrong, but . . ."

The dark man looked at him for a moment, and Scott felt another ripple of fear.

He approached Scott in almost an arc, the way Scott had seen horse whisperers approach skittish colts on TV, and came to stand close by . . . too close. Scott found himself staring, his breath catching, at the weird necklace the man wore, a heavy pendant set in silver. The stone caught some light that Scott couldn't see and seemed to glow.

"What's your name?" the man asked, voice just loud enough to carry. It was the kind of voice that traveled directly from Scott's ears to his cock, and even through the fear he felt his jeans tighten.

"Scott Summers," he answered. "Like on *X-Men*."

"Well, Scott, here's what you're going to do," the man said, leaning even closer so that all Scott could see were the endless pools of his eyes. His voice became hypnotic, rhythmic. "You're going to go home and throw your coat in the garbage, and in the morning it will be as if this never happened."

"But . . ."

"Repeat what I just said, Scott."

"I'm . . . I'm going to go home and throw my coat in the garbage, and in the morning it will be as if this never happened."

"Very good. I'm sorry you had to see this. It's not your concern."

"It's not my concern."

The man smiled. It was a blindingly beautiful smile. "Is there anything you need besides a cab, Scott Summers?"

Scott smiled back, his world full of blue eyes. "Your phone number?"

A chuckle, low and beguiling. "Tempting. But you're better off going home alone tonight."

He walked away. The large man who had helped Scott to his feet guided him out of the alley, over to where a Yellow Cab was already waiting. "Wow," Scott muttered, twisting his head to watch the retreating form of the man in the long black coat.

His guide laughed. "I think the saying goes, 'That's too much car for you.'"

Scott shrugged, allowed himself to be bundled into the cab, and was already asleep before the car had pulled away from the curb.


The sensor network was years ahead of its time, technologically speaking, but it wasn't the most attractive thing in the world. He'd essentially cobbled it together out of the existing resources at the Haven, not wanting to waste time making it pretty while lives were at stake.

The Prime sat in his chair in the workroom, going over the latest diagnostics on his laptop. Things had been a bit turbulent since they'd gone live—the grid worked, yes, but during periods of high activity in the city, like rush hour or Saturday night downtown, sectors had a nasty habit of overloading from too much data and crashing the whole network. The processing power to handle that much information simply didn't exist.

So he'd built it.

The hard part was getting the entire thing coordinated, a process similar to trying to time all the city's traffic lights. Each of the thousands of sensors was tied into a hub, and those hubs routed back to the Haven. Eventually he'd be able to link his entire territory this way via satellite, but for now he had to be content with the Austin metropolitan area.

The thing that drove him, however, was that it was working. War had come to the city in the form of a symbol painted in vampire blood over the corpses of three insurgents: the Seal of Prime David Solomon. The message was clear, and it was heard.

He hadn't figured they would go gently into the darkness, and they didn't. The attacks tripled in frequency. The difference was that since that first night there had been no human fatalities.

The rebels had no idea what hit them. They had their victim chosen and isolated, but before they could put a scratch on the human, they were surrounded by Elite, all under the order to show no mercy. They were executed without question and without trial. Due process was for mortals. This was the Shadow World.

He had trained two of the administrative staff to monitor the network, and they took shifts, but regardless he had reports sent to his phone every ten minutes. The network took readings every three minutes and immediately reported every single vampire moving in the city. Any group of more than two on the streets had a patrol unit in its wake in ninety seconds. Any vampire approaching a human outside a known hunting ground was detained and questioned. The insurgents rarely worked alone, but he wanted it absolutely clear: The vampires of Austin were being watched. His eyes were everywhere and his reach was endless.

It was only a matter of time before they grew desperate and either tried something stupid or slipped up. Taking the heads of their henchmen wasn't enough for David. He wanted the Blackthorn themselves. He wanted their blood spilled, and he wanted his own hands to spill it.

"Have you fed?"

He nodded absently. "Yes."

"Are you lying?"

"No."

For some reason Faith had taken it upon herself to act as his babysitter. He didn't mind most of the time, but he hadn't been terribly patient with her, or anyone, since autumn.

"What did you have?"

He stopped what he was doing and looked up. His neck hurt from being bent toward the monitor for so long; he knew she was about to tell him to take a break, and for once he was inclined to agree. "I had Esther bring me a bag. Ask her yourself."

He noticed she was holding what looked like a newspaper; when he raised an eyebrow at it, she bit her lip a second before saying, "I thought you might want to see this. It's this week's *Chronicle*."

"The entertainment newspaper? Since when do I care about that?"

"Since now," Faith replied, opening the folded periodical and tossing it onto the table in front of him.

He sat back. "Miranda."

The slightly grainy black-and-white picture showed her sitting on the edge of a stage, her guitar in her lap. She was smiling and looking directly at the camera.

He stared at it silently for a while, and then said, "She looks happy."

Faith shrugged. "She's making quite a name for herself. There's an interview."

He tore his eyes away from Miranda's face and planted them firmly back on the computer. "I'll read it later. I have more work to do."

He could practically hear Faith shaking her head, but she left him alone obligingly enough. He tried to go back to his calibrations, but he could see the picture in his peripheral vision, Miranda's lovely pale face fixed on him, eyes whose color was still burned into his memory watching him in shades of gray.

David started to shut the paper, but he couldn't help seeing the header beneath the image:

**Rising Stars of Austin**

Giving up, he turned away from the monitor and picked up the paper. There were profiles of three hot new acts: Gerry Ford, a band called 3 Tequila Floor, and Miranda Grey. Some of the facts in Miranda's profile made David smile, and others made his heart want to crack into slivers inside his chest.

Birthplace: Rio Verde, Texas, "though Austin will always be my hometown."

Favorite instrument: "My first love is my Martin 12-string, but not long ago I got to play a Bösendorfer Imperial Grand, and I think may have found the love of my life."

Genre: Eclectic, more or less. "Well, I curse a lot and I don't sing about how much my life sucks without a man. I think music should be about creating something beautiful out of even the worst of humanity. Whatever genre that is, I'm it."

Plans to record: "I'm hoping to go into the studio this summer, which will be a new experience. I think I'll always be more of a live performer, though. The audience's energy is the greatest inspiration I could ever find."

Favorite Austin restaurant and local beverage: "Take me out to the Texican Café for their frozen margaritas and veggie fajitas and I'm all yours."

Response to rumors that have her dating the drummer for 3 Tequila: "No offense meant to any of the guys I've met in the last few months, but . . . hell no. I've been off the market for a while now. I'm waiting for someone extraordinary to catch up with me, and until then, I'm not going to settle for less."

David didn't realize how badly his hands were shaking until the last paragraph was impossible to read.

He pushed his chair back from the table and left the server room, taking the *Chronicle* with him back to his suite. He was still staring at her picture and barely nodded to Samuel as he passed.

At his desk, he took out a pair of scissors and cut the picture and interview out of the paper, then dropped the rest into the recycling bin. He crossed the room to the locked cabinet.

Inside, in addition to the Queen's Signet and everything else he kept safe, was a leather-bound copy of Shakespeare's comedies; he opened it and tucked the clipping inside, where it rested along with several others like it, mostly paragraph-long announcements of her performances. This was the first one to have a picture with it.

He carefully closed the book and started to lock it away, but one of the clippings slipped out and fluttered to the floor like a fallen leaf. He placed the book on its shelf and bent to retrieve the paper.

He frowned. It wasn't a newspaper clipping. It looked like a page from a lined journal torn out and hastily folded.

His name was written on it in hurried but precise script.

David shut the cabinet and took the note to his chair by the fireplace. Esther had kindly added extra logs to the blaze to combat the icy January night, and she'd thrown a few sprigs of rosemary in for the scent. It occurred to him that Christmas had passed several weeks ago. He'd been buried in his work, but he vaguely remembered most of the Elite having the night off for something.

He didn't want to open the note, but he knew he had no choice. His fingers were already unfolding the paper.

The scent that wafted up from the note would have knocked him over if he'd been standing. A thousand blades of longing stabbed him.

*Dear David,*

*I'm going to make you promise I'll see you again, but I won't say why. I may not even admit it to myself for a while. But if it's ever safe . . . come to me. If it takes fifty years, I don't care. Come to me. Maybe by then I'll be ready to tell you what I'm too scared to say tonight.*

*Thank you for everything. I'll miss you. I know your life is long but please don't forget me.*

*~Miranda*

He lifted the paper to his lips, closing his eyes, just inhaling the fading wisps of her presence for a moment.

"Soon," he said to the empty room. "I will see you soon."

Miranda's fists pounded into the punching bag, each strike sending a cloud of chalk, or possibly dust, into the air. She ducked backward and kicked, causing the bag to shudder and, on the other side of it, Sophie to adjust her stance to hold on.

"Harder!" the vampire ordered. "Move your feet!"

A few minutes later Sophie stopped her, and Miranda stood panting, sweat running down her face and neck in rivulets. Her tank top was soaked, and she was burning up despite the fact that it was about thirty-four degrees outside and not much warmer in the studio.

"All right," Sophie said, walking over to the electrical panel and flipping several switches. Some of the lights dimmed and others brightened until the entire room was flooded in simulated moonlight. Then Sophie snatched a pair of crossed swords from the wall and handed one to Miranda hilt first.

Miranda automatically fell into a ready stance, and she sensed Sophie's approval. She knew that Sophie held back with her—she had to—but it seemed lately that she'd been gradually increasing the force of her attacks, so much so that Miranda went home after every session bruised and sore and cursing like she had their first week.

She didn't ask why Sophie was pushing her so hard. She didn't ask Sophie questions; she did as Sophie said and figured out her own answers one step at a time. It was a maddening method, but an effective one, sort of the anti-Socrates.

"Time for the inspirational power chords," Sophie observed. "Do you want me to sing 'Eye of the Tiger'?"

"You're too young to remember the eighties," Miranda retorted, earning a snort.

"Fuck, girl, I barely remember *my* eighties," Sophie shot back. "I went through magic mushrooms like Super Mario."

With that, she dove in, sword flying; Miranda did her best to parry, making up for the second's lapse of attention by spinning out of the way. She brought up her blade as she turned, meeting Sophie's swing with the loud clang of metal on metal.

The sword was familiar in her hand and, according to Sophie, was balanced just right for her size. She didn't know much about weapons, but she knew it wasn't nearly as dangerous as half the objects hanging on the walls; it was a step up from the wooden one she'd started on, though, which Sophie said actually made her more nervous than steel, what with the whole stake-through-the-heart thing. Nevertheless, wood was safer for a human than something with an edge. The blade she was using now was relatively dull.

The end was a foregone conclusion, of course. Sophie knocked the sword out of her hand, spun around, and kicked her off her feet; a second later Miranda felt the usual pressure of the vampire's booted foot on her neck.

Standing on a fallen opponent's neck was apparently symbolic among their kind, a show of dominance; the Elite hadn't used it because, philosophically speaking, they were all friends. Miranda had never seen any of them fight an actual enemy. Cutting their heads off didn't exactly count.

"I yield," Miranda panted.

Sophie stepped back, lifting her foot and letting her struggle to her feet. The diminutive woman's expression was as calculating as always. "Not awful," she pronounced. "You stayed on your feet for four more seconds this time. Keep it up and you might actually beat me in about a hundred years."

"Thanks a shitload, Mr. Miyagi."

She let Miranda take a break for once, and Miranda gulped down half a bottle of water and sank into one of the folding chairs on the room's perimeter. Sophie, nary a hair out of place, wiped the blades of both swords and hung them back in their spots.

"If you're such a great warrior, why don't you work for the Prime?" Miranda asked.

"You have a piss-poor memory. Remember what I said about getting involved with Signets? You work for the Prime, you follow his orders and end up taking a stake to the chest before your time. Besides, if I joined I'd have to work my way up through the ranks and what, play second fiddle to someone else when I could be doing my own thing? I'm not really what you'd call a team player."

"Good point." Miranda yanked the elastic from her hair and smoothed it out to pull back again. "Lucky for you they don't have a draft, what with a war on and all."

"War is for people who believe in something. Me, I believe in drinking blood, fighting, and fucking, in that order. I outlived Auren and I'll outlive Solomon, too."

Miranda felt the urge to do something like cross herself. Obviously Sophie saw the flash of anger on her face, because she laughed merrily.

"Oh, sorry, I forgot, Your Highness." Sophie bowed theatrically, then dodged the empty water bottle thrown at her head. When she straightened, she looked Miranda in the eye, suddenly serious. "You're not just doing this for him, are you?"

"No," Miranda said without having to think. "Look, I don't have any control over the war. It could go on longer than I live. I'm not going to lie around on a chaise longue waiting for my prince to come rescue me from my tower. And if he were the kind of guy who'd ask me to, well, he could go fuck himself anyway."

Now Sophie gave her a rare, genuine smile. "Atta girl. Now get up—we've got to do something about your footwork."

Feeling like she'd passed some kind of test, Miranda smiled back and did as she was told.


Kat had been out of town for more than a month, so the look on her face when she saw Miranda wasn't entirely surprising.

"Holy Christ on a tortilla," the blonde said. "You look awesome!"

Miranda laughed and fell into step beside her. "Welcome back. How was Beaumont?"

"Hell, of course. I hate Houston. Even in the middle of January the place feels like a swamp, and I got stared at from the minute I got off the plane. Dreads and tattoos aren't the norm over there, did you know?"

"No kidding."

"Seriously, you look great—have you been working out?"

"Yeah. A lot. I got a personal trainer."

"Damn, girl. I said you should take a self-defense class, not turn yourself into Linda Hamilton from *Terminator 2*."

Miranda made a face. "I don't look anything like that. It's been a month, Kat. I haven't changed that much."

As she said the words, though, Miranda wondered if that was true. She had gained back all the weight she'd lost when she started drowning in her gift, but at least some of that was muscle—she was working out almost every day and all her spare time was devoted to music. She ate like a horse, but to avoid Sophie's wrath, she avoided most of the junk that she'd stuffed in her mouth the first month back in Austin. She was feeling remarkably well. It was possible that Kat was reacting to her aura more than her physical appearance. That, she knew, was very different than a few months ago.

They walked up the sidewalk toward Kerbey Lane Café, one of their old haunts from college and a popular all-night eatery for the entire city. Miranda had eaten her way through a thousand plates of scrambled eggs and pancakes in the battered green booths of Kerbey and downed about a million cups of coffee during finals. Kat had been with her for many of those cups.

"Okay," Kat said, pulling her to a halt before they reached the building. "Um . . . please don't be mad."

Dread. "God, Kat, what did you do?"

"Well, remember that guy I was telling you about, Drew? The teacher?"

"Tell me you didn't."

Kat grimaced. "We were working together on starting the center in Beaumont, and I told him how great you are, and he really wanted to meet you, so I kind of invited him."

Miranda punched her lightly on the arm—well, she thought it was lightly, but Kat said "Ow!" and flinched. "Kat, I can't believe you! You know why I don't want to date anybody right now!"

"So don't date," Kat insisted. "Just be friends. Nobody's going to force you to hop in bed with the guy. I just think you need to get out more for stuff that's not playing guitar or lifting weights. I just . . . I worry about you, sugarbean. You get all obsessed about things and you . . . get weird and disappear."

The caring in Kat's voice eased Miranda's aggravation somewhat, and she relented enough to say, "Okay, okay. I won't run screaming. I'll meet the guy. But I'm not dating him. And if he ends up having a swastika tattoo like that guy you tried to fix me up with two years ago—"

"I had no idea! I just thought he was prematurely bald!"

"—I am going to kill you," she finished. "Come on."

Miranda steeled herself as she saw the figure waiting for them outside the café. She rolled her eyes inwardly—anyone with brains would have gone inside, where it wasn't fifty below.

"Hey!" Kat was saying. "What are you doing out here? You should have gone inside!"

The guy turned around, and Miranda froze. For just a breath, she thought she was looking at David.

He had black hair, and was slender, and wore a black jacket, but as soon as he moved, the similarity ended. There was no preternatural grace, no nobility; just the slightly awkward posture of a man who was nervous about meeting a woman. His features were more angular, too, and his eyes, though blue, were pale and had a gray undertone.

Miranda's heart still hammered. She had been ready to believe that split-second impression . . . she had wanted to believe.

"Hi," he said, offering a hand. "I'm Drew. You must be Miranda."

Miranda shook his hand firmly. "Guilty as charged."

She made up her mind to be friendly, and over the course of dinner and dessert, she decided to approve of him, at least conditionally. He was well mannered and well spoken, thoughtful, and definitely handsome; he knew music and was enthusiastic about it, avidly listening to her talk about performing. He even had a decent sense of humor.

Kat kept the conversation light, steering around anything potentially hazardous like Miranda's entire history, her family, or where she'd been last summer. It wasn't too difficult; since the interview in the *Chronicle*, she'd been recognized in public once or twice, and anyone remotely interested in the Austin scene had at least heard her name by now.

Drew paid for dinner and insisted on walking Miranda home when Kat begged off—Kat's old heap of a car was in the shop again and she had to hurry to catch the bus or she'd be stranded on South Lamar.

Drew, it turned out, rode a bike everywhere, but in the ghastly late-winter weather he'd taken the bus. She added that to the approval list: no gas-guzzling car, but he was a licensed driver, which was always handy.

"Look, I'm sorry Kat's been trying to throw me at you," Drew said, walking alongside her.

"It's okay," Miranda replied. "She just wants me to be happy, and she's really fond of you. She's played matchmaker as long as I've known her. She loves seeing people fall in love."

"Well, that's just it. I mean, I just got out of a long-term relationship with April, my last girlfriend, and I'm not . . . I mean, I think you're beautiful, and you seem like a really fascinating person, but I don't know if I want to go there yet, you know? And Kat said you'd had some stuff a long time ago and you aren't much into guys, so I thought it might be safe to get to know each other, be friends. Then someday maybe more, but no pressure."

Miranda looked at him, marveling. "Are you sure you're straight?"

"One hundred percent."

She nodded. "Okay, Drew, I'll tell you this, then. What Kat's talking about . . . it wasn't that long ago. I got hurt, and it left scars."

"Literally or figuratively?"

"Both." She paused in her walking and lifted the hair off her forehead, showing him the white line.

"You're shivering," Drew said. "Here, take my scarf."

She started to protest, but he seemed genuinely concerned with no ulterior motive, so she took the proffered garment. It was hand-knitted and warm, and even one of her favorite colors, dark red. "Thanks. This is nice—where'd you get it?"

"My grandmother made it for me. She lives in Florida and she's always worried about me being cold."

Miranda smiled. "Must be nice."

Drew grinned. "Yeah, it is. I miss her a lot."

They reached Miranda's complex, which was conveniently close to Kerbey, and she said, rather than inviting him in, "So . . . in the spirit of being friends, how about you come to my show tomorrow night? I'll get them to comp both you and Kat at the door."

Drew smiled and nodded, suddenly clumsy in his excitement. "That would be great. Mel's, right? Eight o'clock? I'll see you then."

Miranda let herself into her apartment, sighing out of her outerwear, hanging Drew's scarf on the hook under her coat. She'd have to return it to him tomorrow. It was best not to lead him on, even subtly. Friends was fine . . . friends was, in fact, very nice. It had been years since she'd had someone to talk music with, and even longer than that since the friend had been male. She needed to relearn how to relate to the opposite sex even on a purely social level instead of arguing with herself whether to cower in fear.

Drew was sweet, charming, and touchingly human. Totally harmless to her inner senses, and easy on her eyes.

He was also safe. She would never get that close to him, never be afraid of his groping hands, because she would never let him get that far with her. She wouldn't have to worry about him hurting her, as long as she was honest and forthright. She wouldn't lure him into a false paradise with promises of apples. If he wanted to admire the trees, that was fine.

She also knew just from sizing him up tonight that if push came to shove, she could kill him bare-handed.

It was a disturbingly comforting thought.

Yes, Drew was safe. Drew was safe because he was human, and because she had already decided no human man would ever touch her again. The doors to her body and her heart were already closed and locked, and she would give the key to only one man, perhaps someday . . . perhaps never . . . but all the same, she didn't care about falling in love, or getting married, or any of that, any-more. It was too late for mortal men to stake any sort of claim to her affections. If she grew old and died alone, it would be in full possession of her heart.

And if she ever gave it, she would give it eternally, and without regret.

# Thirteen

Faith sprinted along the street, weaving in and out of the crowds that barely noticed her except for the wind of her wake. Her coat and hair flew out behind her, and her feet hit the pavement with the rhythm of a drumroll.

*"Suspect is approaching Lavaca Street,"* the network monitor said at her wrist.

"I'm closing in!" Faith shouted back, running even harder. Less than a block ahead she could see the thin figure darting from one side to the other, deftly avoiding the humans as Faith did. "Where's my cover from the west?"

*"Closing from Eighth Street,"* came the breathless answer. *"You'll catch her first."*

Faith pounded around the corner with her arms and legs pumping, adrenaline and wrath fueling her pursuit, her senses in overdrive. The hot, dark drive of the predator coursed through her until the universe reduced to her and her prey. Half a block. Closing in.

Out of either desperation or stupidity, the suspect veered suddenly off to the right, out into traffic. Horns blared all around, but it was just after dark on a Thursday and traffic was so heavy that they weren't moving very fast to begin with. A skinny black-haired girl running between the cars was irritating but not especially noteworthy.

"Goddamn it, Sire, where are you?" Faith demanded into her com. "Now would be a great time for that teleporting thing you do!"

Before the sentence was even out of her mouth, one of the SUVs on Lavaca screeched to a halt as something heavy landed on its roof.

The Prime straightened, his eyes flashing silver in the streetlamps, and jumped down from the car right into the suspect's path. She hissed and threw herself to the left, bouncing off the door of a Jaguar and rolling underneath it.

"I want eyes on every corner!" Faith snapped. "Twenty-eight, Twelve, Nine, fan out!"

David strode among the cars, lithe and purposeful, and the humans in their vehicles either stared openly at him or turned their faces away in instinctive fear of the one creature designed perfectly to kill them. He paused, breathing in the chilly damp air of an early-spring night. His mouth opened slightly, revealing the curved ivory of his teeth, and the woman driving the SUV in front of him shrieked and covered her child's face.

The light in the Signet flared, and he pushed out with one hand, seeming to move only air. The Jag slid sideways with the screech of rubber on pavement.

The suspect, suddenly losing her hiding place behind its tire, dove for another, getting her feet up underneath her to bolt. She made it about three steps.

David lifted one hand and made a tugging motion, and the vampire fell to her knees with a scream, dragged back toward him, her fingers clawing desperately at the dirty concrete until the nails broke and bled.

"Please!" she was screaming at the humans. "He's going to kill me! Please! Call the police!"

David smiled. "We are the police," he said, loudly enough that everyone could hear—and practically everyone had cracked their windows at least a few inches by now. David turned slowly in a circle, and Faith felt him grabbing every last mind on the scene and twisting it hard. Faces all around them bent easily to his will, and his words implanted on their weak mortal minds: "We are apprehending a fugitive. There is nothing more for you to see here."

Then he seized the vampire around her collar and hauled her along with him off the street, leaving the Elite to restore the flow of traffic.

He threw the girl into the wall and waited for her to stop sniveling. Around him, the rest of the patrol unit had gathered, and Faith was waiting, too. They were inside an empty storefront with boarded-up windows; there would be no interference from the local cowboys.

"Ariana Blackthorn," David said, staring down at her. He gestured and the Elite produced shackles. Considering the helpless-damsel number she'd been going for, she fought like a tiger until she was securely chained.

Finally, she seemed to understand she wasn't going anywhere and slowly forced herself to stand up straight and face him head on.

Disgust and hatred were all over her otherwise pretty face. She spat at him, but he'd been expecting it and moved out of the way. They always liked to spit, for some reason. Next came the insults: demon, devil, accusations of bestiality for his known appetite for humans, and on and on.

The Blackthorn had created of him the perfect Antichrist. They had him set up to enslave and destroy all of vampire kind. He had to admit it was flattering.

Faith joined him, panting and sweaty, and muttered, "You couldn't have just teleported and caught her before we'd all run ourselves into a coma chasing her?"

"I told you," he said mildly, eyes still on the girl. "I don't teleport. It's a quantum-level shift that involves loosening the bond among all my molecules, and it requires so much energy that it's advisable only in emergencies."

"Like tonight?"

"No. Tonight I jumped down off a building and onto a car. Can we focus, please?"

He returned his attention to Ariana Blackthorn, who regarded him with utmost loathing. "I'm going to *kill you*!" she screamed, flinging herself forward to the end of her chains, then falling back against the wall. "I'm going to kill all of you! And that little Happy Meal bitch of yours in the city!"

David felt his blood run cold, but he clamped down on the reaction that he knew she'd want to see. "Keep ranting," he said. "We have all night."

He held his hand out to the left, and one of the lieutenants handed him a sheaf of papers. "Ariana Blackthorn," he read. "Youngest of the Blackthorn women, not deemed suitable for an arranged marriage until lo and behold, an unattached Prime came into power here in the South. Your father made a deal to sell you to Auren, if not as a Queen then at least as a whore, in exchange for hunting grounds in his territory and safe harbor if the California war went badly, which of course it did. So your loving patriarch sent you to the bed of a psychopathic killer, and you weren't heard from again."

Ariana strained against her chains again. "I loved my Prime," she spat, "and he loved me. We were a Pair, even if his stupid Signet didn't understand. All I had to do was get stronger. My father didn't like his women strong. So I waited. And I grew."

"And when I killed your one true love, you ran and hid," David finished for her callously. "For fifteen years you've scuttled around the underworld like a cockroach instead of facing your Prime's killer. Then you were contacted by James Wallace, formerly of Auren's Elite, and he helped you build your syndicate and then, quite conveniently, met his end."

"I wanted justice," she said. "I wanted to watch you suffer as you made my Lord suffer. I wanted to see everything you care for bleed and die and then bleed you myself."

"I appreciate the honesty." David replied. "Now perhaps you'll favor me with a little more, Ariana. My Elite have the location of your headquarters, and as we speak they are infiltrating it and subduing your guards. We'll have possession inside ten minutes. Now, unless you can give me a compelling reason not to kill every last soul I find inside, the whole building will burn. If you make sure I know where all your splinter factions are, I can promise you not to kill certain individuals, perhaps family, who might be dear to you."

Ariana laughed, a high, eerie sound that was in no way sane. "Kill them all, I don't care," she answered. "And make sure you get my sister, too. She's a race traitor just like you are, *Sire*, and since I swore to my father I wouldn't kill her, you can do it for me. You owe me that much after you murdered my lover."

"Here's what I owe you, Ariana." David took a step back and drew his sword. Two of the Elite took hold of her arms and forced her to her knees as he said, "I am sorry for your broken heart, or at least your thwarted ambitions. Ariana Blackthorn, you are hereby under an order of execution for conspiracy to murder thirty-two humans within my territory as well as seven of my Elite."

"Do I get a last request?" Ariana asked with false sweetness.

He lifted his chin.

Her voice came out as a feline hiss. "I want to see the look on your face when they drag your precious little princess dead from the lake. I want you to hurt like I hurt when I held Auren's lifeless body in my arms. I want to see your world come to an end."

He stared into her eyes for a moment, then said flatly, "Request denied."

Then he cut off her head.

An hour later Harlan pulled the car into an affluent suburb of West Austin, down a long street lined with the homes of the well-to-do. None of them approached the grandeur of the Haven, of course, but then, they weren't built to house a hundred vampires. There was new growth in many of the front flower beds that would probably die in the last freeze that usually hit just before Easter. For now, though, the exultant breath of spring was in the air, even while the nights were still cold.

They stopped at the end of the street in front of an ordinary-looking two-story house where Faith and half the Elite were already waiting for him. Any human family could have lived there, but the lawn didn't look like it had been mowed recently, and the curtains in the front windows were flat—they had been nailed up with boards behind them to block out the sun while still appearing mostly normal from the street. Considering their hatred for humans, the Blackthorn had been living very close to them, but it was a sound strategy for staying off his radar.

Or, it had been, until the sensor network was up and running long enough for his analytical eyes to discern a pattern among the movements of the vampires that lived here. They covered their tracks well, but not well enough.

"The property is secured," Faith said as he got out of the car. Her voice was oddly strained. "We found twenty-six inside along with . . . Well, see for yourself."

He could smell it before he entered the house. The insurgents had done their killing in the city, but they had done much of their feeding here. Not two days before, almost as an afterthought, he had run a search on missing persons in the Austin area and confirmed his suspicions about how a gang as indiscreet as theirs could stay fed. They left only select bodies in obvious places for him to find—where were the rest?

Now he knew.

There were shallow graves in the backyard. Inside the house were cages.

The entire gang had been taken into the backyard to await execution, and all that was left inside was the amassed garbage of beer bottles and three corpses, each covered with bite marks and left to rot in the closets.

By his count, there should be ten more buried out back. Three were children. Managed with even minimal food and water, a dozen humans could keep the gang fed for weeks as long as they were given a few days to recover in between feedings. Eventually they would weaken and their bodies would give out, but in the meantime all the insurgents had to do was pluck the homeless off the streets and they had an unlimited supply of human blood that no one would miss.

"What did that bitch promise her followers?" Faith asked, walking with him from room to room to survey the damage to the house.

"Freedom," David replied. "Can't you tell? They were free to live in filth among the dying. I'm sure she promised that after the revolution they would all be counted high in her own Elite and have license to feed on every throat they could reach."

"We found the sister. She's alive, but . . . not well. They had her in one of the cages—she's marked, too. I think Ariana was feeding on her exclusively."

"Blood is still thicker than water," he said. "Show me."

She led him to the back of the house and the one bedroom that seemed to show signs of only a single inhabitant. The rest of the building had the cramped energy of a barracks, and beds had been created on every available flat surface, but still, they had to have slept in shifts.

Inside the room several Elite stood guard over a blond woman dressed in rags, her neck and shoulders covered in puncture wounds in various stages of healing. She was barefoot and filthy, skeletally thin, her clavicles standing out sharply.

"Here," one of the guards was saying, handing her a bag of hospital blood. The girl took it and began to suck greedily at the tube, whimpering with hunger.

David went to her and knelt, placing his hand on the bag. "Slowly," he said. "Sip. You'll make yourself sick."

She looked up at him, shaking, and he was struck by the intense blue of her eyes. She saw the Signet and stared but didn't shy away; she was simply too weak to react.

"Have you got anything out of the others about her?" he asked Faith.

"No. They were under orders not to talk about her. In fact, we can't get a damn thing out of any of them about what went on here—she trained them well, Sire. They're all as insane as she was."

He returned his attention to the girl. "What's your name?"

She paused in her drinking long enough to whisper, "Bethany."

"Well, Bethany Blackthorn, my name is David. We're going to take care of you."

She nodded, still shaking, still sucking on the tube. The bag was already half empty.

He stood up. Faith caught his arm and drew him away, saying, "Sire . . . you aren't thinking of taking her back to the Haven with us, are you?"

"That's exactly what I'm thinking, Faith. Where else is she going to go?"

"We don't know anything about her. We have no record of her in the Blackthorn case files. These people are out for your blood and you want her in our house?"

"Look at her," he said. "She's too weak to be a threat, and if there are more of them out there in hiding in the city, we'll need information from her. We take her back, we put her under guard and find out who she really is."

"Doesn't this seem a little suspicious to you? They could be playing on your sympathies—face it, Sire, you are a little softhearted when it comes to crazy girls."

"Duly noted, Second."

"Wait . . . you're not thinking of putting her in Miranda's room, are you?"

He rounded on Faith. "It isn't Miranda's room anymore," he snapped. "And no, I don't want her anywhere near me. Put her in one of the visiting-dignitary suites and make sure she doesn't so much as take a piss without it going on record. Now if you don't mind, Faith, I'm going to go watch twenty-six people die."

He started to walk away, then thought better of it and said, "On second thought, bring the girl outside with us. Make sure she sees everything. If she's her sister's enemy, she'll appreciate the opportunity. If she's not, she'll have fair warning about her own future."

The house went up in flames just before midnight, with the bodies of the insurgents stacked inside.

David waited long enough to be sure the Austin Fire Department and police had arrived and they understood their role in things: keep the blaze from spreading to the surrounding houses, keep passersby clear of the scene, but make no move to extinguish it until everything inside was reduced to ash. There would be no arson investigation. It was clear that faulty wiring was to blame.

According to APD, who had been briefed on the situation by Faith, the house had belonged to a family of four. Two of the dead the Elite had found inside were its original inhabitants; the other two were probably buried in the backyard along with the family dog and nine other humans.

He stood out by the car half a block away watching the blaze, the twin smells of gasoline and smoke brutally overwhelming the scents of a rainy night. Neighbors were out on their driveways, huddled together in clumps asking each other worriedly if the Larsons were okay, if they'd been home when it happened, if anyone was hurt.

He felt a moment of uncharacteristic tenderness for them. They were ignorant of the horror that had lived in their midst all this while; they were simply coming and going, working and sleeping, playing with their children. One street over there were children dying in pain in a cage. If they'd known, they would have banded together and gotten the police involved . . . and probably gotten themselves all killed. This was the kind of neighborhood where everyone knew everyone's business and for the most part all cared.

They were so innocent. They had no idea what real darkness was.

Faith was conferring with her unit nearby. An operation like this required a massive cleanup, coordination with the city authorities, and further investigation to find the rest of the gang before they had time to regroup.

"Everything's running smoothly," the Second said, standing to his right. "We can take it from here, Sire, if you'd like to head back."

He nodded. "Have there been any new developments from the network?"

"Not yet. I'm sure they're out there, but tonight they're running scared. We probably won't hear a peep out of them for a week or more."

"Keep me informed."

He directed Harlan to take him out to hunt, making sure they took a tour through the Shadow District on the way. The whole street was dead silent and empty, and several of the bars had already cut their losses and shut down for the day.

Sixth Street was a marked contrast. On a Thursday night the clubs were doing a brisk business—for college students the weekend started early. There were attractive young women and men lined up half a block from the Signet-owned club the Black Door; he could hear the thumping bass even through the supposedly soundproof window glass of the car.

He disembarked and instructed Harlan to return in fifteen minutes, then bypassed the line, garnering both appreciative stares and complaints about cutting in line. He took the steps up to the double doors, where an enormous bouncer—human—stepped in front of him.

Without speaking, he held open the neck of his coat

so the man could see the Signet. The bouncer practically leapt back out of his way, unfastening the velvet rope to let him in. He gave the man a nod as he passed and received a sketchy, nervous bow in return.

Once inside, he took the side stairs up to the catwalk, where he could survey the crowd and choose what he wanted; the employees all recognized the Signet, and they either bowed slightly or, in the case of waitresses with trays of drinks, smiled broadly and winked so they wouldn't lose their balance. He didn't especially care if the humans acknowledged him here, but they had been carefully schooled by their managers to show him the kind of respect they would their best customer—which he was. Aside from paying their salaries and making sure they were unmolested by their vampire clientele, he was a generous tipper.

The music pulsed all around him, and down on the dance floor bodies surged in time to it, young skin glistening with sweat. He envied them their abandon; all they had to worry about were condoms and designated drivers, followed by hangovers and embarrassing sexual escapades to retell at the next sorority meeting.

Standing there watching them, he felt more removed from humanity than he ever had, and consequently, his heart felt like it was about to break beneath the enormity of what he was. There had been times over the years when he had balked against responsibility, wishing he could go back to California when he was only a lieutenant and followed orders instead of giving them. Being the pinnacle of the food chain was lonely, and there were moments that he hated it.

He thought back to California again, this time remembering the phone call he'd received from Deven months ago just after Miranda had left him. The Prime understood what David was feeling. He had felt it, too. They all felt the burden of the Signet, and deep down they all knew there was a way to share that burden, to lighten the weight of the world.

He leaned forward on the catwalk rail, putting his head in his hands. He was being foolish again, dreaming of destiny when there was only reality. He had no Queen, no Consort. He was alone. And the only person . . .

The note he had found hidden in the Shakespeare book echoed in his mind. *Come to me. Come to me,* she had said, and he wanted to so badly . . . in theory it was safe for now, with the leadership of the Blackthorn syndicate dead and the rest of their recruits scattered all over the city in chaos.

But Ariana Blackthorn had threatened Miranda . . . and they had already tried to kill her once. The reality was that it would never be safe, not as long as any of the insurgents still lived. And as soon as one threat was put down, another would rise. As long as Miranda lived in his territory . . . as long as she lived . . . because of him, she would be in danger.

He stood there for a long time, staring sightlessly at the crowd, feeling empty and alone, until a waitress spoke up from his elbow: "Can I bring you something, Sire?"

He sighed and scanned the dance floor again. "I'd like a gin and tonic, and the redheaded woman at the bar drinking the Grey Goose martini. I'll be in my booth."

"Right away, Sire."

He made his way toward the back of the club's second level and sank tiredly into the leather seat; a moment later a second waiter appeared with his drink. He sipped it listlessly until the waitress returned, a wary young woman at her side.

"Here you are, Sire," the waitress said. He handed her a twenty.

The girl regarded him with narrowed eyes. "They said the owner wanted to see me?"

"Yes," he replied. "Sit down, please."

She raised an eyebrow. "I don't even know you," she pointed out. "And frankly you're not my type."

He looked her over, smiling. Very few humans were openly defiant of him; he liked it. He also liked the spark

in her aura, and the flash of her hazel eyes. She was tall—
she'd top him by a good three inches if he were standing up—and a little thinner than he liked, but overall
quite a beauty, perhaps twenty-four or twenty-five years
old. Graduate student, no doubt. She had a more East
Coast than Central Texas accent, one he'd place around
Maryland.

She was also a lesbian. Part of him was disappointed,
but really, he wasn't in the mood to play the game. It did,
however, explain her immunity to his charms.

"That's all right," he said. "I'm not after your ass,
Miss . . ."

"Sandy."

"Very well, Sandy. Please sit." He reached toward her
with his mind and pulled gently, wrapping the fingers of
his power around her will. She was a strong girl, but he
was far stronger, and she blinked twice, then sat down
next to him, confusion on her face.

He leaned in and brushed the loose strawberry hair
from her neck. She trembled at the touch of his fingers,
and not from fear—he had her, whatever her preferences
were, and if he wanted to, he could arouse her so thoroughly that the continued effort of a dozen women would
do her no good until he gave her release.

He wasn't interested in subverting her desires, though.
If she didn't want men, he wasn't going to force himself
on her. But neither did he want her to fight him, or to
be afraid. He fed just enough energy into her body to
relax and soothe her, then tilted her head to the side and
quickly pierced her skin. If she had struggled, she could
have caused his teeth to hit an artery. This way she was
safe.

*Safe.* What did the word even mean in this world?

He drank, his hand around her throat as if he were
simply kissing her, and she moaned, her hands seeking something to hold on to and grasping his shoulders.
Meanwhile the other humans in the bar walked past the
booth, not even noticing.

He withdrew, satisfaction flooding warm and complete through his body, and held her steady for a few minutes until she began to regain her equilibrium.

"Shit," she murmured, sagging forward. "I've had one too many."

"I think you have," he agreed. "Can I call you a cab home?"

"Yeah," she said. "Thanks."

As the waitress led her out of the club, he finished his drink, holding the alcohol in his mouth to cleanse his palate. She had tasted healthy and strong, intelligent, and so young . . . an undertone of cherries and tobacco, suggesting she smoked the occasional cigar.

There was no honey in her blood, and no cinnamon. No music.

David closed his eyes. It was no use. He could drink every redhead in Texas, and until he tasted Miranda he would never be full. Until he felt her life pulsing beneath his lips, her breath catching as her body shivered around his, her hair tangling around his fingers, he would thirst, and thirst . . . and die wanting.

He left the club and found Harlan waiting at his usual spot; the people still in line outside stared openly as he walked by and got into the sleek black car, probably wondering who he was—old money? New money? A music producer? A model?

"Where to, Sire?" Harlan asked.

David stared out the window. He knew what he wanted to say. But it would be dawn in a few hours. He had to meet with the patrol leaders and network managers and put in a call to the fire department and the mayor's office. Again, that weight; again, the longing.

"Home, please," he answered.

Then, he spoke into his com: "Elite Eighty-Six."

Lindsay's surprise was evident; he never spoke to her directly, preferring to leave the whole subject to Faith. *"Yes, Sire?"*

"Is Miss Grey home tonight?"

As far as he knew, Lindsay kept an eye on all of Miranda's comings and goings, but reported back only when something aroused her concern. He had instructed Faith to keep the guard out of the way and above all not to peep through windows or anything creepy; for one thing, Miranda would know, and for another, he already felt guilty enough about spying on her even indirectly. Still, he had said he would keep her safe, and making sure there was an Elite within safe range was the best way he could think of.

*"Yes, Sire. She got home at one A.M. and hasn't left again."*

"Home from a show?"

*"No, Sire—from a date, I believe. There was a young human male with her."*

He was aware that his breath had suddenly become shallow and pained. "This male, did he stay?"

*"No, Sire. They seemed friendly but not particularly affectionate. I have images of his face in case we needed to run a trace on him—would you like me to?"*

"No," he said hastily. "But do you know what her schedule is like tomorrow night?"

*"She usually has a gig at Mel's on Fridays, but this week it was canceled, something to do with the owner having to spray for termites. It was in the paper. Tomorrow night she's going out with friends instead. She mentioned to one of them that she would be back home before midnight."*

"Thank you, Lindsay."

*"Yes, Sire."*

He leaned back in his seat, trying to force himself to ground; there was no reason to lose his calm. Miranda was entitled to have lovers. She was entitled to whatever she wanted. He had no claim over her, and they hadn't even spoken for nearly six months. He had no right to feel jealous.

He could have laughed at himself. He *was* jealous. Poisonously, shamefully jealous. He wanted to find this boy and snap his neck.

It was only right. She should be getting on with her life, doing all those things that made human life so precious: falling in love, finding herself, even starting a family. Those things had been out of her reach before, but now she was strong and could have whatever she wanted . . . anyone she wanted. She was beautiful and talented, and he wanted her so badly he came very close to telling Harlan to turn the car around.

He should stay away from her. He should put her out of his mind for good, or at least pretend such a thing was possible, for her own sake.

He knew that.

He also knew where he was going at midnight tomorrow, and he knew that nothing, no war or fear or misplaced sense of righteousness, was going to stop him.


"Did you hear about that house fire over in Westlake?" Drew asked.

"Yeah, it was on the news," Kat said. "They said the whole place burned to the ground—the fire department barely kept it under control. They're lucky the whole neighborhood didn't go up, with all those trees around."

Miranda listened distractedly, poking at her ravioli. The cute little pasta pockets had been appetizing at first, but she'd sat staring at them so long that they'd gone cold and jiggly, turning a bit gray in the café's lights.

"Earth to Mira," Kat was saying, tapping her on the arm with her fork.

She looked up. "Oh, sorry."

"Where are you tonight?" Drew asked with a concerned smile. He was always so solicitous of her welfare; sometimes it was endearing, and sometimes it made her want to hit him with her purse. "Are you okay?"

"I'm fine." She mustered a smile. "Just kind of distracted. I'm used to being onstage on Fridays."

Kat blew her straw wrapper at Miranda. "Sorry we're not a huge adoring crowd cheering your name," the

blonde said. "If you want, Drew will throw his underwear at you."

Drew's ears went bright pink. "Jesus, Kat."

Miranda laughed. "It's okay. I'm just in a weird mood.
Have you ever had a feeling like something was about to
happen?"

"Of course," Kat replied. "It's called PMS."

"No, I mean . . . never mind."

"Do you want dessert?" Drew asked. "I'm buying."

Miranda shook her head. He and Kat exchanged a
look. It was unlike Miranda not to have cake—she only
ever ate sweets when they went out, and she looked forward to them all week. But tonight she wasn't hungry; she
couldn't shake the feeling of dread in her stomach that
was taking up all the space. Even the few bites of pasta
she'd had were sitting there like a rock.

Kat drove them all back to Miranda's apartment; the
weather in March was unpredictable, and the forecast
called for rain, but with a cold front coming it might end
up snowing; one could never tell. In a way, she was grateful that her show had been postponed. She'd had to slog
home in sleet and mud before, and she'd nearly broken
her leg slipping on icy patches on the sidewalk. The winter had been so cold and wet this year that she had been
itching for spring since January.

"What's on your mind?" Drew asked from the front
seat.

Miranda's gaze was fixed on the city out the window,
but she said, "I can't believe how fast time goes by. It
seems like it was just summer."

"Yep," Kat said. "Before you know it people will be
bitching about the heat again instead of the cold. I love
Texas."

Miranda let them into the apartment gratefully, feeling the blast of heat from inside with a smile. Speaking
of bitching, they complained every time they came over
about how warm she kept her house, but since she'd come
back to the city she had lost a lot of her cold tolerance and

had the heater running full blast almost all the time. Kat and Drew both stripped off their outerwear as soon as they crossed the threshold.

Just as she was about to follow them in, she felt . . . something. She turned, peering into the darkness, eyes narrowed, and swept the view with her senses. Nothing was amiss.

Shrugging, she went inside.

Kat had excused herself to the bathroom, leaving her alone with Drew. He sat on the couch, smiling a little awkwardly. Miranda had made a point not to spend much time with him without Kat to run interference; she knew very well how he felt about her and didn't want to encourage him. It didn't seem to help. But he was a great guy and fun to be around when he wasn't making moon eyes at her.

"So, Miranda . . ."

She held back a sigh. "Do you want a beer or something?"

"No, I . . . I was kind of hoping we could talk."

She tried to joke off his earnest tone. "Well, talk fast—Kat pees like a speeding bullet."

"I'm serious," Drew said, standing up. "I mean, I know we agreed just to be friends, but . . . Miranda . . ." He reached down and took her hand, not noticing how stiff she was at the contact. "I really, really like you. I think we'd be great together. Could you just please think it over? Last night was a lot of fun, and it was nice to spend time with just you. I'd really like to do it again."

Miranda sighed aloud this time. She knew last night had been a mistake. Kat had dropped out of their movie plans last minute due to some sort of emergency with her at-risk kids, but she'd insisted Miranda and Drew go on without her. Miranda had a sneaking suspicion that Kat had planned the whole thing.

"Drew, I told you. I'm not ready for a relationship right now. You're a sweet guy, and very attractive, but—"

Three things happened at once:

One, Drew took hold of her arms and kissed her on the mouth, causing her entire body to go rigid.

Two, Kat emerged from the bathroom and said, "Oh! Sorry, guys!" and started to duck into the kitchen.

Three, there was a knock at the door.

Miranda twisted out of Drew's grasp and barely, just barely, kept from punching him in the face. She stumbled backward, torn between terror and rage, and snarled, "Don't *ever* do that again."

Drew was blushing crimson, and she almost relented at the obvious shame on his face as he stammered his apology. Instead of replying, she turned away and, so rattled she didn't even remember to look out the peephole, flung open the door.

She froze. The earth and time itself abruptly stopped turning.

There, on her front porch, looking exactly as she remembered him down to the buttons of his long black coat, stood Prime David Solomon.

Before she could speak, he leaned slightly to the left to look over her shoulder. His deep blue eyes fastened on Drew. Miranda heard Drew swallow hard.

David looked back at Miranda, and there was a ring of silver around his irises as he asked calmly, "Do you need me to kill him?"

# Fourteen

"Oh my God," Miranda breathed. Then she came back to herself long enough to say, "No, it's okay. He's okay."

Behind her, Kat cleared her throat loudly.

She half turned, looking from Kat to David and back again, her heart and mind going in a thousand directions at once and her insides threatening to explode from her skin. "Oh . . . um . . . guys . . . here, come in."

Her legs felt like Jell-O, but she moved back out of the way to let the Prime in. He stepped through the doorway and all the air went out of the room; God, she'd forgotten that he did that. His energy overwhelmed the apartment even as tightly shielded as he always was. She might have been the only one who felt it, but still, everything from the way he stood to the unnatural brightness of his eyes set him apart from her friends.

Kat's eyes were wide and speculative, looking David up and down with obvious appreciation for his hand-tailored attire, and no doubt also for his magnificent build. "Hi there."

He took his gaze off Miranda long enough to size up Kat. Miranda could see the calculation in his face: human, female, harmless. "Hello."

He gave Drew a disdainful glance and, after that,

barely allotted him the notice he would give a trouble-some insect. Miranda found that weirdly hilarious.

"This is David," she said. "He's the friend I mentioned from when I was away last summer. David, these are my friends Kat and Drew."

He nodded to them. Miranda's addled mind found it a little offensive that they didn't bow.

"So you're Rehab Guy," Kat was saying, having recovered her aplomb. She strode forward to shake David's hand; for a second he stared at it like an alien object, then took her hand and kissed it, causing Kat to turn pink at the ears and stammer just a tiny bit.

In another time, when her worlds weren't colliding quite so violently, Miranda would have laughed at that, too. Kat was never shaken up by attractive men. Her apparent lack of interest in the male gender was what got her so much sex.

David looked over at Miranda. "Rehab Guy?"

Miranda shrugged. She felt behind her for something to lean on and came to rest on the couch.

"Were you a counselor at the clinic or something?" Kat asked. "Mira says you helped get her back on her feet."

Now David smiled, turning again to Miranda. "Mira," he said. "I like that."

She nodded, unable to meet his eyes just yet, though she could feel every inch of his gaze traveling over every inch of her. "My mom used to call me that. Snow White was my favorite fairy tale when I was little—she'd say 'Mira, Mira, on the wall . . .' you know how it goes."

"This was before Shakespeare, I assume."

She smiled. "Yeah."

Kat looked from him to her and back, then over at Drew, then back at Miranda. Kat wasn't psychic, but she was no fool either. "I think we should get going," she announced. "Drew, honey, grab your coat. Miranda, maybe we'll see you later this weekend? I'll e-mail you."

She grabbed Drew by the arm and practically dragged him to the door, despite his protestations. As they passed by the couch, Kat said in a loud whisper, "I want details."

Miranda rose to lock the door behind them and paused a minute with her hands on the deadbolt, trying to steady her breath. When she turned back, David was standing by the hook where her coat was, his hand touching the scarf that Drew had left that she kept forgetting to give back.

There was a moment of tense silence before David said, "He seems nice."

She snorted. "Sure."

He let go of the scarf. "What?"

"Nice. He seems nice. You said it like you'd say 'nice' to a light blue tuxedo or a case of genital warts."

He frowned. "Are you angry at me?"

She put her hands on her hips. "Well, what do you think? You haven't called or e-mailed or acted like I exist for six months; now you show up on my doorstep and, what, want to go out for coffee?"

"Something like that," he replied.

She stared at him. He stared at her.

"Fine," she said.

His eyebrows shot up. "Really?"

She yanked her coat from its hook. "Yes, really. Come on."

"I don't . . . actually drink coffee," he said, sounding a little thrown by her behavior. "Caffeine makes me jittery."

"That's not where we're going."

To his credit, he didn't protest, but let her haul him along behind her out the front door and into the night.

Perhaps no one else in the city would get the novelty of a psychic musician and the most powerful vampire in Texas sitting together in an ice cream parlor, but

Miranda's creeping sense of the absurd had plenty to take in tonight.

Amy's Ice Cream was the foremost chain of its kind in Austin, staffed by the young and hip—smaller versions of Kat, for the most part, and teenage boys with floppy hair and sleeve tattoos. It was decorated with cartoon cows and piped punk and metal over the loudspeakers, a study in contrasts that was typical of their fair city.

It was the only ice cream chain open past midnight, and also the only one in town that had a rotating selection of alcoholic flavors as well as the standard, mashed up with your choice of toppings from chocolate-covered Gummi Bears to granola.

Miranda took the waffle cone full of Mexican vanilla and fresh raspberries that she'd asked for, and licked the dripping edges off while David paid. She found an empty table and grabbed a handful of napkins before sitting down.

It always surprised her how many people craved ice cream when the weather was cold. Amy's was never without a crowd even in the nastiest part of winter, and here at the leading edge of spring with a northern front about to hit, there were still half a dozen people occupying the tables in the middle of a Friday night.

David sat down across from her, resplendent in his black leather with his Signet glowing from his throat, holding a polka-dotted cup full of chocolate ice cream smothered in caramel praline sauce and hot fudge.

With sprinkles.

"I guess you're not worried about diabetes."

He ignored her and took a bite; the look on his face, one of unexpected bliss, made her forget how cold it was.

"I can't believe you've lived here fifteen years and never been to Amy's," she said.

"God, neither can I."

She smothered a giggle; she'd never heard him talk with his mouth full before. It made her think of the night she'd seen him sleeping—he probably would have been mortified at the idea of being adorable, but there were moments that he was almost human, and rather than lessening his allure, they intensified it.

They ate without talking for a while, but this time the silence was companionable, not strained. She pretended not to notice how his eyes lingered on her when she licked a stray dribble of ice cream from her cone, and he paid no heed to the way she kept catching herself staring at his mouth.

Finally, he couldn't seem to stand it anymore. "So this Drew . . ."

She nearly inhaled her ice cream, recognizing the tone as one she'd never thought she would hear from him of all people. "Are you *jealous*?"

He met her eyes. "Insanely."

Now it was her turn to blush. She suddenly found her napkin intensely fascinating. "It's not what you think," she said. "Kat was trying to fix us up, but I didn't want that. When you got here, he'd just tried to . . . push the issue."

Outrage bloomed in his eyes, and there was a hard edge in his voice. "Are you sure you don't want me to kill him for you?"

"I can take care of myself," she replied with a little flare of anger of her own. "I'm not your damsel in distress, David."

He stared down into his ice cream. "I am aware of that."

"Tell me why you're here. After all this time, why now?"

David sat back and folded his hands in that molecular-level noble way he had, choosing his words with care. "Last night we destroyed the insurgents' base."

She nearly dropped her ice cream. "That house fire. That was you?"

"Yes. I tracked them over the citywide sensor network, and we killed them."

"God . . . you mean it's over?"

He shook his head. "I don't know if it will ever be over, Miranda. There are still more of them out there in hiding. We've found a few, but evidence suggests we got two thirds of the total membership in the raid. Their leadership is gone, but they may still regroup and start again, this time even more aggressively out of the desire for revenge. There may also be other factions outside Austin waiting to be called in."

"What you're saying is that I'm going to be in danger for the rest of my life."

"Probably."

She shrugged and bit off one side of her ice cream cone. "So?"

He stared at her in open disbelief. "Aren't you at least a little concerned for your own safety?"

She looked around the room, gesturing at the other people eating their ice cream in peace. "Look at all of them," she said quietly. "They're in as much danger as I am, but they don't even know it. They don't even know what's sitting right next to them. Worry about them, David. I do. I see all these people living their lives, and I wonder which of them is next. But I don't worry about me, not anymore. I'm strong and I can fight for my life. I know what's out there. And I've lived in fear—I spent months jumping at shadows and crying myself to sleep. I'm not doing that again. Let them come and kill me—no, let them try. I think they'll be surprised how hard it is."

He was still staring, but now with wonder, and something like pride.

"Maybe you have the time to spend your life afraid," she concluded. "I don't."

She went back to her ice cream, letting him take in what she'd said in stunned silence for a minute. "I guess I've changed," she observed between bites.

Now he smiled. "No," he said. "I always knew this was

who you are. Now you know it, too. And now you know why I refused to give up on you."

"Thank you," she replied with a smile.

Another ice-cream-filled moment passed, and then he noted casually, "You look like you've been working out."

"I have been. You look like you haven't been sleeping."

"I haven't been."

She took the last bite of her ice cream and wiped her mouth, then reached over and squeezed his hand lightly. "I'm sorry it's been so hard," she said. "How many Elite did you lose altogether?"

"Seven total. Eight, counting Helen. And forty-five humans. There was even . . ." He set down his spoon, pushing the cup away, saying, "There was a little boy. He and his mother were killed together. There were at least three other children as well, but I never saw their faces. This one . . ."

She held on to his fingers more tightly. "He reminded you of your son."

"Yes. Not physically, really, just that innocence. They lose it so young, even without monsters in the night coming to rip their throats out. There's no reason for it. We don't have to end lives to survive, let alone the little ones. Despite what I am, I've never understood destruction for its own sake."

She knew, hearing him speak, that he hadn't told anyone what he was telling her. "But you stopped them," she said. "At least for now. And if they know what's good for them, they'll leave town and not look back."

He smiled with sad irony. "They never know what's good for them." He toyed with the spoon again, letting the mostly melted ice cream drip from it into the cup. "I failed them, Miranda. Fifty-three people died under my watch."

"There could have been so many more," she told him, trying to reassure him with both her words and her energy. "Not even a Prime can be everywhere at once. There's only one of you to watch over all of us. Not even you can be perfect."

He sighed. She had heard that sigh before. "I think I'm finished," he said. "Do you want a bite before I throw the rest away?"

"Sure," she said.

She started to reach for the spoon, but he lifted it first and held it out with a small mouthful captured in its bowl. She leaned forward and opened her mouth, lips closing around the spoon, but she barely tasted the ice cream; all she could feel were his eyes, and something in them made her shiver inside, a dark liquid heat spreading from her belly all the way down to her toes.

"Let's go," he said softly.

They walked back to her apartment close enough to touch, but not touching; Miranda tried not to let that make her insane. It felt so good just to talk to him again; she put that moment of heat between them out of her mind and fell into the rhythm of conversation.

He asked about her music and listened attentively as she recounted the crippling anxiety of her first few performances and how she had learned to use her gift to enhance, but not violate, the audience's experience. She could gather up surface emotions and shift them little by little. It had taken a lot of practice.

They talked about the new Elite trials and Faith's frustration with the new recruits, who weren't nearly good enough to truly replace the dead. Miranda told him that Faith came to see her every week or two, and he didn't seem surprised.

He told her more about the sensor network and the raid on the insurgents' headquarters.

"Wait . . . you have one of them staying at the Haven?"

He nodded, and she had the sense that it was a subject he'd defended a hundred times already, most likely to Faith. "She's under lock and key. As soon as she's well enough to survive, I'm going to find out what she knows and then release her."

Miranda smiled at that. "You do like to take in strays, don't you?"

They stopped at a traffic light just as a blast of icy wind made its way down from the sky to the street, and she shivered a little in her coat, wishing she'd worn something heavier.

David reached over and took her hand. "Here," he said.

She felt a surge of warmth travel from his body to hers, the way he had done the night he had found her in the alley, but this time it wasn't just energy. When the WALK sign lit up and they crossed the road, he didn't let go of her hand, and she didn't pull away.

"It isn't the same," he told her, returning to the subject. "I don't trust this woman. All we know about her is that Ariana hated her. That's not a ringing endorsement. So far she's done nothing but feed and sleep."

"Please be careful," she admonished.

"Don't worry, Miranda. Not every woman I meet completely blinds me."

"Oh?"

"No," he replied, looking up at the night sky. "Only the green-eyed ones with voices like honey and rain."

She let the words run through her, leaving an almost silly delight in their wake, but then frowned, trying to understand what she was feeling. Were they really flirting? His sudden openness unnerved her, although he had been the one to kiss her, and he had just taken her hand. She didn't know how to react. For months she had wanted to see him, and now he was here, touching her, and she knew that if she invited him in, she could have much more than that. Suddenly what had been so obvious no longer made sense to her heart.

They had reached her apartment by now, and she was digging with trembling fingers for her keys, feeling the beginnings of helpless confused tears in her eyes. She thought of how she had turned to stone when Drew kissed her, and how for months the thought of a man's hands on her skin sent her running for the Xanax. How on earth could David be the exception to that fear? Just because he wasn't human?

"Miranda," he said, gently taking the keys from her, "Talk to me."

She shook her head and pushed past him into the apartment, stripping off her coat and aiming it blindly at the hook. It missed and puddled on the floor.

David picked it up and hung it, along with his own, and watched her sit down on the couch, his worry palpable in the room. He clearly thought he had done something wrong.

"I don't know what I'm doing," she blurted.

"All right," he acknowledged, and came to sit beside her, leaving enough distance between them that she didn't feel cornered. "Go on."

That was one thing she loved about him—he listened to her. He didn't try to push his own feelings and experiences on her the way so many people did. He wasn't simply waiting for his turn to talk.

"You found my note," she said. "You must have."

"I did." He smiled. "That's why I'm here. I promised you I would come."

"But it isn't safe. It will never be safe. Weren't you the one who didn't want to put me in jeopardy? What is this, then? What are you trying to do to me?" She hated the entreaty in her voice, but she couldn't help it. "Don't you understand how this feels? Seeing you like this, hearing your voice, eating ice cream with you like we're a normal couple—it feels like the one thing that's been missing all these months. I could live my life without you, yes. But I don't want to. Are you here just to show me what I can't have?"

"I wouldn't do that," he insisted. "I would never hurt

you. I just . . . I had to see you. It had been so long . . . and you . . . Miranda, you have haunted my thoughts every night since you left. I can't even open the door to your room without my heart breaking all over again. I told myself over and over that it was better just to make a clean break, but I don't think that's possible with us." He took both of her hands and held her eyes, and she felt his words all the way through her, body and soul, the emotion shaking her inside. "I'm here because I don't know what else to do. I don't know what's going to happen or where to go from here. I just know . . ."

She held her breath, waiting, her eyes so deeply locked in his that she could hear every thought through his shields and her own. She waited . . . she wanted . . .

He took a deep breath. "I am in love with you, Miranda Grey. I've fallen so far into you that I can't even see the stars anymore, but it doesn't matter—you're all the light I need."

She was crying, she could feel it, but she didn't try to stop it. "Cheesy," she said with a weak laugh.

He smiled back, lifting one hand and tracing her lower lip with his fingers. "You didn't give me time to practice," he said. "Let me try again: 'I would not deny you; but, by this good day, I yield upon great persuasion, and partly to save your life, for I was told you were in a consumption.'"

Miranda felt a strange rising of something in her heart, something she almost didn't recognize at first, until she realized it was joy. Her voice unsteady but the emotion clear, she quoted back, "'Peace! I will stop your mouth.'"

Her hands slid up his forearms, and she leaned in and put her lips to his. As he returned the kiss she felt his hands against her face, thumbs brushing her tears away. She moved into his arms, her lips parting, mouth seeking mouth with half-fearful desire. His hands spanned her waist and lifted her into his lap.

Miranda fell into the kiss, drowning herself in it and grateful to drown, the taste of him almost too much to bear. His skin was cool at first but heated the more she touched, and before long her fingers were seeking his buttons, trying to find their way in and remove another barrier that stood between them.

He lifted his mouth from hers and began to trail kisses along her jaw, up to her ear, the softness of his breath sending tremors all the way down to her toes. His hands moved up beneath the hem of her sweater, skimming the inside edge of her jeans until they found bare skin.

"Wait," she whispered.

He drew back immediately, his pupils dilated hugely in the lamplight.

"I'm sorry," he said a little breathlessly. "You're not ready."

"It's not that." She pulled away and stood, grateful that her knees didn't give out. "It will be morning in a few hours. The bedroom windows are blocked out. It will be safe for you in there."

He looked at her, the vulnerability in his eyes making her ache. "Are you asking me to stay?"

"Yes."

He rose gracefully and turned away from her, and for a moment she thought she'd stepped over a line, but he merely spoke into his com. "Harlan . . . I won't be returning to the Haven tonight. I'll call for you at dusk."

*"Yes, Sire."*

Then David lifted his eyes to hers again, and, smiling, he reached for her hand.

She took it and, switching off the lights as she walked, led him into the bedroom.

He had her in his arms again before they even crossed the doorway, and she turned in his embrace, kissing him again, this time hard. His tongue snaked into her mouth, and he wove one hand into her hair to hold her against him while she worked impatiently at his shirt, pushing it off his shoulders with hands gone clumsy with urgency.

Something wild had seized them both, and neither had any intention of fighting it. Her nails dug into his upper arms so hard that she heard him growl low in his throat, and he maneuvered her back toward the bed, stripping off her sweater and the T-shirt and bra under it, barely breaking the kiss.

It wasn't until she felt the warm air of the bedroom on her bare legs that she caught her breath and made herself slow down. She looked up and held his eyes as she lowered herself onto the bed, then offered her hand again and drew him along with her, stretching out face to face, their hands moving once more but slower, with more care. She tested the hard muscles of his torso, first with her palms and then her lips, and he let her set the pace, watching her, silent.

Finally, she unzipped and tugged off his jeans, and her heart began to thunder in her chest and throat as she let her eyes roam over the length and breadth of the vampire in her bed.

His hand touched her face. "Are you afraid?"

She swallowed, and at first shook her head, but then nodded. "I don't want to be."

He rose up and pulled her close, the smell and heat of his skin making her feel slightly dizzy; she remembered him talking about the aura his kind gave off, and wondered if this was it. His mouth moved along her collarbone and down her shoulder, and he murmured into her ear, "All you have to say is 'Stop.'"

"I don't want to stop."

He smiled. "Then close your eyes, my love, and lie back."

He began a slow, soft exploration of her body, kissing her throat and her lips again while his fingers hooked in her panties and slid them down over her hips; he moved down and kissed the exposed skin, breath hot on her belly.

She tried to close her eyes as he'd said, but she was too mesmerized watching the way he moved—almost serpentine, almost like a cat, nothing like a human man. Yet she wasn't afraid of him; no, she never really had been.

There was reverence in his touch, but also a deep need that she could feel rising from him like a shimmer of sunlight. The stark black lines of his tattoo seemed alive as he curled around her, one hand cupping her neck to bring her mouth up to his, the other sliding between them, over the curve of her stomach, and down.

She moaned into his mouth and arched up against his palm. God, it had been so long . . .

She wrapped one leg around his waist and pressed full against his body, loving how they seemed to fit each other, as if her hip had been made to lock into his just so, and her arms were the perfect length to wind around his back. His fingers dipped gently inside her, and she whimpered, the feeling not nearly deep enough, not nearly close enough.

Twisting, she moved out from under him and nudged him to his back. She leaned down to kiss him deeply, shifting her hips back, and lowered herself onto him with aching slowness, joining them inch by slippery inch.

Now he groaned, and sat up, letting her rise and fall against him with his arms around her waist. She clawed into his back and rocked up and down, eyes shut tight in concentration . . . then in near-screaming frustration. Alone, the deep driving pleasure of him wasn't enough for her. She needed more.

"I want all of you," she whispered hoarsely. "Please."

Before he could even come up with the words for a question, she lowered her head and bit him hard where his neck joined his shoulder.

He moved so fast she couldn't react—a ragged animal snarl tore from his throat, and he flipped her onto her back, driving into her so hard she cried out and let her head fall back, exposing her throat.

Needles of hot pain thrust into her skin and she felt his mouth clamp on her neck.

"Yes," she moaned, pulling him back into rhythm with her body, holding his head against her with one hand. He entered and withdrew in one slow undulation, and she gave herself over completely, tumbling over one cliff and then another, her body quaking around him, a nova kindling in her heart and tearing the universe into pieces.

The aftershocks rolled through her forever, but distantly she was aware of movement, of him reaching down over the side of the bed for something. She heard a click and saw the flash of a blade in the darkness.

Her eyes focused on the berry-bright droplets that gathered along a shallow cut, hovering over her mouth. Tentatively, she reached up and licked one away, earning a tremor as violent as her own. She tasted again, letting the salt-sweetness burn on her tongue, then raised her lips to his skin, and sucked.

She felt him move into her again, this time so slowly that every tiny motion echoed through her body. His heart was beating hard against her breasts, and she could smell her blood on his breath. It only made her want more.

Over and over again, they found each other, sometimes clawing and biting, sometimes with delicious teasing anticipation. Time lost its purpose, as did everything else beyond each other. She found the knife beneath the pillow and opened his skin again, and his teeth found purchase in hers as well, and they drank each other in nibbles and sips, savoring, over and over.

When at last he collapsed on top of her, sweat soaking them both and the mingled smells and tastes of their bodies heavy in the air, he laid his head on her shoulder, shaking, and they held on to each other tightly as the hours of afternoon passed outside and the world went on with no idea that two wayward stars had collided and nothing would ever, ever be the same.

\* \* \*

*Cold, black water engulfed her, and she tried to scream . . .
hands in the dark, laughter . . .*

Miranda woke with a start, struggling against an
invisible assailant that turned out to be the comforter, her
breath and heart both racing. She sat up into the darkness
and tried to calm herself, torn between the urge to run
and the urge to strike out.

She groped mindlessly to one side and shocked herself
when her palm met something solid.

Memory returned. She gasped.

David was sound asleep beside her, the sheets low over
his hip, the faint watery daylight coming in beneath the
bedroom door just barely silhouetting the line of his body
and the light from the Signet a dim red bathing the places
where there should have been dark cuts in his skin. They
had already healed.

Vampires were sound sleepers during the day; he didn't
even stir in response to her movements. She sat there watching him for a moment while she grounded herself—it
was far easier than she expected thanks to the gravita-
tional pull of his oblivion. Still, she was wide-awake and
anxious . . . not to mention she had to pee. She climbed
out of the bed and, wincing at how sore and strained her
muscles were, went to the bathroom, washed her face,
and tried to get some sense back in her thoughts.

She looked at herself in the mirror. There were three
bite marks in her throat, one on the left and two on the
right, and though the holes themselves were closing, there
was blood dried on her neck, and the pale purple shadows
of bruises forming on her breasts. She smiled a little and
touched each one, feeling fluttery inside at the memory.

The fuzziness refused to leave her mind even after she
splashed cold water on her face and cleaned herself up
with a washcloth—she felt almost high, tremulously weak
in all her limbs, but it was a pleasant sort of weirdness.

She went back into the bedroom to find he'd shifted position, turning over to face away from the door; she smiled again, remembering the silk of his skin against her lips and the way the tattoo had been raised, just a little the way she'd hoped it would be, like a relief map of ink.

She caught sight of his knife on the bedside table. The blade was still open from the third . . . fourth? time, and seeing it almost made her stagger backward as the realization of what they had done hit home.

*I drank blood. His blood. That's why I feel so strange. Oh my God, I drank blood.*

*And I liked it.*

Miranda slid into the bed and curled up against his back, kissing his shoulder and wrapping one arm around him to press her hand against his heart. She ran her hand over his chest, then around the side, sighing happily. He had cooled off in his sleep, but it didn't bother her; the blankets were warm, and she was exactly where she wanted to be, and if she were to give the appropriate attention, he'd be warm again in seconds. She considered doing so, but there was too much going on in her mind . . . and as tired as he had seemed, she didn't want to wake him yet.

She wasn't surprised at the nightmares. What had surprised her was that they didn't come until she was asleep. There had been no flashbacks, no real hesitation except at the beginning—for a few hours her memories had been banished to the past where they belonged.

But now there was something new to fear. She could feel it coursing through her. It was as if every cell of her body had opened up to take him in, and something dark and hungry was stretching inside her, waking slowly from years of slumber. She knew the rules—if it happened again, or if she encouraged it, she would change. Forever.

*It's not too late. In a few days everything will be back to normal. It doesn't have to happen again.*

The body in front of her shifted, muscles flexing and twisting, and he turned over to face her, wide-awake with sadness in his eyes. "Don't worry," he said softly. "It won't."

Regret rolled through her, but she said, "How did you . . ."

"I can hear you," he replied. "Open your shields a little."

She did as he said, parting the barrier like a curtain just enough to let his energy in, and instantly her mind was flooded with thoughts and images, memories . . . and pain. He'd been awake long enough to feel her reaction to what had happened. Her fear had dashed whatever embryonic hopes he'd had.

"No," she said. "No, I didn't mean that. I . . . I just feel so weird . . . I . . ."

She couldn't find the words. It was hard to think straight with his mind so close to hers, the blood between them so strong it hurt. All she knew was that she didn't want him to be sad, and that she needed him to understand. She shut her eyes, not wanting to block him out but her mind reeling from even a few seconds' connection.

"It is a little overwhelming," he affirmed. "But it has its advantages."

"Oh . . . like what?"

She felt him touch her; as his fingers wrapped around her shoulder, his energy pulsed through her in a psychic caress, centered on his hand and spreading out to her toes. His hand moved around over her heart, and this time he sent emotion coupled with the pleasure. It felt like he was touching her everywhere at once, inside and out, and Miranda's breath hitched in her chest. She couldn't help but respond in kind, grabbing his hand in both of hers and projecting her own emotions into him. She felt him shiver slightly.

"You're so strong," David said. "I don't think you realize even a tenth of what you can do."

She smiled. "I'm starting to." She breathed slowly, finally taking the time to actually feel out what was different, and found it wasn't nearly as frightening as she'd initially thought—it was dark, yes, but it was still *her.* Whatever changed inside her, she could still choose what to do with it. She thought about the vampires at the Haven—about the one in her arms right now—and how they used what they were to protect, not abuse, even though the power within them was a hundred times darker and pervaded their entire lives.

Surely, if they could do that, she could . . . and, she realized, she wanted to. Something about this felt right to her. She had spent her entire life feeling out of place, out of step with the world, never feeling completely alive . . . but now, she was starting to wake up to who she could be, and whoever this new Miranda was, she wanted more.

"I'm sorry I freaked out," she said. "This is . . . it's a lot to take in."

"I understand." She could feel that he did; she could feel, in fact, that he was a little freaked himself.

She leaned in to rest her forehead against his, and for a moment they simply breathed in each other's presence, taking strength from it as if their energy came from a single source and all they had to do was share it.

"How long can you stay?" she asked.

"Only until sunset . . . I'll have a lot waiting for me when I get back."

"So that gives us, what, two hours?"

"Two and a half until it's really dark enough for me to go."

"Good," she said, and kissed him. "Show me what else we can do now."

He laughed against her lips and pounced on her, ideas blossoming in his mind with the eagerness of a teenager. She laughed, too, catching his mouth again, forgetting sore muscles, the future, and everything else, surrendering to the perfect sweetness of desire.

He was, in fact, about an hour late in leaving—between their last round of lovemaking, which actually became two once they got in the shower, and the hunt for scattered clothing, and the longing not to leave her side, he left Harlan waiting at the rendezvous point until almost eight P.M.

They stood at the doorway embracing one more time, neither wanting to let go. "Do I have to make you promise again?" she asked into his neck.

"No," he answered. "I'll come back. It may be a few days, but . . . Miranda . . ." He chuckled, almost panicked at the certainty he felt. "I couldn't stay away from you now if I wanted to."

"Is there anything I should do, or watch out for? Should I stay out of the sun?"

"It won't hurt you, but until the blood has burned out of your system you'll probably be extra sensitive to light and maybe even to sound. Your senses will be more intense at times, and at times normal. Just stay grounded, and by the end of next week you'll be fine."

"No," she said, tilting her head back to meet his eyes. "I'll be normal, but I won't be fine. I won't be fine until I wake up next to you every night."

He hugged her even more tightly. There was no use denying it. She would get what she wanted from him, and he would yield gratefully to her will. He could fight it for eternity and condemn them both to misery, or he could listen to the part of him that knew, deep down, he belonged to her. Perhaps the Signet would accept her, perhaps not . . . but one way or another he would have Miranda by his side for as long as she was willing to stay with him. "I know. Just . . . give me a little time. Let this pass, while I make sure the Haven is safe for you. Then I'll bring you home."

"All right." She nipped his ear lightly, and it was all he could do not to throw her back against the door and take her again—he couldn't seem to get enough of her. He'd spent an entire day drunk on her body and he was already an addict.

They kissed again, deeply. When he took a step back,

trying to break contact long enough to walk away, he said, "In the meantime . . . say your farewells to the sunlight."

She grinned. "The sunlight can go to hell." She moved forward and kissed his forehead, then his lips, then the hollow of his throat. "I'll see you again soon."

He squeezed her hands, then let go, and bowed to her. "As you will it, my Lady."

# Fifteen

Faith was already grinning as she strode down the hall to the workroom, and when she entered, she had to stop herself from laughing out loud.

The Prime was in his chair going over network reports, but even with his astounding psychic protections, the edges of his aura were leaking out, and the entire room was saturated with how he was feeling.

She had to double the thickness of her own shields to keep herself from getting so turned on she dragged Samuel off to the broom closet.

"Sire? You wanted to see me?"

He looked up from the computer, saw her face, and frowned. "Something on your mind, Second?"

She gave up and burst out laughing.

The Prime shook his head, looking aggravated, but only on the surface. He was clearly having trouble keeping the lazy satisfaction out of his expression. "Go ahead," he said, more good-naturedly than she'd ever heard him. "Get it out of your system."

"Sorry," she said, not sorry at all. "I trust you're feeling . . . refreshed this evening?"

An eye roll. "I don't suppose you kept this to yourself."

"I didn't say a word to anyone," she insisted, "but, Sire,

you've never stayed out all day before. People were bound to talk. You know how this place is—and half the Elite has had a betting pool going on how long it would take you two to sleep together, so . . ."

"You are joking, right?"

"Partly. It wasn't a betting pool exactly but Elite Fifty-One owes me twenty bucks." She sat down, noticing that while he was working his feet were propped up on a second chair, something else he never did. He was also looking a tad rumpled instead of his usual pressed-and-tailored.

"I want doubled security on Miranda's apartment," he said. "I have no reason to believe I was followed there, but I'm not taking any chances."

"As you will it."

"Also I'm not happy with the sensor performance in sector twenty-eight-G, so get a team assembled to go out tomorrow night and replace several of the units. It will take me until then to get the last two built. Do you have anything new to report?"

"No, Sire. The city's been quiet since the raid."

"What about Bethany Blackthorn?"

Faith wanted to voice her protests again, but didn't; one thing she knew about him was that he hated being nagged, and that he always listened the first time, even if he didn't agree. He could quote word for word conversations they'd had years ago. Repeating herself would only annoy them both. "She's up and moving around but hasn't made any move toward wanting to leave. The guards say she's a little spooky, but no trouble."

He nodded, his eyes back on the monitor. "I'd like to request a personal favor, if I may."

She kept her surprise to herself. "Yes, Sire?"

"I'd like you to go by Miranda's and make sure she's all right, perhaps even several times this week. Let me know immediately if she's exhibiting any potentially dangerous symptoms."

"Dangerous? Dangerous how—oh." Faith nodded, understanding. "You traded blood."

"More than we should have. I'm concerned that she may have a stronger reaction both because she's so outstandingly psychic and because I'm, well, me."

"I'd be happy to check on her," Faith agreed. "I was going to anyway so I could get all the juicy details."

"You are incorrigible."

"Damn right."

A few hours later when Faith got off duty and went into the city to hunt, she doubled back afterward and presented herself on Miranda's doorstep, trying not to look as smug as she felt.

Miranda didn't answer on the first knock, and when she opened the door, all of Faith's humor drained out of her.

"Good God," Faith said. "You look terrible."

Miranda beckoned her inside and returned to the couch where she'd been camped—she was dressed in faded Mickey Mouse pajama pants and a black tank top and had several empty water bottles and a pizza box on the coffee table in front of her. The lid was open enough for Faith to see she'd taken one bite.

"All right, you have to eat," Faith informed her sternly. "You need protein and iron or you're going to feel worse by the end of the night. Do you have any multivitamins around here?"

"Bathroom," was the vague reply.

Faith fetched the bottle and pressed two capsules into Miranda's hand. She took them without protest. Then Faith went into the kitchen and dug through the fridge until she came up with half a leftover giant burrito from Freebird's. It was loaded with beans, rice, and vegetables and wouldn't be as hard on her stomach as all that cheese. Luckily it seemed to be only about two days old, and a minute in the microwave restored it to something of its former glory.

"Here. Eat this. Small bites."

Miranda seemed relieved, for a change, at having someone tell her what to do. She nibbled at the edges of the tortilla and then managed a few larger bites.

"He wasn't kidding when he said you exchanged too much," Faith observed, shaking her head. "Another few ounces and you'd be in real trouble. He shouldn't have left you here like this."

"I don't think he knew it was this bad," she murmured. "I was fine when he left. I went back to sleep and when I woke up I had the worst hangover of my life."

"That's one hell of a hickey you've got there. Eat."

Miranda's hand moved up to touch one of the bite marks on her neck, and a dreamy sort of look passed over her face before it was replaced by an acute pain that made her cover her eyes. "That's not the worst part," she said. "Earlier when I got out of bed . . . I felt so . . . depressed. Like I didn't even want to breathe anymore. I still feel that way, just not as bad. If I knew how to get to the Haven from here, I'd have walked barefoot." She wiped at her eyes. "I did something stupid—look."

Miranda stuck out her tongue, and Faith saw a bright red cut. "How did you do that?"

She reached into her pocket and withdrew a familiar knife—carved into the shape of a bird of prey with an ebony handle and a folding blade serrated along its lower half. Miranda flicked her wrist and the blade snapped out, shining and lethal.

"There was blood on it," she explained. "I licked it."

Faith stared at her. "Jesus."

"I didn't even realize what I was doing. I saw the blood, and I just . . . needed it."

"And how did you feel after that?"

"Aside from the fact that my tongue was bleeding? Wonderful, for a minute. Then I got freaked out and took a Xanax."

"Can't say I blame you. Look, Miranda, I know you feel like hell now, but as long as you eat and rest you should be much better tomorrow. You'll probably feel better than you have in your life."

"Does turning into a vampire suck like this?"

"Oh, it's much worse. But if it's done right you're not aware of most of it. Right now the problem isn't that so much as *whose* blood you drank—for one thing, the stronger your sire, the faster and more intense the change. For another, the two of you already had a connection, so this deepened it, and now you're going through withdrawal."

"God, how pathetic," Miranda muttered. "I'm pining. I'm actually *pining*."

"It could be worse. Some of us aren't lucky enough to be turned by someone who loves us. Imagine if your sire forced you, then abandoned you, without even telling you the rules you had to live by."

Miranda's eyes widened in sympathetic horror. "Is that what happened to you?"

"No. That's what happened to David."

"God." Miranda took a long drink from the half-empty water bottle at her elbow. "Did you love your sire?"

"No. I paid her. I loved the boy I changed for . . . but as it turned out, he didn't love me, at least not for very long." Faith sighed. "Remember how I said love wasn't a good reason to become a vampire? I spoke from experience."

"I'm sorry."

"It was a long time ago. And in the end, I was grateful. All of that misery brought me here, to the life I feel I was meant to lead. I just hope it's easier for you." She gave Miranda a long, searching look. "Are you sure . . ."

"Yes," Miranda said, and despite the weariness in her voice there was also determination. "I never expected it to be easy. Nothing worthwhile ever is." She took another bite of her burrito, then set the plate down, looking a little nauseated. "I know that if I do this, I'll be where I belong . . . and everything I've been through will have some meaning."

"Well, you're going to need to make some arrangements—once you two decide when exactly you're coming back, you'll need to clear your schedule for a couple of weeks. You may have to stop performing—"

"No," Miranda cut her off. "Music is the only thing that's gotten me through all these years. My career's just getting started. I'm not giving it up."

Faith smiled at her. "You will need to take some time off, though. Even once the change is complete you'll need time to adjust. So you might want to start talking to your manager about it now—invent some kind of surgery, maybe."

"Good idea. Everyone dealt with my vanishing once. I don't want to do that to them again." Miranda looked thoughtful, and faintly dismayed. "I'm going to have to figure out what to tell Kat."

"What cat?"

Miranda laughed. "Not a cat. Kat. She's a friend of mine. I'm sure Lindsay has reported my going out with her a lot."

"Oh, right—the woman with the dreadlocks. Yes, we know about her. And about the boy."

"You mean Drew? I'm not so sure he'll be coming around anymore. He probably won't want to anyway. I think David scared the piss out of him."

"I'm shocked," Faith said wryly. "What did he do?"

"Threatened to kill him."

"Of course," Faith said. "How romantic. So, tell me more about this whole thing—what happened? After all that 'I have to stay away for her own good' bullshit, how did you two end up snacking on each other?"

Miranda got that dreamy look back in her eyes and pulled her knees up to her chin. "How much detail do you want?"

"Everything—just do me a favor and stay away from words like *throbbing* and *turgid*."

She snorted. "Fine, but I will say this: Remember what you said about Hades being spectacular in bed?"

"Yes."

"Well . . ." She turned bright pink. "You don't know the half of it."

Sunday evening Miranda woke all at once, with no eye-rubbing transition to wakefulness, and stared blinking at her bedroom ceiling for a full minute before she realized she could see in the dark.

The room was never a hundred percent black despite the heavy curtains—and layer of cardboard—she'd hung over the two windows; a little light always came in through the edges of the door. Still, she had never abandoned her nocturnal habits from the Haven, so she wanted it good and dark in her room during the day to let her sleep; usually the first thing she did once the sun was down was to snap on the bedside lamp so she didn't have to blunder around and knock her shins on things.

This time, she opened her eyes to find that it was unusually bright, yet she knew nothing had changed while she slept. The light level in the room was the same as always . . . but she could see. Everything was blue and lavender and gray, but perfectly distinct.

She sat up and looked around, fascinated. She could read the spines of books across the room. She could read the print on the electric bill she'd tossed carelessly on her desk.

Her mouth went dry with momentary fear. Was this normal? Had she . . .

She got out of bed and walked, without stubbing her toe once, into the bathroom, where she didn't have to turn on the light to see herself in the mirror.

She was still in the mirror. That was something.

David had said her senses would fluctuate. Was this how vampires saw? Everything was sharp and clear, and it was almost as if some things were more than three-dimensional.

Once she got over the newness of it and relaxed into

the difference, she found she liked it. It was certainly going to come in handy reading music in dimly lit clubs.

She stripped off her pajamas—Mickey was getting pretty rank—and turned on the shower, and again found she was mesmerized, this time by the water raining down from the showerhead. If she concentrated, she could see individual droplets and watch the path each one took down the drain.

Shaking herself out of it, she got into the shower, but when she went to lather up her mesh bath sponge, the smell of her lavender body wash was so intense she nearly threw up. She capped the bottle and rummaged around in the miscellaneous half-used toiletries that cluttered her shower shelf, coming up with a travel-sized container of organic unscented soap that Kat had left when she spent the night back in January.

It still had a smell, but it was tolerable. She soaped herself up and, after considering her shampoo selection, used the same stuff for her hair.

Drowsy from the heat and steam, she wrapped herself in her bathrobe and wandered into the kitchen.

On the street outside a car alarm suddenly went off, and she shrieked and dove back into the hallway, hands clamped over her ears. Pain ricocheted off the inside of her skull.

She stared blindly into the fridge for a while. Nothing was remotely appetizing. She'd asked Faith to throw the pizza in the Dumpster when she left, and though there was technically plenty of food, she didn't want any of it. The thought of eating made her stomach churn.

She settled for some saltine crackers and a bottle of Vitamin Water.

Her phone rang; she jumped again but this time didn't panic. The ring wasn't nearly as loud as the car outside had been. Her phone was where she'd left it on the table.

She saw who it was, and her heart leapt.

"Hi," she said.

"How are you?" David asked.

"Better. But I can see in the dark."

A pause. "You can?"

"Yeah. Everything's blue. Is that normal?"

She heard him take a deep breath. "Not exactly. I think it's another sign that we overdid it."

"If you say so. I think it's kind of neat, actually. I can't wait to see what's next."

He laughed. "You are a rare woman."

"I'm something, all right." She sat on the couch, the sound of his voice making her toes curl, and said, "I wish you were here."

"So do I."

"When will you be?"

A sigh. "I can't get away until Friday—perhaps I could come by after your show."

"I'd like that." Almost an entire week; she'd stand it somehow. "How are you feeling?"

The humor returned. "Apparently I'm giddy. The Elite are finding me rather obnoxious."

"You, giddy?"

"Relatively speaking, I'm sure."

She heard something beep, and he said, "Damn. I have to go—I'm in the middle of recalibrating part of the network, and I had a minute while it was running. I just wanted to check on you. And hear your voice."

"I'm glad you called."

"I'll talk to you soon—perhaps even later tonight if you're awake. I love you."

She knew she was grinning like a fool, and she didn't care. "I love you, too."

They hung up. Miranda was thankful that the withdrawal seemed to have faded; she didn't feel like crying this time.

In fact, overall, she felt fantastic. The weakness had left her body, and she wanted to get up and do something, preferably something that involved a lot of running. She didn't have another scheduled session with Sophie until Tuesday, and she had gigs on Wednesday on through the end of the week, leaving her at loose ends at least for the night. She was pretty sure Kat would want to get together tomorrow.

She should go out and get something to eat. Perhaps being at a restaurant, with the smells of food around her, would stimulate her appetite; part of her resistance to eating was the idea of cooking. She could go to Kerbey and have all the pancakes she wanted.

Mind made up, she got dressed and pulled on her jacket. When she looked at herself in the mirror again, she had to smile. Her color had returned, mostly, and she looked awake. There was knowing in her eyes. She looked like a woman with a secret.

Outside, Austin was fairly quiet; there was little traffic, pedestrian or vehicular, and she was glad. As it was, the noise and fuss were a bit too much at first, but she stayed calm and kept breathing. The streetlights hurt her eyes—how did the Elite run around town without sunglasses on?

A fingernail moon hung in the sky, and she could taste the change of seasons in the air: wildflowers blooming, trees leafing out, everything had a scent that registered to her both all at once and individually.

It wasn't until she was on the bus that things started unraveling. There were only a few other passengers, and she took a seat in the very back a few rows away from a middle-aged woman in a shabby coat. As she passed, she could smell each person strongly; several had pretty intense body odor problems, and the only one who wasn't repellent was the woman herself, who smelled like old age and rose petals.

Old age had a smell? Miranda concentrated, and sniffed the air again. Sure enough, the woman smelled like a grandmother, and it was familiar enough—slightly musty, a little sweet. The scent had layers that her mind picked out one by one.

The woman was tired and had sore feet, but she was in good health. Miranda stared at her hard, her eyes fixing on the pale wrinkled skin, and on the faint blue tracings of veins in her neck. She listened . . . she could hear the woman's heart beating . . . air rushing in and out of her lungs . . . the quiet click of her bones against each other as she flexed her arthritic fingers . . . the vein throbbed, and Miranda felt the roof of her mouth start to itch, then burn.

She was *hungry*. Her stomach growled loudly, startling her, and also startling the object of her obsession, who looked up at her angrily when she realized she was being stared at.

"Sorry," Miranda muttered. She couldn't breathe. She yanked the stop cord, and as soon as the bus pulled over she practically bolted down the steps and back into the cool night air.

She grabbed a lamppost and leaned on it heavily, panting.

A man walked by, and her head snapped up at the smell of him. Cancer. In his prostate. He would taste wrong. Gamy.

The couple across the street—the woman was pregnant. Twins. The man was fucking her sister. She could smell sex on him, and the woman he had been inside was related to his wife but not her. She was smiling, talking animatedly about . . . cribs. Their conversation was as loud as it would be two feet away.

Car exhaust. Garbage. Horns honking. A baby crying. Cigarette smoke. Music from a bar three blocks away.

Miranda tried to shield again, but this time it couldn't help; what she was feeling wasn't psychic, it was physical. Her hearing and sense of smell had quadrupled at least, and there was no way to block that out except to find someplace silent and safe.

She looked around, trying to get her bearings. She was less than half a mile from home and there was no way in hell she was getting back on a bus. She'd just have to walk, and deal with it.

This was what it was like . . . this was what she had to

look forward to. How long would it take her to get used to the overload? Was it just affecting her like this because she was still human and her body and mind were too weak to handle it?

She had to handle it. She wasn't going to change her mind. It was going to be hard, but she would deal. There was too much at stake to be defeated by these first baby steps.

Steeling herself and straightening her spine, she began the walk home.

"You know," Deven said, "my Consort is rather put out with you."

David leaned back in his seat, watching the night landscape out the car window. They would be back at the Haven in ten minutes or less. "Is he, now," he said into the phone.

The tone of Deven's voice suggested that Jonathan had been making an issue of his dire predictions for some time now. "He remains convinced that you're going to get this Miranda killed."

"That's exactly what I intend to do," David replied. "I'm going to bring her across."

The Prime on the other end of the line sighed resignedly. "I'll spare you reminders of what a huge responsibility that is, and how badly it went the last time."

"This is different. She's sure, and I'm sure. In fact, she won't take no for an answer. Besides, weren't you in favor of this last time we spoke?"

"I'm not against the idea by any means—just cautious. It isn't something to undertake lightly. Not to mention this woman is still fairly young, and you can be as dense as osmium sometimes. Love tends to blind us to practicalities."

"Was that a scientific reference? Sire, I didn't know you had it in you."

"I thought perhaps if I spoke your language you might actually listen once in a while."

David smiled. "I always listen. Then I do what I want. You know that."

"It is one of your more infuriating qualities. But I worry about you, David." There was a surprising earnestness in Deven's voice—he was almost always serious, but usually with a sharp, dry wit that was notably missing now. "I want your rule to last at least as long as mine—I've seen too many friends die, and you . . . I've always thought of you as if you were my own."

"I practically am."

"Exactly. So bring your love over to the shadows, but be careful, both with her and with your own heart. I helped put you back together once, and I'd prefer not to have to do it again. Are you listening?"

"I am, Sire. And I'll be careful. Believe me, I want to do this right."

"Call if you need help."

"I will."

David replayed the conversation in his head the rest of the drive home, wondering how seriously he should take it. Jonathan's vision hadn't changed, but it also hadn't recurred; and now that he knew what he and Miranda were facing together, he didn't find it nearly as alarming. Yes, she would die; and the next night she would awaken. The fire had already happened when the insurgent base burned. He had found Miranda's note in the book.

He thought back to his brief call to Miranda and felt renewed well-being at the memory of her voice. He would see her in a few days, and he was contemplating telling her that they should aim for the full moon to bring her back to the Haven. That would give her a week to settle her affairs for the time being. He was sure she'd want to be back onstage as soon as possible, but it would be two weeks, minimum, before he was comfortable with her going out into the city, even with bodyguards. Ideally he'd like to keep her close for a month to be sure she was strong enough. This was not something to take chances with.

Most vampires were born on a cruel whim or out of some romantic idiocy involving "eternal love," which tended not to last past the first decade. Real partnerships most often arose between vampires that were unrelated—that first blush of infatuation between sire and offspring was an ephemeral thing. Older vampires, especially Primes, almost never brought over a human for any reason; their power meant that their progeny had the potential to take Signets themselves, and they were usually loath to sire their own competition.

Harlan pulled the car up to the curb, and the Prime disembarked, looking, for a moment, up at the Haven, his home . . . her home. Even with her gone, the place had been stamped with her presence. Faith and several of the other guards of his wing had reported that, more than once, they'd been sure they saw her out of the corner of an eye.

One of the lieutenants met him at the doors as he entered. "Sire, the Blackthorn girl is asking for you."

"Thank you, Patrick. I'll see her now."

He took the right-hand staircase to the second floor instead of the left and made his way to the hallway of suites where the rare visitor from outside the territory stayed. Primes seldom left their realms, but once in a while a second in command or someone high up in another Court came to pay their respects. He'd had a constant stream of guests the first two or three years. Right now there was no one but Bethany Blackthorn.

Two guards stood outside her door; they bowed and stepped aside to let him enter.

He did the polite thing and knocked. There was no reason to start things off on the wrong foot.

"Come in," he heard.

He'd put her in one of the small suites—just a bedroom and bath with a sitting area by the fire, much like Miranda's but nowhere near as comfortable.

She looked small and out of place sitting in one of the chairs, her posture stiff, her dishwater hair hanging board-straight on either side of her face. She might have been beautiful once, but abuse had left her wraithlike, her eyes far too big for her face. Their unwavering azure was the only thing about her that seemed alive.

She sat with the pale spiders of her hands clasped between her knees, as unreactive to his arrival as she had been the night they'd found her, neither cowed by his power nor enraged by his supposed crimes. "Sire," she said. She sounded so young.

"Bethany," he replied, taking the other chair. "Are you feeling better tonight?"

"Yes." She stared down at her hands. "They're taking good care of me. I don't deserve it."

"Why not?"

She frowned and gave a one-shouldered shrug. "I'm a Blackthorn. We're the enemy. Or you are. My father said you were the devil."

"I'm sure he did. What do you think?"

"I think he was probably right. But you saved me. And Ariana . . ." She swallowed at the name as if it stuck in her throat. "What do you do when the angel is worse than the devil?"

He folded his hands, elbows on the arms of the chair. "What can you tell me about her plans, Bethany? It's important that I know so I can stop the remaining members from killing anyone else."

She looked up at him curiously. "You care about humans," she said. "My father said that humans were put here on this earth for our use."

"But we all came from humans," he pointed out.

"That's right. We used their bodies and then we use their blood. Once we have what we need, they don't matter. It's God's will that we are superior."

He nodded. He'd heard this line of "reasoning" before, and as with any form of zealotry, there was no arguing with it. "Even if that's true, your sister's people were responsible for the deaths of our kind as well. And if they're allowed to reorganize, there will be more death. I cannot allow that. What can you tell me?"

She shrugged again. "Not much. I was a pet, not a member of the group. She hated me from the time we lived in California. I was Father's favorite—he wanted me to go to Auren, but she lusted for power. I think secretly she was glad that Father was murdered."

"Can you tell me why there's no record of you anywhere? Everyone from the original family has been accounted for except you."

She made a sound that might have been a laugh. "No, they haven't. There were others. Anyone who didn't want to become warriors for the cause, anyone who disagreed . . . we disappeared, over time. Father had a fondness for me, though, because I looked so much like my mother. He let me stay and kept me safe even though I was a traitor. As soon as he was dead, Ariana got her revenge. She was going to give me to Auren's Elite as a toy."

"I see. And you know nothing about her larger plans for the organization?"

"She had a plan?"

He couldn't help but smile at the unexpected touch of humor. "She did intend to kill me and turn the Signet over to someone."

"Not Ariana. She would have kept it for herself. She only acted demure while Father was alive." Bethany picked at the edge of her sleeve for a moment, then said, "They all believed in her. She pulled them together after Auren died. Without her, they're nothing."

"I wish I could believe that."

She looked up and met his eyes, her own suddenly full of pleading. "They're going to kill me," she said. "As soon as they find out I'm still alive, they'll hunt me down. They'll think I was in collusion with you."

"They won't lay a finger on you," he told her. "I have you under double guard and digital surveillance. No one comes in or out of the Haven without my knowing, even assuming they can find it in the first place. Don't worry, Bethany."

"But . . . what are you going to do with me?"

He rose. "I haven't decided yet. So if there's anything further you know, I would appreciate it greatly if you shared it soon. After all you've been through I don't want to cause you more suffering, but I will if it's necessary. Your family has its cause and I have mine. I'm sorry you've been caught in the crossfire. If you cooperate, I'll do what I can to ensure your safety."

She returned her gaze to her hands. "I believe you," she said.

He started to leave, but her voice called him back. "Thank you."

He turned and nodded to her. "It is my duty to protect those under my rule, Bethany, until they become lawbreakers. As far as I know you've done nothing wrong."

"I didn't mean for that," she said, and for just a second he saw something burning in her eyes. "I meant thank you . . . for killing my sister."

# Sixteen

When Sophie opened the door that Tuesday night, whatever acerbic greeting she'd intended died on her lips. She stared for a minute, looking Miranda up and down.

Sophie shook her head. "Girl."

Miranda gave her the same eyebrow she often gave Miranda. "What?"

Sophie gestured for her to come in, as always, and for a while Miranda didn't think she was going to say anything else; she put Miranda through the usual warm-ups and basic sword drills with only occasional commentary on her form.

Then she took her own sword from the wall and without ceremony dove in for the attack.

Miranda countered, but in minutes she was disarmed. That was normal, but today it left her angry and frustrated. She'd been hoping that the changes in her senses would do . . . something. Help her move faster, maybe, or keep her on her feet longer. If anything, it hampered her; she was so busy being impatient that she kept getting knocked on her ass.

Sophie stood over her, the look on her face unreadable. "Get the fuck up," she snapped.

Miranda did so, but anger bubbled up in her throat. This time when Sophie attacked she was ready, or thought she was. She swung her blade hard, throwing her energy with it, but her carelessness cost her, and Sophie merely kicked her in the stomach and slapped the sword from her hand.

"Quit wasting my time," Sophie told her. "You think just because you've been sucking off a Prime that you're something special? I've got news for you, little girl. You're no better than you were a week ago. In fact, you suck as bad as you did the first time I met you."

"Fine," Miranda bit back. "What's the right way to do this?"

"I told you. Stop fighting like a human. If you want to be a vampire, you can't keep thinking like a meat puppet. Let it go."

"Let go of what, being human?"

"Yes, damn it." Sophie slammed her sword into its sheath and faced Miranda with arms crossed. "Becoming one of us is a gift. It elevates you beyond the limits of mortality. But it's not a game and it's not pretty. It's bloody and dark and dirty and it goes on forever. Once you cross this bridge, *there is no going back*. You're selling your soul to this life, Miranda. Are you ready? And moreover—are you worthy?"

Her eyes bored into Miranda's for the better part of a minute before Miranda said, quietly, "Show me how."

"Get up."

Miranda rose, gripping her weapon tightly. Her entire body felt like it was made of iron.

"Go into your Sight. Set your shields, set your stance." Sophie circled her, her pace deliberate and slow. "Now reach deeper into it. There's a power inside you you've never been able to access before. You still can't, not totally, but it's there, and you can touch it."

"Yes," Miranda said. She sought within herself and found what she'd experienced that first night with David, the sleeping shadow, waiting for blood to call it forth. "I feel it."

"Imagine it's air. Breathe it. Let it fill you up."

The energy crawled up her spine, scalding her, and she nearly lost her ground, but before Sophie could command her to, she hauled herself back under control.

The power of her senses from before was nothing compared to what she felt now. She could feel the entire room around her, stretching out from her own skin, the empty space connecting her to Sophie, to the floor, the ceiling, the walls. The sword in her hand was as light as a feather and felt like it had grown out of her palm.

"Good." Sophie fell into her own ready stance and said, "Now, stay in that place as you fight. Hold on to the shadow. Let it move you. Dance with it."

She raised her sword and brought it toward Miranda, where the blade hit its twin with a sharp clang. Miranda breathed in the darkness, and suddenly she could see Sophie as if there were two of her, the one before her and an afterimage. The afterimage was going to spin and kick—

Miranda wasn't there to feel it. She stepped effortlessly out of the way and spun herself, driving her sword up in a graceful arc to meet Sophie's. For the next few minutes she lost herself completely in action and reaction, point and counterpoint, like two melodies merging into harmony.

It didn't last long, though. Soon her arm felt as heavy as lead, and exhaustion pushed her down to the floor, her sword falling uselessly to the ground. She was breathing hard and drenched in sweat the way she hadn't been since the earliest days of her training.

Sophie, still flawless and unruffled, said, "Now you know what it feels like."

Miranda couldn't speak, but when she looked up at her teacher, she was smiling.

Being friends with the hottest act in town had its benefits. Kat got to watch the whole show from the wings instead of out in the crowd, and she was doubly thankful tonight.

The place was so packed that the heat in the room was as intense as a Texan July, and two people had already been taken out by bouncers to get fresh air.

If Miranda noticed, she didn't seem to care. She was on fire. Kat had never seen her so fierce. It seemed like her energy had ignited the audience, too, and they were dancing and jostling each other and it was a minor miracle a riot hadn't broken out.

The power in the singer's diminutive body was amazing. Her voice soared off the rafters and showed no signs of fatigue after two whole hours of solid performing.

It was a marked contrast to the last time Kat had seen her play, months and months ago. She'd been so sad back then, slave to whatever drug she'd been hooked on. She'd been a pale imitation of the Miranda Kat had first met back in college, the girl who caught everyone's attention with her razor wit and doll-like beauty.

Nowadays a doll was the last thing Miranda brought to mind. She was like a blade that had been tempered, purified in fire. Even her hair was aflame in the stage lights.

No wonder Drew had fallen so hard for her. Kat felt awful about the whole thing. She'd pushed them at each other when, now, it was obvious that Miranda was hung up on this David guy, and all her talk about not being ready for men was a smokescreen for not having the one she wanted.

In the few days since David had come waltzing back into her life, Miranda had changed again. There was something about her that was different physically, but Kat couldn't put her finger on it; regardless, she was acting like an amnesiac who had suddenly remembered she was royalty. It might have been annoying if it hadn't been so . . . believable.

Seeing her now, Kat felt like a fool for even considering Miranda and Drew as a couple. He was a sweet guy and had a lot going for him, but he was way too meek for a force of nature like her. As arrogant and cold as David had seemed, Kat had to admit he had charisma.

She wanted to know more about him, though, before she made up her mind. Not just any guy was good enough for Miranda, no matter how disgustingly hot he was.

One thing was absolutely sure: He was no drug counselor. If she'd had to put him in that world, she'd have pegged him as a drug *lord*. No way someone with the money to afford those clothes worked for human services. Particularly not given how he'd looked at Kat and Drew like they were from another species.

Miranda finished her last song to an eardrum-pulverizing ovation and bowed, saying something to the audience about how awesome they were and good night. She walked off the stage, pulling her guitar over her head and handing it to a sound tech . . .

. . . then stopped, wavered on her feet, and passed out cold.

"I'm telling you, I'm fine," Miranda told the nurse for the hundredth time. "I just got overheated, is all."

"Miss Grey," the round, stern black woman in blue scrubs said, "you're severely dehydrated and you said yourself you haven't eaten in three days. We need to do some blood work—"

Miranda snorted.

"—to find out why you've lost your appetite, and we need to get some fluids into you."

Kat, who was hovering near the entrance to the cubicle, said, "Mira . . . honey, listen to her. You've got to eat."

Miranda hopped down from the examination table, standing at her full height, which barely came up to the nurse's nose. She was in her bra and panties, and the nurse was clearly the don't-fuck-with-me-sugar type, but the woman moved back a foot or so anyway as Miranda's aura hit her.

"I want to go home," Miranda said calmly. "I am refusing treatment. I'll sign whatever forms you need me to."

The nurse looked like she wanted to give her an earful but instead just shook her head and said, "Fine."

Kat was giving Miranda a slightly nervous look. "What the hell has gotten into you lately?" she asked as soon as they were alone.

Miranda looked up at the ceiling. "I'm fine, Kat. Can you drive me home?"

"Sure. But only if you'll let me take you out to dinner first. And only if I see you eat."

Miranda crossed her arms and regarded her friend for a minute. Kat was genuinely worried for her; she was only trying to help, just like she'd always tried to do. There was no reason to treat her badly. "I'm sorry," Miranda said with chagrin. "I don't mean to be a bitch. It's just . . . I don't want them to poke and prod me. There's nothing wrong with me that a good meal and a long sleep won't cure."

Kat stared her down, but eventually looked away, making an *I give up!* noise. "Okay, okay. I'll go bring the car around to the exit. You sign your forms or whatever, and don't breathe fire at anybody else."

"Can you take this?"

Kat took her guitar with a grunt of assent and left.

Miranda pulled her clothes back on, glad she'd had the presence of mind to ask the tech for her guitar before Kat had whisked her away from the club to the Brackenridge Hospital ER. Otherwise she'd have had to go back for it, and all she really wanted was to go home.

As she put her boots on, she had to stop and breathe. This place . . . there was so much pain. Everyone here was afraid. Afraid of disease, of hurting, of death . . . especially death. She could feel the doctors and nurses moving among the patients, their calm heads like stars in the blackness of space. Their way was to find answers, to hunt down and kill illnesses and stitch together holes. What would they find if they looked at her blood right now? She had no idea, but she knew it scared her.

She drew the curtain aside and poked her head out of the cubicle; her nurse was nowhere in sight. Good.

Miranda gathered her bag and left. Halfway to the exit she saw the nurse and ducked into an empty cubicle until she passed.

The nurses' station was near her, and she saw through the edge of the curtain that a man in scrubs was standing there filling something out while a woman in a different style of uniform—white, with a badge pinned to her shirt instead of hanging from a lanyard—waited with a large red cooler at her feet.

"Twelve units," the male nurse was reading off. "Five O positive, five O negative, one AB positive, one AB negative. Sounds about right. Oh, wait . . . wasn't there supposed to be another cooler with the As and Bs? Or was that coming separately?"

The woman opened the cooler and looked inside. Miranda saw dark red in plastic, and her stomach turned a somersault. She recognized that packaging: a bag with a black-and-white label divided into four sections, barcoded with type and donor ID.

The roof of her mouth started to itch again. Her hand tightened on the curtain.

"I think you're right," the woman was saying. "Let me run out and check the van to be sure."

She hurried out of the ER, leaving the cooler behind.

Miranda stared hard at the desk nurse. *Look away. Look away.*

He turned to the left and began to dig around in a drawer for something.

Miranda darted out of the cubicle and, keeping her intention focused on the nurse, shoved her hand inside the cooler. Before she could even think about what she was doing, she had seized one of the bags inside and stuck it inside her jacket.

She all but ran for the exit, letting the nurse's mind go at the last minute before she burst outside, where Kat was waiting for her.

She slid into the passenger seat. "Thanks," she said.

Kat did not look at all happy with her. "Anything for you, sugarbean. Now, where do you want to eat? Kerbey?"

"Okay. That's fine. Actually . . . can we run by my place first? I'd like to get out of these clothes and put my guitar away."

"Sure."

Kat drove away from the hospital, and Miranda kept her arms crossed over her chest, feeling the coldness of the bag seeping through her shirt. What was she doing? Had she lost her mind? She'd just stolen blood from a hospital. It might have been meant for babies or some-one's crippled old mother. She was riding in a car with her friend as if everything was normal, and she had blood in her pocket.

"Wait here," Miranda said when they reached the apartment complex. "I'll be back in five minutes."

She unloaded her guitar and went into the kitchen, taking the bag and stowing it in the fridge—for a second she wondered what shelf it should go on. The crisper? She stuck it behind the milk, then went to change.


She forced herself to eat most of a short stack of pan-cakes, though it was a struggle not to throw them right back up again. She had barely eaten anything since the burrito Faith had fed her, but it wasn't for lack of appetite like the nurse had thought. She had tried to eat. She'd tried tempting herself with all her favorite foods, even ice cream from Amy's. Everything tasted like sawdust and ash.

It had surprised her that she was dehydrated, though. She'd been drinking water continuously, though it never seemed to slake her thirst. She'd bought a case of Vitamin Water so that she'd be getting at least a few nutrients.

The amazing thing was that she felt amazing. She was constantly hungry and thirsty, sometimes to the point of crying, but when she could put it out of her mind, she felt like Superwoman. Since she'd left Sophie's she felt like she could fly. She didn't want that feeling to go away.

As soon as she saw the blood in the cooler, it all made horrible sense.

"So Drew's a wreck," Kat was saying over her coffee. "He feels terrible. Are you planning to forgive him?"

"Forgive him? For what?" Miranda asked, blinking. She hadn't really been listening, but she remembered quickly enough. "Oh, that. I guess. I know he didn't mean any harm."

"You should tell him that. He's really nuts about you—right now he's convinced you hate him and he's on the verge of *hara-kiri*."

"I'll e-mail him," Miranda assured her.

"When are you going to tell me more about this other guy?"

Miranda smiled a little. "What do you want to know?"

"You said you met him at rehab. What does he do?"

She cast about in her mind for a suitable description that wouldn't be too much of a lie. "He's in law enforcement," she said. "He's the one that took me there in the first place."

"And the other night, you slept together?"

"Yes."

"I thought you weren't ready for men."

Miranda cut up the last half of her pancake to make it look like she was eating it. "David is different," she said, though it sounded weak even to her ears without any sort of background story. "I trust him. I don't think I can ever trust any other man again."

"Do you love him?"

"Yes. Very much."

"I guess I'm happy for you, then."

"You guess?"

Kat made a face. "To be honest, honey, he seemed like kind of a dick. But I only met him for about thirty seconds, so I could be wrong."

Miranda laughed. "He's not. I promise. He's just . . .

he has a lot of responsibility, and he's not very good with normal people. He's sort of a fanged teddy bear."

Kat looked even more dubious. "I am going to get to meet him again, right? As best friend I reserve the right to kick his ass to the curb if I don't approve."

Miranda smiled at her, warmly, feeling grateful as well as ashamed. There was so much she wanted to tell Kat, and she wasn't sure she'd ever be able to. The secrecy of the Shadow World was what kept it from destruction. The Signets worked diligently to keep vampire kind out of the media and off the radar. Did she have the right to let a human in on its existence?

"We'll all hang out," Miranda told Kat. "It takes him a while to warm up, but you'll like him once you get to know him."

Kat insisted on paying the bill, and Miranda was relieved to leave the café. She'd gotten used to the pressure of a room full of humans, but it was still a strain, especially after a night of performing and two hours in the ER surrounded by the injured and dying.

She told herself it was that, and not the thought of what was in her fridge, that made her so anxious to get home.

Kat let her out at her door with a hug and cheek-kiss. "Call me," she said firmly.

Miranda agreed, and watched her go, making sure she had pulled out of the parking lot before turning the dead-bolt and switching on the living room lamp.

She felt sick to her stomach from the pancakes, and by the time she got her coat and boots off, she was so nauseated she flew to the bathroom, where her dinner made an inglorious return engagement.

It was Thursday. David had said she should be feeling more normal by now. She contemplated calling him, but didn't want him to worry. She'd see him tomorrow anyway after her show. She just had to keep it together until then.

He was probably going to be angry with her. He'd wanted her to let his blood work its way out of her body this time, and turn her properly at the Haven where she'd be protected and he could control the situation. She knew he was right.

But she was so hungry . . . and nothing was helping. It couldn't hurt to keep his blood alive in her veins for one more day, could it?

She flushed the toilet and washed her face with ice-cold water. Her reflection looked green around the gills, and the flush of power had faded from her face, leaving behind an ashen pallor much like the one she'd had that first night. She couldn't stand to be that sick again.

*Just this once.*

Miranda fetched the bag from the fridge and set it on the counter, wondering how to go about it. Should she heat it? Put it in a glass? Stick a straw in it? She'd never seen David actually drink from one, but she couldn't picture him sucking on the bag like a Capri Sun. Surely he used a glass.

She opened the cabinet. A champagne flute? No, something for a red.

She settled on a coffee mug so that she could put it in the microwave for a few seconds. That had to be better, more like . . . more like fresh from a person.

Snipping off a corner of the bag, she poured enough to halfway fill the mug, and the rich coppery smell of it hit her like a sledgehammer. Her legs almost buckled beneath her, but she held herself up and punched twenty seconds, watching the cheerful I WENT BATS IN AUSTIN! logo turn in circles.

She took the cup out and sniffed it, then took an experimental sip.

Miranda moaned softly. As soon as it hit her tongue, she felt warmth and renewed strength trickling through her. One sip turned into a swallow, and before she knew it she had drained the mug and was refilling it with shaking hands. The orgasmic rush she remembered from drinking David's blood returned, though not as intensely. She had to force herself not to gulp—the thought of vomiting blood was the most disgusting thing she could imagine, and it would be such a waste. She didn't know when she could get any more.

She ended up sinking to her knees on the floor, her hands splayed out on the tile, heady joy and pleasure rocking her back and forth. The painful burning and itching in her mouth was gone, and so was her fatigue and weakness. Her vision was acute again, the colors in the room sharper. She hadn't realized how dull her senses were becoming as the week had worn on. Now everything felt right again.

It was wonderful.

She was laughing as she fell asleep on the kitchen floor.

David Solomon had been the first Prime to computerize all his records. Everything in his Haven was stored electronically; everything was beyond state-of-the-art, because if he didn't have the technology he wanted, he simply created it. The com system, the network connecting all the Signets all over the world, the sensors that now helped protect Austin—he had a dozen patents to his name already and was in progress on several more, including a new kind of solar cell that harnessed the vampires' universal enemy as a source of renewable energy to power not just the Haven, but all its systems and even the cars.

At first the other Signets had laughed, but eventually they caught on to the convenience and efficiency. California was the first to buy a software license and join the network; Deven knew a good thing when he saw it. After that, most of the others fell in line. Even a few Signets who were outright antagonistic toward California, and by extension the South, had expressed interest in upgrading their archaic communications.

The only area where Faith had really seen a problem was when it came to research. Everything David had brought with him from California, including all their information on the original Blackthorn syndicate, was on a server. Anything dated before the Signet changed hands was still kept in hard copies in the archives of the Haven. Auren had been particularly disdainful toward technology, so all his old patrol reports were still on paper, handwritten.

That meant that when David asked her to find out more about Ariana and Bethany Blackthorn by going through Auren's files, she wanted nothing more than to beat him about the head with the 1954–1955 bound reports until he had a better idea.

"All I'm asking is for you to pull relevant files," the Prime said. "Eventually I'm going to try to scan and upload all of Auren's old shit so we can go through it and save what we want, then shred and burn the rest. All it's doing right now is taking up space. Just bring me what you think I should look at."

"How the hell do I find it?" Faith asked. The task ahead was daunting, to put it mildly. The archives consisted of eight rooms lined floor to ceiling with shelves of files, some so old they were falling apart or unreadable. "Is any of it in order?"

"Yes, Faith." This newfound patience of his, though refreshing in some senses, tended to make her even more impatient in response. "Auren's archive will be the most recent, so it will be in room eight. According to Bethany, she and Ariana were only here for about four years before Auren died, so look for anything that corresponds to that timeline, pull it, and bring it to me."

"And why do I get this honor? Am I the secretary in command now?"

David looked at her from the array of electronic bits and half-constructed sensors he was working on to further refine the network in town. "I don't trust anyone else in those rooms," he said. "There could be a thousand kinds of sensitive information in there, and it's for our eyes only."

Grumbling, Faith stalked off to the archive hall, where each room's number was hung on its corresponding door. Room eight was on the left end. She unlocked the door with her com and let herself in, trying not to choke at the dust and the stuffy smell of neglected space.

"Oh, Jesus," she muttered. "This is going to take me all year."

Faith took a minute to get her bearings; near as she could tell, the files were in something like chronological order. She started to sort through the first stack, finding as she'd figured mostly patrol reports that were essentially useless now.

An hour later she was still going through them and her patience was wearing perilously thin. She tossed another handful of papers onto the stack on the floor; at least she'd have a box of them to incinerate later so that in that distant era when David had time to spare for archiving, he could skip over them.

The entire Haven was full of people who could be doing this. Surely she had more important work to be going on with. She could have assigned a couple of green recruits to this and gone back to the city for another round of patrols. She didn't trust the peace any more than the Prime did, but he was using the momentary respite to tighten the network. She wanted to be out on the streets making sure the Shadow World knew who was in charge.

Aggravated, she pushed another stack of papers onto the floor, sending a cloud of dust up into the air. She coughed violently and cursed Auren for not at least using file cabinets for all the accumulated garbage of decades of rule.

Under the stack, she saw something odd: a metal box.

She pulled it out and wiped the lid off. It was a nondescript gray, the sort of thing where people kept important papers locked up in case of fire, and was about legal size; it had no com lock, of course, but regular locks were no real obstacle for her. She took out her pocketknife and jimmied it open easily.

The contents were bundled in plastic sheeting, taped shut, and labeled: AUREN: PERSONAL EFFECTS.

Now *this* was interesting. She took the box over to a table, pushed the files that were on it off onto the floor with a satisfying thump, and set the box down, taking out the bundle and slitting the tape with her knife.

A handful of loose items fell out: a passport, a few expired credit cards, other detritus that was probably in the Prime's wallet when he was assassinated. She wondered who had gone through his clothes; it hadn't been her, and David had been far too busy to care what happened to Auren's Visa card. There was an assortment of keys—she was thankful for the com system, so she didn't have to carry so many. He'd seemed to have one for every locked door in his wing. There were also a handful of pens in half a dozen colors.

The last item surprised her: a black hardbound book, worn with age. She paged through it gingerly.

Auren had been something of an amateur artist. The book had mostly been used for sketches, though there were a few scattered journal entries written in what looked like German. Faith recognized images of the Haven gardens, the stables, one of the huge oak trees flanking the driveway; there was even a sketch of the Signet. The drawings were rendered in pen with touches of color here and there. A few were smudged in a way that suggested Auren had been left-handed, just like David was.

She should take this to him. He spoke German; he could translate the journal entries. Who knew what Auren had written down in his final days?

Faith turned to the last few pages, and her mouth dropped open.

A few rough sketches had been blocked in of a woman's face, and one had been completed. It was a remarkable likeness, and underneath Auren had written ARIANA. He had even drawn her wearing the Queen's Signet that she had never earned in life. She was smiling out from the page, coy and flirtatious.

There was just one problem.

The woman in the drawing was blond.

Ariana Blackthorn—the Ariana Blackthorn they'd executed—had black hair and hazel eyes. This one had blue. She also looked a good five years younger.

"Son of a bitch," Faith said.

She shut the book and rushed from the archive room, calling into her com, "Elite Forty-Three, I need the status of the Blackthorn girl."

There was no answer.

She tried again and got only silence. The same result came from trying to raise the other guard on Bethany's door.

Cursing, she switched to broadcast mode. "Security to the visitor's suites immediately."

A beep. David's voice: *"Faith, report."*

She set off for the hallway where the girl was staying at a dead run. "Sire," she said, "We have a very serious problem."

# Seventeen

Miranda had a hard time concentrating that night. For once she was glad when the show was over. She'd been waiting for Friday long enough.

She bounded down from the stage and barely took the time to gather up her stuff and wave good-bye to the sound and light guys before heading off toward home.

She was in a fantastic mood, almost giggly with anticipation; she wanted to get home, shower off the makeup and sweat that had accumulated in the last few hours—oh, and shave her legs. They were like two bottle brushes, and that wouldn't do.

There was also a tiny bit of blood left in the bag in her fridge. She wanted to be sure it was gone before David arrived. She still wasn't sure how she was going to explain what she'd done . . . but he was just going to have to understand. It wasn't as if she'd turned herself into a vampire. Aside from rebuilding her strength and keeping her from going crazy, drinking that single pint of blood had changed nothing.

Miranda swung down off the bus, smiling at the driver. She'd been riding the same line for a long time now, but only in the last few months had she paid any attention to anything besides her own navel. Now she exchanged jokes with the driver, a flirty older Hispanic man named George who recognized her from the papers.

She could afford a car now, if she wanted, but it seemed pointless when the only places she ever needed to go were on the bus routes and anything was better than trying to park in downtown Austin on a weekend. She was lucky—public transit wasn't exactly at New York City level here. If she had wanted to go anywhere out of her usual neighborhood, it would have taken considerable planning and several hours' travel time.

She walked the last block to the apartment humming softly under her breath. A half moon rode the sky overhead amid clouds that heralded a cool, breezy night. It had been a gorgeous spring.

Summer was shaping up to be even better.

Miranda went about her usual post-show routine, but this time in a little bit of a hurry. It was almost eleven, and David was supposed to be there at midnight. She took a hot shower, still with the unscented soap, and threw on her comfy jeans and a T-shirt while she puttered around the house, her hair bunched up on top of her head, her skin cool in the warm apartment air.

She was about to head to the fridge when she heard a knock at the door. A glance at the clock told her it was only 11:25.

She grabbed her phone from her bag as she went to the door, cuing up her messages. Damn it, she should have checked earlier—there was one from David at 10:00, probably saying he'd be early.

Miranda held the phone to her ear as she unlocked the door.

*"Miranda,"* David's voice said apologetically, *"I'm going to be late. We're having a server glitch that I have to fix before I can leave, but it shouldn't take more than an hour—"*

The door opened.

Miranda lowered the phone, hitting the END CALL button with her thumb. "Can I help you?"

The woman standing outside was skinny and blond, with blue eyes that were at once icy and aflame.

She wasn't alone.

"Samuel," Miranda said. "What are you doing here?"

He didn't respond. He didn't look at her, and neither did the other man—vampire—with the woman. A slow ripple of disquiet went through Miranda's stomach.

She started to slam the door, but the woman caught it and forced it back, shoving Miranda hard into the room. Miranda grabbed the edge of the couch to keep from falling over, her phone tumbling from her hand to the floor.

"You must be Miranda Grey," the woman said, tipping her head to one side, her smile only partly sane. Her voice was as high as a child's, almost singsong.

Miranda stood up straight and crossed her arms. "Who are you?"

"My name is Ariana Blackthorn," she replied.

"That's impossible. Ariana Blackthorn was beheaded."

The smile took on a nasty edge. "Nonsense, child. No one can kill me. I am the rightful Queen of this territory. A bow is appropriate."

"I don't see a Signet." Miranda risked a glance around the room—there was nothing she could use as a weapon except for David's knife in her purse. Even that wouldn't do her much good unless she could saw through Ariana's neck.

*They'll send help. Just buy some time.*

"No matter," Ariana said. "I'll have it as soon as I snatch it from your Prime's cold corpse."

"And how are you planning to do that?"

She snorted. "Do I look stupid to you?"

Miranda shrugged. "Mostly just crazy. And kind of ugly, actually. I'd recommend Paul Mitchell hair care and maybe a sandwich."

"Dear girl," Ariana said, "You really are quite something. If you had ever been one of us instead of a mere insect, you might have been a force to be reckoned with. But you won't get that chance, I'm afraid."

"Let me guess. You're going to kill me."

"First you," she confirmed with a nod. "Then your murdering, meat-fucking bastard of a Prime. But not until I have enough forces to take over the city. All of my allies are converging as we speak. I admit your darling did deal us quite a blow. His little network has been annoying to me. That will be the first thing I tear down once we have taken the Haven."

"How did you get out of the Haven?" Miranda asked. "They had you under guard."

"You ask that as if I were ever truly a prisoner. My boys here had it all under control."

Miranda looked at Samuel. "You betrayed the Prime," she said. "All this time he trusted you, and you've been working for her?"

Samuel spoke almost woodenly. "I am loyal to my rightful leader."

"What's this right you keep babbling about?" Miranda wanted to know. "You were never chosen Queen. Auren died and his Signet passed to someone else. That's how it works."

"No," Ariana snarled, coming closer. Miranda held her ground even when the woman was right in her face. "That isn't how it works. Not for me. I was his beloved, his perfect match. I would have been chosen if my sister hadn't come along and gotten in the way—she thought she could take him from me."

"Auren dumped you for your sister? That's a real shame, a catch like you."

"It's all right. Everything worked out. I got him back, and then I got her to trust me. I'm a patient woman. I was biding my time to feed her to the wolves. We made a plan to switch places, and she would escape while I was taken to the Haven. She was a faster runner and better fighter— she thought she could elude that little bitch of a Second and I would be safer as a fake captive. Now she's out of my way, and when the others arrive, I'll be the one to take the Signet."

"When is that supposed to happen?" Miranda asked.

Ariana's smile returned. "No more monologuing," she said. "I'm a better villain than that. Boys, take her. We have work to do here."

They came at her, but she was ready—she didn't give them time to get the upper hand, but threw herself at Samuel, lashing out with both her power and her right hook. He lurched sideways with a grunt of pain, and she swiveled around to land a kick in the other vampire's gut.

She heard Ariana scream something at them but didn't stop to chat; she threw the front door open and ran.

Miranda's bare feet slapped the pavement painfully, but she couldn't think about it, couldn't think about anything but putting as much distance between her and them as possible. She had to find someplace safe and find a way to warn David. If Samuel could get Ariana out of the Haven, he could get her back in, and if no one told the Prime, Samuel could walk right back to his post without anyone ever doubting him.

She angled left, heading straight for downtown where there would be more witnesses. Her senses were on high alert, and she could feel the others pursuing her, their rage a black cloud closing in quickly, too quickly. There was no way she could outrun them. She had to hide, and the best place was amid the teeming mortal life of South Congress.

Her lungs were full of needles, but she didn't slow down until she was almost at the bridge. Cars passed, their headlights blazing over her, and she nearly mowed down a lone pedestrian as she ran out onto the bridge where, at dusk, millions of Mexican free-tailed bats launched themselves into the sky. Tourists loved to come stand on the bridge and watch them during the summer. Far below, Lady Bird Lake was a black smudge rippled with the reflected lights of the capital city.

She heard their footsteps seconds before she felt hands close around her shoulders. She tried to fight them off, but the element of surprise was gone—they knew she was no weakling, now. Samuel seized her arms and pinned them back, though she struggled wildly, and the other vampire stood between them and the lanes where cars zipped by, oblivious.

Ariana walked up to them, as cool and fresh as if she'd just stepped out of a salon. "Well, that was fun," she said, laughing gaily. The noise was almost lost to the traffic. "You're just full of surprises, aren't you? Such a waste."

"I'm going to kill you!" Miranda was still fighting. "I'll take your head myself!"

Ariana giggled. "Isn't she cute?"

"Should we take her back and burn her?" Samuel asked.

"No," Ariana said. "I want there to be a body. I want him to find her, to see her dead and feel her lifeless and cold in his arms. I want him to know what he took from me. Then on the full moon he can lose everything else."

Ariana held out her hand, and the other vampire placed a dagger into it. The steel blade flashed in the streetlights.

Miranda started to speak again, but Ariana pulled back her arm, and suddenly Miranda's entire chest felt crushed with agony—she gasped, then choked, looking down to see the hilt of the dagger protruding obscenely from her rib cage.

Her limbs went numb, and she sagged in Samuel's grasp, feeling her blood begin to flow down her chest, her heart shuddering. The pain was beyond screaming, beyond anything, but she could only make a strangled sound and stare at the dark pool gathering at her feet.

Ariana nodded to Samuel.

As Miranda's vision went from blue to gray, and then to black, she felt her body being hauled up over the rail, and tossed, useless as a bag of trash, off the bridge and into the darkness of the lake.

She never felt the impact.

The Haven was in chaos.

"I want a full patrol team on apartment two twenty-one

at Cypress Grove," Faith ordered into her com. "Make sure Miss Grey is secure before anything else happens. Lindsay, don't you move a muscle. Do you copy?"

She met David at the now-empty guest suite in time to hear him yell a string of obscenities and burst back out of the room, gesturing to the gathered lieutenants to follow.

"What's the patrol team's ETA?" he demanded.

"Eleven minutes," Faith replied. "Where are Bethany's guards?"

"Unconscious in the room. She's smart—she knew killing them would interrupt their com signals. She can't possibly know about the fail-safe, but she knows I know if someone dies. God fucking damn it." He shot Faith a look. "And if you say, 'I told you so,' I'll stake you right here and now."

"Wasn't planning on it, Sire. What now?"

"I run a network trace and see if we can find her. Meanwhile—" He turned, midstride, to the lieutenants and walked backward. "Double patrols through the metropolitan area. Send the word out through the entire territory that she's on the run and likely going to ground with the survivors of her gang. If you see so much as two vampires in one place, I don't care if they're playing Twister, you bring them in."

He dismissed the others and took Faith with him down the stairs to the server room. "What's that in your hand?" he asked Faith as he took his chair.

"Auren's journal," she said, handing it to him. "That's how I knew something was wrong. Look at the pictures in the back."

When he saw what she'd seen, his face lost all expression and he went pale. "God."

He dropped the book on the table and went back to the computer, bringing up the citywide sensor grid. With his free hand, he pulled his phone out of his pocket and handed it to Faith. "Keep trying Miranda," he said. "I want to know she's safe."

Faith called, but there was no answer, only the ghostly

sound of Miranda's voice mail greeting. "Nothing." She hit her com again. "Elite Eighty-Six. Lindsay, has the backup team arrived yet?"

No answer.

"Fuck—Sire, can you access Lindsay's com from here?"

"Of course." He clicked on something and brought up another grid, this one showing the locations of every com. She saw four dots representing the backup team closing in on Miranda's apartment complex, and there in its usual spot was Elite 86's signal.

"She hasn't moved," David noted. "But she's not answering—she could be unconscious like the others. Elite Fifty-Seven, what's your status?"

*"We're having trouble getting to the building, Sire. There's something going on."*

"What do you mean?"

*"There are fire trucks and ambulances everywhere. They pulled in just as we reached the street. I sent Elite Twenty in for a closer look, but there's so much smoke that it's making visual confirmation impossible."*

David met Faith's eyes, and she saw what he was thinking. Her own insides went to ice.

He reached out with one hand and switched windows to the sensor grid. Every life form with a lower body temperature than a human's and a body mass over a certain size registered on the network.

He overlaid the two grids.

There were three vampires leaving the location of Miranda's apartment as four more approached it from the opposite direction. The approaching four were Elite. The other three were not.

"Oh my God, she's there," Faith gasped.

But when she looked up, he was gone.

David reappeared across the street from the apartment complex, and as soon as he could hear again, the cacophony was deafening. Sirens, radio chatter, and people shouting surrounded him, and the acrid smell of burning assailed him.

There were two enormous fire trucks blocking the street, and police cars lining the block to hold back the crowds.

The air was thick with smoke.

David ran across the street, pushing past the bright yellow barrier and ignoring the officer who tried to call him back. He snaked in between the fire trucks and emerged on the other side, where a blast of heat knocked him back.

It was like staring into hell. The building was an inferno, and several of the others in the complex had already gone up as well.

Slowly, he lifted his eyes to the charring white eaves of the building. Just beneath the roof, painted in dark red that was blackening in the smoke, was the Seal of Auren.

The energy expense of moving himself through such a great distance caught up with him as the shock did, and he felt his knees impacting with the concrete. He couldn't tear his eyes from the flames licking out of Miranda's windows—his mind's eye showed him her furniture cracking and paint blistering, her prized keyboard's casing melting in the heat.

And all the while, he could hear the past: Lizzie screaming as the bonfire rose up to consume her lily-white skin.

"Sire?"

He didn't look away from the fire at the patrol leader who had found him.

"Sire, we found Elite Eighty-Six—she was still alive when we got to her, but . . ."

"What else?" he asked. "What have they found?"

"We don't know. It happened so fast—they're certain it was arson. They found gas cans in the parking lot. They rescued a few of the residents, but at least half are unaccounted for."

"And Miss Grey?"

"I don't know, Sire. All I know is . . ."

"What?"

"Lindsay . . . when we found her, she was saying 'I failed, I'm sorry' over and over again. When I asked her what happened, all she said was . . . was . . . 'She's gone.'"

"No," he said. "She must have been out. She couldn't have been in there. Find her. *Now*."

He tried to think, tried to come up with another explanation. She had been at the club tonight, and he was supposed to meet her at midnight . . . she would have been home, waiting for him, when they came for her. She might even have opened the door thinking he was behind it.

There was no way she could have escaped. A small human woman couldn't stand up to three vampires, not without months of fight training and a miracle. She had been strong, but not that strong, not yet.

*No. No . . . no.*

Desperate, he sought out with his power, trying to find the connection they'd had only days ago. He'd let it fade so that she could go back to normal for a little while longer, thinking it was the right thing to do, that she should have more time to think. But she had already known what she wanted. He was the one who was afraid. And now . . .

He searched for her with his mind, but when he found what was left of the link and tried to follow it, he met only cold darkness where her loving warmth should be. Even after a week there should have been a faint trace of it left.

He didn't know how long he knelt there, staring at the fire, before a voice said, "Excuse me, sir, but I've been asked to show you this."

David rose, absently dusting off his knees and straightening his coat, and faced the paramedic. The young woman was sweaty and dirty, and he could see that she was a seasoned professional who wouldn't let herself feel the loss of life until after she had saved as many as she could.

He nodded, and she led him around the fire truck, past several humans in various degrees of jeopardy with other EMTs fixing oxygen masks on their faces. Nearby, there were already three bodies covered in sheets, awaiting transport to the morgue.

The Elite patrol leader he'd spoken to before was standing at the edge of the triage area. He was staring down at something.

David had never wanted to run away from anything so badly in his life.

He forced himself to walk up to the man's side, stand between him and the EMT, and look down.

He was expecting a body. What he saw was a guitar.

"The fire started in unit two twenty-one," the EMT was saying. "One of the first responders tripped over this and ended up dragging it out with him. The strings got wrapped around his foot. As I understand it, you know the resident here?"

David stared at the remains of the beautiful instrument. There was little more than a scrap of neck and string left, the body so charred it had fallen apart.

He remembered the first time he'd seen her play, that night at the club, when he had no idea how she would throw his world into such welcome turmoil. Then, that night at the Haven, when he'd watched her from the door, his heart so full of love for her that only a liter of Jack could silence it. He saw her slender hands dancing over the strings, the way they had danced over his skin, and her soft mouth forming words, that same mouth that had closed over his.

She was gone. He couldn't feel her anymore. Ariana had gotten to her before the Elite could reach her. He'd been too late to save her. Jonathan's vision had come true, and he had been too blind to heed the warning.

She was gone.

He responded numbly to the EMT's questions, and when she finally left, he turned to the Elite.

"You will stay here until we have a body," he informed the patrol leader. "Have Lindsay's body sent back for a memorial and comb the area for any further evidence. I want this Blackthorn bitch brought to me." He looked back up at the smoking remains of the apartment building, where everything that mattered had gone to ash. "I'm going home."

Faith was waiting outside the front doors of the Haven when the car pulled up. She'd been standing there for nearly half an hour.

She'd tried to contact him over the coms, but he wasn't answering; the patrol unit at the scene had no news, only that the building was a total loss and no body had been found. But if anyone would know, David would know. The connection between him and Miranda would surely still be active, and even if it wasn't he was strong enough to find its echo.

She had to be alive. There was simply no other possibility. After everything that had happened, everything Miranda had been through, it couldn't end so suddenly. They would find her, and she would be fine, and she would come home.

Harlan got out and held open the car door, and after a moment, David emerged, his face smudged with soot.

When she saw the expression on his face, Faith shook her head violently.

"No," she charged up to him, standing in front of him, fighting the urge to shake him. "Tell me you found her, Sire. Tell me she's okay."

In the decades she'd known him she had seen him angry, seen him hate; she had seen him mourn. But she had never seen what she saw in his eyes at that moment . . . complete desolation.

Faith fell back, her hand to her mouth against the sobs that were trying to batter their way past her rapidly fracturing calm.

The Prime lowered his eyes and walked past her into the Haven, silent, head bowed.

Faith followed, struggling to regain control of herself, but she saw tears on the faces of the servants and Elite that she passed. When they reached the Prime's wing, and he went quietly into the suite and shut the door without admitting her, Samuel took her arm.

"What's happening?" he asked. "I just got on duty and everyone's saying . . . God, Faith, is it true?"

She made herself sound professional even if her heart was screaming. "We don't have confirmation yet. As soon as there's news I'll make sure you know."

"What are we going to do?" he asked.

She started back down the hall. "We're going to find Ariana Blackthorn and kill her. And we're going to kill all of her friends. And anyone else who might need it. But first . . . first we're going to find Miranda and bring her back here, where she belongs."

# Eighteen

The first breath she took was nothing but water.

She screamed, but no sound would come. It was cold . . . so cold . . . and she couldn't see. Blackness surrounded her, pulled her feet, dragging her downward . . . and she was so weak, she could barely even move, let alone struggle.

*So cold.*

This was where she had always been headed. It was the nightmare made real. The darkness had closed around her and there was no escape.

Images floated past her mind as she hung suspended between life and death. She saw her childhood, her mother, back when things were good. She saw Marianne back when she could smile. She saw her mother's vacant face and lifeless eyes . . . her lonely grave in Austin, unattended for ten years until her prodigal daughter offered her rosemary. There was an empty plot next to her, just the right size for one more grave.

She heard music, her own voice singing. Piano, deep and rich. She felt keys beneath her fingers, then strings, then muscles. She tasted blood.

Faces came to her, some with names, some without. Kat. Faith. Sophie. Terrence. Helen.

*David.*

*Samuel. Ariana. Traitors. The full moon.*

Memory struck, and from somewhere deep within her that was almost dead, she summoned all her strength and *fought*.

She burst through the surface of the water, flailing on all sides, her lungs burning from lack of oxygen. Her hands were nearly unresponsive, but she splashed out until she found something to grab on to and pulled herself sideways.

She crawled onto the bank, vomiting huge gushes of stinking lake water, then sucking in an enormous breath that made her dizzy. She collapsed into the mud, coughing and gasping and sobbing.

Her chest hurt. She put her hands to her heart, felt it beating. It was beating.

She was alive.

As soon as her lungs were empty and her nose was no longer full of the stench of pollution and dirt, she smelled something else . . . something crisp and light . . . something terrifying.

Morning. Morning was coming.

She had to get inside. The sky was starting to lighten in the east.

Inch by inch, she pulled herself all the way out of the water and got to her hands and knees, then her feet. The world spun around her, but she stayed upright through sheer force of will.

She had somehow ended up a long way from the Congress bridge. She was just off the jogging path that wound around Lady Bird Lake. In a few hours there would be people everywhere. She could get help, find a phone, call . . .

Call who, exactly? She had never bothered memorizing numbers because they were all stored in her phone. She was fairly sure she knew Kat's, but she didn't have any way to call. Her phone was back at her apartment and there was no way she'd make it there by dawn. She had to find someplace dark and safe, somewhere she could rest. She was so tired.

She almost sank back to the ground, but fear of what would happen if she was caught outside drove her forward. Her body hurt all over, and she felt like her insides were coated with sawdust. She was soaked and filthy and had no money, no identification, not even seventy-five cents for a bus.

Her mind was whirling. She had to think. Where could she go?

She stumbled up the path, arms wrapped around herself in a vain attempt to warm up. She made her way up to the street, trying to make sense of where she was, and her blurry eyes made out a street sign: LAMAR BOULEVARD.

That was something. Lamar ran all the way through Austin, parallel to the interstate from one end to the other. If she was at the lake, she was west of her apartment and just south of downtown. She could get home in a couple of hours walking once the sun went down. If she continued south a little farther, she'd pass the Zachary Scott Theatre and a variety of restaurants.

She concentrated on moving one foot at a time, watching carefully where she stepped in her bare feet. She was starting to shiver from the cold, and her teeth were chattering, causing her upper jaw to hurt like it was cracked. The pain in her body was growing so intense that she started to cry without realizing it until she felt tears hit her arm.

Around her the night waned, and her skin started to feel wrong, like it was on too tight. She remembered a similar feeling a long time ago when she'd been stung by a bee and found out she was allergic.

She looked around and saw she'd made it as far as the sandwich shop next to the theater. It was closed at this hour, but an idea seized her, and she slipped around the back of the building to the kitchen door.

Taking a deep breath, she threw herself at the door; it shuddered under her weight but didn't give. She tried again, and again, crying out softly with each hit, and on the fourth, the flimsy wood splintered and fell inward.

She had to take it on faith that there was no alarm. Inside, the air was cool and dark, and she wanted more than anything just to curl up in the corner and sleep, but she'd be found; instead, she looked behind the counter until she found a phone.

It took several tries to get the number right. The last two digits were hazy in her mind, but providence was with her, and after a couple of rings, a sleepy voice answered, "Hello?"

"Kat," she all but wept, "It's Miranda. I need your help."

"Oh my God, Mira! Thank God! I've been trying to find you—are you okay? Were you hurt?"

Miranda half laughed, half cried. "Please, Kat . . . I need you to come get me. I'm at the Newman's Deli on South Lamar, by the Zach. Please hurry—and bring a blanket."

"But—"

"Please," she begged. "I'll explain everything later."

"I'm on my way," Kat said breathlessly. "Hang on, honey, I'll be there in five minutes."

Miranda was sitting on the curb outside when Kat pulled up in her battered old Corolla. Miranda pushed herself to her feet and all but fell into the car, taking the blanket Kat offered and wrapping it around herself until every inch of her skin was covered.

"Hurry . . . I have to be inside before the sun is up."

For once Kat didn't ask any questions. When she saw the state of Miranda's clothes and hair and the way she was shaking, she simply floored the accelerator and drove them to her place at twice the legal speed limit.

She bundled Miranda into her rented duplex and sat her on the couch. "Okay, start talking."

"Not yet." Miranda poked her nose out of the blanket. "Are there any windows in your guest bathroom?"

"No, but . . ."

Miranda shook her head and stood back up; Kat made a noise of impatience but helped her into the bathroom.

There, Miranda stripped off the blanket and heard Kat gasp.

"What the fuck happened to you?" Kat asked. "Your shirt!"

She looked down. There was a hole over her heart, and her T-shirt was stained with the blurry remains of the blood that had gushed from the stab wound. Miranda touched the hole, the memory threatening to engulf her.

"Someone tried to kill me," she said.

"Jesus, Mira . . . first your apartment, now this— you've got to tell me what's going on."

"My apartment? What do you mean?"

Kat leaned on the bathroom door, looking utterly mystified by the whole situation. "It was all over the news last night. Someone burned down your complex. There are at least ten people dead—weren't you there?"

Miranda sat down hard on the closed toilet lid, putting her head in her hands. "They burned it. They burned it. All those people . . . everything . . . was anything left?"

"I don't think so. The fire started in your building."

Miranda was crying again, out of rage and loss, thinking of all her things—her guitar, her computer . . . her mother's picture, framed and hanging on the living room wall. She had nothing, not even her wallet left, only the rags she had had on when she crawled from the lake.

"Can I borrow some clothes?" she asked in a small voice.

Kat's eyes were wet, and she nodded. "You take a shower. I'll get you something to put on." She wiped her eyes and said, "It's going to be okay, Mira. We'll figure this out."

Miranda pulled off her T-shirt and the sodden, muddy jeans, added her underwear to the pile, then gathered it all up and shoved it in the trash. She ran the water as hot as she could stand it and stood beneath the spray for a long time, scrubbing at dirt that couldn't seem to come clean.

By the time she got out, she was on the verge of losing consciousness. She had to sleep. Something was happening to her body, and she was losing what was left of her strength rapidly. Her belly hurt unbearably, as if something were twisting her intestines and squeezing them hard; if there had been anything in her stomach she probably would have lost it. Her head was throbbing, and the roof of her mouth felt like it was on fire.

Her vision was swimming and she fell back against the bathroom wall, sliding down until her butt hit the floor.

Kat opened the door. "Here," she said. "This should fit—it's just sweats but I thought you'd want something warm."

"Thank you," Miranda managed, struggling into the unfamiliar garments. The legs and arms were too long, but they were dry, and soft, and smelled like fabric softener.

"What else do you need?"

Miranda stared at her hard, her eyes traveling over her friend's face and down to her neck. She could see the tributaries of Kat's veins flowing into the greater river, and how it pulsed.

"Oh, God," Miranda moaned, doubling over. Realization hit her as the pieces flew together.

*I died. Ariana killed me. And then I woke . . . and now I'm . . . changing . . . it's not over yet. It's only just beginning.*

"I need someplace to stay for a few days," she whispered. "Someplace dark. Does your guest room have windows?"

"Yeah, it does—and I'm asking again, what the fuck is going on? Why do you need dark? Miranda, we have to call the cops. Somebody tried to kill you. You just said so."

She smiled sadly. "The police can't help me now."

"You said you were going to explain, Miranda. Don't I deserve that much?"

"I'm not sure you'll believe me," Miranda told her. "I'm going to have to stay here . . . do you have spare blankets? Maybe a pillow?"

"You're going to sleep in the bathroom?"

"I don't know what's going to happen to me. The bathroom might be the best place." She grabbed the blanket she'd arrived in and folded it, laying it out on the floor as a pad. "Kat . . . whatever happens . . . thank you. I couldn't ask for a better friend than you."

"Just tell me, damn it—"

"Okay." She tried to find words, but her head was hurting so much she could barely think; she lay down on her side on the folded blanket, not caring that the floor was hard and her hair was wet. "I'm sick, Kat. I'm going to be sick for a few days. The sun will kill me. I just need to be in the dark and safe until it passes. Then everything will be fine."

Kat was staring at her as if she'd lost her mind, and really, she wasn't far off. "Miranda, tell me right now. Are you back on drugs?"

Miranda laughed out loud at that. "No. I promise you it's not drugs. It was never drugs. I want to tell you . . . you don't know how much. I've wanted to tell you since you came to see me play last summer. I just don't know how."

"Let me take you to the hospital, then."

"No hospitals. No police. Please, Kat . . . if you want to help me, bring me some more blankets, then shut the door and stay away until I come out. I don't want to hurt you."

Kat stormed off and returned a moment later, practically throwing an armload of linens at her. "You know, you are really stretching the whole 'above and beyond the call of friendship' thing. You call me at five in the morning asking for help, and I come and pick you up looking like you've been dropped in the lake, and now you say you need to sleep something off in my bathroom— I ought to throw you out on your ass!"

Miranda tried to organize the blankets into something like a bed, but her arms weren't cooperating. She couldn't seem to get up, though she tried and nearly cracked her head open on the clean white tile. Tired . . . so tired . . .

Kat saw her struggling and, with a sigh, knelt and started tucking and arranging things around Miranda's body. "You owe me big-time," she muttered.

"Turn the light off and lock the door on your way out, please," Miranda said, closing her eyes.

When he returned to the Haven, he shut the world out of his suite. He went into the bathroom and showered, washing the soot and smoke away, and put on clean clothes. He added another log to the fire.

Then he lay down on the still-made bed, curled into a ball, and closed his eyes.

He didn't move again for three days.

He was aware, from a great distance, of movement around him. Esther came in and tended the fire; Faith tried to talk to him. He heard voices from his com and he heard his phone ringing, but he didn't stir, didn't even bother silencing the noise.

Outside the sun rose and set, rose and set. A rain shower passed during the afternoon. The gardeners came and trimmed the hedges. None of it mattered.

He was so cold. There was nothing but cold, ice forming inside him, the fire dying in the room beyond. With a thought he could have made himself warm again, but he didn't. There was no reason to.

The city might have fallen apart. It might all be burning. Every human in the territory might have had their throats torn out by now. The world might have come to an end.

Let it.

He might have slept, or not; he didn't notice. His body might be craving blood. It might already have died of starvation.

If only. If only he could let go, break free of his flesh, and with it shed the weight he had taken on his shoulders. He had been fool enough to want it, for a while. For a while, there had been the possibility that he might not have to bear it alone.

But the vast emptiness in his heart was proof against even the most mindless optimism. Whatever had been there, whatever tenuous bond had been forming, it was no more. He hadn't even realized it was there until too late, when the soft kiss of her presence was abruptly torn from him. How long had it existed? Much, much longer than a week. It had perhaps formed the night he laid eyes on her. Some part of him had always known.

He heard the door open again, and ignored it at first, but there was something strange . . .

A presence he hadn't felt in years moved through him, settling on the bed at his side. A hand touched his arm.

He opened his eyes and looked up.

"Sire," he said, his voice hoarse and thin from disuse.

The Prime of the Western United States regarded him through his gentle lavender-blue eyes. "I can't stay long."

"What are you doing here?"

"Faith called me. I came as soon as I could."

"Where's Jonathan?"

"Out in the hall. He was afraid you might blame him."

David didn't answer; his strength seemed to have failed. *Failed* . . . the word had a thousand new meanings to him now.

"I can't do this anymore," David whispered.

Deven had been about seventeen when he became a vampire, and his face was still young, with a touch of the fey about it. Dark, shining brown hair fell straight around his shoulders, and he had always made David think of a renegade angel content to be cast out of paradise, especially when he had a sword in his hand. He bowed his head beneath shared pain and said to David, "Yes, you can. And you will. Millions of people depend on your rule. You took up the Signet, and there is no putting it down."

"We're supposed to die when this happens," David said.

"I know."

"I don't know what to do."

Dev's hand moved up to his face. It had been a long, long time since David had felt that touch. "You're going to mourn her, and then you're going to go on. You have work to do yet, my friend, and you must do it as much for Miranda as for all the others. Don't belie her faith in you. Stand and fight."

"I don't even know what I'm fighting for anymore. It isn't as if it matters anyway—if I die, there will be someone else. There's always someone else."

The Prime gave him a wryly affectionate smile. "Believe me, there will never be another you. I don't think the world could take it."

David felt his resolve to remain numb breaking beneath waves of despair, and he knew there was no holding back the tide. Hot tears spilled from his eyes, and out of instinct he tried to ward them off.

"Don't," Deven said. "She was worth your grief."

He opened his arms, and David fled into them, buried his face in his friend's shoulder, and wept.

He let the sorrow pour out, knowing he was with one of the few people who wouldn't judge him for it, the rare strength of a Prime the only thing that could understand, and withstand, such pain. Deven didn't speak, but he offered solace that meant far more than mere words ever could.

Gradually, one shuddering breath at a time, he felt himself grow calmer. The emptiness was still there, and it still felt like it was dragging him down with it, but at least, for the moment, he could think a little more clearly.

He sat back. "Thank you for coming," David said, trying not to sniffle like a child. Deven lifted a corner of the comforter and wiped David's eyes, causing him to smile in spite of himself. "Thanks, Mom," he added.

The Prime chuckled. "I wish we could stay longer."

"It's all right. I understand. And you're right . . . I have to finish what I've started. They're still out there, and if I don't stop them, this will never end."

"That's my boy." Deven rose, taking David with him; David was a little unsteady on his feet, and Dev grabbed his arm to hold him up. David felt an inrushing of energy, strength into strength. He took it gratefully and brought himself back to center.

"I'd recommend a shower," Dev said, "and a shave. You're starting to look like my pedophile uncle."

"Your uncle was a bald Irish monk who weighed two hundred fifty pounds."

"It's the facial hair," the Prime replied. "I hate facial hair. Now, go. I want to see this sensor network of yours before we leave."

David was used to giving orders, but even he knew when to do as he was told.

Clean and dressed and feeling a little more like himself, David accepted the wineglass of blood that Deven pressed into his hand when he emerged from the bathroom but didn't take the time to savor it; there was no more time to waste.

He left the suite to find Faith standing outside with Jonathan, the two of them in conversation that stopped as soon as the door opened. Neither of them looked entirely comfortable with seeing him.

"It's all right," he told the Consort. "I don't blame you."

"Damn right you don't," Jonathan retorted, though he was grinning. "You didn't give me credit when you got your Signet. Don't blame me for this."

They shook hands, and when Deven came out of the suite Jonathan immediately stepped to his left side. They were an odd couple, to say the least; the Consort was twice his Prime's size, but it was Deven who traveled armed, a sword beneath his coat and half a dozen knives concealed over his seemingly delicate frame.

David turned to Faith, who wasn't looking at him.

"I'm sorry," he said. "I shouldn't have shut you out. I know you're hurting, too."

Faith nodded. "Permission to speak freely, Sire?"

"Granted."

"You're an asshole," she said, and hugged him.

He returned the hug, saying, "Let's get back to work."

Miranda had known pain in her life, but not like this. For days she writhed on Kat's bathroom floor, her fingers clawing at the tile, her entire body scalded from within. Fever gripped her, washing her with unbearable heat one second and freezing cold the next. She held the pillow to her mouth and screamed when she couldn't stand it.

Kat pounded on the door more than once, asking if she was okay, but she couldn't answer. She had locked Kat out—no one should see her like this.

It felt like every bone in her skeleton snapped and knit itself over and over again. Her cells seemed to have turned to acid and were eating their way out of her skin. The worst part was her stomach—her bout with salmonella in college had in no way prepared her for the torturous cramps and nausea. She retched almost constantly for the first day, at first water, then nothing but air; her thirst was so great she stuck her head in the sink and drank from the faucet, then threw it up, and drank again.

It went on past the point when she thought she could endure no more. It went on past when she prayed to die. Every few hours she passed out, only to be driven awake again by a fresh punishment, thousands of knives in her gut or a vise grip around her head.

At one point she was aware that she had bitten her tongue and it was swollen and raw in her mouth, bleeding from two holes. The taste of her own blood made her insides twist so hard she would have wailed, but she had long since lost her voice.

*I'm alone . . . I'm dying and I'm alone . . . I can't do this. It's too much. It hurts so bad . . .*

She lay on her back, sweat pouring from every pore of her body, so worn out she could hardly breathe, and for a moment a strange sort of peace descended over her.

She thought of the night she had been raped, and of the raw power that had taken hold of her. She thought of all the nights before that when she had let her psychic abilities use her. She had been beaten, and violated, and murdered. She'd had everything taken from her by force. Her illusory crown had been stripped away. There was no music to hide in, no Haven to run to, no Prime to show her the way back. There was only Miranda, and one final decision.

She could die here, a sad broken heap on a bathroom floor . . . or . . .

Another stream of thoughts, or rather feelings: the ecstasy that filled her when she performed. The joy of turning music into emotion and sharing it. The pride of getting up one more time when she fell down and picking up her sword. The heat of beloved hands on her skin and a body meeting hers. The possibility . . . the endless possibility. Power, and love, and belonging were all hers, if she could find the will to reach out and take them . . . no . . . to reach *in*.

Miranda pulled her attention back to her breath, then followed it, as Sophie had shown her, down into the shadow coiled inside her. It was waiting for her to let it finish its work. If she fought it, she would die. If she took its hand . . .

She smiled into the darkness . . . and chose.


"I'm glad you're here. I don't know what to do."

"Is it drugs?"

She heard the voices so clearly it took a minute to realize they weren't in her head.

Voice one: female, mixed race, approximately thirty years of age. Southern drawl evident on vowels. Voice two: male, slightly younger, Caucasian undertone but accent from farther north than Texas.

She opened her eyes and blinked at the unexpected light. At first she thought it must be daytime, but a scent of the air told her otherwise; it was about eight o'clock. The overhead fixture was not switched on. The room was bathed in watery blue and gray shades, and she could see every detail down to the spidery cracks in the grout.

She felt out along her body, curious. No pain. She felt light, buoyant. She lifted her hand and looked at it, amazed at how distinct its edges were, how strong it seemed; she curled it into a fist, admiring the feeling of muscle and tendon sliding over each other. She lowered her hand to her body, running her fingers down the length of one arm, then over her breasts and belly. The sensation was so exquisite that she lay there for several minutes touching herself, every inch alive.

A light knock at the door interrupted her exploration. "Miranda?" the female voice called. "Can you hear me?"

She spoke, and her voice was a wonder: it had the same smooth golden timbre as always, but now there were layers of nuance and meaning to even the simplest of words: "Yes."

"Honey, Drew's here. We want to take you to the doctor. Will you let us in?"

She focused on the door, and on the two human figures beyond it. She breathed in, and could smell them both.

They both worked with children. One of them had varnish under his fingernails. The other used cocoa butter on her hair. They had had sex recently.

The male smelled lovely, like old books and rosin, yes, but underneath were the mingled scents of sex and masculinity. He was healthy and bright. An occasional meat-eater, active, had smoked pot at some point in the last month.

Her teeth pressed into her lower lip.

Slowly, she turned over onto her stomach, then rose, allowing her body to unfold as gracefully as a deer rising from the brush. She extended a hand and unlocked the bathroom door.

"Thank God," she heard the woman say. "Mira, you've got to . . . holy shit."

They stared at her, the woman's mouth open as she lost the sentence, the man's eyes huge. They were both very attractive; the woman had power, and she knew it, and the man was caring, kind. Both of them were very worried about her.

Why?

She lifted her hands again and ran them down her sides, looking down to see what she was wearing. Sweatpants and a sweatshirt. It was absurd. Her hair was a tangled mess. What were they staring at?

She tilted her head to one side, watching them watch her.

"Um . . . Miranda . . ." the man said hesitantly, "Are you feeling all right?"

Miranda. Yes, that was her name. And his was Drew; the woman's was Kat. She knew them. They were her friends. He had tried to kiss her, once.

"May I borrow your comb?" Miranda asked.

Kat stuttered something and gestured back behind her; Miranda turned toward the medicine cabinet, opening the door and taking out a large-toothed comb. When she shut the door, she realized what Kat was motioning at.

The door of the cabinet was mirrored. She could see,

behind her, the two people framed in the bathroom doorway.

She couldn't see herself.

She shrugged inwardly and pulled the comb through her hair, wincing at the tangles. It took several minutes of careful work to get it all under control again. Even after she was finished, they were still staring.

"What's happened to you?" Kat asked softly. Her voice was quaking.

"I told you," Miranda said. "I was sick. I'm better now."

"But . . . Mira . . . you're so pale . . . you don't even look human!"

She considered that, looking down at herself, then back at them. Well, it was obvious, wasn't it? "I'm not."

"What do you mean?"

She met Kat's eyes, and Kat took a step back.

"Don't be afraid. I won't hurt you." Then she added, "Unless you run."

She fixed her gaze on Drew. "I'm hungry," she said. "I need you."

Drew turned adorably pink and exchanged a look of alarm with Kat. "But you said . . ."

"Stop talking."

His mouth snapped shut.

"Come to me."

He was about to protest, but she took careful hold of his mind and brought him into the room, walking like a dreamer toward her. She let go enough that he could talk, wondering if he wanted to run, but to her surprise, he didn't. She released his mind completely, and he stayed where he was.

Kat made a faint mewling sound of horror, but Drew said, "It's okay, Kat. She's not going to hurt me. Are you, Mira?"

"Of course not," Miranda replied, cupping his face in her hand, then tilting his head to the side. "You have something I need, Drew. I know you want to help me."

"I do. I'm your friend. So is Kat. We'd do anything for you."

"I know . . . and I promise I'll never ask again."

She leaned into him, inhaling deeply of the warmth and pulsating life before her. She nuzzled his neck, earning a groan, and studied the veins for a moment, trying to choose a place that wouldn't injure him. The veins branched like a tree, and she knew not to open the trunk.

The smell of him drove her hunger to a fever pitch, and she sighed against his skin, feeling the delicious itch of her teeth sliding down over her lip.

He didn't flinch when she bit down, or when she sucked. Even without the influence of her power he was willing.

She whimpered and held on to him, drinking deeply, the taste assailing her senses as the need began to fade one swallow at a time. She felt his heartbeat wild against her breast, and as her own began to come into sync with it, she knew by instinct when it was time to stop.

Miranda lifted her mouth and let him go. He slipped silently to the floor at her feet.

She licked her lips, almost drunk with heady satisfaction. Her teeth withdrew to a more manageable length.

Kat had shrunk back against the hallway wall. She was crying.

Miranda stepped around Drew, who was breathing hard and trying to conceal his erection by staying on his knees facing away from Kat.

She left the bathroom but stopped beside her friend, who refused to look her in the eye.

"I have to go," Miranda said. "I'm putting you in danger if I stay here."

She walked past Kat and through the house. It seemed so small and confining. She craved the freedom of the night air.

"Wait," she heard, and paused.

Kat hadn't left the hall, but said through her tears, "Where are you going?"

"I have work to do."

"Are you . . . are you ever coming back?"

Miranda smiled. She knew what Kat meant. "No," she said. "But I will see you again."

With that, she walked out the duplex door, leaving the mortal world behind her.

# Nineteen

It was going to be difficult to mount an assault on the enemy without shoes.

The full moon already hung in the sky, and she knew there was no time to waste, but there were things she needed: one, shoes; two, weapons; and three, some kind of plan.

A slightly less trailer-park outfit might be nice, too.

She tried to remember what part of town she was in. There was a bus route a block away that would take her close to where she needed to go, but she didn't have any bus fare . . .

She laughed to herself. Money was not going to be a problem.

When the bus pulled over, she stepped up into it, surveying the other passengers and deeming them harmless. The bus driver cleared her throat and nodded at the fare box.

"I have a pass," Miranda said, and bent her mind toward the driver's.

It was almost too easy. "Oh, okay," the driver said. "Sit down."

Miranda took the only free seat, one in the middle. The minds of the others started to lean on hers, but she added more energy to her shields and it was quiet in her mind again. There had been a time when such a simple act would have exhausted her or at least given her a migraine. Now it was as effortless as breathing.

As the bus bounced and rattled, she looked around at the humans traveling with her and felt the stirrings of pity. They were so sad. Some were homeless, and others were just as lost even though they had someplace to go. Perhaps three were genuinely happy and lived with purpose and passion. She had been one of the others, once. She had been a wanderer with a homeless heart.

Now what was she?

She would know tonight, once and for all.

A couple of the humans were staring at her, and she couldn't blame them, really. Without knowing it they saw her kind every night, but probably never this close, and probably never someone so new to the shadows, her fledgling power mantling around her like the still-wet wings of an infant butterfly.

She knew that this, too, would change. She was already starting to feel a bit more grounded, her true personality settling back a few thoughts at a time. She reviewed her memory of the last few days and was relieved she hadn't caused more damage—she could have killed Drew, or Kat, or both. The sheer horror on Kat's face had been heartbreaking . . . but it could have been worse.

She needed to call Kat as soon as this was over. Kat might never speak to her again, but she owed her friend an explanation, and a long one. To hell with secrecy. Kat had saved her life. She deserved better than an enigmatic farewell and her boyfriend left on the floor with a raging hard-on.

Although that had been kind of funny, now that she thought about it.

Miranda leaned her head forward on the back of the next seat. She was still tired. She felt like she could sleep for a week . . . but not yet. There were miles to go.

"You okay there, young lady?"

She lifted her gaze to the grizzled old man across the aisle. "Yes, sir. I've just . . . had a long day."

"I know what you mean." He was reading a newspaper, something she'd never been able to do in a moving vehicle, and nodded down at the headline: AUSTIN GANG VIOLENCE ESCALATES. "World's getting scarier, isn't it? People burning down buildings, gangs . . . Wasn't that long ago Austin was a safe place to let your kids play outside."

"It will be again," Miranda said, sitting up. "I'll make sure of it."

He gave a gap-toothed grin. "That's right," he said. "It's up to you young people now. My generation's on the front porch these days, and that's where we should be. You get out there and change the world."

Miranda smiled at him. "I plan to."

The bus let her off slightly west of her destination, so she walked along the road, her eyes roaming around the shabby neighborhood of taco stands, run-down warehouses, and public assistance offices. She felt like a visitor from a foreign land, even though only days ago she had walked these same streets with recognition. Her vision, in the blue-grays of night, picked out colors and shapes she couldn't before. She passed a dog chained in someone's yard that stared at her, ears up and eyes wide, trying to decide whether to sound the alarm. She met its eyes, and it backed away, tail down.

A block later she felt a stabbing pain in the bottom of her left foot.

She stopped and lifted her ankle. Her foot was already black from the pavement, but there was a rather large shard of glass sticking out of the middle, oozing blood. She yanked it out and watched, fascinated, as the cut began to close, and within ten seconds it was gone.

She put her foot back down, testing it for soreness, but it was healed. "Wow," she said out loud.

Suddenly dizzy with the reality of it, she sought out

a nearby tree and leaned on it for a minute. *Oh Jesus. I'm . . .*

*I'm a vampire.*

She would never see the sun again unless she wanted to die. She'd never see her own reflection again. No children, no pigging out on pizza, no tanning by the lake, no matinees, no Fourth of July barbecues. It was one thing to give those things up in theory, but now . . . now it was done, and there was no undoing. Everything was different now.

She wasn't human anymore.

She rapped her forehead lightly against the bark. "Later . . . later. Think about it later," she told herself. "You've got to hurry."

She pushed herself away from the tree and broke into a jog, then into a run.

The movement woke her entire body up and energy surged through her muscles, propelling her faster and faster. The freedom of it, knowing she wasn't going to get a stitch in her side, made her laugh as she ran, no doubt giving any passersby something to talk about in her wake.

She stumbled to a halt outside the warehouse building and pounded on the door.

This time she could hear the footsteps approaching all the way from the inside. "Password?"

Miranda pushed her hair back from her eyes. "I mock you with my monkey pants."

She heard a bitten-off curse, and the door opened.

Sophie stared at her, something utterly unexpected and, Miranda had thought, impossible on her face: shock.

"I need weapons," Miranda said. "And your help."

Wordlessly, Sophie let her into the hall, barring the door behind her with a quick, hunted glance out onto the street.

Miranda strode into the studio and studied the wall of weapons. She heard Sophie walk up behind her, then do her usual circle around her student, but this time instead of detached speculation, there was something akin to wonder in the vampire's face.

"This is new," Sophie said.

Miranda turned to look at her. "Are you surprised?"

"A little. The word is that you're dead. Burned up, left as a warning. The Signet declared blood feud on the Blackthorns and it's been holy war for a week. Where have you been hiding?"

"With a friend," she answered. "I have to call the Haven. Do you have Faith's number?"

"No. I have her e-mail."

"That's not going to be fast enough. Ariana and her followers are going to attack the Haven tonight."

"How are they going to get past security?"

"They have a man inside. He's one of the Prime's bodyguards—he's worked there for years. They'll never see it coming. We have to warn them." Miranda walked over to the wall and pulled down the sword she'd been working with. "Can you get me to the Haven?"

"I can draw you a map."

Miranda turned to her, frowning. "You have to come with me. I need you."

Sophie laughed. "Are you kidding? I told you, I'm not getting involved in Signet bullshit. I'm going to do what I always do, keep my head down and wait it out."

"No," Miranda replied. "You're going to help me. You don't want Faith to die and you don't want some holy rolling crazy bitch to take control of this city."

"I've done my part. I'm finished with this. If you want directions, I can give them to you. You want weapons, I'm your girl. But this is not my fight."

Miranda's eyes narrowed. "I suppose this is the part where I give you an inspirational speech about what's right, and the value of freedom, and persuade you to risk your life for the greater good."

She spun around, swinging her arm up, and stopped short with the blade hovering a millimeter from Sophie's throat.

"I don't have time for that crap," Miranda said. "I'm not asking you to fight. All I need is a ride. Then you can crawl back under your rock and pretend the rest of the world doesn't exist all you like. But first, get your keys, little girl. We're leaving."

Sophie, unfazed by either the sword so close to her jugular or Miranda's imperious tone, just stared at her for a minute . . . then burst out laughing.

Miranda lowered the sword. Sophie shook her head and went to the weapons wall, then started removing blades, still laughing as she said, "You, my Lady, are pure fucking awesome. I'm going to get a finder's fee for you, right?"

Miranda smiled back at her and caught the knife Sophie tossed her way. "I'm sure we can arrange something."

"Just one problem," Sophie pointed out.

"What?"

"No way in hell I'm going anywhere with you in that outfit."


"Sire."

He didn't answer.

"Sire, you need to sleep."

Since the night of the fire there had been three attacks on humans in the city, but none had resulted in fatalities. Thanks to the network, the Elite were there in time to apprehend the fugitives.

Speed was still with them, but the insurgents were on to them and knew to expect a counterattack. They traveled in larger numbers now and were better armed. Each time an Elite unit descended upon them, the battle was bloody and ended in casualties on both sides. By Thursday, four Elite were dead, but they had taken out twice as many of the enemy, and five humans walked away without a scratch.

Well, they would probably need some therapy. But at least they were alive.

The city was crawling with vampires. Most were his. The Prime had them triple-teaming their patrol areas and checking in every twenty minutes instead of on the hour.

"I can't, not yet," he finally said to his Second. "I have to debug this search routine."

"Which means?"

"I'm close," he muttered, his eyes full of code. "Another hour and I'll have it."

"And you're sure it's going to work?"

"Positive . . . but it's a very detailed routine."

"And you've been in that chair for two days. Your ass is growing into the seat. You've only fed because I brought it to you, but I can't bring you sleep unless I hit you over the head with a chair."

"I'll sleep when I'm done, Faith."

She waved her hand between his face and the monitor. "Could you at least pretend to listen to me? Do I have to call California again?"

He didn't stop typing, but shot her a poisonous look. "I'd really rather you didn't. Is there any news from APD?"

Faith sighed. "Nothing we haven't already heard. They're still going through what's left of the building. They've found eleven bodies so far and identified six. Three additional people are still missing. I told Sergeant Winters to have any personal effects sent here."

"Good."

She sat on the edge of the table, crossing her arms, saying hesitantly, "You don't suppose there's any chance . . ."

"No," he cut her off. "If Miranda were alive, she would have found a way to contact us by now. It's been almost a week, Faith."

He heard the hardness in his voice, hardness she didn't deserve. He should let her have her hope. He had abandoned any such thing and accepted the truth, and if his heart was still howling in pain, he could ignore it. He had to. He had lost three days wallowing in self-pity and people had died.

He raised his eyes to her. "As soon as we have this under control, you can have some time off. I'm sorry you've been running nonstop since the fire."

"So have you . . . and I'm in much better shape than you are. I lost a friend, yes, but not a Queen."

"She wasn't my Queen," he said shortly and went back to the simple, heart-numbing task of proofreading lines of characters and symbols. That black-and-white place of numbers and letters, if and then, had been his escape, letting him focus on something that didn't make him break things and scare the servants.

"There." He sat back and rubbed his neck.

"You're done?"

"No. I've got a check running. It'll be done in a few minutes."

He watched the progress bar on the screen inch its way from left to right. Thankfully he'd upgraded the server's processors two weeks ago, otherwise there was no way he'd have the computing power for what he was doing. As it was, he'd had to do a lot of the work by hand instead of letting the network run it for him.

The sensors were programmed to take readings of body temperature, body mass, and speed of movement, then weed out anything above or below average human parameters; what fell into a certain range was most likely a vampire. So far he'd had a 98 percent accuracy rate with a couple of glitches involving large dogs and an immortal midget. He knew that Ariana Blackthorn fit perfectly in the range, so all he needed to do was isolate her specific set of readings from every other vampire in Austin.

He'd gone back over the grid from the night of the raid, when her hench-vamps had all been taken outside and the only vampires in the house had been him, her, and the Elite. Everyone who was in the building that night had a com except Ariana, so he could eliminate anyone whose signal corresponded to one of the Elite. The remaining readings he was currently running against those of every vampire that had entered or left the city limits Friday night.

He'd found four likely candidates and was now letting the computer do the rest. Once he had a profile for her he could track her down within the grid.

It wasn't a perfect plan—far from it, with so many variables—but it was the best thing he'd come up with since returning to his duties on Tuesday. They could continue to catch the attackers, slapping bandages over the city's wounds until it bled to death by inches, or they could go to the source.

He wanted Ariana Blackthorn's blood to spill over his hands. He wanted to see her head fall to the ground and her skull crack on the concrete. He wanted to see her body twitch and spasm into stillness.

Then, and only then, would he rest.

He heard a noise like a wind chime, and Faith slid off the table and took out her phone. "I'll be damned," she said. "An e-mail from Sophie."

He looked up at her again. "Sophie . . . not Sophia Castellano?"

"You know her?"

"You mentioned her once before—something about her being a former agent of the Red Shadow."

Faith frowned down at the screen of her phone. "The hell . . . Sophie says that the Blackthorn gang is planning to attack the Haven."

David laughed. "And they're going to find it, how?"

"I don't know. She doesn't say. She just says they're coming . . . tonight."

"What makes her think so?"

"Again, she doesn't . . ." Faith trailed off, and when she looked up, her eyes were wide. "She says they have a spy in the Elite."

"Even if that's true, there's no way they can get in."

"Not even if they had someone inside?"

David's laughter faded. "Impossible."

"I'm e-mailing her back—damn it, I should have gotten her phone number, we could make short work of this."

David moved to his laptop and pulled up the com system. "There's no way they could have someone inside," he muttered. "I'd know. I've gone over everything a hundred times since Elite Seventy turned on us. There's been no unusual signal activity going in or out of the Haven . . . they'd have to communicate somehow. What the fuck are they using, then, Morse code? Smoke signals?"

He ran a secondary search for transmission anomalies, but he knew there wouldn't be anything—everything from cell phones to radios showed up on his monitors, and he watched them all.

Something beeped.

"What is that?" he asked. "There's something . . . or, there was something . . . Saturday night, there was a single burst transmission from the room where we had Ariana. It was less than a second long . . . and it came twice more this week."

"What kind of transmission?"

"I don't know. With all the com chatter that night it got lost. It's not from a com, it's . . . Christ."

"It's Christ?"

"No, no . . . Who's the guard in the visitor's wing right now? Send him to that suite immediately."

"What's he looking for?"

"Anything that looks like a GPS device."

Faith gaped at him. "Bitch stuck a GPS in the Haven?"

"That's what it looks like. It transmitted three times—Saturday, Tuesday, and yesterday—and then shut down. It was such a short-lived signal it was logged in the system but didn't trip security. She planted it the night she escaped and I wasn't watching the transmission logs." He all but slammed the screen of his laptop shut. "They've got us mapped, Faith. Sophie's right. They're coming."

Faith and the Prime stared at each other.

He said, very, very calmly, "Plan Alpha Delta Nine."

"Yes, Sire." She lifted her wrist and hit broadcast mode. "All Haven Elite and personnel, incursion code Alpha Delta Nine. Battle stations. Double coverage on every door. Windows closing down in twenty seconds."

David leaned over and hit the override switch that would close the metal shutters, then flipped several more security switches, turning on firewalls to protect the network and scramble any outgoing frequencies.

"I don't suppose you've got sensors covering the Haven, too," Faith said hopefully.

David smiled wickedly. "As a matter of fact, I do. They were the first test system before the grid went live. I didn't think we'd ever need it, but I left them in place anyway."

A diagram of the property came up, and within seconds each vampire within its borders was highlighted as a red dot; most of them were in motion, the Elite headed to their stations for an invasion, the servants migrating to the secure rooms belowground.

Faith leaned over his shoulder. "Holy fucking mother of shit."

There were red dots moving steadily toward the Haven in groups of ten or twelve, approaching through the forest from three sides. David added them up quickly in his head.

"Eighty-three," he said. "How many Elite do we have?"

"Thirty-two in house," she replied. "The rest are out on patrol. I can send out the recall signal—"

"No," he told her, rising. "They need to stay put and defend the city. We can handle a siege here. Secure all the entrances as well as the underground tunnels. There's no way they can get in—all we have to do is keep them out until sunup. I'm going to get the rest of my weapons. You check the entrances."

"On it!"

David quickly connected his phone to the computer

system so he could monitor the sensors from anywhere in the Haven and left the server room, locking it down; the door and walls were steel-reinforced, and the only way anyone could break in was with a battering ram.

He emerged from the stairway and strode down the hall to his suite, and Paul, the second door guard, said, "Sire, is it the Blackthorn?"

"It looks that way—where's Samuel?"

"He said Faith called him to the front doors and he took off running."

David took his sword down from the wall, then grabbed two long daggers with smooth, tapered wooden blades and strapped them to his waist.

As he was about to leave the suite, he saw something out of the corner of his eye that made his blood run cold.

The cabinet where he kept Miranda's book and the Queen's Signet had been pried open, the door cracked and splintered and hanging partway off its hinges.

He jerked it the rest of the way open and saw that someone had torn through the contents of the cabinet, tossing things aside until they found what they wanted.

The metal box had been jimmied open, the wooden one inside left empty.

Someone had stolen the Signet.


Faith ran down the hall out of the East Wing, checking as she passed that everyone she saw was at the ready, weapons drawn; they had been trained in how to handle an invasion, even though such a thing hadn't happened in decades. Few interlopers were ballsy, or stupid, enough to lay siege to the Haven. Almost every assassinated Prime was killed beyond the walls of his home.

"Elite Twelve, is the West Wing secure?" she asked.

*"Secure and ready."*

"Sire, what's your position?"

David's reply was terse. *"I'm in my suite. Tell Samuel I*

*need him back here. I think Paul's gone rogue on us—he broke into the suite and then abandoned his post."*

She halted. "Samuel's not there?"

*"No—he's not with you?"*

"No."

Normally she enjoyed hearing David curse, but lately it seemed to be happening with unfortunate frequency. *"I'm running a trace on his com,"* he said. *"He's in the building, near the front doors. I can't raise him or Paul. The insurgent signals are converging on the entrance— get everyone there* now."

"Sophie said they had a man inside," Faith realized, starting to run again. "I'm on my way." She hit broadcast. "All available Elite to the front doors!"

Faith raced down the hall and around the corner toward the front entrance . . .

. . . just in time to see Samuel swing the double doors open.

Then all hell broke loose.

# Twenty

Sophie pulled her little black car up behind the stables and parked; before she even had the key out of the ignition Miranda had leapt out.

The horses were out in the paddock, clearly distressed, whinnying and pawing the dirt the way they did before a storm broke. Miranda climbed up on the fence to get a better look at the Haven.

An animal hiss escaped her lips. She could see dark figures streaming into the Haven like ants and the broad front doors standing open. Even if Faith had believed their warning, it had come too late. The enemy had taken them by surprise and found no resistance at the doors. Miranda could only hope that the Elite were strong enough to drive them back.

"Hurry," she called to Sophie and hopped down. "We have to get in there."

"Hang on a minute. Do you have any sort of strategy here, or are we as stupid as I think we are?"

Miranda was staring at the Haven, wishing she could see through the shutters; from out here it looked almost normal, but even at this distance she could hear breaking glass and the clear ring of metal on metal.

"We fight our way in and take out as many as we can."

Sophie snorted, hard. "Not to be a pain, here, but there are exactly two of us, and you've never even been in a real fight, much less as a vampire. You can win one on one, but if we go in the front it's us against all of them. If we want to help, we need a plan, which is what I told you in the car."

"Fine, fine. Ideas?"

"We need to go in where we'll have the greatest advantage and do the most damage."

"Side entrance," Miranda said. "There's one over there—but the doors are electronically locked."

"Locks are the least of our worries. Come on."

They slipped past the stables and around to the side of the main building. Miranda was grateful for her borrowed clothes; Sophie had dressed her all in black, and though the T-shirt was tight across her chest, the rest fit well enough. The two of them looked like paramilitary, except that instead of guns, they were armed to the teeth with swords, and Sophie had insisted she also carry a wooden stake in her belt.

Once on the far side, Miranda looked back around the corner at the front entrance—seconds later, something whistled down from the roof, and one of the insurgents fell to the ground with a cry, a crossbow bolt in his chest. There were more whistles as the Elite picked the enemy off from above. The rest of the insurgents—Miranda counted at least thirty still pushing their way in—clogged the doors, trying to shove their cohorts out of the way before they, too, were shot.

They were trying to destroy her home. They were killing her friends. They might already have killed Faith . . . or David . . . They wanted to tear apart everything the Signet stood for. Her vision seemed to turn red, but she kept her anger under control—she had to save it for what was ahead.

Miranda ducked back and joined Sophie at the garden door that she and Faith had walked in and out of a dozen times when Miranda lived here. Sophie was fiddling with the door handle. Miranda was about to remind her that the lock was electronic, when Sophie grabbed her arm and hauled her back, saying, "Move!"

There was a small explosion, a puff of black smoke, and the door swung open.

"Hasn't been a lock made that I couldn't get into," Sophie said. "Some require a little less finesse than others."

"It's too bad you didn't bring anything else that blows up. We could use a nice flamethrower or something."

Miranda risked one last look at the front. Suddenly the broad double doors slammed shut, crushing at least one invader between them and blocking the others from getting in. The enemy were shouting among themselves, dividing up to find other ways.

"Shit, they're coming this way!" Miranda exclaimed. "Get in!"

They both ran through the door side by side and Sophie flung it shut, while Miranda dragged the nearest table in front of it to at least buy time. She shoved the table sideways up beneath the door handle while Sophie took a wad of some kind of gray chewing gum and stuffed it into the lock.

"Pressure-sensitive explosive," Sophie explained. "When they try to open it, boom! It won't do that much damage but it'll make them shit their pants. Let's move."

There was no guard at the door, which told Miranda that everyone who was able had been diverted to the front entrance. It seemed like a bad idea—how could David know that all the insurgents were there, not trying to come around like she and Sophie had?

Her answer came seconds later when four Elite came pounding down the hallway straight toward them. Miranda recognized one as Theo, who had served as an East Wing guard a few nights during her stay.

"Stay where you are, hands in the air!" Theo yelled. "Show your coms!"

"We don't have coms!" Miranda yelled back. "We're friends of the Haven, we came to help. There are Blackthorn coming through this door."

"We're aware of that, we're tracking them," Theo snapped. "Who are you?"

"Sophia Castellano," Sophie said, steel in her words. "Formerly of the Red Shadow and an ally of this Signet. I am also the bodyguard to your Prime's lover. We need to find the Prime immediately."

Miranda blinked at Sophie. "What's a Red Shadow?"

"Better that you don't know."

Theo gaped at Miranda for a few seconds, finally recognizing her, then deferred to Sophie without question. "Our Lord Prime is with the rest of the Elite fighting in the Great Hall. We've already lost warriors, and they outnumber us three to one. The more swords the better— come with us. Eighty-Three, Forty-Four, stay here and keep that door shut."

They all headed down the hallway at a graceful trot, and Miranda asked, "How bad is it?"

"Bad, my Lady. Samuel and Paul were both in collusion with the enemy and let them in through security after Ariana Blackthorn planted a GPS to trace the Haven's location. Near as we can figure, they were communicating the one way we don't check on."

"Radio?" Sophie ventured.

"No, the mail. Postal mail has never been inspected piece by piece except in suspicious cases. Samuel was sending regular one-stamp letters to Ariana at a post office box. It never raised a single eyebrow."

They took the hall that led out of the Prime's wing, and Miranda stuck her head in the suite to see if David was there, by some miracle, but he wasn't. In fact it looked like a tornado had blown through the room. There were no suite guards—Samuel and this Paul had already abandoned their posts and all pretense of loyalty.

She hoped they both died nasty.

They passed the music room, and again Miranda paused—the door was locked tight, but she felt a moment's fear. "I will protect you," she promised the Bösendorfer inside. "I won't let you down."

Sophie gave her a quizzical look.

"Bastards better not hurt my piano," Miranda replied.

"*That's* what you're worried about right now? What about your boyfriend?"

"He can take care of himself. I know he's a good fighter. I've just never seen him do it."

"Get ready," Theo said at her side, urging them all to the left. "We're almost there."

The sounds of the battle reached them first—screams, shouts, cries of agony, the solid thump of fists on flesh, the clash of blade on blade. Something fell and broke all over the tile floor, probably some statuary or another. The sounds of nearly a hundred people bottlenecked into the Great Hall were deafening.

The Elite defended both staircases and thus far the invaders had fought them halfway to the second floor, but they held their ground.

Miranda ran up to the railing, searching for familiar faces in the din. An Elite screamed in pain as he was run through with a wooden sword, and blood pooled all around his body, blood that another vampire slipped in; Miranda searched their faces, and the faces of the dead, for those she knew.

There was Samuel, decapitated and dismembered. Another Elite lay nearby, and she was pretty sure it was Paul.

Finally she caught sight of Faith in the center of the fight, exactly where Miranda expected her to be. The Second was a blur of motion, her two swords whirling all around her, and attacker after attacker dove in for the kill and never emerged. She wasted no time with banter—Faith had one objective, to put down the insurgents, and she would do exactly that.

Where was David? And where was Ariana? She had to be here. She would have come.

"Draw!" Sophie shouted. Two insurgents had broken through the wall of Elite at the head of the stairs and were making a break deeper into the building.

Miranda joined her, and they outran the enemy and faced them in the hallway, swords at the ready.

The two insurgents looked amused at the sight of two small women spoiling for a fight. Miranda knew exactly what they were going to do—underestimate her.

One of them moved in, blade ready, and Miranda took him on, while Sophie took the other. Miranda fought hard, her sword arm already aching from overuse, but she lost as much ground as she gained until she remembered she had better weapons than a sword.

She lowered her sword, held out her hand toward the man, reached into herself for her power, and *pushed*.

He began to tear at his clothes, and his hair, and scream: "No, Daddy! No! I'm sorry! NO!" He dropped to the ground in a fetal position, head covered with his arms, his sword and the fight abandoned to a less visible but far more potent attacker.

Miranda walked over, put her booted foot on the man's neck and pushed him flat on the floor, and with one swing took his head.

Sophie had already dispatched hers with the wooden stake she'd stuck in her jacket. The insurgent lay in a spreading pool of her blood, eyes wide open.

Miranda's head already felt like it was going to split from that little stunt, but she grounded quickly—she was probably going to have to do it again. In fact, if only she could get control of more than one mind at once, she could take out several at a time, drown them in childhood fears or reliving the death of a loved one. She could choke them on their own histories while Sophie, by far the better fighter, killed them.

She remembered being skeptical that empathy would be useful in combat.

They stepped over the bodies and reassessed the situation. So far the Elite were still holding the stairs, but the insurgents were trying to get the doors back open, and there was no way to know how many might have found other entrances already.

"We need a way to disable all of them at once," Miranda said, shouting to be heard above the din. "I don't think I can work on this many. At that mental depth I have to do them one by one."

Sophie started to speak, then looked up past Miranda and grinned. "What we need," Sophie said, "is a really pissed-off telekinetic."

Miranda's heart nearly burst from her body, and it was all she could do not to jump up and run to him, but Sophie kept her firmly out of the way where they weren't seen.

David Solomon stepped out onto the balcony where the two staircases met over the Great Hall.

He wore his long coat and was fully armed, but the thing that was most frightening—the thing that made the entire fight stop and the hall fall silent—was the churning cloud of wrath that surrounded him, the silver of his aura shot through with deadly black. His eyes were pure silver, the Signet ablaze at his throat.

He stepped up onto the balcony rail. Miranda saw the Signet's light begin to pulsate—she'd never seen it do that before, but it made him look even more terrifying.

"Elite," he said, "Stand down."

As one, the Elite dropped whomever they were fighting, lowered their weapons, and stepped back to line the walls of the Great Hall.

The Prime jumped smoothly off the rail, landing twenty feet below and straightening to level a steely-eyed gaze on the insurgents, who were inching closer to each other and looking like they wanted to pry the doors back open and flee into the night.

Miranda rushed to the rail to look down. David slowly, deliberately drew his sword and stood with it down at his side, and when he spoke, it was with the same calm authority she had heard him use at the Elite trials. No one could look away.

"You have staged an open attack on the Haven of this territory in an attempt to assassinate me and claim the Signet. You have failed. The sentence for such actions is death."

The blade of his sword tilted and caught the light. "I will give you a choice. If you hand over Ariana Blackthorn, you will die a quick and merciful death. If you face me now, you will die with honor in battle. If you try to escape, you will be cut down by my Elite and bleed to death on this floor."

As if on cue, one of the insurgents broke free of the hypnotic hold David had over them and bolted for the doors.

David raised a hand, and the man fell to the floor, screaming, with the sickening sound of breaking bones. Blood spurted from the insurgent's nose and ran from his mouth, and he twitched, still trying to get back to his feet and run.

Faith, at the ready, swung her sword and finished him, then bowed to the Prime.

He smiled. "Next?"

Seconds ticked by before the crowd parted near the doors. The invaders fell back respectfully as a woman stepped out from behind them. She was blond and had huge eyes, a gaunt face that might once have been beautiful, and was smiling that same cruel murderous smile she had worn when she stabbed Miranda through the heart.

She came out into the center of the room and stood facing the Prime without a trace of fear. Then she lifted her hand, and Miranda saw what was dangling from it: a carbon copy of David's Signet, only slightly smaller. Its stone, too, was flashing rhythmically.

A gasp went up all over the room.

Miranda saw David's eyes widen almost imperceptibly. His face went absolutely white. "What's going on?" Miranda whispered to Sophie.

Sophie, too, was astonished. "The flashing . . . that's what happens when a Signet chooses its bearer. When the Prime finds his Queen, that's how he knows."

"Wait . . . it can't be her!"

Sophie rolled her eyes artfully. "Well, now, who else could it possibly be speaking for?"

Ariana and the Prime stared at each other. Then Ariana said sweetly, "Looks like we get to call a truce, my Lord."

He didn't answer.

"Just think," Ariana went on, "You and I, bound together for all eternity—how poetic. I had no idea, when I killed your little human whore, that this would happen. I thought I was merely inflicting the same pain on you that you had on me. But this is so much better."

Miranda started to leap up, but Sophie again grabbed her arm and held her back. "Just wait," she hissed.

Ariana, laughing, reached up and dropped the Signet's chain around her neck.

The second it settled over her chest, the stone went dark.

David's continued to flash, and he glanced down at it, frowning a little before looking back up at Ariana.

"You will never be Queen," he told her. "You will never hold a Signet. You are a pretender to the throne, Ariana, and not worthy of these hallowed halls. I'll cut you down the same way I did your Prime and you'll die the way you lived—as nobody."

Ariana's face became a twisted mask of rage. "Kill him!" she shouted.

Her men rushed forward past her, roaring out their challenge, and surrounded the Prime, who stood waiting, a faint smile on his face.

As the first of the insurgents reached him, he brought

up his sword and said to the Elite without raising his voice, "Attack."

The insurgents, so intent upon following orders, had all run into the center of the room toward David and were now surrounded by Elite on all sides. The Haven warriors bore down on the insurgents, their swords slicing through the air, and the room was suddenly full of the sounds of battle once more.

Miranda pulled her eyes back to the Prime.

He met the first four attackers at once, his sword a liquid flame, his body a blur of motion as he kicked one in the head, spun in midair, beheaded the second man, and opened another's throat on the follow-through stroke. The fourth avoided the first slash aimed at her, but was simply not fast enough—she tried to parry but couldn't, and he punched her, then pulled a wood-bladed dagger from his belt and ran her through. By the time he'd gotten to her, more had come, but he didn't lose a step; she could barely see him, he moved so fast, almost as if he were dancing, each movement graceful and deadly.

Sophie was laughing, a look of recognition on her face. To Miranda's eyebrow, she said, "That style—I've only met one other vampire who fought like that. Come on—let's go get messy."

Miranda followed her from the balcony rail around to the staircase, and they ran down to join the Elite.

Miranda's heart was pounding, but there was no time to think, no time to consider her actions. She simply had to fight. One of the insurgents closed on her, and she felt her awareness turning crimson again, her mind going deeper into the trancelike place Sophie had shown her before she crossed over. Now the power came through her like a breath, and she gave herself to it willingly.

Nearby she heard something crash, and then a scream; she disabled her opponent and rammed her sword into his neck, unable to avoid the spray of blood; it hit her chest and shoulders, and the thick smell of it only fueled her bloodlust. She glanced up toward the noise in time to see an invader fly backward into the wall, then another, and another; they were picked up off the ground and flung without anyone touching them. She jerked her head to the right and saw that David was fending off an attack with one hand and gesturing with the other.

She felt the energy moving through him up and out like a volcanic eruption, and another insurgent fell to the ground, screaming, clutching his head as his skull cracked.

Miranda fought her way toward the center of the room. She could hear Sophie laughing as she did the same—but then her laughter cut short, and Miranda whirled around toward her.

Sophie lurched forward, mouth open. The splintered end of a wooden stake protruded from between her ribs. She seemed to gather the last of her strength to round on her attacker and return the favor, sending the woman who had impaled her to the ground with wood in her own chest. Blood running freely from her body, she threw herself at the next wave of attackers, taking out three more before her strength failed her.

"Sophie!" Miranda cried, diving between warriors toward her teacher, who fell to her knees, then pitched forward onto her stomach.

She turned Sophie over gently. "What do I do?" she asked. "Do I pull it? Sophie—"

Sophie laughed again, weakly. Blood was trickling from her mouth. "Told you so," she wheezed, coughing. Spasms racked Sophie's petite frame, and something rattled deep in her chest.

Then she lay still.

Miranda's eyes burned. She looked up; all around her people were dying. The stench of blood and the chaos were overwhelming.

She caught sight of Faith, still alive, still fighting.

Her opponent was Ariana Blackthorn . . . and Faith was losing.

* * *

Faith yielded more ground to Ariana, who was swinging side to side with a blade as if she had lost any sort of skill to the scarlet rawness of her hatred. The Blackthorn was a horrific sight, her face streaked with blood and her hair filthy around her face. Still, Faith continued to let her drive her back, and back . . .

. . . straight to the Prime.

Faith moved from side to side to avoid Ariana's wild swings, only bothering to parry when her sword sang too close to Faith's head for comfort. Ariana obligingly followed her in their waltz across the hall until they reached the center of the storm.

David dispatched the last two insurgents who had the balls to fight him, throwing their bodies aside as he pulled his dagger from one and his sword from the other. Faith fell back to his side and then jumped out of the way to let him take over.

Again, Prime and Blackthorn faced each other, but where Ariana looked like a walking corpse, David was still cool and collected, a single smudge of blood on his cheek where a knife had gotten through his defenses and left a cut behind. She was breathing hard and ragged, her eyes darting around the room to see that her people were all but wiped out. Likely any that had been waiting outside were long gone by now. Even outnumbered, the Elite had won.

David's Signet was still flashing. Ariana's was still dark.

The Prime followed Ariana's gaze from one end of the Great Hall to the other, and he said, "Surrender."

Ariana's voice was high and cracked, what little sanity it had once possessed long gone. "Surrender? To your tender mercy? Never. I'll spend my last breath spilling your traitorous blood. I killed your beloved and I'll kill you!"

"Wrong on both counts," came a warm, smooth voice, touched with dark honey.

A blade flashed.

Ariana's face was frozen in a look of eternal surprise as her head was parted from her neck and, almost in slow motion, fell to the ground. Her body followed a second later. The second Signet tumbled from her throat and lay on the floor.

The silence in the Great Hall was absolute.

Faith's hand flew up to her mouth.

Miranda Grey stood over the body of their fallen enemy, her sword bloody, her bearing regal. She wore black from head to foot and her jewel-red hair had fallen out of its clip to tumble around her shoulders. Her skin was pale ivory with the luster of immortality. Her green eyes were ringed with silver.

Power surrounded her and shone like a nebula. Faith had never seen anything like it.

Miranda stepped forward, lithe and purposeful as she sheathed her sword and bent down. She picked up the Signet, and as her hand closed around it, the light in the stone blazed to life and began to pulse.

She held it up and fastened the chain around her neck.

The light in the stone brightened and grew steady. Miranda turned in a circle, letting the entire Elite see the Signet. Her voice rang off the walls.

"I am your Queen," she said. "Any questions?"

There was a clattering sound, and Miranda turned to face the Prime.

He was staring at her in stunned silence. The sword had fallen from his hand. All of hell was in his eyes.

Faith could feel the power in the room rising, contracting around them. She could feel currents of energy crackling between them—a circuit was completed, the floodgates opened. Power joined into power, weaving in and around itself and each other, and the foundations of the Haven trembled as David stepped forward, a single tear leaving a silvery track down his face.

Miranda laughed joyfully and opened her arms to him, her own eyes shining. Neither of them spoke.

David drew a ragged, halting breath . . . and then he crossed the last space between them, and throughout the Great Hall a cheer went up as the Queen and her Prime fell into each other's arms.

# Epilogue

Matt was such an asshole. What was she thinking?

Madison stumbled out onto the sidewalk, so angry she was practically shaking, her fingers missing half the keys on her phone while she tried to dial. "Come on," she muttered. "Answer. Come on, Teresa."

"Hey, Maddie, how's the date going?"

"Can you come get me?"

"Are you okay? What happened?"

"It's a long story. We're gonna need cheesecake."

"Okay, where are you?"

Maddie sighed, pushing her professionally streaked auburn hair out of her face. She'd gotten it done special because she'd been waiting for Matt to ask her out for months. She'd even gotten a wax! What a fucking waste of money. "I'm on South Congress near the Paramount. I'm going to walk a little farther south—there's a concert letting out up here and the road's clogged. I'll meet you in front of the Kinko's, okay?"

"Sure, babe. I'll be there in half an hour. Be careful."

As she walked, Maddie made a mental list of all the ways she was going to get back at that bastard. Voodoo dolls, slashed tires . . . she got grim satisfaction thinking of his dick turning green and falling off.

She got farther from the postconcert crowd; thank God there were still a thousand people out.

God, she felt sick. She'd only been drinking since she moved to Austin—she'd been such a good girl in high school, and she was making up for lost time. She'd had a half dozen too many tonight, though. The bartender had called them Pierced Nipples, and they were sugary sweet with a bitter aftertaste and went straight to her head. She was so out of it that it had taken her until her shirt was halfway off to realize what Matt was trying to do.

Thankfully eight Pierced Nipples hadn't affected her ability to knee him in the crotch.

Her phone rang, and she held it up, but she couldn't hear Teresa talking—there was too much noise on the sidewalk. Madison shook her head in irritation and ducked out of the flow of people into an alley where it was quieter.

By the time she could actually hear, Teresa had hung up. Cursing, Maddie dialed her number again.

"There you are!"

Madison started, and her heart did a swan dive to her knees when she saw Matt.

"I've been looking all over for you," he said, his usual swagger uneven from the amount of beer he'd swilled. "Why'd you run off like that? I thought we were having a good time."

"Go fuck yourself," Maddie said. "I told you to stop."

"Come on, Maddie . . ."

"No!" she cried as he came closer and reached out to her. "Leave me alone!"

He got his hands around her shoulders and pushed her back against the wall, and this time she didn't have the advantage of a crowd of people and good leverage. She hit the wall so hard it dazed her and she dropped her phone. She yelled and struggled, but he ignored her and sloppily kissed her neck. He stank of Budweiser and cigarettes, and she could feel his erection stabbing her in the stomach. He held her back against the wall with his weight and groped her breasts, sticking a hand in her shirt.

*Oh my God. Oh God, please, no, please . . .*

She took a breath to scream at the top of her lungs.

Before she could, Matt was wrenched away from her and thrown hard into the far wall. Maddie heard something—she was pretty sure it was his wrist—crack.

Maddie was so relieved her legs turned to water and she fell back again, her planned scream coming out as a sob.

A figure stepped between her and Matt. She saw a long black coat and a wild cascade of red hair.

The woman couldn't have been taller than Maddie, but she reached down and seized the front of Matt's shirt and hauled him to his feet, then punched him in the stomach twice. He came at her, cursing a blue streak, and she took the opportunity to do what Maddie had done in the club—she nailed him in the balls with one knee.

Matt went down with a grunt, and the woman towered over him. Whatever he saw in her face, he whimpered and covered his head with his useless arms. "Please don't kill me—"

Her voice was calm and strong, and Maddie recognized it. "If you ever again hurt a woman in my city, *human*, you will answer to me. Now go."

Matt struggled to his feet and stumbled out of the alley, crying like a little girl.

Slowly, the woman turned to Madison. "Are you okay?"

Maddie stared at her: her luminous green eyes, her proud shoulders, the large red stone at her throat that looked like it was glowing.

"Holy shit," Madison said. "You're Miranda Grey."

The woman smiled. "Yes."

"You saved my life."

"Yes."

Madison swallowed hard and got up, dusting herself off and groping for her purse. "Um . . . can I have your autograph?"

Dangerous, immortal, and thirsting for blood.
Like it or not, "they" are among us.
Laurell K. Hamilton
the Anita Blake series
MaryJanice Davidson
the Undead series
Christine Feehan
the Dark series
Diane Whiteside
the Blood series
Charlaine Harris
the Sookie Stackhouse series
Don't miss the best in vampire fiction from Berkley.
penguin.com